Acclaim for Isla

'Breathless ... appealingly spirited ... sparkiness, freshness and verve' *Mail on Sunday*

'Strong characters, sharp dialogue and a haunting sense of place ... a compelling study of desire, frustration and contentment' *Eve* magazine

'Both wise and funny' Shena Mackay

'Refreshing and powerfully adept' *Irish News*

'A reassuring account of family dynamics and the love that binds people together' *New Woman*

'She knows just what will move us' *Scotsman*

'A Scottish Kate Atkinson, astute, sensitive and a joy to read ... a wonderful author' *Bookseller*

'Compelling' *Options*

'Acute observations . . . a wonderfully strong female character' Glasgow *Herald*

'Funny, sad and poignant, this is a brilliant observation of family life and childhood . . . Isla Dewar paints a picture with words, sights, sounds and smells and such warmth in an incredibly evocative novel' *Yorkshire Evening Press*

'Dewar's gift is to pull you into the minutiae of her people's lives . . . few writers are so good at making the reader empathise' *Scotland on Sunday*

'You will wish that this magical, poignant and funny story never has to end' Glasgow *Evening Times*

'Dewar is an accessible storyteller with a wry sense of the comic . . . Comfortable and sweet' *Kirkus Reviews*

'Dewar draws characters with acerbic wit, and also love – recommended' *West Australian*

'An amusing and compelling read' *South Wales Evening Argus*

'Frank, funny writing . . . Reading her books is a bit like listening to fantastic gossip' *The Big Issue in Scotland*

Also by Isla Dewar and available from Headline Review

Keeping Up With Magda
Women Talking Dirty
Giving Up On Ordinary
It Could Happen To You
Two Kinds Of Wonderful
The Woman Who Painted Her Dreams
Dancing In A Distant Place
Secrets Of A Family Album
Getting Out Of The House

The Consequences of Marriage

Isla Dewar

headline
review

First published in 2006 by HEADLINE REVIEW
An imprint of HEADLINE PUBLISHING GROUP

First published in paperback in 2007
by HEADLINE REVIEW

1

978 0 7553 2592 4

Typeset in Cochin by Avon DataSet Ltd,
Bidford-on-Avon, Warwickshire

Printed and bound in Great Britain by Clays Ltd, St Ives plc

Headline's policy is to use papers that are natural, renewable and
recyclable products and made from wood grown in sustainable forests.
The logging and manufacturing processes are expected to conform to the
environmental regulations of the country of origin.

HEADLINE PUBLISHING GROUP
A division of Hachette Livre UK Ltd
338 Euston Road
London NW1 3BH

www.reviewbooks.co.uk
www.hodderheadline.com

To Bob

Voices

Voices, spilling down the corridor, all male, in harmony and unaccompanied. A strange but not unpleasant new sound that mixed with the usual sounds of an April morning – wind rattling the old sash windows, a car starting up, footsteps on the pavement outside. Seven o'clock; the world was waking up.

Bibi sighed; she was awake and didn't want to be. Light seeped round the edges of her old grey velvet curtains, drizzled into the room. She listened, trying to decipher what she was hearing. A choir, she thought, Gregorian probably. It would be quite lovely at some other time of the day, but right now it was annoying. She shifted, trying to rearrange her body into a new sleeping position, shut her eyes and willed herself back to her dreams. But no, she couldn't; she had joined the living and now she had to know why an old a cappella chant was humming through the flat.

She climbed out from under her duvet and shivered. It was cold; a bitter wind swept under the ill-fitting window and her kimono, a present Callum had brought her from Japan over twenty years ago, did little to keep her warm. She thought it had aged a lot better than she had. Mornings these days she was stiff, sore, her bones ached.

First movements of the day were slow, arthritic. Every day, when she rose, she felt at odds with her body. It was, she felt, a lot older than she was. She shoved her feet into a pair of old trainers, and stood for a moment staring sadly down at them. They seemed too distant to reach. She left the laces undone and shuffled from her room and into the hall, following the sound of singing.

Of course, she knew where it was coming from – James's room. The draught from his window, never shut at night, whatever the weather, had sucked open his door, which didn't shut properly anyway, so she could see him, his young body, thin, too thin, absurdly thin, Bibi thought. He was sitting cross-legged in the middle of the floor, his back to her and wearing only his underpants, which were a startling shade of red. His ribs stuck out, his skin was shockingly white; there was a mole just below his left shoulder blade. He seemed, even from behind, to be transfixed by a candle burning on the dresser in front of him. The man's a fool, thought Bibi. He'll catch his death. Meditating at this time in the morning, half naked in front of an open window and the temperature hovering just above zero. Bloody idiot.

She left him to it, turned and made her way back to bed. No matter if she slammed her door; he would not hear anything, so lost was he in the pursuit of nothingness and light. Still, an early morning sight of the flat was cheering; it was always at its best at this time of day. She was rarely up to appreciate it; she hated rising before ten. The walls throughout were painted ochre, a dulled, mellow antique yellow that glowed when the sun streamed in and looked burnished, beautiful to Bibi when that bright sunlight was muffled by drawn curtains. The woodwork was lacquered black, a good contrast to the soft yellow of the walls. In the evening, lamps strategically placed to illuminate corners and create shadows lit the whole place. Bibi abhorred overhead lights. She thought them cruel, heartless, showing up dust on the surfaces as well as being merciless about the sagging cheeks and the wrinkles on her seventy-two-year-old face. No, she would not have them and refused to put bulbs in them.

She slipped off her kimono, threw it on the chair and crawled back into bed. Ah, warmth, comfort; she should never have left it. Head on the pillow, she shut her eyes. The singing still poured down the corridor, but she would try to blot it out. She would sleep. That man, she thought, is too thin, too fussy, uptight. All this meditating and eating health foods is not good for him. A proper hot meal is what he needs, a pie, a heap of sausages and a mound of buttery mash. Carbohydrates. Proper sustenance. He's a fool, self-obsessed, nervy and more than likely a virgin.

Lying in bed, Bibi sighed. Seeing James meditating had reminded her of Graham, who had developed an interest in Eastern religion shortly before he left home. Though he had not sat in a trance at dawn, thank goodness. Graham's interest had been inspired by kung fu films on television. There had been posters of karate masters on his wall alongside giant pictures of motorbikes and The Jam. The boy had worshipped Paul Weller.

'Ach,' said Bibi, rolling her head on the pillow as if this would shake her thoughts out. She didn't want to think about Graham. She preferred to think about Callum first thing in the morning; it set her up for the day. Thoughts about her husband were also good last thing at night. They made for a better class of dreams. She slept so deeply, she thought she touched death nightly. Her dreams were often odd collages of places she had once lived – the house, not far from Inverness, where she was born, the cottage she'd shared with Callum when they were first married, the tiny apartment where she'd sweated through an airless New York summer in the sixties. Her other recurrent dream was of Graham. She'd be running after him through dusty, rubbled streets, following him into the dark heart of a city that was nameless and strange to her.

She shook her head again. This was not Graham's allotted time of day. She let herself visit her memories of him – a skinny, dark-haired seventeen-year-old when she last saw him – when she was gardening. She would chip at the earth with her hoe or furiously dig her vegetable patch, then lean back cursing herself. 'I was a fool. Pig-headed. Pig-bloody-headed.' She could never forgive herself for what she'd done to Graham.

At last the singing stopped. The meditation was over. She heard the pipes clank. James was in the shower. In a while she would hear him move about the kitchen as he prepared his breakfast. He'd put the kettle on to make ginseng tea, his morning brew. He might toast a slice of organic stone-ground wholemeal bread, or have a bowl of the hideous muesli he made himself using oats and dried apricots and other indigestible things. 'A decent bacon sandwich, at least, is what the man needs,' she muttered. He'd wash his dishes and wipe the surfaces, then put on his puffa jacket, quietly tiptoe up the hall, and leave. He'd be back, as he always was, at quarter to seven. Prepare himself another healthy, organic vegetarian meal, then go to his room to sit reading, or watching television, before retiring to bed at half past ten.

Such a dull man, Bibi thought. I'd hoped for someone more vital, lively. Like Megan. Megan had been her last lodger. She'd been a popular girl, studying for her doctorate in biochemistry. The flat had been full of people, laughter, music. Bibi had loved that. But James was a solitary soul, friendless, Bibi thought. He kept himself to himself. They rarely saw one another.

'He's a strange one,' Bibi had told her daughter, Beth. 'Uptight, tense.'

'Well, tell him to leave,' said Beth. 'Get someone else.'

'I can't do that,' Bibi said. 'Not without good reason. I don't think uptight qualifies.'

'I don't know why you have to have a lodger anyway,' said Beth. 'It's not as if you need the money.'

'Whatever makes you think that?' said Bibi. 'Of course I need the money. My savings are tiny. The pension's absurd. I have bills. I have you. You are always borrowing. Though why you call it borrowing, I do not know. You never give it back.'

Beth had shrugged. 'One day.'

'I like having people about,' said Bibi. 'Now everybody's gone, I miss movement. I like hearing someone in another room. I like knowing there's someone else in the house. James just doesn't fit the bill. He's quiet. We don't speak much. I like speaking. People don't chat like they used to on buses, in queues. I don't know what's wrong with everybody.'

That was what she missed. Talking. Someone to chat to. And she liked hearing voices, people calling, laughing, singing. Once, when her family was younger and still living at home, the whole place rang with voices, all sorts of voices and tones, high and low, male, female, all young. She missed them, her children and their voices.

James McElroy had been lodging with Bibi Saunders for six months now. He had wanted a small flat or even a bedsit to himself, but the prices in central Edinburgh were beyond his means. He'd found these two rooms he occupied through a leasing agency, and even before he viewed the property he had fallen in love with it. Well, not really the property, more the notion of it. Two names – Bibi Saunders and Saxe-Coburg Street – had captured his heart. He'd fantasised about them both. The street had not disappointed. Tall terraced buildings, old and grey and grand, with black railings between them and the passers-by on the pavement. The moment he turned the corner and saw it, he wanted to live here. He wanted to walk down this street every day; he wanted to say the name with pride: 'I live in Saxe-Coburg Street, actually.'

Bibi, however, had been a surprise. James had been so taken with the name, he'd put a face, body and personality to it. The woman he'd imagined was in her early thirties, professional, with a busy career, foreign, probably Swedish, with a charming accent, who was looking for a lodger to help with her mortgage. She was small, lively, quick to laugh at his jokes. He'd tease her, gently, of course, about her eating habits and try to tempt her to some of his steamed vegetables and Quorn sausages. He'd make her ginseng tea in the morning and camomile before she went to bed. He'd tut and tenderly shake his head if he came across her standing in the kitchen, leaning on the sink, eating Ben and Jerry's Phish Food ice cream straight from the carton.

Bibi would wear designer business suits, charcoal grey or black, with silk shirts. But in the evenings she would slip into a pair of loose-fitting velvet pants, or maybe tracksuit bottoms and a T-shirt. She'd run in the mornings before leaving for work, and probably visit a gym a couple of times a week. She'd go out most nights; she was bound to have a full social life. James would get along with her lovers, but sometimes might express a little disapproval if someone not quite up to snuff turned up in the kitchen in the morning. 'Not good enough for you,' he'd say. 'Thinks too much of himself.' Bibi might laugh, but she'd respect his opinion. They would banter, joke and, from time to time, talk seriously about themselves, their lives, their ambitions, disappointments. But they would give one another room. A person needs his own space, James thought.

He had fantasised so much about Bibi Saunders, she had become real to him. So real, in fact, that when a woman who was obviously in her late sixties or early seventies opened the door on that October afternoon when he'd come to view the flat and said, 'Ah yes, Mr McElroy, you've come to see the rooms. I'm Bibi Saunders,' he had almost told her that no, she wasn't. Bibi Saunders didn't look a bit like her.

This rather ancient woman standing before him was not in the least small or pretty. She was tall; her hair was white and cropped into a neat bob. She wore a pair of jeans and a sweatshirt bearing the words Harvard University that had seen better days. On her feet was a pair of battered blue canvas shoes, the sort of thing favoured by weekend sailors. James had to admit that, though not beautiful, this woman was striking. And once, many years ago, she must have been stunningly so. Still could be, James thought, if she cared. Her eyes were large, hauntingly brown, the lids hooded. Her lips were full, but probably not as full as they'd been thirty or so years ago. Once, she must have had cheekbones to die for. Once, she must have turned many heads.

'Come in,' she said, and started down the hall in front of him. 'Shut the door after you.'

He'd done as he was told, then followed her. He would tell her, he decided, that he would let her know, he had other places to look at. Since this was not the Bibi of his imaginings, he did not want to live here.

Then he saw the rooms. They were ideal. Their perfection as a living space was beyond his dearest desires. They were, of course, ochre, the woodwork lacquered black. Neither of them was particularly large. But who wanted large, James thought, when small looked like this? The bedroom had an old four-poster bed, a dresser, black lacquer again, and matching wardrobe that looked to him to be Chinese. There was a small armchair covered in oatmeal linen; on the floor a pale but thick carpet.

'The door on the left leads to your bathroom. It's very tiny, but adequate. A shower, basin, loo, everything you need. My bathroom is down the hall. Don't use it, please. I do not like sharing. And this,' said Bibi, opening the door on the right, 'is your living room.'

It was smaller than the bedroom. Beside the large window that overlooked the street was a huge plant, lustrously green and shiny. There was a sofa and an armchair that both matched the one in the bedroom, a table on which stood a television and a small CD player. On a grey marble mantelpiece were a clock and a collection of tiny jade boxes.

Bibi stood at the door watching James take in the rooms. She was never comfortable in here. Once, this had been Callum's domain. Once, it had been littered with books, magazines and papers. There had been a thick, blue-grey layer of fug from his cigarettes floating above him, around him. His desk had a spreading of ash among his notebooks. He'd worked in what was now the bedroom, and the little living room was where he'd lain on an old day bed, thinking, planning, dozing. He'd been dead for three years before Bibi could face clearing it out. She'd shut the door and left it as it had been the day he died – a sort of shrine. Time passed; money was tight. Bibi knew the only way she could ease her dwindling bank balance was to take in a lodger, and the only way she could feel comfortable with a stranger in the house was to let him have Callum's rooms. There was a living room, so she wouldn't have to sit in the evening watching television with someone she hardly knew, and might not like. And there was a small bathroom – she would have hated to share that particular space with a person she was not related to.

She had moved the books to her bedroom, the kitchen and bookcase in the living room. The desk, also, went into her bedroom; Callum's typewriter sat on top of it. Celia, her daughter, took the day bed. She had the rooms redecorated, and paid for a carpet, a sofa and a couple of chairs. It looked lovely, she thought. But still, every time a new lodger arrived to view her property, she watched them gaze about, and felt guilty. Sorry, Callum, she'd say under her breath, but it had to be. It was either this or starve.

'Not much to it, really. But my last lodger was happy here. I will leave you to yourself, but I do come in here once a week to water Henry,' she said to James.

He looked puzzled.

'The plant. A bit twee to give plants names, I know, but I've had him for years. I think he merits some sort of acknowledgement for staying alive for such a long time. I'll let you see the kitchen, which, I'm afraid we'll have to share. Still, it won't be too bad, I'm rarely in there.'

The kitchen was huge and a bit neglected. There was a large table, round which stood seven or eight assorted chairs. Its top was cluttered with newspapers, mail, books and pot plants. Pine units ran the length of one wall, a cooker in the middle of them; the tops were white-tiled, littered with crumbs and coffee stains, illuminated by sunshine streaming through the window. Copper pots hung from hooks overhead, and the wall opposite the units was covered with a collection of oil paintings. James could tell that once this room had been the hub of a household; it had been alive and busy. It had stories to tell.

'You can have the three cupboards on the right,' said Bibi. 'And that fridge is yours.' She pointed to the newer of two fridges standing side by side behind the door. 'The other's mine. Like I said, I don't like sharing.'

'You don't like sharing?' asked James.

'Well, some things. A bottle of wine, my bed once upon a time. I shared everything with my husband – food, obviously, toothpaste, some clothes even, a child or two. I have even shared a child with another woman, but I don't talk about that. These days, I like to keep some things to myself. I come from a large family, six brothers and sisters. Personal belongings become precious.'

James said, 'Ah,' and asked if he could take another look at the rooms.

Bibi led the way. 'The bed is an heirloom. My family, not my husband's. It was among the few possessions my mother spirited away from her home before everything had to be sold to pay death duties on my father's estate. My husband's family had nothing worth inheriting.'

'Your husband?'

'Callum, died fifteen years ago. A man of many passions, socialist, trade unionist, poet, orator, but in the end he was faithless. Believed in nothing, not politics, unions, literature. Except love, he believed in that. Though, of course, love never comes without complications, don't you think?'

James nodded. Sympathetically, he hoped. He wanted to make an impression. He wanted to come and live in these rooms.

'It must have been quite a squeeze at home with all those brothers and sisters.'

'Good heavens, no. We had an enormous house. A mansion, really. Twenty rooms. There was always somebody getting lost, usually me. I was a wanderer. Lovely times, huge parties, picnics, guests every weekend. After my father died, we lost pretty much everything. I always meant to go back and look at that old house. Never did get round to it.'

'Where is it?' asked James.

'North, Inverness way.'

James nodded again. He went through the bedroom to the small living room, where he stood quite still and looked around him. He breathed the air and smelled . . . what? Lilies? Sandalwood? He didn't know. But there was peace here, stillness. Who among his old acquaintances – for he never did have many friends – would believe he might live in rooms like these?

Bibi watched. He seemed to have forgotten she was there. She had been about to tell him there were other people interested in viewing the rooms. She'd actually been hoping for a woman. But, right now James reminded her of somebody, and her heart stopped. Something strange happened inside her – a rush and tumble of emotions. This surprised her. She'd long forgotten such things could happen. It was the way he stood, the concentration on his face, the intensity of his scrutiny of the furniture, the view from the window, the jade boxes on the mantelpiece, as if he could see something others couldn't.

Graham, Bibi thought. My God, it could be him.

Though, of course, it wasn't, Graham had left many years ago. For a moment she wondered if perhaps he had returned to her in some mystic way to let her know he was all right. But she didn't believe in such things. Besides, the young man she was looking at was smaller than Graham, slighter, and with fair hair, while Graham's had been dark. And, of course, he was much younger. Graham would be in his forties now. Still, in this light, watching his face – the high cheekbones, the thin lips, the long forehead – the resemblance was uncanny.

So she didn't say that there were others coming to view the rooms. Or that she was waiting for a decision from a previous viewer. Instead she said, 'So, when can you move in?'

'I can have the rooms?' asked James.

'Absolutely. I thought that was the purpose of the visit. I'm certainly not going to put up with a huge crowd of potential lodgers arriving every half-hour or so to view them. No, you seem fine to me. You're not a rapist or murderer, are you? You don't play loud rap music at unspeakable hours of the morning? You're not going to be entertaining dubious people like drug-pushers, I assume.'

She wanted him here so she could look at him. This

might have been what Graham was like in those early years when he was first away from her. The time in his life when he'd moved from being a boy to becoming a man. The time, too, when he'd been angry with her. She didn't know if he still was.

'No.' James shook his head, quite appalled that she might think he was a rapist or murderer who played loud rap music and invited drug-pushers round.

'Well, you'll do then. I'll contact the agency and they'll get you to sign the lease. There's three months' rent in advance, returnable when you leave, less any money for breakages. You're not prone to breaking things, are you?'

'No,' said James. And he blushed. He was. Sometimes he got nervy and things just fell from his hands, or he felt his elbows were out of control and seemed to knock over things he hadn't noticed were there.

'Excellent,' said Bibi. She'd noticed the blush, and thought, Yes, he looks like someone who doesn't fit his body. It acts on its own without him being able to do anything about it. He has an elbow problem. She led him up the hall towards the door. 'I don't supply linen. But your electricity and heating are included in the rent.'

'Fine,' said James. He paused, staring at a framed photograph on the wall. A family gathered round a table outside a long, low building. It was sunny; there were pots of begonias by the open door, a vine climbed a pergola, sprawled green and vibrant over the gathering below. The table was spread with plates of food, bottles of wine, glasses. James longed to know what it was they were all eating, but didn't like to peer too closely.

'France, about twenty-five years ago,' said Bibi, coming to stand beside him. 'A family holiday. That's Callum.' She pointed to the man, smiling, raising a glass of wine, nearest to the camera. He was tall, wore a straw hat and small wire-rimmed spectacles. His shirt was denim, collarless, his trousers white, worn and baggy. On his feet was a pair of sandals. He looked to be in his sixties, but he was tanned, handsome.

At the far end of the table was a woman, also tall and tanned. She wore a long calico dress, was leaning on her elbow, head in hand, smiling, a tumble of dark chestnut hair falling past her arm. She was, James thought, the most strikingly good-looking woman he'd ever seen. Her face was open, humorous, sensual. The dress was low cut; James could see her breasts: not all of them, but enough to know he was looking at someone who was earthy and very sexy.

'Me,' said Bibi. 'Not altogether sober, I have to tell you.'

James nodded. He was swamped with envy. He wanted to be there, with those people, drinking wine, joining in the jokes and banter, laughing. 'There's a lot of children there,' he said.

'Mine,' said Bibi. 'All five of them. Liz, Roddy, Celia, Graham and Beth. Though not necessarily in that order. Roddy's the oldest,' she pointed to a young man of about twenty, 'and that's Beth. Three at the time.' Squatting by Callum's knee was a round and happy child wearing nothing more than a pair of yellow knickers; she was waving a spoon. 'Nothing like that now, of course. She's twenty-eight and full of herself. There's always a tendency to spoil the youngest. You'll meet her, no doubt. She usually drops by when she's short of cash or when some steamy romance goes awry. And I'm afraid these things happen rather a lot.'

James smiled and nodded. Steamy romances that go awry; yes, he knew about that. 'You had a big family.'

'Yes,' said Bibi. 'Making babies was one of the few things Callum and I did together. We got rather good at it. We disagreed about most things: politics, religion, books, music. But when we got into bed, well, we did rather enjoy ourselves.'

James said, 'Yes, well.' There was something about a woman of Bibi's age talking so candidly that embarrassed him. He didn't think they should. Old ladies, he thought, should leave carnal doings behind them and never mention them. 'Is this a big flat?' he asked. 'Where did everyone sleep?'

'It's enormous,' said Bibi. 'Far too big for me on my own. The family is always trying to persuade me to move into something smaller. But this is home, has been for the past forty-odd years. I'm settled, won't leave unless it's in a box. Which may be soon enough.'

James smiled. 'Surely not.' He didn't want that to happen. He'd have to find somewhere else to live.

'My room is down the hall a bit from yours, opposite the kitchen. Then there's the drawing room, as Callum liked to call it. Beyond that there's a further four bedrooms. All empty now the family has flown the nest,' Bibi said, heading for the front door. She turned, held out a hand for James to shake. 'See you next week then. I'm sure you'll be very happy here.'

16

James had walked back to the leasing agency in Dundas Street. He signed the lease and wrote a cheque for the deposit, thanked everyone very much indeed, and left. He walked towards the town centre, looking for somewhere to have a cup of coffee. It was cold, a wind sweeping up from the Forth; people busied past him, clutching their coats, huddled against the chill. He stopped. What a strange old woman, he thought. All that stuff she told me, and me an absolute stranger. He frowned, remembering the conversation he'd had with Bibi. He hadn't taken it all in at the time. What had she meant when she'd said she'd shared a child? He shrugged. Old ladies, they rambled.

A Chance to Make a Statement

Celia phoned Beth. 'You'll have to take her, I can't. I have clients back to back all day. Two root canals and some bridgework on a policeman who has a phobia about dentists. Huge bloke, reduced to jelly by the sound of a drill. Then I have to be home by six, it's Olivia's school concert tonight. She's doing a solo on her flute, some Mozart thing that frankly I've heard so much I'm not sure I want to sit through it again. The state she's in, she's worse than my policeman.'

'She'll be fine,' said Beth. 'She'll get on that stage and dazzle everyone.'

'I know. But I'll have to sit on one of those hard little school chairs for two hours, and my back's killing me.'

'Dentist's back,' said Beth. 'A well-known condition.'

'I know. I'm going to a chiropractor next week. Anyway, our mother, can you take her to the clinic? I'm not going to manage it.'

'When's her appointment?'

'Two o'clock.'

'My lunchtime ends at half one.'

'Well change it. You can do that. You're sleeping with the boss, for heaven's sake. That should get you some privileges.'

'I don't like to take advantage of my situation. It annoys my colleagues,' said Beth. 'There is jealousy and aggravation.'

'Just change your lunch hour and take Mum to the clinic.'

Beth said she would but that she wasn't staying to drive her home. 'She'll be ages. She'll pester the doctor and try to sort out the National Health Service. Will she be at home?'

Celia sighed, 'No, she'll be at the allotment. She goes there every day if it isn't raining. God knows what she does.' She looked round at her reception area. She was proud of it. It was relaxing, pale green, a colour known to be soothing. There were paintings of tranquil landscapes on the walls. A sofa, a couple of leather chairs stood beside a table with a selection of mind-enhancing books about meditation, keeping calm, finding inner peace. Celia desperately tried to convince her patients that a visit to the dentist could be an enriching experience. She played music as she drilled and poked inside people's mouths – Mozart, Chopin or Schubert trilled out, barely audible above the whine of her expensive equipment. But somehow this decor, a call for inner peace, didn't work for her if she was talking about, or even thinking about, her mother. Bibi always made her nervous.

'She sits in that little shed talking to other old gardening types, drinking red wine, sorting out the world. Look, it's quarter to nine, I have to get up and get ready for work,' said Beth.

'You're not up!' said Celia. 'What sort of job do you have? I'm calling you from work. I've been here for an hour. I've already seen two clients.'

'God,' said Beth, 'going to the dentist is bad enough; going at dawn must be hell.'

'It's the only time of day some people can manage. They have responsible jobs.'

'*I* have a very responsible job. I may not get into work before ten, but I never leave till well after six. And I often have to work really, really late.'

'Taking people to dinner isn't work,' said Celia.

'Is too,' said Beth. 'You have to project, smile, keep the conversation going. It isn't the same as going out with friends.'

Celia snorted and said she had to go. Deirdre, the receptionist, had arrived and was making coffee, and she had a lot of paperwork to get through before her first root canal at nine fifteen.

Beth put the phone down and lay back, her head filled with things she didn't want to do – get up, go to work, fetch her mother from her allotment and take her to the clinic. But then her life these days was so packed with things she didn't want to do, she'd lost track of what it was she did want. She told herself often that she had to take hold of her existence, get some direction, find something that roused her passions, gave her a reason to get out of bed in the morning.

She would have liked to blame this apathy on her mother, but couldn't. Both her mother and her father, when he was alive, had doted on her. They'd encouraged any interest she showed in anything. So there had been dancing classes, piano lessons, horse-riding, trips to the cinema, books about horses, astrology, biographies of rock stars and actors she'd taken an adolescent shine to, posters, CDs. They'd cuddled her when she was little, carried her on their shoulders, laughed at her jokes, which were mostly pathetic, welcomed her friends into their home, accommodated her eating fads. No, she couldn't fault them, though she desperately wanted to. In fact, and she was loath to admit this, they'd given her more of their time, affection and actual material things than they had any of her four siblings. And look at them, all in good jobs, buying houses, bringing up children, and all of them happy. Or making a show of being happy. Except Graham, of course, but then he might be happy now. Beth didn't know. Nobody in the family knew. Graham was lost to them, nobody knew where he was.

And look at me, she thought. What am I? A marketing liaison assistant. What the hell is that? People looked impressed when she told them what she did. They also looked blank. 'I liaise,' she'd say. 'I work for the PR department in an advertising agency, and I liaise between departments and with financiers and clients.'

'At the moment,' she'd once told a woman at a dinner party, 'I'm working on an exhibition of graphics used in advertising and I'm liaising between the people who are mounting the exhibition, the exhibitors, and the people who are financing the whole thing.'

The woman had looked mildly impressed, and more than a little blank. Beth thought she had sounded pretentious and absurd. In truth, she'd been sleeping with Bradley, who owned the agency and who was bright, hardworking and creative. And when she'd complained of having nothing to do, and needing money, he'd put her on his payroll. Then he'd thought up a name for the job he'd given her, which was a very creative bit of thinking. Now she did at the office the same things she'd done when she wasn't working: she emailed and phoned her friends, chatting and arranging outings to the cinema and restaurants. 'I'm a sham,' she told herself.

The allotment was fairly large. Bibi had rented it from the council for the past thirty years. She grew a selection of vegetables – onions, cabbages, cauliflowers, broad beans and mangetout peas. Herbs flourished, as did the fruit bushes. Once, everything had been brought home and put into the freezer or made into jam. Now, with nobody around but herself, she gave most of it away. The flowers she kept, though she rarely picked them. She liked tall blooms, ones with a swagger – delphiniums, dahlias, hollyhocks – and rarities: black lilies, dark purple poppies, a selection of unusual fritillaries. The front of her borders was thick with clustering green and black pansies. She had fifteen or so assorted clematis and several different kinds of lavender. She had planted salmon-pink verbascum and tall white daisies to add to the mix.

These days, the allotment, with its winding brick paths, small white picket fences and vibrant flowerbeds, was a little neglected. Weeds had pushed up through the cracks in the path, and the small shed where the tools were kept, and where Bibi sat by an old electric heater, needed painting. But that was not why the council had, a couple of years ago, tried to evict her. The notice to vacate the premises had been issued on account of the marijuana.

She had vehemently denied growing it. *I'm old*, she wrote to the council, *very old indeed. Why would I grow such a thing? I don't even know what it looks like. I fear it must have been planted by some local youths up to mischief. Had I discovered it, and known what it was, I'd have whipped it out immediately.*

The council had replied that in the circumstances, Bibi could keep her allotment. But they advised her to keep a close eye on what might be growing in it, and should they find any more illicit substances on the small plot of land, they'd terminate their agreement.

Bibi had decided to stop cultivating her marijuana anyway. It wasn't the same, she'd decided. She'd puffed a little dope in the sixties, but that had been to get high. Now it was to dull her aches and pains and to help her dwindling eyesight. And that was a bit sad, she thought. Still, it had been pleasant to sit of an evening with two or three of the other gardeners, all pretty much the same age as herself, and drift into a mutual reverie of calm. She'd told her fellow indulgers – Dave, Wilma and Brian – that from now on they'd have to get their kicks from something else. They all started to drink wine after their hoeing and weeding and watering. They took this as seriously as they had their rolling and sharing of spliffs. The red was opened before any gardening started, to allow it to breathe; the white was kept in Brian's shed in the small chiller he'd bought. In the end, Bibi decided, she preferred the alcohol. It loosened their tongues; they'd chat, exchange gossip and complaints about the modern world: mobile phones, motorways, credit cards, computers and call centres. They laughed a lot. The spliffs had made them drift into a smiley silence. Wine, Bibi decided, was a lot more sociable, even if it did nothing for her arthritis.

In time, they'd bring some food along. Evenings, when the work was done, they'd sit on deckchairs outside Bibi's shed with its glass-fronted extension where she nurtured her seedlings, and over Merlot or Chardonnay, sandwiches and Wilma's fruitcake, discuss the state of the world, their miserable pensions and the best organic spray to get rid of greenfly. What she loved about the allotments was the number of new people who'd turned up over the last few years. Gardening was chic. They were mostly young, mostly keen to grow organically, and enthusiastic. They planted exotic things – small fig trees, squash, okra. Some were discussing forming a collective so they could buy the land and put an end to the threats from building corporations eager to take over the plots and cover them with new upmarket houses.

Once she and Callum would have been in the forefront of such a movement. They'd have organised meetings, petitions, leafleted all allotment holders in the city. They'd have made placards, written to the press, given heated interviews, held a rally outside the main offices of the building company concerned. Now, Bibi was happy to hear all the discussions going on in neighbouring plots without taking part in them. Doing nothing felt a little indolent and apathetic, and made her slightly guilty, but only slightly. Mostly, after years of campaigning for various causes, doing nothing was delicious.

This space was hers, always had been. Callum had not been welcome here. At first, when Bibi started renting the plot, he'd come along. He had helped to lay the brick paths. But then he'd begun to tell her what to plant, and where. He'd mocked her decision to grow Brussels sprouts: 'Nobody will eat them,' he'd said. He'd scoffed at her plan to have roses climbing over the shed and to put lupins in the flowerbeds. 'You're just a little suburbanite at heart, aren't you? You'll be wanting a small square lawn and a perfect row of tulips, I suppose.'

'No lawn and a clump of tulips,' said Bibi.

'This is land,' said Callum, spreading his arms, swirling to embrace the area. 'Leave it alone to grow as it's meant to, encourage natural plants, nettles and the like. Watch it go wild and enjoy the life that will come to it – foxes, badgers, field mice.'

'Rats,' said Bibi. 'I hate rats.'

'You're prejudiced. You have no right to hate rats. What have they done to you? They are part of the environment.'

'Not my environment,' said Bibi. 'You leave me alone to do what I want. This is my garden.'

'It's your chance to make a statement,' said Callum. 'You can say what you feel about small houses, small gardens and small minds. You can give this spot back to nature. You can liberate it.' Callum had been keen on liberating things.

'I've got a statement to make,' said Bibi, 'and my

statement is bugger off.' She poked him in the belly with the end of her hoe. 'Get off my land. Let me cultivate my space as I want to. Like I said, bugger off.'

Callum had turned and left. He'd taken the car; Bibi had had to walk home. Not that she minded. In fact, there had been a spring in her step; she was feeling jubilant. This hadn't been the first time she'd stood up to Callum. It had, however, been the first time she'd won.

Callum had not been gracious in defeat. He poured scorn on Bibi's gardening efforts. He mocked when he came across her poring over market garden catalogues, ridiculed the fruit bushes and packets of vegetable seeds that arrived through the post. But when Bibi came home after a hard day working her soil, arms laden with radishes, lettuces, rhubarb, new potatoes, raspberries, strawberries and gooseberries, and when the fruits of her labour turned up on his dinner plate tasting fresh and juicy, he changed his tune.

'From our own garden,' he'd tell guests. 'We grow nearly all our own food now. We're practically self-sufficient.'

Bibi let his boasting pass. That was Callum, she told herself. He described everything they did together, every idea they concocted as a couple, in the first person. 'I did that,' he'd say. Or 'It was my idea.' Every achievement that was Bibi's own was referred to in the first person plural: 'We grow our own food.' He was not a man who liked to be excluded.

Sitting in her shed, remembering her husband, Bibi smiled. There was not a day passed but she did not revisit scenes from her marriage. They haunted her mostly at home, in the flat where they'd lived, fought, had discussions, prepared food, made love. This was why she came here to this shed to sit, when there was little or no work to be done, on her old deckchair by the heater, drinking tea from her Thermos. Callum and her children had rarely come here, so this was where she was nobody's mother and nobody's wife. She was Bibi.

She heard footsteps outside and stiffly heaved herself from her chair to see who was coming. It was Beth, wobbling up the cracked old path on absurdly high heels. She saw Bibi's face bob up at the window and waved.

'Ready?' she said as she entered the shed. 'I've come to take you to the clinic. Celia can't make it. She's up to her eyes in root canals and other hideous dentisty things.'

Bibi pointed out that Celia was always busy. 'If it's not one thing it's another. She doesn't know how to relax. Never did.'

Beth folded up the deckchair, then leaned down to unplug the heater. 'I tried to phone, but you'd already left to come here. You should get a mobile.'

'What on earth for?'

'So we can keep in touch,' said Beth.

'The world is obsessed with keeping in touch,' said Bibi. 'What would we keep in touch about?'

'Things. Life. How you're doing. Where you are.'

'Things,' said Bibi. 'What things? What life? You know what my life is like; why would you want constant updates? And you know where I am; if I'm not at home, I'm here.'

Beth held the door open as Bibi packed her Thermos into her bag. 'But what if you fell down in the street? You could call me or Celia and let us know.'

'If I fell down in the street, I'd be flat on my back. The last thing I'd be thinking of doing is making a phone call.'

Beth sighed.

'Next thing you'll be wanting me to get a computer so I can email people,' said Bibi.

'You could easily keep in touch with Roddy. It takes seconds. Press a button and off goes your letter.'

'I can talk to people on the phone,' said Bibi. 'I like to hear their voices. Email is impersonal, and how do you know your letter has got to the person you sent it to? It shoots off into the ether, and you have no idea where it is.'

'You know it's got to them because they'll reply.'

'And what if they don't? You're left thinking you've said something rude and they're not speaking to you. No. No email and no mobile phone for me. The modern world has gone too far. People don't chat any more. I like voices. I miss voices.'

Bibi padlocked the shed door. They walked slowly down the path.

'I don't know why you come here in the winter,' said Beth. 'What do you do?'

'There's always something to be done. Tools to be taken care of, flower pots to be scrubbed out, a bit of snipping and pruning here and there. Besides, it's peaceful.'

'It's peaceful at home,' said Beth.

'Yes, the flat's very peaceful. It's just I'm not at peace

when I'm in it. Too many memories. They lie in wait for me, hiding behind doors or in drawers, waiting to leap out and destroy my calm.'

At one time, this would have been the cue for Beth to tell her mother she should move, get a smaller place to live. But she knew better than to do that. Bibi would only say, 'I can't move out of that flat. Too many memories.'

Beth looked round. The plots were empty now, winter still. Plants, snipped back, had slid below the earth and out of sight. She didn't know how many garden plots there were, but there seemed to be about twenty or so small sheds. Some painted, some covered with clematis or climbing roses, all leafless now. It fascinated her how many different personalities were expressed here. Some plots had small lawns, some had rose beds, some large vegetable patches. There were fruit trees and clumps of heather and winter-flowering pansies in pots.

She smelled earth, Bibi's perfume (Calvin Klein that she'd been given for Christmas last year) and drifting from the houses nearby the smell of cooking. Something foreign, Beth thought, curryish. She felt exposed here. Out of place in her business suit, black with a short skirt, and pale pink silk shirt, and high heels. Once she had come here with her mother every Saturday. But that had been years ago, when she was eight. Her interest in working the soil, weeding and hoeing and watching plants push up through the earth, had waned as her interest in music, makeup and boys waxed.

'Why are you going to the clinic anyway?' she asked.

'My yearly checkup, for my angina.'

29

They reached the car. 'You're not going to die, are you?' said Beth.

'Of course I am,' said Bibi. 'We all are. But it's not in my immediate to-do list. Also, I've just paid my gas and electricity bills. If I was going to die I certainly wouldn't have bothered with them. I'd go out on a spree with a credit card and leave you lot to pick up the pieces. You've all got a good deal more money than I have.'

Beth snorted. 'We all need more money. Things cost a lot more now than they did in your day.'

Bibi told her that people wanted to buy a lot more than they did in her day. 'We made do with less. We weren't caught up with consumerism.'

They got into the car. Bibi fumbled with her seat belt. 'I think about your father when I'm sitting at the allotment. I didn't used to. But these days he just floats into my mind. I was young and innocent when we met. It was at one of my father's parties. Not one of the grand affairs. This was more low key. Dinner, then we danced in the drawing room. There were only about fifteen people there. Somebody, I don't know who, brought him along. It was very fashionable then to have some sort of bohemian at get-togethers. He was quite famous. A poet and communist. We thought we were very bold associating with him. I thought he was gorgeous, so handsome. We put Duke Ellington on the radiogram; everyone was drinking gin and tonic or champagne. He was wearing a pair of baggy corduroy trousers. His shoes were a disgrace, hadn't seen a lick of polish in their life. My father disapproved. He said you could tell the cut of a man by his shoes. My father also disapproved of Callum's shirt, which was red. Back then a red shirt was unheard of, shocking. And his tie looked like it had been knitted by his granny. He came over and held out his hand to me. He didn't ask me to dance, just held out his hand and smiled. He knew I'd take it. It was almost as if this was why he'd come, to meet me, and take my hand and lead me into the middle of the room and dance. He always loved dancing, your father. So we danced. And that was that.'

Beth smiled. She'd heard all this before, many times. But like a child with a favourite bedtime story, she didn't mind hearing it again and again.

James

James hadn't always been James. Until recently he'd been Jimmy. Looking back on his Jimmy years, James recalled himself as an ordinary meat-eating bloke. He lived in Manchester and loved it. He could see no reason why anyone would want to live anywhere else. He went to pubs, clubs, he liked clothes, had a fairly large collection of CDs and loved cars. They were his passion. Mornings, in the bus on his way to work, he'd note every one he saw, whispering their names under his breath. 'Renault, Fiat. Oh, Audi convertible, excellent.' He thought he had the perfect job. He sold cars, and was considered to be surprisingly good at it. Yes, he thought, ordinary, that was what he'd been. And now he was a disillusioned fool. A dupe who'd been taken in by a liar, and a young female one at that.

Back in his days of being ordinary, he'd had a way of watching people, knowing exactly when and how to approach them. Relaxed, he would saunter up and compliment them on their taste in automobiles. He'd put his hand gently on the car's roof, strike a relaxed pose and say, 'Nice, isn't it?' He'd enthuse quietly about the car's petrol consumption, its acceleration, its gadgetry, its colour. He'd invite the customer to sit at the wheel, and offer a test drive, and make it seem as if he wasn't selling a car at all, just sharing his delight.

He'd started in the showroom at sixteen, cleaning and polishing cars. He'd hosed, shampooed, vacuumed, buffed, seen paintwork and chrome start to gleam, and buffed some more. Watching the shine deepen pleased him. He was happy. He was working with cars. Could anybody ever want to do anything else? In time, his eagerness was rewarded; he was offered the chance to work in sales on Saturdays. 'Learn the ropes,' the manager said.

Nobody in the sales team considered James to be noteworthy. The lad, they said, hadn't the personality to sell cars, or indeed anything. He was too shy, too introverted, he spoke too quietly, he'd no oomph, no swagger. He wasn't, they'd laugh, a contender. But James did well. He sold cars to people who only bought one because they needed it, and not because they loved cars or saw them as status symbols. People who only knew that you switched on the ignition, released the brake and put your foot on the accelerator, and did not want to think about what went on under the bonnet. And he sold cars to people who were a little ashamed of how little they knew about them. He could flick open a small compartment on the dashboard, provided as a handy space to keep money for parking meters. 'Cool or what?' he'd say, as delighted with the novelty as the potential buyer. He could point out that there was plenty of room for a handbag or shopping, or that the boot could be opened by pulling a lever on the inside of the door. 'Isn't it fantastic?' he'd say. 'I mean, don't you just love it?'

He was so charming, affable and gently persuasive, he was soon making two or three sales most Saturdays, always to people who knew nothing about cars and found them daunting, and their need for one irritating. It was not long before he was promoted permanently on to the sales team. His colleagues admitted they'd been wrong, 'Who'd have thought it?' they said. 'He can sell cars to people who don't like cars, just need them.'

James, when he was not talking to customers who knew nothing about cars, spoke the language of the enthusiast. Read all the magazines, watched the television programmes, and when he went to the cinema he didn't follow the plot line or listen to the dialogue; he looked at the cars. One day, he promised himself, he'd own a Ferrari.

Most of his colleagues thought this unlikely. He'll make it to an Audi, second-hand, maybe, or a Volvo. He's not a Ferrari man, they said. They all thought James was one of life's unfortunates. He just could not cope with the simple business of being alive. The smallest of dilemmas unnerved him. Even something as minor as stepping off the pavement without checking the traffic, then being harshly tooted at by some passing driver, seemed to upset him more than was warranted. He'd jump back and stand apologising to people around him and to the tooting vehicle long after it had disappeared down the road.

He'd been ten when his mother died, and had been brought up by his father, a retiring, gentle soul who worked as a postman. Their life together was placid. They spoke in quiet voices, moving about the council flat they shared in an easy mutual rhythm. Evenings, they would prepare a meal together, James peeling potatoes and setting the small table in the kitchen, Nigel, his father, making chips, frying eggs or sausages, putting on the kettle for a pot of tea. As they ate, they'd exchange gossip, though it was mostly Nigel who spoke. He'd tell tales of a postman's life – the people he met, their hallways, their pets, their garden paths. 'You see the world delivering the mail,' he'd say. 'You meet all sorts.' He secretly hoped James would follow him into the postal service.

They had two running disagreements, one about James's refusal to join his father in church on Sundays, the other about James's job, which Nigel thought beneath him. Not that they argued; there was no raising of voices. Rather they had the grumpy exchanges of two shy, stubborn people who hated confrontation.

'What do you want to sell cars for? That's no way to make a living, getting people to sign up for years of payment, encouraging them into debt,' Nigel might say.

'It's a good thing to do. It's rewarding to see people's faces when they pick up their new motor. Cars give people freedom. They are beautiful.'

'Flowers are beautiful, trees, birds. The sky is beautiful. And none of these things costs a penny. God gives people freedom. That's what life is about. Not big lumps of metal.' And Nigel would express his disapproval of the red Ford Escort ex-demonstration model James had bought. The love of his life that would take him four years to pay for, and that he polished every Sunday morning when Nigel thought he ought to be in church. He was a deeply religious man who found the worship of a shiny metal thing horrifying.

But James stood firm. He was an atheist and a petrol head, and proud. Just walking up to the beloved Ford caused his heart to quicken, his breath to catch in his throat. He tinkered with the engine, added alloy wheels, a leather steering-wheel glove and a natty gearstick. The very smell of petrol fumes in the morning made him heady. He was aglow with the joy of ownership. Buying the Ford Escort had been the pinnacle of his achievements. 'Dad,' he'd say, with a sorrowful lowering of his voice, 'you just don't understand.'

Nigel died on a bitter February morning when he had finished his rounds and was on his way back to the main post office: a heart attack. James was nineteen at the time, and racked with guilt. He thought it was his fault. He'd had a grumpy exchange with his father that morning.

Nigel had expressed his regret, for the umpteenth time, that James had not become a postman. 'Good, healthy, honest work,' he'd said. 'I don't sell people things they can't afford. I don't get them into debt.' He was a man who had never borrowed money to pay for anything in his life.

'Who'd want to be a postman?' James had said. 'Heaving sacks of mail through wind and rain, delivering bills and bad news.'

'I bring people good news as well as bad. Love letters, news from folks abroad, presents, birthday cards, exam results, university acceptances, Valentines, offers of jobs, all sorts,' Nigel had said. 'It's a grand job I do. People need a postman.'

James had said that cars were beautiful, they brought pleasure and freedom to travel anywhere people wanted. And that one day everyone would have email and nobody would need postmen.

Nigel told him he was wrong. 'No, son. There's nothing better than a letter. The world will always need someone to deliver the mail. There's always someone looking out for the postman to call.' And with that, he'd left, shutting the front door quietly behind him. James always thought he'd broken his father's heart speaking badly of the job he loved.

James's boss helped him arrange the funeral. They'd both been amazed at the crowd that turned up. James hadn't realised his father had been so popular. The mourners were mostly colleagues from work and friends from church, but quite a few people who had seen Nigel arrive at their door every morning for years and had welcomed his friendly face had come along to say goodbye. There were no relatives; both Nigel and Mary, James's mother, had been only children. Their parents had died years ago.

Afterwards, alone in the flat, missing his father – the quiet way he'd bustle in the kitchen preparing the evening meal, and how, after they'd eaten and washed the dishes, he'd spread newspaper on the table to keep it free from boot polish as he brushed, then buffed his shoes and held them at arm's length admiring the shine ('A man needs proper shoes,' he'd say. 'Look after your shoes and your feet will never suffer') – James imagined Nigel walking alone through that bitter morning, wind and sleet in his face, feeling broken-hearted at his son's cruel words. Guilt and grief took a grip of him.

The next day, James returned to work. He'd been given time off, but didn't know what to do with himself. As if on autopilot, he rose from bed, showered, ate a bowl of cornflakes and went to the showroom to move among cars. Shiny and solid and smelling of newness, they were a comfort.

Evenings now, he sat in front of the television, hardly aware of what he was watching. In bed he'd lie staring into the dark, listening to the sounds of the night outside, cars passing, people calling, footsteps on the pavement. He felt that he had stopped; he was still and empty and around him everything carried on as if nothing had happened.

It was round about then that he developed his reputation for being an unfortunate. Every so often his emotions welled up within him. He found it hard to breathe. He'd be overly aware of tiny things going on around him, as if they were happening in vivid Technicolor – a bird landing on a telegraph wire, a chocolate wrapper blown by the wind scraping along the pavement, someone in the car showroom laughing. These minuscule events had seemed to distract him not just from what he was doing at the time – talking to a customer, filling in his paperwork – but from thinking. He was numb.

At such times, perhaps because he was concentrating so much on suffocating his feelings, he forgot about his body. It often looked as if his arms were not only out of synch with the rest of him, but also out of synch with each other, moving independently, crashing into cups or knocking over a display stand. Occasionally his head appeared to be either tagging along behind, or bobbing in front of him as he walked. Entangled in feelings he had no notion of how to express, he lost the knack of communicating.

Then again, he had a gift for being in the wrong place at the wrong time. If a football, kicked too hard and too wild, was flying out of a playing field, James would be passing and would get hit. If a bird sailing overhead suddenly relieved itself, James would be underneath, directly in the path of the descending shit. James tripped on kerbs, bumped into lampposts, dropped things, lost things, sat on things. Once or twice he'd caught his tie in a customer's car door, and had to run alongside, tapping the window, saying, 'Excuse me. Excuse me,' as the vehicle pulled away. Watching this, the manager's secretary had said that the lad was suffering. 'He's bottled up all his sadness. He'll come to himself in time.'

James did indeed come to himself, on a Saturday night in June. He met Vicky. It was balmy; the streets were alive with young people moving between pubs. Throngs drifting. There was laughter; music blared from bars and thudded from the open windows of cruising cars. James was wearing a dark green shirt hanging loose outside a pair of new Armani trousers he'd bought in a sale. His hair, a pale sandy colour, was cropped short. There was something about the night, the air silky soft, summer still new; he could tell something good was about to happen.

He was in a pub, looking round, smiling, swigging lager straight from the bottle. He was standing, as always, on the edge of the crowd he was with – some friends from work, and some of their friends. Vicky, on the edge of her crowd, was standing next to him. Excluded from the banter, mostly because he couldn't be heard over the roar of the Stone Roses CD that was blasting, he spoke to her instead.

He fought his way to the bar to buy her a drink, vodka and Coke. They exchanged names. She was a student doing English and history. He'd sold two cars today. They both liked the same television programmes. Neither of them particularly followed football, but she loved tennis. At nine o'clock, when the others decided to move on to another pub, then a club, James stayed put.

He asked her if she'd like to go for a meal. 'Not really,' she said. 'I'm veggie.' She lit up, her face and body engulfed in the surge of joy brought on by a really good idea. 'We could go to McDonald's for a shake and fries.'

'Excellent,' said James. This was his kind of girl. She wore an orange top that revealed her tanned midriff, and tight black satin jeans. On their way there she smoked Marlboro Lights.

They sat inside, at the window, watching the night. He asked how old she was.

'Nineteen,' she said.

He thought that perfect. He was twenty-three, four years into being an unfortunate. He still lived in the council flat he'd shared with his father.

He found her easy to chat to, but then she was the first person he'd met who didn't mind his commenting on every car that passed. 'Merc, nice.' She was his ideal woman – small, very small in fact, blonde, skinny and blue-eyed. He did notice she was prone to giggling, and sometimes put her hand over her mouth to hide her laughter. But that only endeared her more to him.

Outside, the summer hummed and buzzed. Inside smelled of burgers and coffee. The place rattled and sizzled. He asked where she lived.

'Still at home with my mum and dad. He sells carpets. He has a chain of carpet warehouses. He says you can tell everything you need to know about a person by his carpet.'

James thought about the old pale green carpet in his flat. What did that say about him?

'I've never bought a carpet,' he said. 'I'll have to be careful when I do.' He looked out of the window. 'Renault.' He told her he loved selling cars. 'It's the biggest thing people buy, apart from a house. You should see how they smile when they drive away. It's rewarding.' He looked out of the window again, watching the traffic. 'Ford Escort. Golf GTi. Nice.' And all the time he was thinking, Wonderful, wonderful, wonderful.

At half past ten, she told him she had to go. 'I have to get up early tomorrow.'

He asked why. She told him, 'Stuff. You know.'

He nodded, though he didn't know. He asked if he could see her home. She shook her head. 'Nah. I'll get a taxi.'

He held her hand as they walked, lifting their entwined fingers now and then to look at them and take delight in this new small intimacy. When he asked if he could see her again, she said, 'Yeah, sure.' When she climbed into the taxi he heard her give the driver her address. 'Chorlton,' she said. Nice, thought James. A lot nicer than Hulme where he lived.

It became their routine to meet on Friday and Saturday nights. They'd go to the cinema or for a meal. When they kissed, James could tell she was a lot better at this than he was. He pleaded for her to come home to his flat and go to bed with him, but she never would.

'I like it in town, the lights and noise. I don't want to go to some old flat,' she said.

'It isn't that bad,' he'd said.

She had just said, 'Nah.'

Then at eleven o'clock she'd get into a taxi. He never did accompany her home.

Over the months, James stopped being an unfortunate. He lost his awkwardness. He stopped bumping into things, knocking things over, and he stopped having these numb moments when he couldn't think, couldn't breathe, and thought the world was closing in on him. He became so much more alive. He had a girlfriend, and told everyone he knew whenever he had a chance. Asked if he wanted to go to the pub, he'd say, 'Love to. But I'm seeing the girlfriend tonight.'

She told him her secrets, hoping to shock him. 'Sometimes me and my mate go out at night and run through the park without any clothes on.'

'You do what?'

'We take everything off and run about naked. It's lovely. I feel free.'

'Please don't do that. You could get attacked. I'll worry about you now. Promise me you'll stop.'

'Yeah, well,' she said.

She told him she smoked dope in her bedroom at nights.

'Goodness,' he said. 'I've never done anything like that. You're quite a girl.'

She'd smiled and said she liked to experience things. And he suspected he must appear quite dull to her.

For Vicky he grew his hair longer, bought himself new clothes and painted the flat. It had hardly been touched in years. He got new sheets and duvet covers for the bed and a new sofa, hoping for the day she'd come to see him here.

He'd thought a lot about why she always refused to come to his flat. He thought it could only be because she was a virgin, and was a little afraid of what might happen if they were alone together in a place where they would be free to let their passion rip. He wondered if she *was* afraid, or if she worried he'd think less of her if she let him make love to her. Beneath all the confidence, the tales of running naked in the park, was a shy and insecure little girl. If they became lovers, he thought, he would only love her more. He'd be kind to her; he wanted to take care of her.

Imagining how his life with Vicky would unfold was his favourite daydream. On their first night of love, he would light candles, cook her a meal, pasta perhaps; he'd play soft music on his hi-fi, he'd be gentle. After that, they'd often spend nights together. She might even come and live with him while she finished her degree. Then they'd marry. She'd teach, he'd be regional sales manager of a chain of garages. He'd have an estate car; a Volvo was a good safe bet. He'd buy Vicky a small convertible, a Mazda, he decided. She'd love that. Sitting at his desk, he'd swing on his chair, a wistful smirk flickering on his lips. He only saw Vicky twice a week, but he conjured up a whole future for them both. He no longer saw how few friends he had; he moved into his own world of cosy fantasies.

He'd text her and email her a couple of times every day. Sometimes when he phoned her mobile she'd tell him she was with her friends. But he never met any of them. 'You're mine,' she told him. 'I'm keeping you to myself.' And always, whatever they were doing, wherever they were, come eleven o'clock, she'd go home.

He offered to take her there. He offered to come and pick her up. 'I want to meet your mother and father. I want them to meet me.' She always refused. Often, during the week, on days when he wasn't seeing her, he'd drive slowly past her house, staring in. It was huge, in an expensive part of town. There were two cars in the drive, a BMW and an MG sports car. The garden was landscaped, with clipped hedges and two symmetrical bay trees in large pots, one either side of the front door.

He'd park and sit in his car looking at the building, wondering what was going on behind the vast bay windows. He imagined a group of rich, designer-dressed people sitting round a candlelit table eating some kind of food he didn't even know about. Fabulous food. Or maybe they'd be lounging on some sumptuous sofa in front of a magnificent television, watching a documentary about the secret life of dolphins. Or they'd just be moving about, softly, on lush carpets, wandering occasionally to the kitchen to remove an ice-cold drink from the fridge, like people did in the movies. He desperately wanted to go through that glossy black front door and join them.

'Why don't you want me to meet your family?' he asked. 'Do you think they won't like me? You're ashamed of me, that's it, isn't it?'

Vicky said, 'No. It's fine like this. It's lovely. Don't let's spoil it.'

But spoil it he did. On the twenty-second of December at nine o'clock in the evening – he knew the date and time by heart – eighteen months after they met, he asked Vicky to marry him.

The weekend before, he had decorated the bed he hoped to share with her, wrapping multicoloured fairy lights, tinsel and baubles round the ends. 'It's all Christmassy,' he told her.

'I love Christmas,' she said. 'We have a huge party on Boxing Day. Everybody comes. There's champagne and everything.'

'Who is everybody?' asked James.

'Just everybody,' said Vicky.

'But not me,' said James.

'It's people we know,' said Vicky. 'My mum and dad invite them. They don't know about you. You're my secret.'

James said he didn't want to be a secret any more. He wanted everybody to know he loved her. Vicky said what she usually said in awkward moments: 'Yeah, well.'

In the week that followed, James made his big decision. He'd propose. Vicky would wear his ring, and everyone would want to know who had given it to her.

Then he'd get to meet her parents. Then he'd get invited to the party.

His bedroom twinkled, lit only by fairy lights and candles on the dresser. A dozen red roses stood in a beer mug; he hadn't realised he'd need a vase. Beside the bed were a box of chocolates, a bowl of Kettle's crisps and a bottle of vodka. On the bed was a new fur throw he thought Vicky would love. The baubles glistened. He would propose to her, let her know his feelings for her were honourable. Then he'd bring her to this flat, this bed, and make love to her.

He took her to an Italian restaurant. He had penne with crabmeat and chilli; she had vegetarian lasagne. They drank wine.

He bought her a huge chocolate pudding. As she worked her way through it, he brought out the ring. 'Marry me,' he said.

She slipped the ring on, and held up her hand, fingers splayed, admiring it. 'It's gorgeous. This has been the most gorgeous night of my life. Everything is gorgeous.'

'So will you?' he said. 'Marry me?'

'I can't. I have to finish my studies.'

'After you've graduated,' he said.

'I want to get a job. I want a career.'

'I won't stop you. I'll support you.'

She said, 'Yeah, well.'

He'd planned a speech about how he'd always love her and would work hard to keep her and help her do whatever she wanted after she graduated.

'We'll be engaged,' said Vicky. 'Then we'll talk about

getting married and everything later.' She flung her arms round him. 'I'm the first of all my mates to get engaged.'

She still went home at eleven o'clock. As the taxi drew away, James saw her take out her mobile, clamp it to her ear and start to chat excitedly. He went home, sat on the fur-covered bed and poured himself a vodka and Coke. He wasn't sure how his proposal had gone. He still hadn't been invited to meet Vicky's family. He was sure he wasn't going to the party.

He'd imagined it all. Arriving at the glossy door, ringing the bell, hearing the bustle of footsteps coming up the hall inside. Everyone smiling, greeting him: 'Hello, Jimmy.' It was warm in that house, busy and friendly. He would have taken a bottle of single malt for Vicky's dad, chocolates and flowers for her mum. He'd have been welcomed into the family. Her dad would have put his arm round his shoulders and said, 'Come away in, Jimmy. Make yourself at home. You're one of us now.' In time he'd have become a regular in the house, watching television with them all, helping in the kitchen with the dishes, talking to Vicky's dad about football or the rising interest rates, chatting with her mum about the garden or where to go on holiday. He'd seen it all on television; he wanted to be part of something like that.

Two days later, driving into the street where he lived, he noticed a black BMW gliding past him. He watched it in his rearview mirror as it oozed into the stream of traffic: 730i Sport, he thought, great car. Nothing to sixty in under seven seconds, top speed one hundred and fifty-two.

He parked and walked across the small area of scrubby

grass in front of his building, jingling his keys. Not that he needed them. His door had been forced open. He stood in the hallway, breathing, sniffing. There was a strange smell. Burning, he thought.

He went to the kitchen, and on the table was Vicky's engagement ring. He picked it up, stood turning it over in his fingers, wondering why it was there, then went down the hall to the bedroom.

It had been trashed. Some fury had been unleashed. The fairy lights and baubles had been ripped from the bed ends and trampled into the carpet. Multicoloured shards of crushed glass were spread thick, ground into the pile. His clothes had been pulled from the wardrobe and flung about the room; the drawers in his dresser yanked out, emptied and tossed to the floor. Someone had pulled the fur throw from the bed, set fire to it, then doused the flames by tossing the beer mug of roses over it. His small hi-fi lay wrecked on the floor.

He stood looking at the devastation, still turning the ring over in his fingers. He couldn't quite take in what he was seeing. But he was, he realised, shaking. 'Vicky?' he said. 'Vicky?'

He ran to the phone, repeating, 'Vicky? Vicky?' Dialled her mobile.

'Jimmy,' she said. 'You're not to phone me. I've got to stop seeing you. They found out about us.'

James said, 'What do you mean? What are you talking about?'

Another voice, a woman, came on. 'Are you the man who has been seeing my daughter?'

James said, 'Yes.'

'What sort of person are you, giving an engagement ring to a child? Have you no sense of decency?'

James said, 'Child?'

'Yes, a child, a schoolgirl.'

James said, 'School? Vicky?'

'Yes, Victoria,' said the voice, icily furious. 'It is as well she has at least one sensible friend, who told her mother that you'd asked her to marry you. Tracy Millington phoned me last night and gave me the whole story. What sort of inadequate pervert are you? Can't you find someone your own age?'

James clenched the ring in his hand. 'Vicky,' he said. Then, 'I'm not a pervert. I love her.'

The phone went dead. He sat looking at the receiver, listening to the hum of the dialling tone. He didn't know what was happening. He said, 'Vicky, Vicky,' so softly his lips moved but hardly a sound slipped from them.

He remained on his sofa in the dark, phone in his lap, for a couple of hours, staring, frowning, trying to make sense of things that came to him in a series of questions. Vicky was at school? He'd been seeing a schoolgirl? He'd proposed to a schoolgirl who'd shown off her ring to her friends? One had told her mother, who'd told Vicky's mother?

The car, he thought, the BMW was the same as the one parked outside Vicky's house. Vicky had been here in that car? Or maybe her mother or father had been here. Her father, he decided. Vicky's father had been in a rage, thinking he'd been sleeping with his daughter.

He got up, switched on the light and went through to clean up. He moved slowly, putting the drawers back in place, folding his clothes, hanging them up. He picked up shards of glass, throwing them into a black bin bag along with his wrecked stereo, the ruined fur throw and the roses. He vacuumed. Made up his bed with fresh linen. Then carried the bag down to the bins at the back of the building.

He stood looking up at the flats, windows lit up, Christmas trees, the blue tint of televisions. Happy Christmas, he thought. He remembered Christmases with his father. They'd decorate the fake Christmas tree they'd bought from Woolworth's and put up the few cards they received. They'd exchange presents – socks, books and aftershave, usually – and cook pork chops since neither of them fancied turkey. Sometimes they played cards, then they'd drink beer and watch television. He wondered what his father would make of all this.

'Talk,' Nigel had often said, 'people should talk more. It's our great human gift, talking. You can sort anything with a chat.'

James thought that was what he should do. He should talk to Vicky's parents. He could explain to them that he hadn't known Vicky was at school. And that he definitely had not slept with her. He'd let them see what a kind, reasonable and reliable person he was. He would let them know he would wait till Vicky had finished school, wait till she'd graduated from university, wait till she'd settled in a career. Why, he'd wait for ever if he had to.

They'd chat quietly. They'd have a cup of tea and

discuss everything. In time they'd become friends. He could do all that, he was sure. He was good with people. Wasn't he the one who could sell cars to people who didn't like cars?

He had stood turning his keys over in his pocket, looking up at his kitchen window. He was in his shirtsleeves; he should go back upstairs and fetch his jacket. But no, the decision was made. He'd go now while it was all straight in his mind.

It was almost ten when he parked outside Vicky's house. He had practised everything he was going to say on the twenty-minute drive. It was clear in his head. He just had to explain.

Gravel crunched beneath his feet as he walked up to the front door. The night was bitterly cold, frosty clear, and he wished he'd brought his jacket. He'd look smarter, he'd be warmer. The curtains moved. Someone, he didn't know who, peered out.

He rang the bell, waited; nobody answered. He rang again, and again; still nobody answered. He banged on the door with his fist. Maybe they were watching television and hadn't heard. But then they'd seen him walking up the path, they knew he was here. He just wanted to talk. Why didn't they answer the door? He was filled with a desperate desire to see Vicky, to tell her he loved her and to tell her parents he only wanted the best for her. He ran to the middle of the front garden and shouted, 'Vicky. Vicky.' The curtains remained closed, nothing happened.

'VICKY! VICKY!' he yelled. He stood on the lawn, feeling wretched, fists clenched.

Lights went on in neighbouring houses. People stood at windows, watching. And a man appeared at Vicky's front door. He was small, thickset, with cropped hair, wearing jeans and a white shirt. He started walking towards James, who smiled. 'I need to see Vicky. I need to explain. I didn't know she was at school. She told me she was at university.'

The man kept coming. Walking faster now. And James realised he wasn't looking very friendly. In fact, he'd never seen anyone look so anguished and angry. He was standing, feeling slightly shy, a small smile on his lips, and this man was walking too quickly, coming horribly close.

The punch caught him just below his left eye. Crunched against the side of his nose and his cheek. Then there was a change of view. He was lying on the grass, holding his face. Salty blood was running down the back of his throat. Then the man kicked him and kicked him, kept kicking him. He tried to get up and run, but couldn't. Instead he curled up, squirming, trying to avoid the flailing boot.

'She's fourteen, you fuck,' the man said.

'I didn't know,' said James. 'I didn't know. I want to talk to you.'

A woman came to the door and started screaming. 'Barry, stop it! Someone will call the police.'

But Barry picked James up by the shirt collar. 'My daughter, my daughter, you little arse.'

James couldn't breathe. He had his arms protectively round his head. Barry punched him again, 'My little girl.'

The woman, in white jeans and thin slippers that

slapped on the ground as she ran, reached Barry, started to haul him back into the house. 'Stop it. Stop it,' she screamed. 'He's not worth it.'

The pair backed towards the house. 'She's fourteen,' said Barry. 'My daughter is fourteen.'

James got painfully to his feet. He didn't think his legs would hold him upright. He ached; blood ran down his face. 'I didn't know. I didn't know. She told me she was nineteen, at university.'

'University?' the woman, Vicky's mother, said. 'She's a child. You must have known she was a child.'

James could see Vicky standing on the doorstep. She had her hand over her mouth. Indeed, at this moment, she looked like a little girl.

'You've ruined our Christmas,' said the woman.

'And you haven't ruined mine?' said James. 'You can still have your party.'

'What party?' said Vicky's mother.

'Your big party, the one you always have on Boxing Day.'

'What are you talking about? We don't have a big party on Boxing Day. You must suffer from delusions. Please go away, and if you ever come near my daughter again, we'll have the police on you. You must be aware that what you have been doing is against the law.'

James stared. No party? he thought. No party?

He wiped his face with the tail of his shirt. The true awfulness of his situation trickled into his mind. Vicky was fourteen and her father was convinced he'd slept with her. Horror dawned. He could be reported to the police, arrested, accused of having sex with a minor. He could go to prison. 'I never touched her,' he said.

He started to walk slowly, still bent against his pain, towards his car. He turned, pointed to Vicky. 'That is no little girl. She's a bitch and a liar. And I never touched her.'

He looked in his mirror as he drove away, and saw the family standing on the lawn watching him go. They seemed as stunned as he was.

He spent Christmas Day in bed. Everything hurt. He gazed in the mirror at his bruised face. When he returned to work, he said he'd fallen down the stairs. They believed him; well, how else would a quiet lad get so beaten up?

James tripped over things, dropped cups and pens and car keys. He jumped whenever the phone rang. Drifted off into his private thoughts and fears in the middle of sentences, worrying that he would be arrested for sleeping with a minor, and failed to sell cars.

His euphoric fantasies turned to nightmares. What if Vicky's parents took her to a doctor to find out if she was still a virgin? And what if she wasn't? How did he know? What if they reported him to the police? How could he prove he hadn't slept with her? If the police didn't come for him, Barry would, probably bringing a couple of heavies to help avenge his little girl's loss of virtue. Coming home alone at night after working late, James would walk swiftly from his car to his building, turning often, checking there was nobody stalking him, preparing to leap on him from behind. He developed a rash, red and itchy, on his arms and legs. He was a nervous wreck.

After some months of this, his boss called him into his

office. 'Jimmy, Jimmy, Jimmy,' he said, rubbing the bridge of his nose with his finger. 'What's got into you?'

James said he didn't know.

'You're a good lad and I like you,' said his boss, 'but I've got to let you go. It's not just that you're not selling any cars; you are actually putting people off coming to the showroom. Look at you. You're a mess.'

James agreed, he was. He was sitting scratching his arm; his mouth was open; there was a bruise on his cheek where he'd tripped on his untied lace and hit the side of a desk as he fell. He said he was sorry. 'I can't help it.' He couldn't explain what had happened. He was too ashamed.

'Got a cousin in Edinburgh,' said his boss, 'owns a few health shops. Funny teas, veggie food, tofu, oils and balms, whale music, herbal remedies. That sort of stuff. Can't be doing with it myself. Hippy nonsense. But I spoke to him about you. Said you were a fine lad, quiet. He says he'll give you a trial. It might be just the thing. Maybe the car business is too stressful for you.'

'I love cars,' said James. 'They're the only thing I love.'

'Still, I think you should think about this offer.'

James nodded. He said he'd take the job. Not that he wanted it. He had no interest at all in health foods, balms, oils, herbs and whale music. But he knew he had to get away, live in a new city. Vicky and her family would not know where he was, and he could set about forgetting them.

Floating

It deeply irritated Bibi that when she was talking to her doctor, he would sit behind his desk consulting medical notes, while she sat in front of the desk with nothing to look at. She thought they should look at the notes together. It would be friendlier.

She longed to know exactly what these notes said. In fact, she thought she ought to be given them to read; they were about her, after all. So when Dr Martin was called away during his chat with her, the temptation to take a sneaky peek at her file was hard to resist.

She sat shifting her glance from the door to the notes. When the urge to look got too much to bear, she slipped round to the doctor's chair, opened the file, and read. In a panic she skimmed the words before her – *no medical intervention advised*. That was all she got to see; that was all she needed to see. Shocked, she returned to her seat.

Up till this moment she'd felt fine; having read that, she suddenly felt very frail indeed. What did *no medical intervention advised* mean?

Dr Martin returned. He told Bibi she was fine and he was happy with everything; her angina was under control, her blood pressure was good. 'Excellent,' he said. Considering how robust she was, he secretly thought Bibi

Saunders might outlive him. He walked her out to the reception area then bade her goodbye and told the nurse he was ready for his next patient, Barbara Simpson, an eighty-five-year-old with a serious heart condition and liver cancer. He suspected she would not survive a bypass operation. It was her notes that Bibi had sneakily read. Dr Martin, sensing Bibi's curiosity, had taken her file with him when he'd left her alone.

On the bus heading home, Bibi pondered her discovery. *No medical intervention advised* must mean that she was not worth operating on, or resuscitating, should her heart cease to function. She figured they must think this likely to happen, or they wouldn't have noted that it wasn't really advisable to intervene medically when the moment came.

It was clear to her that her doctor thought she was going to die, sooner rather than later. Well, she thought, it comes to us all, and now it is coming for me. She had, since passing seventy, been flippant about death, saying she wasn't afraid of it and that she hoped she would be told it was nigh so she could spend a huge amount of money and leave her children to pick up her debts. But now she wondered if she had touched her own mortality, and she didn't feel quite so flippant.

The bus was rumbling down The Mound, and she looked out across Princes Street Gardens. She had seen these gardens year after year, season after season, and soon – she had now convinced herself – she would never see them again. Bugger that, she thought.

She had walked in these gardens with her children and

Callum. They had come to watch the shows put on in the outdoor theatre and to swoon at the fireworks every festival. She and her mother had strolled here, when Bunty had moved to Edinburgh after Bibi's father died. Bibi and Callum had, at the time, been living here for several years in a tiny-roomed flat in Easter Road.

Every Thursday Bibi and her mother would meet for afternoon tea at Jenners, followed by a slow amble along the top of the gardens. Tea at Jenners was always pleasant, something of an Edinburgh ceremony. Bibi remembered the cluck of ladies chatting, clattering crockery. Each table was served two pots, one of tea, the other filled with steaming water to top up the tea after the first cups had been poured. She and Bunty ate scones. Bunty would thickly butter a small area of scone before each bite and tut at Bibi, who would cut her own scone in two, coat each half with strawberry jam and bite deeply, eyes shut. It was a method Bunty found upsetting. 'That is not the way to consume a scone,' she'd say. 'You should put things delicately into your mouth. Eating in public is an art. Be discreet. You can eat, but you must not be seen to be eating. No huge bites, no violent chewing.'

Bibi would shrug. Bunty would say she should have taken more interest in her when she was a child. 'I was always too busy to look after you properly. I regret that.'

Bunty always wore a flamboyant hat and a fur coat that she didn't remove, preferring to slide it off her shoulders. 'You should wear a hat, Bibi. It simply doesn't do to go out dressed like that. Look at you, all in black. You look like some sort of refugee waif.'

Bibi smiled, slightly pleased; it was the look she was after.

Thinking about it now, she realised that the women in fur coats, flamboyant hats and jewellery who took afternoon tea in Jenners were an extinct breed. They've all died off, she thought. She hoped they were happy in tearoom heaven, wearing their coats, eating scones properly and slipping shiny silver coins under their saucers for the angels in old-fashioned black-and-white waitressing outfits who served them.

Whatever they spoke about, Bunty would weave her impending death into the conversation, listing what she was leaving to whom, and who should and who should not be invited to her funeral. Unwaveringly polite in life, she was planning to snub a lot of people when she died. These were mostly people who had 'let her go', as she called it, after her husband Humphrey had died, leaving her with huge death duties and debts incurred by his misjudged business dealings. She was now, for the first time in her life, impoverished, and she didn't like it very much.

Bibi's childhood memories of her mother were of a busy woman, involved with many committees and arranging endless dinner parties. They seemed to have one a week, at least. She spent a lot of time on the phone, laughing with friends or quietly and deftly bullying people into doing things they did not want to do – taking part in a charity auction, arranging flowers for a bridge evening, giving a talk to the Women's Institute. Whatever it was the reluctant person was inveigled into doing, they'd end up thanking Bunty profusely for thinking of them. But in the middle of this Bibi was ignored, left to her own devices. 'Not now, Bibi,' her mother would say. Or, 'Ask Cook, she'll help with your homework.' Bibi owed a lot of her outlook and attitudes to Cook.

Sipping tea, Bunty would say, 'I deeply regret the number of times I sent you to Mrs Henderson. She was a splendid cook, but a communist. Well, she voted to the left and not the way I told her to. It was an act of rebellion.'

Bibi would smile at this.

'No point in asking you how *you* vote,' Bunty would say to her. 'Look at you. You might as well have *Leftie* stamped on your forehead. I haven't the time, before I die, to sort you out.'

She'd slip a silver coin under her plate and tell Bibi it was time for a walk through the gardens, then a taxi home.

During their small get-togethers, it was Bunty who did most of the talking. Bibi would smile and nod and very rarely mention Callum. She was aware of how intensely her mother disliked him, not really for luring Bibi away from her family; rather for influencing her to vote for left-wing parties. 'How could you?' Bunty said to her.

Once, while strolling through the gardens, Bunty had slipped her arm through Bibi's. It was spring; daffodils were in bloom, 'You're a good person, Bibi,' she had said. 'I'm afraid I rather neglected you as a child. I feel I hardly know you. But I like you, I think we may be friends.'

Three days later Bunty had died. Alone in her small Edinburgh flat, she'd had a massive heart attack.

Bibi got off the bus and walked down Dundas Street. It

was spring and warm, the sort of day that she always thought of as hopeful. Soon there would be swallows overhead, and her allotment garden would overflow with blooms. It was on such a day that her mother had told her she hardly knew her.

Thinking about it now, Bibi wondered why she hadn't told Bunty that she hardly knew her either. There had been phone calls when she'd first married Callum, but these had been strained and furtive, as her father had disowned her. He had heartily disapproved of her marriage. Then there had been the afternoon tea rituals, when Bunty had done most of the talking, but they hadn't really ever communicated with one another. They had never had a heart-to-heart, exposed their fears and embarrassments, hopes and moments of happiness. Dreadful, Bibi thought. Dreadful and remiss of both of us.

There had been a small funeral, attended by a few of her mother's friends. Bibi's brothers and sister had shown up, stayed around for a day, then gone their separate ways. Two of her brothers had been in the army, one worked in the city, the fourth had gone to seek his fortune in Australia; he did something in the media, Bibi didn't know what. Her sister had married well and lived in Washington for a while. Now Bibi didn't know where any of them were; they hadn't kept in touch. They had all been older than her, twenty years between her and her oldest brother. If he was still alive, he'd be in his nineties.

She headed for home, thinking how dreadful it was to lose touch with your closest kin. And what an awful thing it was for a mother to think she hardly knew her child.

She turned into Saxe-Coburg Street, walked the few familiar yards to her building. Won't happen to me, she thought. I will visit them all, I will make my peace with each one. She stamped up the stairs to her front door. I will talk to them. They will become my friends, she vowed. She thought it odd that, having discovered she might be on the brink of death, and was not worth medical intervention when it came for her, she felt unusually fit. Well, she decided, since she felt so fit, she would take a trip. She would visit her family and let them all know how much she loved them, and indeed, how well she knew them too.

On Sundays, Bibi would make a pot of coffee and take it, along with the newspapers, back to bed. Today, however, the paper delivery was late. She sat at the kitchen table, waiting for the familiar dull and heavy thud of papers and supplements landing on the doormat, drumming her fingers, mildly irritated at her routine being interrupted and looking about for something to read. 'Hate just sitting,' she said.

She took a book from the shelf behind her. The books on this shelf were what she thought of as life manuals: cookbooks, dictionaries, an atlas, a thesaurus, tomes to be consulted rather than read. But her life was in them, slipped between the pages: birthday cards, Christmas cards from people she loved; photographs of her children; a few of their school reports and drawings; a piece of thrift picked on a coastal walk; postcards, theatre tickets. The books all had cracked spines, they were so stuffed with mementoes.

Chinese Kosher Cookery caught her eye. A book she had picked up at a church sale many years ago; the title had amused her. She had only once tried a recipe from it, when Callum had invited a publisher from Seattle, Joe Abraham, and his wife Maureen to dinner, telling her they were Orthodox Jews, keen on Oriental food. This was one of his assumptions; the Abrahams turned out to be lapsed Catholics who weren't awfully keen on Chinese cooking.

She opened the book and found a photograph of Graham, four years old, tanking along the pavement on a red three-wheeled bike. There were old train tickets from Edinburgh to London; a thank-you note from the Abrahams: *we had a wonderful time, fabulous wine and such invigorating conversation*, they'd written, not mentioning the kosher Chinese food; a Mother's Day card Beth had made at school when she was six, and a postcard from Callum. It was from Cornwall, and his experience there would lead to a poem called 'Floating'.

Bibi reached for the bottle of wine left on the table from the night before, and poured herself a glass. Callum's notes always had this effect on her, whatever the time of day, and 'Floating' in particular made her need a drop of alcohol. The argument surrounding it had lasted for months, but had reached a peak in the week that Callum finished the poem. It remained in Bibi's memory as the floating argument.

She always recalled things by bringing to mind what

had been going on around her at the time. That was 1968, she thought. The Beatles everywhere.

It hadn't been a good time. Early August, and the children were on school holidays, complaining of being bored. Graham was four and enthused about dinosaurs. Celia spent most of her time looking at her picture books, which was a relief. Roddy, almost nine years old, had said to Callum's horror that he wanted to work in a bank when he grew up. 'There's lots of money in banks and I can get some of it to give to you. You never have any.'

'He did it to shock me,' Callum said. 'It's an act of rebellion. A son of mine a banker. I'd never live it down.'

And Callum was exhausted. He'd been campaigning, giving passionate speeches up and down the country on behalf of a group of workers in a factory in Glasgow who, on hearing they were to be made redundant, had staged a sit-in. For a week Callum had joined the workers, locked inside the factory to protest about the cruel injustices international corporations impose on ordinary working people.

But he'd grown bored with this. 'To tell the truth, Bibi,' he'd said, 'the food was awful. And I got virtually no sleep.' So he'd left the workers to sit in, while he went out into the world to spread word of their despair, and to urge other workers to down tools and join them. In his trademark black collarless shirt and buff waistcoat, black trousers and shoes, he'd delivered passionate speeches. Wind ruffled his hair, now greying and always too long, as he spoke at factory gates and gave interviews to journalists.

'This is about expense accounts over wages, executives over workers. This is a wave of new management that cares nothing about people, and we are going to see this happening time and time again in the coming years. This is about lives. This is about humanity.'

He pleaded with other workers to strike in sympathy; he called for a national strike. People had listened, roared their approval, clapped and cheered, then carried on as normal. Nobody had downed tools. After a month, the workers in the factory in Glasgow gave up their sit-in and went home. The factory closed, and other items of interest grabbed the headlines. Callum was a disappointed man. And there had been uproar at home in the flat, where an old friend from New York had been visiting.

To help him recover from his weariness and disenchant-ment, some friends, Robin and Franny Mackintosh, had invited him to join them on holiday in Cornwall. Callum always had friends; he was charming, good at drawing people to him.

'Cornwall,' Bibi had said. 'How are we going to get to Cornwall? We can't afford the fares. Not for all these children.'

'Um,' said Callum. 'They haven't invited you. Only me.'

Bibi said, 'Ah, I see.' She'd packed his bag, and told him to enjoy himself. In truth, she was quite glad to see him go. A week without The Grateful Dead was appealing.

On his third night in St Ives, Callum had drunk too much wine. He'd sat up late with Robin and Franny, talking about books, socialism and love. At two in the morning his hosts retired to bed, exhausted. But Callum was fired up, his mind racing and heady with alcohol. The night was warm; he'd gone for a walk. He strolled through narrow cobbled streets down to the beach. Nobody was about, so he'd stripped off and waded into the sea. He swam out as far as he dared, then rolled over on to his back and floated, arms spread.

A few seagulls skimmed past him, black shapes. Above him the sky was alive with stars, millions of them. He drifted; the water was dark and calm. I'm done with politics, he thought. I'm a poet. He told himself to free his mind of all the clatter and noise and pleading of the past few weeks. Let go, he thought. Feel the water, feel the night.

And as he floated, breathing the tangy air, delighting in the stars, it seemed to him that he left his body and moved up above himself, soaring between sea and sky. He was looking down at himself even as he was lying on the water looking up at himself and the heavens beyond. He slowly drew a breath. 'Magical, magical, magical,' he said. He did not want to leave this moment. He wanted to stay here coasting in the water for the rest of his life.

But eventually, fearing he might drift too far, be caught in currents, swept out to sea and drown, he rolled over and swam back to shore. Back at Robin and Franny's holiday house, he'd found a postcard, a naughty picture of a woman with a huge bum in a red bathing suit, chiding a small man in a cap, and had written a message to Bibi: *Now I know what exquisite is*. He'd gone out and posted it right away.

Bibi refilled her glass, and took a chocolate biscuit from

the tin that was also on the table. She vividly remembered getting that postcard. Roddy was sitting at this very table eating breakfast. Graham was messing about with her pots and pans. Celia was looking at her picture book. 'Now I know what exquisite is,' said Bibi. 'Excellent, I'm glad someone does.' She'd put the postcard into her Chinese Kosher cookbook, and forgotten about it.

Callum, meantime, had told Robin and Franny about his magical experience floating beneath the stars. 'An out-of-body moment,' he'd said. By the end of the week, he'd talked about it so much, they were both happy to see him go. He had told people he'd met on the train about it, then the taxi driver who'd taken him from Waverley to Saxe-Coburg Street.

At home, he spoke about little else. His senses had been electrified by his moment. He couldn't sit still; halfway through meals he'd stand up and almost shout, 'It was magnificent. Magnificent.' He'd be pulsating with excitement. And all Bibi could say was, 'Swimming out to sea in the middle of the night, you could have drowned.' Feeling a little dull as she did so. The children all looked glazed with boredom. At night, in bed, he'd lean over to Bibi. 'I floated. I saw myself above me, looking down on me, and it was beautiful. The stars shone, water rippled round me, and something mystic happened.'

At last, after phoning everyone he knew to tell them of his exquisite experience, he settled down in his study to write a poem about it. But he couldn't. He'd burst out, and pace up and down the hall.

'I can't do it. I can't get it down on paper. I can't define it. I can't explain it. I can't even describe it properly. What does it mean? A thing like that happening to you, is it an omen? Was some greater spirit trying to communicate with me? Was it mystical? Was it religious?' He'd stormed into the kitchen. 'I can't do it. I can't write. I have spoken it all out. There's nothing left. I can't describe the mystery of floating.'

Graham had been on the floor at the time. He'd been lining up a row of toy cars, but had stopped when Callum had thundered in, and had stuck a thumb in his mouth, watching the tiff between his mother and father.

Bibi, tired of all this angst, had said, 'Callum, shut up. I'm sick of all this. Why can't you just be? Like other people can just be. Why do you have to define things, explain things, tear things apart, look for meanings? So, you floated and had a magical experience. Do you have to make a melodrama out of it? You've become a bore. Why didn't you just float? When you're floating, float.'

Callum had stared at her, then turned and stormed back to his study. He hadn't thanked her or even told her she'd cracked it. When the poem appeared, in a volume that was not dedicated to her but, Bibi noted sadly, to Maureen and Joe Abraham – *Oh, what a gorgeous evening we had* – it was called 'Floating – for all my children: the born and those yet to come.'

'No mention of me,' said Bibi. 'Me who put up with all his nonsense. The man was a brute.'

The poem described a man who had ruined a magical moment by talking about it too often.

Moon on water, stars and breezes, joy
And I ruined them all

It ended,

Oh my child
Swim out far, take risks, enjoy the deep
But when you're floating, float.

Dedicated to his children. 'Not that any of them ever read it,' said Bibi. She poured another glass of wine. Outside, it had started to rain. She couldn't count all the memories she had of sitting at this table watching rain spill down the window. Callum had a major role in every single one. Callum reading his latest poem to her and asking what she thought. She always said it was wonderful. No other reply was acceptable. If she said it was the best thing he'd written, he'd ask what was wrong with all his previous poems. If she loved it, he'd demand to know what exactly it was about it she loved, and did she love one particular part more than another? Then again, if she said she thought it needed work, he'd say he knew that, but didn't need any criticism at this moment, thank you very much. You never could win with Callum.

This kitchen, hot, steamy, noisy and crowded. *The Archers* on the radio, Graham demanding food. Celia working at her colouring book. Roddy reading *The Beano* and asking when supper would be ready, he was going out in a while. And Callum would stride in and tell them all to be quiet: 'I'm working. Is there no respect for what I do round here?'

'Damn you and your bloody work,' Bibi remembered saying. 'You just don't care about any of us, do you? It's all you, you, you. The only thing about your children that interests you is their conception. Then it's all up to me.'

Callum had looked at her for a moment, then said, 'Of course.' And he'd gone back to his study. There had been a few seconds of shock and silence. Everyone in the room had watched him go, then they'd returned to what they were doing. The noise resumed. Bibi had gone to the cooker, to stare glumly at the stew.

Memories. Memories. Memories. Bibi was haunted by them. Anything could trigger them – a sight, a smell, a song. She felt as if her brain was cluttered by recollections, not all of them happy, and she wished there was something she could do to stop them floating to mind. A switch on the side of her head, perhaps, that she could just flick off when an unwanted memory visited her. She took another chocolate biscuit. Sometimes a bit of comfort eating helped.

She heard James come in. He'd been out for his morning run. He appeared at the kitchen door, the hood of his tracksuit top pulled over his head. He was soaked through. He handed Bibi the Sunday papers she'd been waiting for. 'Met the boy on the stairs.'

She thanked him, looked him up and down. 'You'd better get out of those wet things. You'll catch your death. And take off your shoes, you're getting mud on the carpet.'

He looked at her, that slow gaze he had. Then nodded, 'Sorry,' and bent down to untie his laces.

Bibi watched, smiling. Excellent, she thought. I can still nag. Once you've got it, you never lose it.

James went off to shower. Bibi started on her newspapers. She wanted to go back to bed, but since James had seen her at the table and they had exchanged a few words, she thought this might appear rude. So she sat and absently sipped her wine. She didn't feel like coffee now.

She turned to the horoscopes, a vital part of her reading routine. Not that she paid much attention to what was forecast for her own star sign. She read her children's; this, she was sure, kept her abreast of what was happening in their lives. Not that they didn't keep in touch. But Bibi knew there were always things they didn't tell their mother. According to the astrologer Bibi swore by, Celia had meddled in someone's life and was regretting the expense, Roddy was on the verge of having an affair, Beth was broke and unhappy at work. Liz would have to make major decisions soon. Graham, wherever he was, would appear to have found a new kind of contentment. Bibi pondered all that, and felt a certain motherly satisfaction that she was keeping an eye on her brood.

Ten minutes later James reappeared, slightly pink, his hair wet. He wore his jeans and an extraordinarily white T-shirt. Once more he gave Bibi his slow gaze, and now she realised it was directed at her breakfast: wine and chocolate biscuits.

'Very good for me,' she said, lifting her glass. 'Reduces the blood pressure.'

'And the chocolate?' he said.

'Good for the blood pressure too.'

71

'Not first thing in the morning.'

'Now why should something be good for the blood pressure in the evening and not the morning?'

He shrugged.

'And it's an aphrodisiac.'

'You need an aphrodisiac?' he said.

'Oh yes. Well at my age you would, wouldn't you? There's powdered rhino horn, but how do you get hold of that? Oysters. Asparagus, apparently. But chocolate will do me.'

James sniffed disapproval. He reached into one of his cupboards and brought out his selection of vitamin and mineral pills. He laid out his tablets and capsules in a neat row on the unit top. Vitamins E, C and D, zinc and selenium and iron, plus one large bullet-shaped multivitamin pill, bright orangey yellow. He swallowed them one by one with a glass of Evian.

Bibi watched. 'You think all that works?'

'Of course,' he said. 'I believe in looking after my body.'

'So I see,' said Bibi. 'Have you always been so obsessive about taking care of yourself?'

James said he hadn't. 'Never knew half of these things existed before I went to work in the health shop.'

'But now you have heard of them, you religiously swallow them,' said Bibi.

'They help. This is the only body I've got. I don't pollute it with rubbish.' He turned and looked pointedly at her.

'Like I do,' said Bibi.

James shrugged. 'You should take better care of yourself. You don't eat properly.'

He checked Bibi's fridge regularly, and was shocked by what he found in it – out-of-date cartons of yogurt, wrinkly tomatoes, packs of bacon, chocolate puddings, milk and several bottles of wine. He wanted to tell her his good news. His discovery of the benefits of fresh organic food, the healing properties of fish and evening primrose oils, the joy of B vitamins, the energy boosts of a daily intake of minerals. Since starting to work at the health-food shop, he'd become a fanatic. Not only did he swallow vitamins and minerals, he ran every morning and went to the gym twice a week. He'd bulked out.

He cooked porridge using organic stone-ground oats and soya milk, and brewed a cup of green tea. 'Full of polyphenols and antioxidants,' he said.

'So's chocolate and red wine,' said Bibi.

James didn't answer that. Bibi spoke with such conviction, he had to wonder if what she'd said might be true. He changed the subject. 'Funny name that, Bibi.'

'Yes,' said Bibi. 'It's a nickname. I'm actually Barbara, but nobody's ever called me that. Apparently my older sister called me Bibi shortly after I was born. She couldn't say Barbara.'

'Maybe she was saying baby,' said James.

'Maybe, I never thought of that. No matter. I've been called Bibi all my life. We all had nicknames in the family. My mother and father were Bunty and Humph. He was Humphrey, obviously. She was Margaret. God knows where Bunty came from. My sister was Dodie. Then there was Rog, Pip, Harry and Seb. I don't know where any of them are; scattered across the globe, I suppose.'

James leaned against the unit, bowl in hand, eating his porridge. He didn't want to sit nearer to Bibi. He wasn't comfortable with people, especially female ones.

Bibi, sensing how unsettled her presence made him, smiled. He was looking well. Quite handsome, in fact. Her mother would have called him dishy.

'It was considered jolly to call people by some affectionate private little name. And I suppose it helped to keep outsiders at bay. You weren't invited to call some- body by their nickname till you'd known them for an awfully long time.'

James gazed down at his bowl, moving the porridge about with his spoon. He didn't like a mouthful that didn't contain a deal of honey. He sympathised with the outsiders, who'd be frowned upon for using a nickname when they weren't yet accepted. He'd be one of them.

Relishing how disconcerted James was, knowing he was identifying with the outsiders, Bibi smiled at him once more. 'You'll be pleased to know I'm going away for a while.'

James said, 'Oh. Why should that please me?'

'I unsettle you. You're ill at ease around women. Especially old ones. Perhaps you didn't get along with your grandmother.'

'Never met her,' said James. 'She died before I was born.'

Bibi said, 'Ah.'

'So where are you going?' asked James.

'Up north to see Liz, my daughter. I thought I'd take a detour to look at the house where I was born. Then to Yorkshire to see Roddy.'

'Long trip,' said James.

'Indeed.'

'How are you going?'

'By car.'

'You have a car?'

'I have an excellent car, a wonderful and splendid car. A Volvo.'

James nodded. It figured. An old woman would have something solid and reliable. 'Good cars, Volvos.'

'You like cars?' she asked.

He nodded and shrugged. 'Yeah.'

'Do you know anything about them?'

He shrugged once more and told her, 'A little.' A sad memory flashed through him. 'I used to have one, but I had to sell it when I moved up here. I needed the money.'

'Well, a little's a lot more than I know about cars. You can finish your breakfast and come and take a look at the Volvo. I haven't driven it in a while.'

'What model is it?'

'Green,' said Bibi. 'It's a green one.'

James nodded. He should have known she wouldn't know what damn model she owned.

'It may need an oil change and a jump-start if it's been idle for a while,' he said. 'When did you last drive it?'

'Can't remember. About ten years ago, I think. But Peter, Celia's husband, looks after it. Keeps it ticking over.'

James asked if she wasn't worried about driving so far after not being behind the wheel for such a long time.

'Not at all,' said Bibi. 'It's like riding a bike, or swimming, or even sex, a skill once mastered you never forget. One thing I do very well indeed is drive a car.'

For some reason, James didn't believe her.

A Splash of Happiness

On Sunday, Beth phoned Celia. 'What's with our mother and the credit cards?'

Celia, sitting at her breakfast bar, writing her shopping list, said she had no idea what Beth was talking about. *Sugar snap peas*, she wrote. *Tomatoes on the vine*.

'She's applied for about a dozen credit cards,' said Beth.

'How do you know that?' said Celia.

'I dropped by last night to see how she'd got on at the clinic, and there she was sitting at the table filling in the forms.'

'Why would she do that?' Celia abandoned her list. This was worrying. 'She hates credit cards. In fact she hates anything that happened after nineteen seventy-two. She hates the modern world.'

'Exactly,' said Beth.

'She hates the clothes people wear, and the way they walk about with mobile phones clamped to their ears, and motorways, and car crashes in films,' said Celia. *Pasta*, she wrote. *Pesto. Parmesan*. After that she started to doodle a row of long loops.

She and Bibi went to the cinema on Thursday evenings. Remembering these outings, the row of loops became wilder, rounder. A night at the movies with Bibi was hell.

She always insisted on buying a huge tub of popcorn. 'It isn't the same without popcorn.' But then there were films that were too sad, too distressing to eat through, *Schindler's List*, for example. 'They should warn you before you go in,' Bibi had said, tossing her large, still full tub in the bin as they walked out into the night. 'They should tell you it's a no-popcorn film. It should be in the ratings. This is a NP, no popcorn film.'

Then there was the choosing of the seats, which had to be mid-row so Bibi could see the film full on and not from the side. This meant she had to try several seats, squeezing along rows, making other members of the audience stand to let them pass. All that before the programme started. The worst part for Celia, however, was watching a film in a public place with her mother. Bibi always, always joined in. She had opinions about the action, and she never kept them to herself. She remarked loudly on watching a torrid sex scene that she'd never done it like that, and she wished someone had told her about it before she got to this age. She commented on the actors' clothes, and frequently spoke along with the dialogue.

Her observations on car crashes caused sniggers. Watching a film where a couple of men on the run had driven top speed up a motorway the wrong way into the flow of traffic, causing blasting horns, screeching brakes and multiple crashes, cars spinning out of control, careening into one another, metal crunching into metal, Bibi had been horrified. 'There's no need for all that, it's totally irresponsible,' she'd said loudly. 'All these people will have to fill in insurance forms. What are they going to write in them?'

People in the row in front had turned to look. There had been snorts, tuts and sighs. Celia had squirmed in her seat, and tried to look as if Bibi was with the woman on the other side of her.

Garlic, she wrote. *Parsley. Basil. Tomato purée*. God, she thought, my life, my parents. There wasn't a day one of them didn't embarrass me. She thought she'd spent her young life squirming. There had definitely been a lot of time, effort and intrigue put into trying to stop them visiting school on parents' day. She'd hide the letter telling them the date and times of their appointments with her teachers. And she'd tell the school her parents were away in America. But somehow they'd hear about it and turn up.

Celia winced. She could still see them, Callum and Bibi, coming down the corridor, Callum striding slightly ahead in his tattered jeans, grandfather shirt and waistcoat, on his head his John Lennon cap. His shoes, suede, would be worn and weary, as if he'd walked a thousand miles in them. Which, considering how old they were, he probably had. And Bibi in her long, flowing skirts, bought from the Indian shop in the Royal Mile. They'd be decorated with beads and sequins. Her hair, always long in those days, would hang straight almost to her waist. She'd have bangles on her wrists and several strings of heavy multicoloured wooden beads round her neck. Sandals on her feet, whatever the weather. Surrounded by parents who'd obviously scrubbed up, put on something smart to impress their children's teachers, Bibi and Callum looked illuminated, trailing wafts of patchouli behind them. They were so appallingly hippy, Celia would pretend she didn't know them. But Callum would always give the game away. 'I've come to talk about Celia Saunders. I want to know who is educating her, and why she is being encouraged in the sciences. Chemistry and physics. This isn't what our family does.' Then he'd turn to Bibi. 'Are you sure you brought the right child home?'

Thinking of all this, Celia's doodles got wilder, the loops fatter, larger. She put her hand to her face, agonising. All her friends had had ordinary parents, mothers who came home from work and cooked a meal, fathers who made jokes, wore suits and drove normal family cars. They were mums and dads. Celia always felt her parents were not mum and dad sort of people, and she couldn't remember calling them by anything other than their first names. Her father, she was sure, hadn't owned a suit. He'd stalk the flat, waving his arms in the air, demanding silence; he needed to work. He'd appeared on television in his collarless shirt, braces and bright red corduroy waistcoat, long hair tousled, talking heatedly about freedom – freedom for the workers, freedom for the arts, freedom to speak out against dictatorial governments, freedom to make love to whomever whenever you wanted. This last had embarrassed Celia, especially at school. Fellow pupils would come up to her saying, 'Saw your dad on telly. He's weird.' Or, 'Your dad needs a haircut.'

All this had made her long for a quiet, mild-mannered and humorous man in her life, which was why she'd married Peter. He was a small man, thinning on top, stocky and not jovial so much as pleasant. Yes, she often thought, my Peter is a pleasant man, pleasant to be with, pleasant to share a bed with; plain, ordinary, down-to-earth pleasant. He was an engineer, disappearing to work every morning at quarter past eight, arriving home sometime after six. He rarely spoke about his work, and Celia did the same. He loved sport, spent Saturday afternoons watching football and Sunday mornings on the golf course. Celia never went with him.

Perhaps it was his absences that made Celia consider Peter the perfect man. She had time to herself. But he had other attributes that endeared him to her. He never raised his voice, he never burst into rooms waving bits of paper and bawling for silence. When he had a report to write at home, he wrote it, put it in his briefcase and was done with it. He never strode into the living room, switched off the television and read it out loud to her, then demanded a critique, which had to be favourable. He never wore flamboyant clothes, the soles of his shoes weren't taped on, his shirts were ironed and he went to the hairdresser regularly.

Sometimes, at work, Celia would think of Peter and sigh with contentment. How lucky she was to have such an agreeable man. They'd moved into the house where they now lived a year after they'd married. It had taken them two years to get it the way they wanted, painted in pale, soothing colours; they'd installed a new kitchen and bathroom, laid pale carpets and added a conservatory, which was also painted in a pale, soothing colour. Bibi thought it all very bland. But Celia loved her house.

At last, she thought, she could start living the life she'd

envisioned, quiet, contented domestic bliss. She felt her shoulders relax. She exhaled. She was twenty-eight at the time, and always felt she'd spent her time up till then holding her breath, waiting for the next storm to erupt. Of course storms kept erupting, things happened – exorbitant bills arrived, the car would break down, pipes burst, sinks got blocked, keys got lost. Minor things, really, but major storms came along too. Once, Peter lost his job and was unemployed for six months before he found another. Her father died. She'd had to take six months off following an operation on her back. Then there was Olivia, her daughter, who was shaping up to be alarmingly like her grandfather. Olivia's school reports were disturbing. Disruptive in class, they said, prone to outbursts, overemotional, has no understanding of maths or the sciences and is unwilling to work at them. And if Peter never burst into rooms waving bits of paper and demanding silence as he read from them, Olivia did. Olivia said there was no point working at subjects like physics or geography. These were things that were not vital to the life she had planned; she was going to be a poet, songwriter and actress. Celia worried about this.

'Where's the calm?' she once asked her mother. 'Where's the peace? The contentment? The domestic bliss?'

Bibi had looked at her as if she was a fool. 'Don't be absurd. Calm, peace, domestic bliss come in ten-minute splashes of gratification as you move from one upheaval to the next. Did you think you were going to buy a house then sit in it quietly till you die? Things happen and mostly they are shitty. Get real, Celia. There's no such thing as happiness, only the pursuit of happiness. You're old enough to know that by now.'

Now, looking down at her shopping list, Celia saw a page covered with loops and whorls and exclamation marks. At one point she had written, *Lamb chops, bacon, free-range eggs, aaahh!!*

At the other end of the phone Beth was saying, 'Celia? Celia? Are you there?'

'Yes. I'm here.'

'So, what about the credit cards and our mother? You'll have to talk to her.'

'Why me? You talk to her,' said Celia.

'No bloody way. You do it. She listens to you.'

Celia sighed. Sunday mornings were precious. It was a time when she took pleasure in small activities. She pottered, wrote a shopping list, watered her plants, read the papers, listened to the radio. Now she felt a knot tightening in her stomach. Her mother was about to do something embarrassing. She just knew it. It was an instinct, a vibe.

'Damn woman,' she said.

'I know,' said Beth. 'But I'm worried. She won't tell me what the doctor said. What if he told her her heart was giving out? She might not have long to live and is planning to go berserk with credit cards, leaving us all with a pile of debt to pay off.'

'Won't happen,' said Celia. 'She's not like that. Besides, her flat is worth a fortune. No, that's not it. She's planning something sillier than that.'

'What?' said Beth.

'How the hell do I know? I'll talk to her.' Celia put down the phone, ripped her shopping list from the pad, crumpled it and threw it in the bin. 'Damn, damn and damn again.' Her Sunday morning was ruined. There was no way she could potter now, she was too worried. She'd have to go round to her mother's flat and find out what was going on.

Bibi's garage was in Circus Mews, a relatively short walk from her flat. James strolled by her side affecting a cool, detached manner. Trying, Bibi thought, to look as if he wasn't with her. Quite like old times, she thought. She well remembered Graham and Roddy adopting the same casual hands-in-the-pockets style of moving along the pavement when they went anywhere with her. Still, at the time of their stylised indifference, they'd both been about thirteen or fourteen. James was a little old to be so truculent.

In fact Bibi was wrong. James was just depressed. A Volvo, an old lady's Volvo; he could imagine it: dull, neglected, with a dicky gearbox after being driven for miles and miles in the wrong gear. It depressed him further to think that *anybody* had a car and didn't use it. He scuffed his feet, stared down at the pavement, thinking back to happy Sunday mornings when, if he wasn't working, he'd spend time with his Escort.

'So,' said Bibi, 'does meditating in the morning do anything for you?'

'It helps,' he told her.

'Helps with what?'

'I want to have inner calm,' he said. 'Peace. Happiness.'

'That's why you sit cross-legged on the floor listening to strange chants, staring into space in your underpants?'

Embarrassed by this, James kicked a stone, sent it spinning to the middle of the road.

'Suppose,' he said.

Bibi said, 'Happiness: sometimes I think it will be the ruin of us all.'

'That's an odd thing to say. Surely everybody wants to be happy.'

'So it seems,' said Bibi. 'But it's impossible. Nobody can be happy. Not totally, utterly happy all of the time, or even most of the time. It just comes in splashes, moments. I think we are happiest when we are doing something, utterly engrossed, enjoying the challenge. But it's only when the challenge is over that you realise how happy you were rising to it. You sort of regret it being completed. Even something so small as a crossword, you quietly wish you had it to do again. Happiness only comes in retrospect, when you look back and think, I was happy then.'

Remembering his time with his car, when he'd worked to make it shinier and to make the engine growl and purr, but hadn't stopped to consider his state of mind, James agreed that could be true. 'But what about standing on a mountain, taking in the view, feeling on top of the world?' He hadn't ever done this.

'A splash,' said Bibi.

'Or at a picnic, sitting in the sunshine, drinking wine with friends?' He hadn't done this either.

'A splash,' said Bibi.

'When your first child is born?'

'A splash. A big splash, a beautiful splash. But, considering what comes afterwards, definitely a splash.'

'I think you're a cynic,' said James.

'Yes,' said Bibi, 'and proud of it.'

After that, they walked in silence, James feeling resentful that Bibi had enjoyed moments of happiness on top of mountains and at wonderful picnics with friends. Bibi was rather pleased with herself. She'd got a reaction from the boy, though it was irritation. She'd have preferred a smile. Nonetheless, good for me, she thought.

When they reached the garage, James leaned against the wall as Bibi fiddled with the lock. Watched her heave open the old blue wooden doors and disappear inside.

'Here it is,' she called. 'My car, isn't it beautiful? I used to hate it, and this garage. Callum bought them both with some award he won, some poetry thing. I couldn't even get to the ceremony. No babysitters. I was so angry with him for blowing his money on all this when we needed a new washing machine and the kids were growing out of shoes every five minutes. I said he was a wastrel squandering good cash. But I got a washing machine anyway. The kids buy their own shoes now, and I've got all this. The garage alone is worth a bit. But the car, it's a beauty. They don't make them like this any more . . .'

James listened to her enthuse. He made a face, then heaved himself from the wall he was leaning on and walked into the garage. And there it was, just as Bibi had said, a thing of beauty. It was long, shiny, low-slung, with cream leather seats.

'It's a sports car,' he said.

'I know,' said Bibi. 'That's why I was so furious at Callum. There's only two proper seats and a bench at the back, and we had five kids.'

James looked at her, a little shocked. Kids, in a car like this? He didn't think so. Why, they'd leave sticky things on the seats. They might even pee; you never knew with children. James had no experience of them, but suspected they all had unreliable bladders. 'You couldn't have children in a car like this,' he said. 'They might make a mess.'

'You sound like Callum,' Bibi told him. 'He said he didn't want the children in it. This car was his. He wanted to be himself in it. Just Callum, the man, the poet. Not the father or the husband. A bit insulting, don't you think?'

James didn't know what to say. He supposed it was a little insulting. But then this was a Volvo P1800, top speed over a hundred miles an hour, designed in Italy, built by Jensen. A person would want to be alone in it. In a car like this, he thought, you could be everything you wanted to be. A god, a king, Superman. Driving it would make a statement about who you were: not rich, but stylish, someone who took risks, who knew what he wanted, and who he was. It was a beautiful, beautiful thing.

When it came to cars, James was on Callum's side. He wouldn't want to be a father or husband either. He looked at Bibi and shrugged. 'It's beautiful.'

She smiled. Cars certainly did strange things to some people. She handed James the keys, 'Why don't you get in and see how it feels?'

He opened the door, slid into the driver's seat, ran his hands over the steering wheel, touched the gearstick. It smelled of leather in here. This was wonderful. He felt a warmth in his stomach, a glow in his cheeks; he was smiling. This was something he hadn't experienced in months and months. A little splash of happiness.

Blame it on Florence

Liz knew that her problem was that she never complained. Or if she did complain, she did it to herself, a quiet inner mumble. She chastised herself for never learning to shout. It was an inadequacy she blamed on her mother and father. She felt they had always shuttled her off into a corner, called her Our Lizzie and expected only one thing of her – that she should be at all times good natured. She always thought she had wasted her childhood being not so much good as complacent. 'You were always such a good baby,' Bibi often told her. 'So easy. All you did was eat and sleep and smile. You never cried.'

Well, I've made up for that now, she thought.

Mornings, these days, she worked in a local shop, after she'd dropped off her children at school. Afternoons, after she'd got home and before she had to pick up Louis and Lara, she would lie on her bed, staring out through the window at the sky. It was a couple of hours she cherished; the house would be silent and she could be still and think, or, even better, not think. Thinking only filled her with guilt about all the things she should be doing instead of lying staring at the sky – the vegetable patch needed weeding, the parsley and sprouts had run to seed, there were dishes piled in the sink, she should iron, she should vacuum, dust, wash the windows. She should. She should. She should. But no, she would lie here and sift through the decisions and events that had brought her to this house, and she would try to face the truth. Drew would not come back. And, if she was honest, she didn't blame him.

Looking back, she decided she must have been about fourteen when she realised how intensely she disliked her mother and father. 'Bibi and Callum,' she'd say to her friends at school, her upper lip curling. 'Hate them. Hate them. Hate them.'

Had they heard her, the passion, though not the words, would have surprised Bibi and Callum. They were well versed in the ways of teenagers and expected their own to hate them; would, in fact, have been disappointed in them if they didn't.

'Excellent,' Callum had said once when Graham had expressed his loathing for his father. 'Glad to hear it,' he had continued. 'I'd be surprised if you didn't hate me at this stage in your development. You are starting to think for yourself, form your own opinions and reject authority figures. Good for you.' And he'd patted his defiant son on the head.

Liz's passion, however, would have been a revelation to Bibi and Callum. They had her down as the placid one. Roddy was the go-getter, Celia the brains, Graham the rebel and Beth a sweetie-pie.

Evenings, sitting at their kitchen table, Bibi and Callum would discuss their children, decide their characters and bring them up accordingly. Liz had from early adolescence resented being dismissed as placid. She'd rebelled, but only in the privacy of her room, throwing pillows and cushions at the wall and kicking her wardrobe.

She'd left home at eighteen to study at St Andrews, and hardly ever gone back. She'd lived in a flat in Bridge Street with six other students. One of them was Drew, who was studying maths and physics almost as half-heartedly as she was doing English and history. They fell in love, and their first year was lost in a whirl of sex, beer, drugs and music. Neither of them did well in their exams, but they shrugged and laughed off their shame by getting drunk celebrating their bad results in the Central Bar. They would, they decided, leave all of this behind and spend the summer travelling in Europe.

It was the summer of 1993. Liz was twenty, Timberland boots on her feet, Oasis on her Walkman, a pack on her back laden with T-shirts, jeans, shorts and knickers, and love in her heart. She was happy. She phoned her mother from Calais to tell her she wasn't coming home for the summer. 'I'm travelling,' she said. 'Spain, France, Italy and wherever the notion takes us.'

Bibi, still quietly grieving for Callum though he'd died two years ago, had remained silent for a long time. 'If that's what you want to do,' she said at last.

'It's what I want to do,' said Liz. 'I'm happy. I'm really, really happy.'

'I'm glad someone is,' Bibi said, then asked if Liz had enough money.

'Of course I have,' said Liz. 'I always have enough money. It's just a matter of not buying material things.'

Bibi said, 'Ah. I never thought of that.' She wished this

denial of material things had been mentioned when Liz had wanted training shoes, CDs and clothes when she was younger. Still, she told Liz to take care and keep in touch and resolved to put some money into her account anyway. She thought her daughter might need food.

Liz and Drew travelled through Spain, then France and on to Italy. They took buses, hitched lifts and walked. She would always remember it as a time of heat and dust, wine, bread and the drifting scent of wild thyme from hillsides. Now she grew thyme, and lavender too, in her garden in a thick fragrant border that hazed into blue in summer. Just brushing against it as she walked down the path to bring in her washing or to fetch some vegetables for supper, the air around her would flood with that same tang she'd known in France, and she'd feel happy. The emotion always hit her before the memory. A warmth tumbled through her. She'd smile. What is that? Happiness. She'd recall a time when the sun was on her back and Drew was by her side, and they were full of joy.

She remembered foreign voices, small cafés that smelled of coffee and cigars. She remembered aching muscles and sore feet from walking long, empty roads; sometimes she'd walked backwards surveying the path they'd trodden, rather than contemplate the distance yet to be covered.

She remembered their small bickerings, but had let the huge arguments fade from her memory. Except for the one in Italy. He wanted to go south, to Sicily; she wanted to go to Florence. She said it was beautiful, bathed in golden light. She'd been reading brochures. Her heart was set on seeing it. She wanted to tell people back home she'd been there. She planned to casually drop it into conversations: 'We found the most wonderful little restaurant down a little back street in Florence,' she might say. Or she could quietly mention that something – the light, a painting, a cup of coffee sipped al fresco somewhere sunny – reminded her of being in Florence. Really, she wanted to impress people, and was a little ashamed of this. She certainly didn't want to mention to Drew that this was why she so desperately wanted to go.

He said it would be full of tourists, hot, sticky and expensive. She took a tantrum, told him if they didn't go to Florence she wasn't going anywhere. She won; they went to Florence. He was right. It was hot, sticky, thronging with tourists; the streets were narrow and the signs so old on the sides of crumbling buildings, they were unreadable. It was also beautiful and bathed in golden light.

Short of money, they'd avoided the cafés with tables sprawled across wide squares, and bought a bottle of red wine, some cheese and bread to eat on a bench by the river. It was evening, the light was golden. They watched a lone rower scull past on the water below them, took a swig apiece from their bottle, and sighed. 'You were right,' he said. 'This place is magical.'

Still a little smug at winning the argument, she conceded that he had been right too. 'It's heaving with people. You can hardly move.'

He took her hand and said he wouldn't have missed it for the world.

She said, 'It's ours. All this is ours. Nobody can take it away from us. And the good thing about being at uni is we don't have to write an essay about what I did on my holidays when we get back.'

He said he wasn't going back. 'Uni's not for me. Hate it.'

Liz's world stopped. The magic was gone, everything was ruined. A group of American tourists, laden with cameras, talking loudly about the beautiful light, bustled past them, heading for the Ponte Vecchio. Further along the street a man, standing before an easel, was drawing caricatures of a young Japanese couple. Everywhere there were people lingering, staring, strolling, busy making holiday moments. And here she was having her heart broken.

'But you have to go back,' she said. 'What are you going to do?'

'Self-sufficiency. The good life,' he told her.

He'd bought a house. 'Up north, overlooking the sea. Three bedrooms, a living room and dining room. And a good whack of land round it.' He spread his arms wide. This place was big.

'You bought a house?' she said. 'How could you do that?'

'My grandmother left me thirty-five grand.' It was in her will; when her house was sold, the money was to be divided between her grandchildren. 'Thirty-five grand. And I've blown five already. Five grand, Liz. Pissed it away. Beer, wine and pizzas. Not good. I thought I'd better do something before it was all gone. So I bought a house. Best thing you can do with money.'

'But,' said Liz, 'you can't just give up your course.'

'I can. I have,' he told her.

Liz was standing with her mouth open. Shock had reddened her cheeks and brought the first glint of tears to her eyes. 'But what about me?'

He looked at his fingers and mumbled, 'You could come too.'

'Come where?'

'Up north. Gairloch.'

'But I can't quit uni,' said Liz.

'Why not?'

'I need a degree.'

'Why?'

'To get a decent job.'

'Why?'

'I'll have to work.'

'Why?'

'I'll need money. I want to work.'

'Why work? Why does anybody work? To pay the mortgage. I bought the house outright. I won't need money for that. People work for money to buy food. I'll grow my own. I won't need to work. I'll be my own boss, make my own rules, keep my own time. I've got it all worked out.'

She didn't say anything. But there in Florence, bathed in golden light, what he was saying made sense. More than that, it sounded romantic, exciting. Liz imagined herself living in a beautiful house by the sea. In this dream, she was walking up a lush and bountiful garden carrying a basket laden with vegetables. She was smiling, and her skin was peachy fresh, touched by sunlight and light breezes.

'We'll sell our surplus to pay for electricity and stuff. We won't be wage slaves,' said Drew. 'Our food will be fresh. We'll smell earth and wind and sea as we take it from the ground. Potatoes, onions, carrots, garlic.'

The air around her was alive; scents flooded round her: coffee, bread baking, the hot smell of an early Italian evening in August. And she was in love with a notion.

'A pig,' said Drew. 'We'll have a pig.'

Liz imagined herself leaning over the wall of a pen, patting the pig. They'd call her Myra, she thought.

'Chickens,' he went on.

They'd come clucking at her feet when she scattered corn in the morning. She and Drew would eat speckled brown eggs, boiled lightly, for breakfast. Their kitchen would be warm and steamy.

Children's voices drifted from across the river; somewhere someone was playing a flute.

'We'll live our own lives. We'll do it right,' said Drew.

'Yes,' said Liz. 'Let's do it.'

It was a whirl of a moment, dizzying. They kissed, hugged, whooped for joy. Picked up their backpacks and started heading home.

All the way, on buses, the ferry, then the train to Edinburgh, where they intended to drop in on Bibi and give her their news, they planned. They'd install a wood-burning stove, heat their home with driftwood from the beach. They'd sell their fruit and veg to local hotels, or they'd set up a delivery service taking boxes of fresh organically grown produce to customers' doors. They might even set up a table at their gate, so passing tourists could buy freshly picked strawberries. 'Yes,' they said. 'This will work. This will be perfect.'

In Edinburgh, Bibi took the news of her daughter's life-changing decision with a sigh of resignation. When one has five children, she thought, one should expect a little emotional turbulence. She was aware of repeating, somewhat incredulously, everything Liz said.

'You're giving up your education?'

'You're going to live off the land?'

'Sell your surplus to hotels and passing tourists?'

'A *pig*?'

Liz hadn't noticed her mother's scepticism, she'd been too excited. It had been months since she'd last been in this flat, and in her absence Bibi had redecorated. Every room was now ochre. This had been part of Bibi's emergence from her grief over Callum's death. It had happened two months ago, when she had finally managed to take some of his clothes to a charity shop. It had taken her over two years to accept that he would no longer need them. He was dead. Along with this came the realisation that she could paint the flat any colour she wanted; he was no longer around to criticise her taste.

Liz had loved it. 'Everything's ochre,' she said. 'Golden. It reminds me of Florence.'

There, she'd said it. The thing she longed to say. The remark she'd gone to Florence to make when she got back. Not that Bibi noticed. She was rummaging through the kitchen drawer, looking for her chequebook.

While Liz had been wandering from room to room, marvelling at the new goldenness in the flat, Bibi had questioned Drew. 'If you don't mind me asking, how much did your house cost?'

'Twenty-five grand,' he told her.

She said she supposed property was cheaper that far north. 'But wasn't that extraordinarily cheap for a house that size with a considerable area of ground attached?'

'It was a snip,' he said. 'I got in there before anyone else saw it.'

'What did the survey say?' Bibi asked.

'Didn't need a survey. Didn't borrow any money. No building society for me. I bought it outright.'

Bibi said, 'Ah.' Then asked what he'd thought about the state of the house when he viewed it.

'Didn't view it. I wanted to get in there quick, so I made an offer as soon as I saw it for sale. I've lived in that house. My parents rented it for a holiday. I loved that house. I loved being in it.' He loved the views from the windows, the long garden that stretched to the shore and that had apple trees, fruit bushes, an enormous vegetable patch, a little summerhouse. 'Everything,' he said.

'But you haven't actually been in it recently?' asked Bibi.

He shook his head. 'Not since I was seven. Fourteen years ago.'

Bibi said, 'Ah,' again, and went to fetch her chequebook from the drawer.

Watching her write a cheque, Drew said quietly that he and Liz had no use for money. They were going to grow their own food, heat their house by burning driftwood. They would have everything.

Bibi got up from the table, crossed the room and closed the door so that Liz, who was still wandering from room to room, marvelling at the goldenness of things, wouldn't hear.

'Young man, this money isn't for you. It's for my daughter. There are things she'll need. Food, warmth, clothes. There are tools to be bought – spades, rakes, a hose. Seeds; you won't get many vegetables without seeds to plant. Your money will all go on repairing the stupid house you've bought. Twenty-five thousand pounds will have bought you twenty-five thousand pounds of house. Not much these days. Just pray it doesn't need a new roof.' She sniffed. 'I used to think my Liz was sensible. Seems she isn't, she's taken up with you. And you are all testosterone and dreams.'

Now, lying on her bed, staring at the sky, Liz thought Bibi had been right. Drew *was* all testosterone and dreams. But how they'd laughed when, all those years ago, they'd been in a taxi on the last lap of their journey to their new home. It had taken hours: a train to Inverness, a bus to Gairloch, then, at last, this taxi to take them on the narrow road along the coast to their house.

They'd caught a glimpse of the house as the car bumped over a rise in the road, and it was beautiful. It was white-washed and set in a garden that was a haze of whites and pinks. Drew clutched Liz's hand, 'It's gorgeous. I was right. It's wonderful.'

They looked at one another, faces bursting with joy. It was almost as if there was not enough room between their ears to contain their smiles.

'Your ma was wrong,' Drew said. 'I'm not just testosterone and dreams. I've got a vision. And I'll make it work.'

Liz put her hand on his face, kissed him and said, 'I know.'

The car stopped at the gate; they climbed out, paid the driver and watched as he turned and drove back down the road, leaving a small cloud of late summer dust in his wake. They stood looking at their new home; the smiles waned.

The house from close up was not as full of promise as it looked when glimpsed from afar. A window on the ground floor was broken, the paint on the front door was peeling, the roof looked as if it might, at any moment, cave in. The tantalising drift of pinks and whites in the garden turned out to be a mass of waist-high nettles in full flower. And Drew thought, Ah, the old bag was right. In a time when the average house costs about a hundred grand, when you spend twenty-five grand's worth of house is what you get.

It was three o'clock. Time to drive to the village to collect her children. Liz sighed. They had scythed down weeds, they had dug the garden, they had painted, plastered, renewed windows, unblocked chimneys. They had argued. They had known hunger. Their potatoes had been small and slightly green; lettuces, sprouts and cabbages had been decimated by rabbits. Clouds of soot had billowed into their rooms when they'd lit a fire. The bedroom was so damp, they'd found mushrooms growing in the cupboard. It had been hell.

Last year, Drew had decided to go back to his studies.

He'd enrolled at Aberdeen University, and with a wife and children to support when he graduated had worked hard. His days of beer, rock'n'roll and pizza were behind him. For the first couple of months, he'd phoned every day. Then he'd thought this was costing too much, and had got in touch twice a week. Soon it was once a week. He hardly came home at weekends, and when he did, they had very little to say to each other. Their lives had slipped apart. His was full of his new friends and his studies. Hers was all about the children, tending their huge garden, and the gossip she picked up at her job in the local shop.

The end, when it came, started over a conversation about vegetables. He'd come home to see the children and had been sitting at the kitchen table when she'd asked him to dig up some potatoes for supper.

'Do I have to?' he'd said. 'I hate digging up potatoes. I hate potatoes. In fact, I've started to hate vegetables.'

'Well, that's going to be tricky when you come back. I know you'll have a job, and won't be here as much. But I can't manage this place on my own,' Liz had told him.

He hadn't looked at her. Instead he'd studied the table mat. Plain cork; there wasn't much to study.

'You're not coming back, are you?' said Liz.

Drew shook his head.

'What's her name?' asked Liz.

'Maggie,' he said.

'How long have you been seeing her?'

He shrugged. 'Months.'

'But we made love last night. How could you?'

'I thought you'd want to,' he'd said.

'I did. But then I didn't know I was sharing you with Maggie.' She'd spat out the name.

They had stared at one another for several minutes, neither of them knowing quite what to say.

At last he said, 'Sorry. I didn't know this would happen. I met Maggie, and it all just ran away with me. I didn't want to hurt you.'

'But you have,' she said. Then she'd snorted and said she'd better go and dig up some potatoes. 'The children still have to be fed. Probably, you shouldn't be here when I get back.'

He wasn't. Now he phoned at weekends to talk to Louis and Lara. She got by. Her job earned her a little money, but she could bring home out-of-date food. She sold some vegetables to a local hotel. But still, she could scarcely pay her bills. The phone had been cut off.

She hadn't told her mother what had happened, though she knew, in time, she would have to. For the moment, she couldn't face it. She had made one or two friends who came by and chatted and whose children played with her children as they sat in the kitchen drinking tea and exchanging what they considered to be the small details of their small lives.

Still, running through the moments of her life, considering the things that she'd done, she cursed herself for never quite being able to come up with a satisfying reaction to things said to her, when they were said. Bibi was right, she thought. I am a dumb, placid fool.

When Drew had told her about his affair, she now

thought she should have shouted, screamed, thrown things at him. What had she done? Gone out and dug up some potatoes for supper. She'd screamed silently that night in her bedroom, thrown pillows at the wardrobe. She'd let her fury and frustration fly in the same pathetic way she had done back home all those years ago, when she was a teenager in Edinburgh.

And now I am in hell, she thought. It had all sprung from a crazed moment in an Italian town when the light and the scents had robbed her of her reason. All the cold and damp and poverty had come from that. This awful life she now lived was down to a stream of golden light. I blame Florence, she thought. It's all Florence's fault.

Just a Little Bit of Freedom

For days after his drive around town with Bibi, James raged. He sulked and was prickly with jealousy. He lusted after Bibi's car. Why should an old woman have such a car, especially when it was plain she hardly ever drove the thing? It wasn't right. A car like that was more than a car, it was a thing of beauty. It should be beloved. It deserved to be stroked, polished, to have its engine tweaked and souped up. He could do all that. He would take it out, cruise the streets, and let the whole world see what a handsome thing it was.

Bibi had driven him to Crammond, a small village on the edge of Edinburgh. She took the inside lane on the Queensferry Road, moving serenely through the quiet Sunday traffic. She was not, as she claimed, a wonderful driver. She was sedate behind the wheel, something James found embarrassing. He liked speed whenever he could get it. Bibi obeyed every rule of the highway, and criticised those who didn't. 'Signal, you fool,' to the driver in front. 'Just where is going so fast going to get you?' to the driver who whizzed past her. She was affable. When a pedestrian stepped off the kerb as she was pulling away as a traffic light turned green, Bibi knocked on the windscreen, then wagged a scolding finger. And smiled. On spotting a woman wearing a particularly vivid green hat, she had tooted her horn, then pointed to her head and waved, shouting, 'Excellent hat.' James cringed.

But when he tried to chat, Bibi had flapped her hand at him. 'Don't talk to me when I'm driving. I can't chat and drive. I have to concentrate on the road.'

'Well you shouldn't be looking at people's hats,' said James.

'True,' Bibi agreed. 'But someone bold enough to go outside in a hat like that needs all the comment and encouragement she can get.'

At Crammond, they parked and walked by the shore. Old buildings, painted white, eiders in the water, yachts moored, people drinking outside the pub; Bibi and James strolled, taking it all in.

'You drive going home,' said Bibi. 'I'm a wonderful driver, but I'm even more wonderful as a passenger.'

James looked at the keys; the temptation was overwhelming. 'Are you insured for me to drive?'

Bibi didn't really know, but said she was. She made a mental note to check this out when she got home.

James smiled and took the keys.

'That makes you happy,' Bibi said.

James smiled again. 'You think?'

'I think you like to drive. You want to be in control,' said Bibi.

'Do I?'

'You know nothing about yourself, James,' she told him. 'You are not, as they used to say, in touch with your emotions. You need your consciousness raised.'

'Do not,' said James.

'Do too,' said Bibi. 'You have no concept of happiness. The only time I've really seen you smile, smile properly, was a few moments ago when I gave you the keys. And you don't seem capable of celebrating it, other than with a small smile. I don't think you have ever jumped for joy. Or spread your arms and shouted just to let the world know how ecstatic you are.'

James stared at her in horror. 'I'd never do anything like that.'

'I know,' said Bibi. 'You're too shy. Too introverted. And when you add that you don't know who or what you are, I'd say you were gullible. Easily taken in, too eager to be liked. I suspect you've had your heart broken.'

James was shocked. How dare she say this to him? What made it really annoying was that she was right.

'My dear,' said Bibi, touching his arm, 'you have to learn to show your enthusiasm. You've got to stop being so uptight.'

James stared down at the hand on his arm. How strange to see it there. Nobody ever touched him like that. Vicky had put her arms round him when they kissed, but she'd never just put her hand on his like that. It was a tiny intimacy, but it went to the heart of him. Then there was *my dear*. Nobody had ever called him dear, or sweetheart or love. These two words rocked him. He didn't know what to say, so he turned his eyes away from her and looked out at the water.

At work, thinking about what Bibi had said, he'd fill the baskets in the central aisle with the selection of organic breads, delivered fresh every morning – raisin bread, walnut bread, onion bread. He'd keep the shelves filled with bottles and cartons of vitamins, oils and potions. He made displays of marigold shampoos and vitamin E moisturisers. He'd chat to customers.

But inwardly he raged. That old bag Bibi, what did she know about anything? My dear, she'd said. He wasn't her dear. He was filled with a strange fiery hatred for her and her family. They were soft, privileged. Reading books, listening to classical music, drinking wine, calling one another dear and love and sometimes even sweetie. What did they know about real people with real jobs leading real lives?

He'd dig his nails into his palms, clench his teeth, stare out of the window, lower jaw grinding against upper jaw, damning her – for she'd been right, he was uptight, he didn't know how to express enthusiasm, his heart had been broken – and cursing his luck and his stupidity.

He'd been a fool. He'd taken up with a girl who'd lied about her age. He'd fallen hopelessly in love, duped by her stories. All he'd wanted was someone to be with, to walk beside him into pubs and clubs, to sit with him in the evenings, to share his meals, listen as he told her about his day. Someone who'd hold him at night, breathe with him in the dark. In exchange he would have given her everything he had.

He didn't want to be here. He missed his old life, his old flat, his old job. Mostly, he missed his car.

And there was a thing – his car. Why, when he'd had it, had he not gone anywhere in it? He'd been happy to drive about town, or to polish it. He'd loved to look at it. Indeed; just walking up to it jingling his keys had given him a thrill. But he'd never driven it for miles and miles and miles. He'd taken Vicky on short runs out to the country. That didn't count, though. Not when he considered that he could have gone to Cornwall or up to the Highlands, or even to France. He'd never been abroad. Now, he couldn't think why not. On holiday from work, he'd stay in bed till noon, watch films on television. But he'd never gone anywhere. What was that all about? he asked himself. He'd expected nothing. And nothing is what I got, he thought. Now he wanted to drive Bibi's car, window down, radio on. He wanted to see long roads winding, unfolding in front of him; to feel the steering wheel in his hands as he travelled along. He longed for the sense of freedom that a road, a car and unlimited time would bring.

He blamed his father for telling him that there was no point going abroad. 'What does abroad have that we don't have right here? It's all funny food and funny drink and people speaking a language you don't understand.' James had believed him, and had stayed home. Reviewing his time on earth so far, he considered he'd walked a narrow path, lived a small life.

He stopped meditating. He could no longer find any calm; emptying his mind was impossible. He was plagued by self-doubt and recriminations. He stopped playing his Gregorian chants and started to listen to his favourite hip-hop CDs. He'd hoped they would annoy Bibi. But she would smile when she heard the throb of bass thud and tell him it was nice to have some young noise about the place again.

Evenings, he no longer stayed in his room, reading. Instead, he'd sit with Bibi as she watched television quizzing her about her travels, torturing himself the while about his small stay-at-home life.

'Have you ever been to India?' he asked. He was in the armchair opposite hers, slouched low, legs spread in front of him. He was trying to look only mildly interested in her reply.

She picked up the remote, turned down the volume. 'India? No.' She turned up the volume.

'Well, America then. Have you ever been there?'

Bibi turned down the volume and wondered why this boy did not understand it wasn't on to question a person when she was watching her favourite soap.

'America, yes.'

'When?'

'Years ago. In the sixties.'

'Did you like it? How long did you stay?'

'Yes, and six months. I had to come home. I was expecting Celia.'

'Why didn't you have her there?'

Bibi sighed. She really, really didn't want to talk about this. More, she didn't want to think about it. 'I wanted to be at home. It was a hormone thing. Then again, we didn't have insurance, and we didn't have any money.'

'Did you eat burgers and Hershey bars and Twinkies?'

'Yes. Yes. And no.'

'Well, did you go to a drive-in movie?'

Bibi sighed. The soap ended and she hadn't seen what happened. 'I suspect you get your notions about America from sitcoms, cop shows and films about rampant teenagers. No, I did not go to a drive-in movie.'

'What did you do?' James wanted to know.

'What do you think I did? I had a child. I cooked, cleaned, made beds. I shopped. I did more or less exactly what I did over here. Only the accents around me were different.'

'But,' said James, 'it was America. Everybody wants to go there. You must have done some American things. Eaten apple pie. Sat in the back of a yellow cab. Seen long, long roads stretching into the distance, endless rolling wheatfields, rodeos, lone cowboys on horseback, motels, little bars in the middle of nowhere where drifters go to shoot the breeze and drink a coupla beers. Did you drive around in a Cadillac, roof down, him steering with one hand, the other arm round you? You'd be wearing a thin cotton dress, he'd have a Stetson pushed back on his head. Country and western on the radio.'

'You have definitely been watching too many films,' said Bibi.

'It was America, for Christ's sake, you must have done something more than cook and clean and look after your kid. Did you see Montana in the winter? Vermont in the fall? Fog in San Francisco? Did you see the Knicks play? Eat hot dogs from a street vendor, extra onions?'

Bibi pushed herself stiffly from her seat. 'I think I need a glass of something,' she said.

James followed her. He was too caught up in his visions

of America to notice the pain on Bibi's face. Too naïve to know he ought to shut up. He was furious that someone would go to that golden land and fail to do anything golden.

'Why are you suddenly asking me all this?' said Bibi. She took a bottle of white wine from the fridge. Poured a glass and silently scolded herself. Today had been delegated as alcohol free.

'Because,' said James, 'I haven't been to America. In fact, I haven't been anywhere. I haven't done anything. I looked back on my life so far and thought it was small, narrow. I thought about the things I've let happen to me and the path I've taken and decided I've been a fool.'

Bibi took a second glass from the cupboard, filled it and handed it to him. 'Me too,' she said. 'I have made bad decisions, I have failed at many things, I have let people I loved go. Yes, a fool, that's a fair definition of me.'

'Who have you let go?' asked James.

'Graham,' she told him. 'My Graham. I don't know where he is. I've lost him. Every day I think about him and I wonder if he ever thinks about me.' Then she did the thing that James dreaded most – she touched him. Laid a bony hand on his arm. She smelled of chiffon and lavender. 'My dear, we have this in common. We are both fools.'

James was in turmoil. That touch made emotions broil within him. He wanted to run from the room, slam the door, and press himself against the wall staring wildly ahead. Then again, he also wanted to cry.

A Monstrous Mistake

These days Bibi would often walk into a room then stand gazing ahead wondering why she'd come in here. She put it down to her age, a diminishing short-term memory, but she was aware of the blank look on her face as she stopped just inside the door and realised she'd forgotten the purpose of her mission. It had, after all, been uppermost in her mind only a few steps ago. That blank look perplexed her, because she now felt it was the way her face fell most of the time, and not just when she halted mid-stride and said, 'What am I doing in here?'

This emptying of expression from her face happened because she was living in the past, swimming through memories. Everywhere she went, her past trailed behind her. Anything – a sound, a smell – could bring long-lost moments reeling into her mind. Staring into space, she would concentrate on the pictures in her head, things she'd thought she'd forgotten. And her face would be fixed with a bemused blankness.

Her recollections were mostly of Callum. He had been part of her life for over thirty years. When he'd died, Bibi's days became a whirl; there was so much to do. The flat had filled with grieving friends. There had been a lot of weeping, but she hadn't done any of it. She had arranged the funeral, answered letters and cards. There were flowers everywhere; the phone was rarely silent. Bibi was so busy, she'd wished she could chat to Callum about it.

She hadn't accepted he was dead, and that was what kept her going. Later, when the fuss had calmed, the phone had stopped ringing and Bibi was alone, she would lie in bed rigid with grief. Sometimes she'd reach over to the empty space beside her, not quite believing Callum wouldn't be there. She'd often turn to him in the kitchen to ask what he thought of some item in the news, and cry at his vacant chair. To this day his black coat hung on the hook by the front door. By the time she had resigned herself to the fact that he would not be wearing it again, she'd got too used to it being there to bring herself to throw it out. When she was leaving the flat to go anywhere that caused her anxiety – the dentist, the heart clinic – she touched it for luck.

For a while she'd been angry, filled with sudden fury at Callum for dying. 'Bloody man,' she'd say, stamping about, 'always doing something to upset me.' But once she'd realised her life was now her own, she had small moments of glee. Dining on a carton of yogurt and an apple, she'd said, 'You wouldn't like this, now, would you?'

Last night, James questioning her about America had distressed her deeply. Her memories of being there were painful. She thought she had definitely been a fool. Her days in New York came to her as a time of loneliness, long evenings when she sat waiting to hear Callum's footsteps on the stair. Roddy was two and she was twenty-eight.

It was 1962. Bibi's mother had died the year before, leaving her three and a half thousand pounds, a princely sum back then. Callum had wanted to blow it all on a world tour. Bibi had refused. She opened a bank account in her name only, and tucked the money away before Callum could get his hands on it. She bought the flat in Saxe-Coburg Street. She loved that it was so big. Two of the rooms were vast. It cost two thousand pounds. These days, Bibi could hardly believe a property could have cost so little. But then, it did need a lot of renovating.

As soon as they moved in, Callum unleashed his silver tongue on her, persuading her, willing her to spend what was left, money she'd planned to use on rewiring and decorating, on a trip to America.

'We have to go,' he said. 'It's where all poets go.'

Bibi wondered about this, but had no facts to back up her doubt.

'They love poets over there. It's America, for God's sake, the land of opportunity. We can't live our lives and not go there. It will be a wonderful experience. An education. It's the golden land. Everybody in the world is a little bit American.'

So they went, and within two months of arriving, Bibi was pregnant with Celia.

They lived in Greenwich Village, which, at the time, was cheap and the haunt of writers, poets, artists and musicians. Callum loved it. Later, he was to say how happy he was there in his little cold-water pad.

At first, Bibi loved it too. It seemed to her to be a city on a constant high. The cafés, at that time, were called luncheonettes. There was one not far from the apartment she and Callum rented. It was alive with voices; there always seemed to be some kind of drama going on, usually concerning a small disagreement. She loved the noise of the city – there was, she remembered, music everywhere. She supposed in such a vast and thrumming place there must be some shy and retiring New Yorkers, but she never met one. She was often told her Scottish accent was cute.

But in time, as Callum made more and more friends, she felt out of place among people who talked the night away about their stuff and other people's stuff. She was not a poet, didn't paint or make music; she had no stuff. She had a child who filled her life, but there seemed to be no place for them among Callum's friends. And Callum made many friends.

As did Roddy. The little Scots boy captured hearts. In the deli round the corner he'd be swept up into eager Italian arms, twirled, tickled and showered with gifts – an amaretto biscuit, chocolate, a stick of red and white striped candy. People who lived nearby said hello to him as he went by, clutching Bibi's hand. They'd ruffle his mass of dark curly hair. 'Hi, Roddy.' He spent his time there saying, 'Hi,' and smiling. Bibi didn't fare so well friend-wise. In the end she reckoned she wasn't a hi kind of person; she was more a good-morning sort.

Callum was high. This was where he wanted to be. 'Everything that's happening in the *world* is happening right here in this little bit of New York. The people here now are going to change everything. Books, art, music, everything.' In later years he was to claim he'd been in the room when Bob Dylan played his first gig at Gerde's Folk Club. He told interviewers he'd rushed home to Bibi and declared he'd just heard the future of popular music, a voice of protest that spoke to millions. 'Frank Sinatra is dead,' he vowed he'd said. Bibi had no recollection of this, but held her tongue.

The apartment in Greenwich Village had been small: three rooms – two cramped bedrooms, a tiny bathroom with a shower and a main room where the family watched television, cooked and ate. This room was not large enough for all the demands made on it. The heating was inadequate, and there was no air-conditioning. It had been March when they arrived, but still cold, and they sat huddled by the radiator. In summer the heat was excruciating. It seemed to Bibi to be a solid thing, a wall she walked into whenever she went out. Roddy cried and whined a lot. Callum complained and left them alone.

In all her six months living in that apartment, she did not go out in the evening. Instead, she sat by the window sipping, that stifling summer, iced tea. She'd observe life in the street below and spy on Polly, the woman who lived directly across from her.

Polly was an artist. She made collages using anything from old soup labels to her own pubic hair. Bibi knew all this not just because Callum had told her, but because she could see Polly at work. Polly never drew her blinds. She fascinated Bibi.

They had met once, when Callum brought her in for a drink. He'd met her at a party and they'd shared a taxi home. He'd invited her up, they had opened a bottle of red wine and talked heatedly about poetry, art, blues music and their mutual love of good ice cream. At the time, Bibi was three months pregnant, and suffering. She felt bloated, fatigued and nauseous. Her fingers were waterlogged and fat. Because there was a limited supply of hot water, she washed her hair only twice a week. Her clothes were old, and no longer really fitted her properly. She was, she felt, at the peak of her career as a frump.

Polly, on the other hand, was delicate, a fragile thing in a long skirt and gipsy top. She had sandals on her feet, her toes painted scarlet. She was blonde, fragrant, with a slow Texan drawl, a voice like melted honey. She was overflowing with gorgeousness. Bibi, tired after a day of heat and Roddy, had gone to bed. She lay with the covers pulled back, listening to Polly and Callum talk. She could not hear what they were saying. She did hear intonations, rhythms of speech, zest, enthusiasm, passion. She had none of those things, and was jealous.

Over the next couple of weeks, Bibi's fascination with Polly became an obsession. She could not wait for Roddy to go to bed so she could take up her position by the window and spy. She was ashamed of this. It was a ghastly thing to do – shabby, sleazy. But she couldn't help herself. She was convinced the glamorous, sexy and intriguing woman across the street was stealing her husband. She wanted proof. She was in torment. As soon as she saw Callum and Polly together, she could let go and engulf herself in agony. She felt that, in some absurd, perverted way, this would be a relief.

Polly performed for her. She emerged from the shower wrapped in a towel, and paraded up and down the room almost naked. She drank coffee, poised in front of her latest masterpiece, considering it. She had lovers, and when one of them came to her, she kissed him by the window, lights on, blinds up. Bibi knew that Polly knew she was watching her.

One night in August, when the heat was unbearable, Bibi sat in her underwear by the window, sipping iced tea, spying. She'd put the flat's only fan in Roddy's room to cool the air, help him sleep. She sat legs apart, wafting a newspaper in front of herself, sweat trickling slowly between her breasts and down the back of her neck.

Polly wore a thin black dress, low-cut, buttoned down the front. She set two glasses on her table, glanced across at Bibi, a slight smile on her lips. She put a single rose in a long glass, Billie Holiday on her turntable loud enough for Bibi to hear. Then she turned and said something to someone in the room, held out her arms. A man came to her, kissed her, slowly opened the front of her dress, kissed her again. He was tall, dark haired, wore a blue and white striped shirt. It was Callum.

Bibi went to the lavatory and threw up.

Next morning, Callum had not come home, and Bibi left. She packed her things, took the return tickets to Heathrow, her passport – Roddy was on it – and all their money from the drawer in the kitchen, then got a taxi to the airport.

I've gone home, you bastard, said her note. *Hope you have a wonderful time with Polly.*

After a long, gruelling flight home, in the days before in-flight movies and smoking bans, and a horrible train journey from King's Cross, they had arrived back in Edinburgh. Bibi bathed and fed Roddy and put him to bed. She had a long bath herself, then lay on her bed. Her own bed. Wonderful, she thought. She tried to imagine what Polly and Callum were doing now. Were they relieved to be rid of her? Planning their future together?

She let the events leading up to her flight from New York run through her mind. The man she'd seen had worn a blue and white striped shirt. Callum certainly had such a thing, often wore it. But it occurred to her now that as she had stormily packed her bag, stuffing clothes into it, hadn't there been a blue and white shirt hanging in the wardrobe? Hadn't she put it there only the day before, after washing and ironing it?

And the man's hair had been short, while Callum's, even back then, curled over his collar. The arms that had enfolded Polly were brown; Callum's arms, arms Bibi knew well, were pale, a fine, slightly freckled Scottish white, beneath the thick fuzz of black hair. Bibi put her hand to her mouth. She had only seen what she dreaded seeing, willing it to be Callum making love to Polly to justify her jealousy, to put her mental anguish on solid ground. Now, one heated note and six thousand miles later, it came to her that the man making love to Polly hadn't been Callum after all.

Bibi was in her kitchen, standing at the sink, remembering all this, when she became aware of someone else in the room. It was Celia, who was staring at her, as she gazed out of the window, lost in memories.

'Are you spying on me?' said Bibi.

'No,' said Celia. 'I came to see you. And there you were staring into space. Are you all right?'

'Of course I'm all right,' said Bibi. 'I just don't like being sneaked up on.'

'I'm not sneaking up on you.'

'Tiptoeing into someone's kitchen and standing silently watching them is sneaking. It's also spying.'

Celia sat down at the table. 'I wasn't spying. I just didn't want to disturb your reverie. What were you thinking about?'

'America,' Bibi told her. 'I was remembering New York.'

'You don't talk about that much,' said Celia.

'Nothing to tell, really,' said Bibi. 'We went over there. I got pregnant with you and came home again.'

'On your own?' said Celia.

Bibi nodded. 'Your father was busy. He was making contacts. Doing readings. The whole scene in New York suited him. He was writing a lot. He came home after you were born. You were very little at the time. You won't remember.'

Celia said that she didn't. She watched Bibi tidy up some papers, avoiding eye contact, and knew there was a lot she wasn't being told about her parents' American experience. She vowed silently to find out everything. 'Beth is worried about the number of credit cards you've been applying for,' she said, changing the subject. There was no point in quizzing Bibi about what had happened in

New York over forty years ago. Celia sensed a shameful secret, and knew her mother would clam up. No, finding out about this would take cunning, subterfuge and a bottle of wine.

'Beth is only worried that I might run up huge bills, then die leaving you lot to pay up.'

Celia sighed. 'No she's not.' Though in fact this was exactly what bothered Beth.

'I'll need the cards for my trip,' said Bibi. 'I'm going up north to see the house where I was born, and I will also drop in on Liz.'

'Are you taking the train?'

'No, the car.'

'You can't drive that old thing. It isn't up to it.'

'Cars like that were built to last. Besides, I'm not going to drive it. James is. Only he doesn't know it yet. I haven't told him.'

'James?' said Celia.

'Yes, James. He doesn't realise who or what he is. I have decided to take him in hand.'

Last night, as James was grilling her, Bibi had become uncomfortably aware that his resemblance to Graham was more than physical. He acted the same way, too. He followed her through the flat, quizzing her. Did you eat hot dogs? Did you go to a drive-in movie? Graham had done that, asked those same questions about her time in New York. Sometimes, she'd feel hounded as he came along behind her, battering her with questions. Where are my sun glasses? Why do I have to be home by eleven o'clock?

If one of his girlfriends phoned when he was out, she'd be grilled. What had the caller said? How had she sounded? Friendly? Angry? On and on, questions, questions, questions. Last night, replying to James's grilling had been quite like old times.

Celia stared at her. 'You can't just take him in hand. You can't force someone to drive you for miles and miles. James has a job. He can't give it up merely to satisfy some whim of yours.'

'Of course he can. He hates it. He should come with me, it will be an education.'

'Stuck in a car for hours and hours, yes, that would be an education,' said Celia. She got up and went to the fridge. 'I came for some lunch, but you don't seem to have any food.'

'There are tins of soup in the cupboard. I don't eat much. Can't be bothered. There's no joy in cooking for one.'

Celia put the contents of a tin of tomato soup into a pan. 'You should cook for James,' she said.

Bibi said, 'Food means very little to him. It's kindness that tears him apart. He can't cope with it.'

Celia stirred the soup in the pan, then laid two bowls on the unit. 'So you are going to be kind to him. Poor soul.'

Bibi picked up her spoon. 'I'll have to be careful. The slightest touch brings him close to tears. He knows nothing about affection.'

Celia brought the food to the table. She wanted nothing to do with her mother's plans.

'You think I'm mad,' said Bibi. 'But I'm not. I just want

to go back. See places I used to know. See Liz. All that before I die.'

'You're not going to die,' said Celia. 'Look at you, fit as a fiddle. What did they say at the clinic the other day? I bet they said you were fine.'

'Yes, they did. But I don't believe them. I am going to die. Sooner rather than later.'

Celia sighed. She didn't want to talk about Bibi's impending death. She wanted to hear about New York. In fact, now she thought about it, there were many things she wanted to know about. Throughout her childhood there had been incidents – people who turned up in the middle of the night, stayed a couple of days, then disappeared never to be seen again; her father's occasional long absences; a woman she had never seen before sitting weeping at this very kitchen table – that had never been explained to her.

But Bibi was talking about her death. 'I've made my will. I know exactly what songs I want at my funeral. And I want someone to read the last verse of *Hiawatha*. What I must do is take you round my things. I have pictures and ornaments you must never sell. They are to stay in the family.'

Celia nodded. She'd heard all this before. The last time Bibi had mentioned it she'd wanted everyone to sing 'Great Balls of Fire' and 'Hey Jude'. Before that it had been 'All Along the Watchtower' and 'I'm Feelin' Good'. 'The Nina Simone version,' she had insisted. She thought it slinky.

'There are your father's manuscripts. Future generations might treasure them,' Bibi said now.

Celia doubted this. In fact, she was sure that future generations would have no idea who her father was.

Bibi said she'd been contemplating death, and was fully prepared for it. 'Odd, when you think about it, because I won't be around to have the satisfaction of seeing my plans work out. And I've never been prepared for a single thing in my life before. I certainly wasn't ready for any of my children. Every single one took me by storm. Such a shock, a baby. All that howling and sleepless nights and vomit and plastic things everywhere. And the guilt, oh my goodness. I lived on guilt and bacon sandwiches with each of you for months.

'Then, before all that, I wasn't prepared for my marriage. Suddenly there I was living with a damn poet of all things in a cottage in the middle of nowhere. Him scribbling away, me in the kitchen having a tantrum because I didn't want to do the dishes. I had never washed a dish in my life.'

Celia looked at her watch. She didn't mean to be rude, but she'd heard all this before, except for the bit about her mother never having washed a dish before she married, and knew that when Bibi got on a roll it was hard to find a moment to reasonably stop the flow.

'Always had someone to do that for me,' said Bibi. 'I got married for the sex. Dishes never occurred to me.'

Celia said she had to go. 'Work,' she said. Really she did not want to listen to details of her mother's sex life. She thought that Bibi might be on the verge of divulging some memories that were not the ones she wanted to hear about.

Bibi nodded. 'See you later then.'

As Celia left, she turned and glanced at her mother. Bibi was sitting at the table, lost in thought. Her expression was bemused, that look that fell over someone's face when they walked into a room and wondered what the hell they were doing there.

Bibi, sitting at the table, had gone, in her head, back to her return from New York. Realising her mistake, she'd sent Callum a telegram. *I'm sorry*, she said. *I've made a monstrous mistake. Please forgive me.*

When, a week later, she had heard nothing, she sent another. *Come home to me. I love you. I was wrong.*

Mornings, she'd wait behind the door for the postman. But there was never anything from Callum. During the day she never strayed far from the phone; often she'd lift the receiver, checking it was still working. It was. But Callum didn't call.

She considered flying back to New York, but by now she was too pregnant. Besides she had Roddy to consider, and she needed all the money she had to get by. All she could do was wait and hope and curse her foolishness.

She remembered herself, tired and frumpy, wearing a navy print dress, the only thing she could get into, standing staring in despair at the silent phone. Oh, the gloom, she thought, and wondered if that was why Celia was the way she was. If the mood of the expectant mother drifted down to the child in the womb, the only emotions passed on to poor Celia would have been desolation, regret and loneliness. That would be why she now busied herself keeping her house perfect, looking after her family and reading *The Little Book of Calm*. She'd suffered all the angst she could bear before she was born.

Gathering the soup dishes, Bibi noticed a headline in the newspaper she'd been reading – *Do Creases in the Ear Lobe Signal a Heart Attack?* She carefully investigated her own ear lobes, tugging them, feeling for creases. 'Definitely,' she said. 'I have definitely got a crease or two. Bugger. I'm going to have a heart attack. I am going to die. And I'm just getting the hang of being alive.'

Celia didn't go straight back to her surgery. She went, instead, to Stockbridge, to the health shop where James worked. It was busy. She stood at the end of the only aisle, pretending to read the label on a jar of honey as she observed him. How odd, she thought, he looks like Graham. She wondered why she hadn't noticed this before. Of course, Graham's hair was darker, and his movements, his whole body language, a lot more assured. The man she was looking at was unsure of himself. He moved quietly. Gently, Celia thought. Still, there was a facial resemblance – the same long lashes, high cheekbones and full lips. She wondered why she hadn't noticed this before.

When the last customer had gone, she took her jar of Manuka honey and a bottle of hemp oil to the counter, and smiled at James. 'Lovely shop,' she said. 'I'm Celia, Bibi's daughter. We've met at the flat a few times.'

'Yeah.' He nodded, but not very enthusiastically.

'You like working here?'

He shrugged. 'It's OK.'

Celia smiled harder, and drew a deep breath. She was about to ask a favour, something she hated to do, especially when she hardly knew the person she was asking. 'Um,' she said. 'I have a proposition for you.'

James raised his eyebrows.

'I was wondering if you would consider driving my mother on her trip. Only she's getting on, and doesn't see very well, especially at night. And I worry that her car might break down and she'd be stuck on her own in the middle of nowhere.'

'Can't you do it?' said James.

'I'd love to,' said Celia. A lie. 'But I can't take the time off.'

James thought, Posh bitch. But asked, 'What makes you think I can take time off?'

'I just wondered if you'd consider doing it,' Celia said. 'I worry about my mother.'

James paused, contemplating this. 'I haven't been here long enough to get much time off.'

Celia said, 'Ah.'

They stared at one another in silence. Then Celia said, 'I'll pay you, of course.'

James said, 'You want me to give up my job and drive your mother about? I can't do that.'

Celia looked at her feet. 'I'm sorry,' she said. 'I shouldn't have asked.'

'How much?' said James.

Celia didn't really know. She debated inwardly; she'd

never done anything like this before. 'Five hundred pounds.'

James pulled at his ear lobe. He mulled this offer over. Five hundred pounds for driving a car – tempting. Of course, that woman would be with him. He dreamed of driving for miles and miles alone. He could always ignore her. But five hundred pounds was probably not enough to tide him over when he returned to Edinburgh. He shook his head. 'Sorry, I can't do it.'

Celia said she understood. 'I shouldn't have asked you,' she said.

James said he didn't mind being asked. 'You rich people always think you can get whatever you want. You think you can buy anything, including people.'

'You're wrong there,' said Celia. 'Rich people don't think they can buy anything and anybody. I don't think they even want to. Anyway, what makes you think I'm rich?'

'You act rich, you look rich.'

'Well, I'm not, so nyah,' she said, and left.

Rich, she thought as she headed for her car. If only he knew. Behind the glossy black door of that huge flat, the family had lived in searing poverty. She'd been one of five ragamuffin children dressed in hand-me-downs and a selection of garments bought from charity shops. They'd eaten baked potatoes and thick soups her mother had made from cheap bashed vegetables from the local grocer's.

One of her most vivid memories was of Bibi and Callum fighting over a couple of slices of bread he'd eaten that she'd been saving to make toast in the morning. There had been nothing else in the kitchen. Celia well remembered being hungry and cold, for her clothes did not keep out the weather. There had been bickering and tantrums at the dinner table, often over a single leftover potato. The electricity and phone had often been cut off. Once, her father had come home looking triumphant. He'd won a prize for his poetry and had blown the money on that car and a garage to keep it in. Bibi, enraged, for she'd needed a new washing machine and had been for the last six months cleaning their clothes by hand in the kitchen sink, had thrown a lump of sweatily hard cheese at him. It hit him on the forehead, bounced to the ground and rolled under the fridge. Celia remembered this because later she'd seen Bibi retrieve that cheese, grate it and spread it on toast to grill for their supper. Ha, rich, she thought. That young man knows nothing.

An Offer He Can't Refuse

Bibi spread a map on the kitchen table and plotted her route.

'I'm not just going to see Liz,' she said. 'I want to have a look at the cottage Callum and I lived in when we first married. And I want to see the house where I was born. I'm going to visit my old stamping grounds.'

James was leaning on the kitchen unit eating a cheese sandwich and came across to look.

'I'm going to go through Perth,' said Bibi. 'Up the A9, then along here to Aberlour.'

James said she might be quicker going up to Aberdeen.

'No, it has to be Perth,' said Bibi. 'That's where I met up with Callum when we ran away together.'

'You ran away to get married?' said James.

'Yes,' said Bibi. 'It was very romantic.'

'I don't know anything about running away,' he said.

'You do too,' said Bibi. 'When you came here you were running away. From what, I do not know, but you definitely had an air of fleeing about you.'

James said nothing.

'I mean,' said Bibi, 'you just turned up in town with a job that seemed to be any old job. I don't mean to knock working in a health shop, but it isn't you, is it?'

He shook his head.

'What is it you'd like to do really?' she asked.

'Cars,' James said. 'I want to get back into the motor trade. I want to be a mechanic. I want to work with cars rather than sell them. I want to be involved with them, get my hands dirty. That's real, honest work.' He was uncomfortably aware of Bibi looking at him. 'I'd have to do a course,' he said. 'It's all specialised now. You have to take your car to a garage to get a headlight bulb changed. It's all computerised, too . . .' He thought he saw a glaze coming over Bibi, and tailed off. He was boring her.

Bibi stared at him. She wasn't glazed at all; she'd been fascinated, though not by any information about cars, rather by the way James had spoken in exactly the way Graham used to speak. He had wanted to do something physical when he left school. 'Real work. I want to be tired and dirty at the end of the day. I want to really need a cold beer. That's what earning a living should be about. Fixing things, making things, getting your hands dirty. Not writing bloody poetry.'

'Why have you stopped?' she asked James.

'I thought I was boring you,'

'No, not at all. You just reminded me of somebody. If you really like driving so much, you should come on my trip with me. You could drive. It would be good for you. You'd see mountains, rivers, wild places; you'd travel through history. Besides, my family worry about me. They think I'm too old to go travelling on my own. They imagine me getting stuck alone on lonesome roads in the middle of the night when storms are brewing.'

James said he was sure that wouldn't happen. He took a large bite of his sandwich and wished he *was* going on the trip. Driving for miles and miles along strange new roads appealed to him. He wished he had taken Celia up on her offer. But five hundred pounds was not enough to tempt him to quit his job.

On Tuesday, returning from an afternoon of planting her seedlings, Bibi stopped outside an internet café. The place was usually busy, but today it was relatively empty. She went in, ordered an espresso, sat at a computer and was told it would cost a pound to operate it.

'Don't know how to,' she said. 'The modern world baffles me.'

A student who was sitting nearby showed her how to log on, and how to use email. Bibi was amazed. 'This is all I have to do?'

She found a letter from Roddy that had his email address in the heading and sent him a note telling him she was in an internet café and that the weather today was lovely, and she hoped he was taking an Omega-3 tablet every day. Then, remembering what she'd read in his horoscope about having an affair, she added that she hoped he and Ruth were both fine.

She knew this might perplex Roddy, since he was aware of how much she and Ruth disliked one another. Bibi's main objection to Roddy's wife was that she made her feel like the worst sort of mother-in-law – interfering and disapproving. She had to admit that Ruth was right on the second count. Bibi did disapprove of her. She had told Roddy not long before he married that she thought Ruth quite the wrong sort of person for him to settle down with. 'She is neat and tidy. She will be up at dawn, cleaning. She'll nag you to better yourself. She won't be happy if you don't provide her with two holidays abroad every year and all sorts of status symbols.'

Roddy had told her she was being judgemental. Ruth was sweet and gentle and he loved her. Proving, Bibi thought, that love is truly blind.

Soon she got the hang of Google. This was amazing. She googled Callum and was delighted to find him listed; less delighted to find him described as a minor Scottish poet and essayist. He was never minor to me, she thought. She tried googling her children. Roddy wasn't mentioned, but she found Celia under Dental Practices in Edinburgh and felt proud. There was no mention of Beth. 'Well, she hasn't found herself yet,' said Bibi. She didn't think Liz would have found her way into Google, but there she was, having won a competition for growing the largest beetroot in her area. She'd got a rosette for her efforts. I didn't know that, thought Bibi. You never told me. And what else have you not told me? I wonder. She tapped the screen. Very soon I shall be on my way to find out.

She looked for Graham Saunders, but none of the people who came up seemed to be him. He's gone, she thought, lost to me. And really, I am to blame.

❊　❊　❊

On Tuesday evenings Celia usually had Beth round for supper. It was a casual family thing. They'd eat in the kitchen. Beth would bring a bottle of wine and a tub of pralines and cream ice cream or a chocolate cake. Celia would cook pasta, Peter would make a salad.

Beth would talk about how she hated her job, and how she worried that her life was slipping by without her having anything to show for it. Celia would console her and tell her something would turn up, 'Something always turns up.' Peter would have loved to talk about golf or football, but knew nobody was interested. Olivia would talk about school and her friends and her ambition to be an actress, 'Or something like that.' Always, always they'd end up talking about Bibi.

'I'm worried about her going on that long drive on her own,' said Celia. 'She isn't getting any younger.'

'She's a tough old bird,' said Peter. 'She'll make it. Don't think the car will.'

Beth said she would drive Bibi, but didn't dare take any more time off work. Celia and Peter agreed; they couldn't either.

'I went to see James and asked him to do it. But he said no. I even offered him money – five hundred pounds.'

Beth and Peter said she'd done her best.

Olivia disagreed. 'That's a crap offer. I wouldn't do it for five hundred pounds, and I'm a schoolgirl with no taxable income.'

They all looked at her.

'I mean,' said Olivia, 'where's that sort of money going

to get you these days? It would cover his rent and food for a month, two at most. Then what?'

Celia supposed she was right.

'You'd make a crap godfather, Mum. You know nothing about making people offers. You have to suss people out, find their weak spots. You have to make them an offer they can't refuse.'

'She's right, Cel,' said Beth. 'What can you offer James that he can't refuse?'

'Sex,' said Olivia.

'And who is going to provide that?' asked Peter.

'Well, not you, or me. Mum's too old. It'll have to be Beth.'

Beth didn't think so. Celia thought her daughter had been reading the wrong sort of newspapers, and furthermore she was not too old. Peter wondered if there was anything else they could offer James. 'What sort of thing would he be interested in?'

'Football? Motorbikes? Cars?' suggested Olivia.

'Yes, cars,' said Beth. 'Bibi said he used to sell them.'

'You think I should offer to buy him a car?' said Celia.

'No,' said Olivia. 'You should go and find out what he really wants, then negotiate. That's what you'd do if you were a Mafia boss. Get a sense of his weaknesses and go for them. It's a good job you're just a dentist. You're crap at corrupting people.'

Celia said she'd take that as a compliment. 'Why don't you go and corrupt James, since you seem to know all about it?'

Olivia said she couldn't. 'He wouldn't take me seriously.

I'm a kid. Anyway, I've got music class after school. And French homework to do now.' She finished her ice cream and left the table.

When she'd gone, Beth said, 'Well, you have to hand it to the girl, she has a savvy I never had at her age. You won't have any worries about her getting ahead when she goes out into the world.'

Celia said she was a little bit shocked. 'She never got any of that from us.'

'Makes you proud,' said Peter. Then he turned to Celia and said, 'I sometimes wonder if you brought the wrong child back from the maternity hospital.'

The next day, Celia went again to see James. She waited till the shop was empty, and bought a walnut loaf and a carton of zinc tablets. 'I wondered if you have thought about my offer,' she asked.

James said he had.

Celia sensed a certain relaxing of his attitude towards her. 'It's still on the table,' she said.

He shook his head.

'What, then?' said Celia. 'What do you want?'

This question took James off guard. He didn't realise Celia was asking what it would take to get him to drive Bibi on her trip; he thought she meant what did he want out of life. What were his hopes and dreams. He was aware of looking vacant, so he said, 'I want my old life back. I think I used to be happy. I can't remember.'

Celia said she couldn't do that. 'I can't make you happy.'

James said he knew that. Remembering last night's conversation with Bibi, he said, 'I don't mind working here, but there's no future in it. I'd like to go on a course to study car mechanics.'

Celia said, 'That's it? That's all? We need to find which colleges offer such a course. Get you an application form. Maybe you'll have to do an interview. Then we can find out about grants. I could ask Bibi to lower your rent if you don't get much. We could perhaps help you find part-time work in a garage.'

'You could do that?' said James.

'I'm pretty sure I could. Peter knows people who could help.'

She saw a smile spreading on James's face and thought that Olivia had been right. To get someone to do what you wanted, all you had to do was find their weakness and make them an offer they couldn't refuse. 'You'll drive Bibi, then?'

'OK.' A mild reply, but it had been a while since he'd enthused about anything. He'd lost the knack of it.

But Celia gushed. She didn't mean to; it was a reaction. The relief of knowing her mother would not be alone in what she imagined to be a wilderness – mountains, bogs, tumbling rivers and winding single-track roads. Celia had travelled the world, visited America, India, gone backpacking in Peru, cycled across France and Italy, sailed in the Caribbean, but she hadn't explored her own country. 'Oh, thank you,' she said. 'I can't tell you what this means to me. I'm so grateful. It's wonderful of you to agree. Just one thing, though. You must never tell my mother I asked you to do this. She's so independent, she'd be furious if she found out I thought she wasn't capable of driving herself.'

James said, 'OK. No problem.'

'Thank you. Thank you.' Celia reached over to grasp his arm. If he'd been nearer, she'd have kissed him.

He stiffened, drew back. Stared at her, tugging his ear lobe. So Celia patted his hand and said thank you once more. 'I can't tell you how grateful I am.'

As she drove back to her surgery, she thought how easy that had been. All James had needed was some encouragement. A little help along the way, the sort of thing your family did. A mother, she thought. She wasn't up for that; she had one child and that was enough. But he was welcome to share her own mother. It might take some of the heat off herself and Beth. If James needed a family, she decided, she had one, and it was big enough to allow a little room for one more on board.

In the evening, James asked Bibi if she still wanted him to go with her. 'You said last night it would be good if I came along.'

Bibi was watching a cop show, one of her favourite programmes; a detective was driving a really old car along a narrow road, listening to opera as he mused about a murder.

'It would be a relief,' she said. 'I get tired easily these days and my eyesight isn't what it used to be. But I have a mind to be on my own – driving, listening to music, thinking about my life so far.'

James nodded. This sounded good to him.

'I expect you feel the same. You fancy driving my car, but secretly you'd prefer it if I wasn't in it with you.'

When he answered, 'No. Not at all,' a little too loudly, a little too quickly, she knew she was right.

'You can tell me all your stories, about how you ran away to get married and that,' he said.

Bibi said she might; it would while away the hours on the road. 'I would like it if you came along.'

James said fine, he'd like to go too. He could do with some time off.

As he headed for the door, Bibi said, 'Is Celia behind all this?'

He didn't answer.

'How much did she offer you?'

'Five hundred pounds, but I didn't take it.'

'I should think not,' said Bibi. 'It's not that princely a sum when you think you may not be earning when you get back.'

'She said she'd help me get into college to do a course on car mechanics, and she'd also ask her husband to find me a job working part-time in a garage.'

'You should have insisted on the five hundred pounds as well. You really mustn't undervalue yourself, James.'

Having the Thing

Bibi and James were travelling north, at fifty-five miles an hour in the inside lane. They were half an hour into their journey when Bibi suggested stopping for a cup of tea. James was against the notion, protesting that they had hardly started.

'But I never feel like I'm away till I stop and do something I wouldn't be doing if I'd stayed at home,' said Bibi.

James pointed out that they were on the motorway, and that she wouldn't be, obviously, if she'd stayed at home. Wasn't that enough?

'No,' said Bibi. 'I like to be somewhere, not just moving from one place to another. It's good to be in a strange town, sitting in a café watching the world go by. It's one of the best things about being on holiday, don't you think?'

'I wouldn't know,' James told her. 'I've hardly ever been on holiday. And when I did go, I went with my dad. He wasn't one for sitting in cafés; he'd buy fish and chips and we'd eat them as we walked about.'

Bibi said that fish and chips were excellent, but sitting in a café with some bread and butter and a mug of tea was best. 'Haven't you been abroad, then?'

'No,' said James. If he sounded sour, it was because he felt bitter about this.

'Goodness,' said Bibi. 'I thought everybody your age went abroad. All that drug-taking and boozing in Ibiza.'

'Not me,' said James. 'I got the impression drugs and boozing were more your thing.'

'No,' said Bibi. 'I missed out on all that. I had children. They change everything. Added to which, they didn't hand round spliffs at the toddlers' group. Callum indulged, though.'

'When?' asked James.

'From nineteen sixty-six till nineteen seventy-two. He was one of those people who can't remember the sixties. He was very proud of that.'

James said that Callum sounded a complete prat. 'If you don't mind me saying so.'

'I mind very much,' said Bibi. 'Callum was a lovely man. Witty, gifted, unpredictable, tender, humane, passionate and curious. That's what makes the world go round in my opinion – passion and curiosity. And you seem to lack both, young James. If you don't mind my saying so.'

James also minded. He sulked. The journey continued in silence. Bibi stared out of the window, watching the landscape shift past. James put his foot on the accelerator. Every time he swung out into the fast lane to overtake some slower car in front, Bibi drew her breath and gripped her seat. She did the same when towering lorries, ten times taller than they were, hurtled past only inches away. The silence turned deeper, blacker. Bibi switched on the radio, Classic FM. Though the adverts annoyed her.

James returned it to Radio 1. Bibi put it back to Classic FM, and glared at him. And the silence became filthy.

When James did not take the slip road leading into Perth, Bibi continued to stare out of the window. She would not give him the satisfaction of a sigh. She rested her head on the window and felt the vibrating hum of the road. It was something she'd done long ago as a child, long ago when the world was slower and, she liked to imagine, a lot less complicated. She found it comforting. Every so often she glanced across at James. He was staring fixedly at the road ahead, but sometimes he'd clench his teeth and the muscles in his jaw would move.

And the silence continued.

At last Bibi said, 'You're sulking, aren't you?'

'No,' said James. 'I'm not.'

'Yes you are. You're sulking because I accused you of lacking passion and curiosity.'

'Well, no wonder,' said James. 'That wasn't a very nice thing to say. You rich people think you can open your mouths and just say anything that comes into your heads. You don't care who you hurt.'

'I care very much about hurting people,' said Bibi. 'But tell me, where did you get the idea I was rich?'

'Well, aren't you?' said James.

'I live in a flat bought in the sixties with a small inheritance when property in that area was cheap. My furniture came mostly from my childhood home, the few pieces my mother rescued when she had to sell up to pay death duties. We are driving along in a thirty-year-old car, the only one I have ever owned. And I didn't buy it, my husband did. It became mine when he died. For many years I have grown a lot of the food I eat. So where does rich come from?'

James didn't answer this. The silence returned. Eventually he said, 'What food do you grow yourself?' He was thinking about the contents of her fridge – wine, cartons of yogurt, apples, and sometimes a pack of bacon.

'Vegetables,' said Bibi.

'Vegetables? I've never seen you eat a vegetable.'

'Well,' said Bibi, 'for years my family ate what I grew. Now they've all flown the nest, I still grow vegetables. Can't seem to help it. It's an urge that takes hold every spring. But I no longer have to nag anybody to eat their greens, and there's nobody to nag me to eat mine. I can return to my normal state. Hate cleaning, quite like cooking, but not awfully fond of devouring my own dishes. I am a slut, was born to it. Now I can return to being one, I'm happy.'

James told her she should be eating five portions of fruit and vegetables a day. 'At least.'

'At least,' Bibi agreed. Then she told him to take the turn-off for Dunkeld. They could buy some sandwiches for lunch at the deli there. 'We'll picnic by the river,' Bibi said.

They parked in the square, bought sandwiches and fruit juice, then walked down to the river. It was a pretty place: old buildings painted white, and busy with tourists. But it was quieter by the Tay. They spread a rug on the grass, and watched the water flow by.

'Always liked this river,' said Bibi. 'I've always thought McGonagall was right when he said it was silvery. Though it's more pewtery today.'

James nodded. He was still irritated at being told he was neither curious nor passionate, and he hadn't wanted to stop. When travelling, he was always intent on his destination. Bibi told him to relax and stop fidgeting.

'I want to get up the road. It'll be dark when we arrive.'

'When we arrive where?' said Bibi.

'Where we're going. Inverness,' said James.

'There are stops to be made along the way. I told you I want to see the cottage Callum and I lived in,' Bibi told him. 'That's the whole point of travelling, stopping to look around and ponder.'

So James ate his sandwich and pondered the matter of Bibi not being rich. 'But,' he said at last, 'you and your family act rich. You all talk loudly. Beth wears expensive clothes.'

'You're not still on about that,' said Bibi. She sighed and told him he was mistaking style and confidence for wealth.

He bit into his sandwich, thinking about this. Then, 'But you told me you were brought up in a big house.'

'I was,' said Bibi. 'My father had money. I never saw any of it. He cut me out of his will when I ran off with Callum. But by the time he died, he'd gambled and drunk most of it away. And what was left went on death duties. Not that I'd have inherited much even if I hadn't run off, or if there had been any money left. I made the mistake of being female. Father thought daughters a waste of time. He refused to educate them. All we were good for was marrying into more money. Obviously, I didn't do that.'

She lay back, propped on her elbows, remembering the house where she was born.

'I was very clever, you know. Science and maths. But

my father wouldn't pay for me to do anything with it. My brothers went to boarding school, then university. Several of my friends went on to finishing school. But I stayed home to help with the estate and work at the local riding stables. The thing I remember most clearly about my childhood was being cold.'

'Cold?' said James. 'You were cold? I thought servants would light big log fires in every room.'

'Hardly,' said Bibi. 'There were fires in the drawing room and dining room and my parents' bedrooms, but nowhere else. I wore my brothers' hand-me-down sweaters. I was a child with a shiny face, frost-nipped cheeks and chapped lips.' She smiled at him.

James said, 'Really?' He thought Bibi looked rather lovely today. Or, at least, as lovely as somebody quite old could look. She wore a black linen jacket over a pink T-shirt, jeans and her usual training shoes. Her reminiscences amused her; her face was soft, relaxed.

'We had wonderful dinner parties, though. The table candlelit, fire glowing, glasses glinting; sometimes thirty people in evening clothes gathered, laughing and sparkling. As a child I'd watch from the upstairs landing. Clad in pyjamas and a dressing gown the colour of a teddy bear, peering through the banisters.' She turned to him. 'Next morning we'd race to the kitchen checking out the leftovers. Especially the puddings.'

He smiled back. 'That's what I'd have done too.'

'That's where I met Callum. At one of my father's dinner parties.'

'He came to dinner?' asked James.

'Good heavens, no. He was a poet. Working at the time on a neighbour's estate. He came for drinks, after dinner. One didn't have poets at the table, unless, of course, they were famous. And Callum wasn't then.' She laughed out loud at this. 'It didn't do to encourage the socialist classes.' And she laughed again. 'Callum's first book had just been published and our neighbour had seen a review of it in *The Scotsman*. He was very impressed and told my father that the chap living in one of his cottages was a poet. Published and everything. So my father drove over and invited him for drinks. He'd said dress was casual, and Callum had taken him literally. Of course, when Father said casual, he didn't mean *that* casual.'

James asked what Callum had been wearing.

'Corduroy trousers, very baggy, very old. A striped black and grey waistcoat, black jacket, faded and worn, red shirt, very red, and suede shoes.'

'That sounds all right to me,' said James.

Bibi agreed, it did. 'It wasn't the clothes. More the way he wore them. He'd stand, hands in pockets, surveying the room, looking uncomfortable and kind of sneery. People always noticed him, especially women. I think it was the shoes that got my father. Suede. He was of the opinion only communists wore them.'

James said, 'My father thought that anybody who didn't polish their shoes every night was suspect. A person of dubious cleanliness and morals, and not to be trusted.'

They both gazed down at their feet and took in Bibi's neglected training shoes and James's Converse high-tops, and smiled.

'It seems,' said Bibi, 'you can get a kick out of parental disapproval no matter how old you are. And no matter that your parents are long dead. There's something very satisfying about being naughty.'

'Rebelling,' said James. 'Even if it's only with your feet.'

A small troop of ducks floated past, Bibi threw them the remains of her sandwich. Further along the bank, a family were also picnicking. Bibi watched them. The mother was laying out food and the father was swinging a small child, heaving her high into the air, then bringing her down, holding her close, kissing her cheek, before tossing her up towards the sky once more. The infant's squeals of glee bounced through the still afternoon air.

'Callum used to do that with Beth. He adored her. A late child, and he had time for her. He'd settled down by the time she came along. When the others were young, he'd been too busy writing and campaigning and, to be frank, beating himself up about his work and lack of spectacular success to play with them. Beth was his chance to be a proper father.'

'Was it love at first sight? You and Callum?'

'It was something. The shoes did it. Anything my father disliked, I took to. No, it wasn't love. It was chemistry at first sight. I wanted to go to bed with him.'

'I didn't think people did that back in the olden days,' said James.

'Of course we did,' said Bibi. 'We just pretended we didn't. We certainly didn't talk about it all the time like people do today. I suppose we felt guilty about our lusts and desires, but that made them all the more pleasurable.'

She thought there wasn't as much guilt about as there used to be. It was guilt lite, as far as she could see. People fretting over eating too much chocolate or having spent too much on their credit cards. The filthy, black, all-encompassing, soul-destroying guilt of her childhood days seemed to have gone.

She remembered herself as a painfully thin child, prone to chilblains, solemn and obsessed with God. She prayed every night, hands clasped as she pressed her knees into the hard wooden floor of her bedroom, small, pale lips moving as she fervently vowed to be good, honest and pure in thought, word and deed. Oh, the guilt, the dense, stifling cloud of it that filled her mind, gnawing at her conscience if she committed one of the seven deadly sins. Should she have eaten one too many slices of cake, lusted after a school friend's pencil case, forgotten to thank Cook for making her supper or uttered a nasty word, she would punish herself by standing alone in her father's wine cellar, where spiders lurked, mice scratched, sudden shadows moved in corners and cruel demons, ghosts and spirits shifted round her, running icy, bony fingers through her hair and whispering mocking threats. Goodness, she was glad she'd grown out of all that. The older she got, the more free-spirited and wilful she'd become, so that on that autumn night when Callum had come into her life, she was ready for him.

'It was a wonderful night,' she said. 'Callum was outrageous; he spoke about Marx and how wrong it was to be rich. He advised our guests to sell their houses and donate the money to the less privileged.'

'Proving your father to be right about his shoes,' said James.

'Yes,' said Bibi. 'I never thought of that. Anyway, we drank cocktails and played records on the gramophone. Bing Crosby and Frank Sinatra, Mario Lanza and Duke Ellington. He asked me to dance. When he touched me, the thing happened. Have you ever had the thing?'

James shrugged; he didn't know what she meant.

'You know, when someone touches you for the first time and your stomach flips over and a wild tingling spreads through you, starting in your stomach, shooting all the way to your head, and coming down again, ending at your groin.'

James nodded. Yes, he'd had the thing. But he didn't think it had made the journey up to his head.

'Well, that was it. If Callum didn't have the thing too, he certainly knew I had it. And from that moment, I was a goner.'

She heaved herself slowly to her feet, dusted down her trousers and told James to pick up their litter. 'It's time to go.'

Not a Popping-in Sort of Person

Celia had been trying for days to phone her sister Liz, to warn her about Bibi's visit, but the line had been disconnected.

'She hasn't paid her bill,' Celia said to Peter. 'She always was a bit dreamy.'

Peter said there was nothing they could do about it.

'I hope nothing's wrong,' said Celia. 'I haven't been in touch with her for months and months. This is a bit worrying.'

'Bibi will find out what's happening when she sees her,' Peter said.

'That's exactly why I wanted to speak to her. A person should know when their mother is about to descend on them. In fact, I don't think anybody should visit anybody unless they've been invited.' Celia herself was not a popping-in sort of person. The very phrase made her shudder. Should anyone pop in on her, there was a certain stiffness in her welcome, a briskness in the way she made the uninvited guest a cup of tea and then sat across from them at the kitchen table, legs crossed, making a poor show of being friendly that ensured her popper-inner never did it again.

It wasn't that she didn't like the people who turned up

on her doorstep; it was the unexpectedness that disturbed her. She needed to be in control of who came to her house, and when. That way, she would never be caught in compromising situations. Like she had been when she and Peter had both taken the afternoon off work so they could have a little time together in bed.

Their sex life had been going through what Celia called a dry patch. They'd both been stressed and overtired. Going to bed together had been a matter of slipping under the duvet and kissing one another briefly, before falling into a deep sleep. Often they had promised each other that tonight would be the night. They'd winked and smiled, anticipating the pleasure ahead. But then they had hit the sack, exhausted, and gone through their same old chaste routine. The morning after, they'd woken, said, 'Damn,' and cursed themselves.

It had been Celia's decision to take matters in hand. She told Peter they needed to do something to de-stress, to keep the physical side of their relationship healthy and active. They needed to take an afternoon off work to do some naughty things together. 'And the fact that we both ought to be working will make it all the more fun,' she said.

They consulted their diaries and found they both could make a window the next Thursday.

They'd had champagne and oysters followed by chocolate pudding for lunch. 'Skip the main course,' said Celia. 'We don't want to be weighed down by overly full stomachs.'

She had meticulously planned their afternoon delight.

Candles filled the bedroom with scents of jasmine and sandalwood, soft music played on their small hi-fi, the curtains were drawn. They took their bottle of champagne upstairs with them. Celia wore a black basque and black stockings, Peter a thong. Things were going well. Peter was discovering that the afternoon Celia was more abandoned, noisier and more open to all sorts of innovative suggestions than the evening Celia. As the activities got hotter, the music on Celia's pre-recorded tape got louder, faster. Every now and then they'd look at one another, faces pink and damp with sweat, and promise to do this again. And soon. They were having fun.

When the doorbell rang, Peter said they should ignore it. 'It'll be someone selling something.'

But Celia froze. She wasn't one to ignore bells. Her response to ringing – phones, doorbells, alarms – was Pavlovian. She felt compelled to answer.

When the bell rang again, a series of loud, long rings, she heaved herself off Peter (she'd been on top), run across the room to get her robe from the back of the chair and started down the stairs. 'It might be the police. Something might have happened to Olivia. She might have been run over. Or my mother. Maybe she's had a heart attack and died.'

She thundered towards the front door, leaving Peter hot, sweaty and disappointed. It was not the police, of course. It was Natalie, Celia's friend, who'd been passing, seen the car parked outside and thought she would pop in.

'Pop in?' said Celia, her horror plain to hear. She was

too irritated at being denied her moment of sublime pleasure to hide it. 'You thought you'd pop in?'

'Yes,' said Natalie. 'You don't mind, do you? I haven't caught you at a bad time, have I?'

Celia said, 'No. Lovely to see you.' And showed Natalie into the kitchen, where she sat at the table, hands folded in front of her, sensing the awkwardness of the atmosphere as Celia put the kettle on.

'Is something wrong?' asked Natalie.

'No,' said Celia. She couldn't stop her voice slipping up an octave. 'I'm just off work with a touch of the flu.' She took a tissue from the box on the table and blew her nose to add dramatic authenticity to her lie. 'Thought I'd have a day in bed, nip it in the bud sort of thing.'

'Good idea,' said Natalie. 'You do look a little flushed.'

'Do I?' said Celia. She took a second tissue, blew her nose again, and coughed. The kettle boiled; she made two mugs of tea, set one in front of Natalie and leaned against the kitchen unit, taking a sip from her own.

Celia had known Natalie since they'd been at school together. She was small, shy and prone to saying the wrong thing at the wrong time. The woman would be mortified if she discovered what she'd just interrupted. Celia thought it best to have a cup of tea together, then get rid of her.

Then Peter appeared, also wrapped in his robe.

'Goodness,' said Natalie. 'Have you got flu too?'

Peter said nothing. His mouth opened and shut as he searched for words. Flu? He knew nothing about flu.

'Handy to have it together,' said Natalie. 'You can offer each other comfort, and share the Lemsip.'

It was only then that she sensed a frisson in the atmosphere. She caught the scent from the candles. She saw that the flush on Celia's cheeks was not the sort of flush caused by flu. Then, from upstairs, the specially prepared afternoon-delight tape started to play the hot selection Celia had recorded for when the passion got juicy. Natalie, at last, realised that there were no invalids in this house. She had interrupted a deeply private activity, and probably at a very crucial moment. She made her excuses and left. Celia didn't see her very often now.

'Come back to bed,' Peter said.

'No,' said Celia. 'It's not the same. I was just getting into a flow when the doorbell rang.'

'The flow will return,' Peter said. 'I can make it.'

'I've gone off it now,' said Celia. 'I feel silly.'

'Of course it's silly. We're both being silly. Isn't it fun? I am here being naughty and silly when I should be at a meeting. I'm loving it. Come on, we've got an hour before Olivia gets home and we've got to put on our grown-up clothes and pretend we're responsible, mature people.'

'Which we're secretly not,' said Celia.

'Which we're secretly not,' said Peter. He took her hand and led her back to the bedroom.

After that, Celia didn't just dislike popping-in, she hated it. She thought there ought to be a law banning it. People should feel free to frolic in their own homes wearing little or nothing, should they choose, without fear of disruption from the doorbell. 'It's a basic human right,' she said to Peter.

She felt horrified on Liz's behalf that their mother was

about to drop in on her. Celia thought this the worst possible act of popping-in. The uninvited visitor will have travelled a long distance and will, therefore, have to stay overnight. What consternation this would cause. What if there were no fresh sheets available, or not enough food? And what about Liz's everyday routine, feeding her children, running their baths, helping with their homework? How was she going to get on with things when she had the irritation of an extra person hanging about? All this would be made doubly worse when the unasked guest was her mother. A person couldn't just sit about and chat with their mother, Celia thought. There were too many unresolved issues, unasked and therefore unanswered questions. And from Bibi there would be a lot of unspoken criticism. She would gaze out at the garden, saying nothing, but her disapproval of what was going on out there would show on her face. Her eyes would rove over what Liz was making for her children's supper, and she'd purse her lips and pull in her breath. All this was bad enough, but Bibi was bringing a second popper-inner with her, James. Two extra mouths to feed, two beds to be made up, two extra breakfasts to worry about – Liz would have to be warned. 'I mean,' said Celia to Peter, 'this popping in on Liz is my fault. I was the one who bribed and nagged James into driving my mother. I have brought dreadful things on my own sister. I have to let her know that our mother is on the way.'

So she phoned and phoned and phoned. But Liz's line was dead. Her phone had been cut off.

She had mentioned her concerns to Peter, who'd told

her that, really, it was none of her business. Beth had also been uninterested. 'Haven't spoken to Liz in months. Sometimes we're on the phone a lot, then ages pass and we hardly speak. Don't worry about it. She will be delighted to see Bibi.'

'Would you be delighted to see our mother turning up out of the blue, knowing she'll probably stay for at least a week, and bringing James with her?'

Beth didn't answer that. But she thought, Probably not.

Celia phoned Roddy. In moments of confusion, despair, or when she didn't know what to do, she always got in touch with her older brother. Other than the fact that it gave her some comfort, she didn't really know why. Roddy, she knew, would not particularly care that Bibi was about to descend on Liz. The older Roddy got, the less he seemed to care about anything.

'I worry,' she said to him, 'that Bibi will say something about Liz living in that remote place and not keeping in touch, and they'll argue. Then Bibi will leave in a strop and they won't speak for ages and ages, and one of us will have to sort it all out. Probably by going up there to talk to Liz. It will be awful.'

Roddy told her to lighten up.

'How can I lighten up?' said Celia. 'Our mother is on a visiting spree, and I helped her. It isn't right to go calling on people uninvited.'

'When has anybody been able to stop Bibi doing anything?' said Roddy. 'She gets an idea in her head and she carries it through. When has she ever listened to anybody?'

'Never,' said Celia. 'I'll never understand what goes on in her head.'

'So,' said Roddy, 'let her go on her travels, and just be thankful it isn't you trapped in that car with her.'

Celia said she supposed that was true. 'Still, I worry about her.'

'Don't. She'll be bowling along enjoying the scenery, listening to Classic FM and telling young James her life. Sounds good to me. Go have a glass of wine and forget about it.'

Celia went to the kitchen, where Peter was pouring wine.

'It's as if you knew what he said. He told me to have a glass of wine and forget about it.'

'So you should,' said Peter, handing her a glass.

'What's up with Roddy these days? What's happening to him? Remember the last time we went down to visit him and Ruth? He went off to work wearing jeans. He's a bank manager, for heaven's sake. They don't wear jeans, not in the office anyway. And he wears pink shirts, and red ones. He'll get the sack. Then he spent hours and hours sitting outside on his patio, wearing Dad's old straw hat, gazing into the distance and smiling. That's not right. We were visiting; he should have been entertaining us.'

'How?' asked Peter. 'Doing party tricks? Juggling? Telling jokes?'

'You know what I mean. Spending time with us, chatting. Roddy used to be so charming. Charismatic, I'd say. He always took time to talk and ask how you were and what you were doing. He used to help me with my homework when I was little. He took me to the movies and bought me ice cream.'

'Ah,' said Peter, 'isn't it a sad day when you discover that your idols are only human after all?'

Celia took a swig of her wine and supposed it was. 'I don't want to be too grown up to have a hero. And that's what Roddy was to me. I just adored him when I was little. I used to listen for his footsteps on the stairs. I hung about him when he was in the flat. I wouldn't look near a boy if Roddy didn't like him. I didn't want to marry unless I could marry someone like him.'

'Good job you changed your mind when you found me,' said Peter.

Celia smiled and agreed. 'Good job.'

Roddy put the phone down. He stood by the window. It had stopped raining; blackbirds were calling, the sun was slipping down below the horizon. From here he could see for miles and miles; the greenness of his view always delighted him. He wished he was on the road, like Bibi, going somewhere, anywhere. Ambling along, he thought, with time on my hands.

He was a bank manager. A job he hated. Still, he figured he deserved that; he'd only studied accountancy and started work in a bank to horrify his father. He fondly remembered the moment he'd told Callum the direction he planned to follow in life. Callum had paled, and slumped into a chair. 'You're going to do what?'

'I'm going to take accountancy exams, and if I pass I'll look for work in a bank.'

'You can't do that,' Callum had said. 'No son of mine would do such a thing.'

Callum had prepared himself to cope with almost anything his children might do. He had speeches ready for moments of crisis should they end up in prison or slaves to drug dealers. He had primed himself to travel to Turkey, Greece, Saudi Arabia, anywhere, to grapple with the authorities should any of them get into trouble. He wanted his children to be explorers, if not of the planet, then of their own minds. He wanted them to be mystics, poets, philosophers, actors or any kind of artist. Mostly, he wanted them to be outrageous. It had never crossed his mind that one of them might become staid, conservative, wear a suit and embrace the nine-to-five. This business of Roddy wanting to work in a bank blew his mind.

'Well, this son is going to do exactly that.' Roddy had grinned as he spoke. 'There's a solid career structure in a bank, a pay cheque at the end of every month and a sound pension scheme. I could make manager by the time I'm thirty.'

Callum had said, '*What?* A bank manager? Have you any idea how corrupt banks are? How they treat people? You have joined the capitalist society; how could you?'

Roddy had smiled, spread his palms and said, 'Easily.'

He'd been nineteen at the time, home after a year in Australia, and even today, twenty-seven years later, that moment of truly horrifying his father still gave him pleasure. He'd studied accountancy, passed his exams, taken a job in a bank and risen to manager. He'd married Ruth, had two daughters and now a grandson. He had it all, really. Only snag was – he was miserable.

'Why are you telling me all this?' he'd asked Celia when she phoned.

'Bibi's on her way to visit Liz. Liz's phone isn't working, so I can't warn her. I thought you might be able to do something,' said Celia.

'What?'

'I don't know,' said Celia. 'Don't you know somebody up there, a bank-type person who could go round and let Liz know her mother is about to arrive?'

'No,' he said. Though he did have a friend, a colleague, who'd taken early retirement and moved into a house not far from Liz's. The difference in prices between houses in the north and houses in the south meant his friend had sold a four-bedroomed semi in Ruislip for a large modern bungalow with a veranda and a huge garden that led to a private jetty where he kept his boat. Roddy was jealous and had suggested to Ruth that they do the same. She'd taken a tantrum and said it was bad enough they were living here – a small town in Yorkshire, not far outside Leeds – without moving to the back of beyond: the Highlands of Scotland.

She still hadn't forgiven him for turning down a plum job in London and taking, instead, the post of manager at a small bank in rural Yorkshire. She'd had dreams of a rich social life and a house in Primrose Hill.

Roddy had scoffed at her. 'You know nothing about life,' he said. 'You only want to move upwards to impress your friends. I want to get back to the roots of what I do. I remember when I was young, not much more than a lad. Twenty-three, assistant manager in a tiny branch in Kirriemuir, a small place, but lively, full of humanity. I remember farmers would stop you in the street to discuss a loan for their new financial year, and I'd be happy to talk to them. I remember one day I was locking up the bank when a young couple ran up the steps. They'd been held up on the road, caught behind a tractor. They needed money for the weekend, but the bank was shut, and I gave them ten pounds from my own wallet. They paid me back first thing Monday morning. That was what banking was about then. It was about people. Not this modern rubbish: emails, sales, clients, credit rating, business plans, databases. I want to get back to talking to people: farmers, shopkeepers, housewives, anybody. It should be about knowing, trusting, shaking hands. That sort of thing.'

Ruth had dismissed him as an old-fashioned dreamer. 'Times have changed. Deal with it.'

Roddy dealt with it by trying to be a bank manager of the people. His suits were grey moleskin or beige corduroy, his shirts pink or navy. He waved to people in the street, calling out their names. Ruth said he was behaving as if he were in an old James Stewart film. He travelled to work on his new, and much-loved, Harley Davidson. Ruth said this made it obvious he was a middle-aged man with a problem. None of it worked. He was perceived as a man who liked to linger with his customers and talk about books, films or what was on the telly last night, when all anybody wanted to do was attend to business and get out of the bank as quickly as possible. It was agreed he was the worst bank manager the town had ever known. But a nice enough chap, nonetheless.

He could hear Ruth downstairs clearing up the supper dishes. She'd wipe the unit tops and sweep the floor. Then she would settle down on the sofa and watch television till it was time to go to bed, half past ten, usually. He rarely watched television these days. He liked to go out. He'd walk through the fields beyond his house to the woods; he always took his camera, hoping for shots of the foxes that lived there. Then again, he could take his bike into Leeds, where he had rented a small flat. He could sit and listen to music or read one of his art books. He never could read when Ruth was in the room with him. They hardly spoke to one another any more. They hardly touched.

It was time, he knew, to give up on this marriage. He should leave her. He was sure they'd both be happier, but he didn't know how to broach the subject. It might be easier if he was having an affair; he could say he'd fallen for someone else and wanted to be with her. Only there was no someone else. How could he tell his wife of twenty-odd years that he didn't want to live with her any more for no reason other than he no longer liked her? What were the words? He could say he wanted some time alone to think, or that he didn't think the marriage was working, but it still pointed to his desire to get away from her. He thought that pretty insulting, and Ruth was at an age when it would be hard to make a new life.

He sighed, crossed the room, put on his walking boots and picked up his camera. He walked down the hall and paused at the living room door to tell Ruth he was going out. 'OK,' she said.

Outside, he climbed the fence to the field across from his house. Walking towards the next field, then the woods, he spotted Jim Finney. Jim, a large and affably hearty man who owned and farmed most of the land in the area, was a client of Roddy's. Roddy didn't like the man – there was something sly about him. He was, Roddy thought, overly friendly in a superior way. Roddy always felt Jim patronised him. He supposed it was because he worked in an office and Jim worked the land, kept his eye on the weather, knew his livestock and thought himself to be more in touch with life, nature, the way of the world. Bankers to him were a boring necessity – little men who filled in forms. Still, Roddy raised his hand and shouted, 'Grand evening.'

Jim shouted that indeed it was and continued on his way. It was their usual greeting; they never stopped to chat.

The woods this evening smelled of damp earth and greenness. Roddy would have liked this to be the smell of his childhood. He would have liked his young days to be filled with wild and secret places, messages in the hollows of trees and adventures. The smell of his childhood was of coal fires, vegetables stewing and books. He could not hold an open book to his face and breathe in the tang of ink and paper without thinking of his father. Evenings, he'd sat on Callum's knee, rapt at his reading of *Treasure Island* and *Swallows and Amazons*. This, he was aware, was where he'd got his notions of a childhood filled with wild places, hideaways, secret messages and adventures.

He sat in his favourite spot, on a fallen log at the far edge of a small clearing, where he had a view over the fields beyond. From here he could watch early lambs frolicking and making small sorties away from the safety of their mothers. He saw a hawk soaring on the thermals above him, and took a photograph of raindrops hanging from the leaves of a primrose. He hoped the fox cubs would come out, but doubted they would. He'd made too much noise as he approached and was downwind of their earth. He felt a little guilty that his presence would curtail their evening's games. It started to rain, but still he sat, thinking himself absurd. How pathetic to prefer sitting in the woods feeling chilled and wet to being at home on the sofa in the warmth with a cup of tea and a good film on the television.

He saw Jim Finney heading home across the fields in front of him and wondered where he'd been. He didn't really care. But then, he didn't care about anything much these days. From time to time he wondered how it had come to this.

Romance is Tricky

Bibi was travelling north, watching the scenery and flicking through scenes from the early days of her marriage to Callum. It always embarrassed her to remember those first months they spent together. She had known nothing about living with someone, except that they could go to bed together every night, and wake up together every morning. This was what appealed to her. In her young mind, the more practical matters of day-to-day existence had been fuzzy. She was, after all, a woman who had never so much as boiled an egg.

It had been November when she ran away with Callum. Even then, her father had been in trouble financially, though she had known nothing about it. Staff in the house had been reduced to a cook, Mrs Henderson, and a maid, Hilary, who did all the cleaning and bed-making and who laid the fires in the drawing room and dining room every day. It had never occurred to Bibi that this might be a sign of a money worry. She'd thought that since her brothers and sister had all left home to marry or to work in the city, there was no longer any need to employ a number of people to maintain the household.

She had started seeing Callum after his appearance at the dinner party. They'd gone for walks together on the moor on her family's estate, a hundred acres of heathered land where they roved and talked and kissed. He'd opened his coat and invited her in out of the cold. An old coat, she remembered, thick tweed with a dark red lining. There had been room for two inside. He'd wrapped it round her, and kissed her. She'd slipped her arms round him, wanting him. She'd always felt she couldn't get close enough to him.

Once, he'd taken her for a drink at the hotel in the nearby village. Gin and tonic, she'd had. He'd bought himself a pint of beer. They'd sat in the corner whispering to one another.

'You will marry me,' he'd said. Not a proposal, more an order.

'Will I?'

'Of course,' he told her. 'What else is there for us to do? We must be together.'

She'd smiled. 'I think we must. You have to ask my father, though.'

He'd told her he didn't know about that. He knew her father wouldn't approve of him.

Bibi had a feeling he was right about that. Her father had strict views on who would be an appropriate match for his children. She didn't think a left-wing poet, outlandishly dressed, with very little money, no prospects and twelve years her senior would come up to snuff.

She was right. In a small place, word spreads swiftly. Bibi supposed that apart from sex, there wasn't much else to do other than gossip. And she had to admit, the locals around where she lived were excellent gossipers. News of her gin and tonic with Callum reached her father the next day.

'You were seen with *that man*,' he said. 'Making a display of yourself in public.'

They were in his study at the time. He was standing behind his desk; she was hovering by the door, anxious to get away. His face was a blistering red, lips tight; slow streams of sweat gleamed on his forehead, slid down his cheeks. He coughed. The phone rang, but he ignored it. 'Don't answer that,' he said. 'I've got a lot to say to you. How dare you go out drinking with a man like that? Don't you ever think of your family, of our reputation?'

Bibi had shrugged. 'We were only talking,' she said.

'He's beneath you.'

'No,' said Bibi. 'It's me who is beneath him.'

She meant that she was in awe of Callum. Constantly astounded by his wit and lyricism. She was sure she would never be his equal, and was baffled that a man of such talent could be interested in her. Her father thought she was making a cheap, sordid remark and told her she was a slut.

'I didn't mean that,' said Bibi. 'I meant that Callum is better than me.' She was about to add that she loved him. But until this moment, she hadn't realised it. This sudden dawning surprised her.

'You are not to see him again. I forbid you to see him.'

Bibi had laughed at that. 'How Victorian of you. I don't think you can forbid me from seeing anybody I want to see.' She had turned as she left the room. Her father was leaning on his desk, glaring at her.

It had never been a tidy room; her father didn't like paperwork and had come in here to smoke, read the papers and chat to his bookie on the phone. Now it was dusty, his desktop cluttered with papers, unopened bills and letters. The phone started ringing again; he picked up the receiver and dropped it back on to the cradle. 'I can do many things to stop you associating with someone I think unsuitable. Don't push me on that one.'

Bibi had slammed the door as she went out. That was the last time she'd seen her father. The next day, she packed her bags in the morning and cycled to see Callum in his cottage. 'Did you mean it about getting married?'

Callum had been in the kitchen at the time – dishes heaped in the sink, an old gas cooker thick with grease; the floor was stone slab, grubby with scattered mud from his boots and twigs that had strayed from the heap of logs he had piled in the corner. He was wearing his trousers and a striped pyjama top; a cigarette hung from his mouth. 'Good dramatic entry,' he said. He was filling the kettle.

Bibi got the impression he'd gone off the notion of marrying. It had been the beer speaking last night.

'My father has forbidden me to see you again. He says he can do many things to stop me seeing someone he thinks unsuitable. You, for example.' Even as she spoke, the absurdity of this struck her. It felt like she'd been thrust into an overblown melodrama.

Callum was delighted. If he'd gone off the notion over-night, suddenly he was taken with it again. The prospect of slipping off with someone's forbidden daughter was incredibly sweet. It was the quiet way he continued with what he was doing – he put the kettle on the stove, struck a match and held it to the gas – that made Bibi aware that he did not love her. He didn't rush to hold her; he didn't kiss her and tell her that everything would be all right. Instead, he made a pot of tea.

This was not about her, or even about them both as a couple – it was about him. He recognised an opportunity to raise a single rebellious finger at a man he did not know, but despised anyway. Callum hated Bibi's father because he was rich and a landowner. 'Nobody has a right to own land,' he had said. 'The ground beneath our feet should belong to the people.'

In years to come, Bibi came to think Callum's loathing of the gentry was a passion bordering on jealousy. But at that moment, all she knew was that she was about to run off and marry a man who was using her to hurt her father. It was in his eyes, and in the way he quietly poured a cup of tea, took a sip and turned to smile at her.

Hurtling north now, she turned to James and said, 'He didn't love me, you know.'

James, who had been lost in his own worrying, mostly about what he would do if he didn't get into college, said, 'Who didn't love you?'

'Callum. Not at first, anyway. My father forbade me to see him, and I went to him and told him I'd marry him. I could tell then he didn't love me. He only wanted what he couldn't have. But what was I to do? I'd left a note at home, in my father's study. I knew he wouldn't get it till at least six in the evening, and by then I planned to be far away out of his reach. So I told Callum we had to run away together.' She sighed. 'It was all so absurd, really. But I thought it romantic. I was in love with romance.'

James said, 'Romance is tricky.'

'He loved me in the end, of course. After we'd been married for years, we were one life. I was him. He was me. It was hard to know where one began and the other ended. We knew what the other was thinking. But marriage does that; all its stupidities, fights, jokes, misunderstandings, meals shared, a bed shared. I mean, you'd have to love one another after all that.'

James said he supposed that could be true, he wouldn't really know, not having ever been married.

'Oh, trust me, it's true,' Bibi assured him.

'So did you run away together that morning?' asked James.

'I had a plan. After I left the note and went to Callum . . .'

'What did the note say?' James wanted to know.

'What difference does it make what the note said?' said Bibi.

'I want to know. It makes a lot of difference what the note said.'

'It said, *I love Callum. We are going away to make a life together. Please don't try to find us.*'

'Is that all?' said James. 'That's not very much to say. You could have made it a bit longer. I mean, that sounds a bit hostile.'

'I *was* hostile. I was very hostile,' said Bibi. 'Anyway, my plan. I thought it best if Callum and I left separately. First

I went into the village, cleaned out my bank account and caught a train to Edinburgh. Then, hours later, Callum got on a train to Glasgow. I'd got off my train at Perth, waited till his train came in, got on it, and there we were on our way to Glasgow. We stayed with his friends Brian and Jane. A couple of weeks later we married. The fourth of December. It was snowing, great swirling fat flakes. I thought it magical, a sign that we were doing something wonderful and that we were always going to be happy.' She sighed. 'I was so stupid.'

'Why?' said James. 'It doesn't sound stupid to me. Running away because your father forbade you to see someone. Like you said, it's romantic.'

'I didn't see it,' said Bibi. 'All the signs were there, and if I'd been older and wiser, I would have recognised them. My father's rage, the mess in his study, the unopened letters and bills, the phone ringing and ringing and him not picking it up. He was ill, stomach cancer, but he hadn't told anyone. He knew he was going to die. He knew he was ruined, financially, and that it would all be worse after he'd gone. My mother would have to sell the estate to pay death duties. He had wanted me to stay home, to be with her, to help her through the chaos.'

She sniffed, ran her fingers through her hair. 'If he'd told me, if he'd sat me down and explained everything, I would have never gone off. But we were never a family who did that sort of thing. We put up with things, stiff upper lip, no discussions. So, he shouted and I ran away. And my elaborate plans were for nothing. My father never did try to find me. He cut me out of his will and forbade

171

anyone in the family to ever mention my name in his presence.'

James said, 'Heavy.'

'Exactly,' said Bibi. 'After the wedding, we went back to Brian and Jane's flat and had a celebratory meal, spaghetti bolognese with whisky. It was splendid.'

'Spaghetti bolognese with whisky,' said James. 'I don't think so. You should have drunk wine.'

'We didn't have any wine,' said Bibi. 'We were high as kites. We didn't care. A couple of weeks later we went back up north to the cottage Callum had rented. Smack in the middle of nowhere. Six miles to the nearest shop. At first I thought it would be heaven; we were so in love we wouldn't need people round us. I was wrong.'

James said they'd be in Inverness in an hour. But Bibi said, 'No. Take the next turn-off. I want to go see that cottage. It's been over forty years since I last saw it. I want to look at it again. I have memories of that place, the things that happened there. There are paths I walked every day. I want to walk them again.'

James said, 'But . . .'

'No buts,' said Bibi.

'We need to get on,' said James. 'We've got miles to go.'

'We've got a destination, but no set agenda on how we're going to get to it. This is a trip. I sometimes think you have no idea what a trip is. It means we can go anywhere, wherever we fancy. And I have taken a fancy to see that cottage again. So do as you're told, take the next turn-off.'

Mugged by
Elizabeth Barrett Browning

The cottage had been smartened up, painted white with a shiny new roof, and the beech hedge that surrounded the garden was neatly clipped. Bibi opened the gate, walked up to the front door and knocked. James lingered some distance behind her. He wasn't sure about this. He didn't think it proper to go barging in on complete strangers on the grounds that once, many, many years ago, you had lived in their house.

Bibi had dismissed his doubts. 'I'm sure they'd be delighted to know that a distinguished poet stayed here. Beautiful things were written under their roof.'

In the end, James's doubts were for nothing; there was nobody home. Bibi walked round the cottage, stopping to peer inside, hands cupped against the windowpane. 'It looks pretty much the way it was. Same fireplace, anyway.'

She had looked in at the kitchen. 'Same old sink, same stone floor, I remember it all.' She walked round the garden, which was overflowing with flowers, and had a tightly packed vegetable patch. 'Isn't this lovely? I started this garden, you know. It was all mud and weeds when we came.'

She wandered down to the end of the garden, cupping blooms in her hand and breathing in scents. 'It was bliss living here. Endless happy days.'

James stood at the side of the house watching her, and watching the road, fearful that the homeowners might turn up and ask them what the hell they were doing. It was a relief, then, when at last she walked back through the gate and out on to the road.

'There used to be a track just along here a bit,' she said. 'I used to walk it every day, summer and winter, rain, hail or shine. It led up to a small moor where I used to sit and read, weather permitting, of course. Sometimes, I'd just think.'

She set off. 'It's still here. Look, the same track. Isn't it wonderful to find things haven't changed?'

James said that they should get going. It was getting late. They had miles to go. But Bibi waved her hands. 'Oh, nobody's expecting us. We can do what we like.' She set off up the track. 'I used to know every twist and curve of this path, every stone underfoot, where the rain gathered into puddles, where it was muddy and where the deer walked past on their way to the river. I knew it all like the palm of my own hand.'

She glanced back over her shoulder. 'I must see it all again. The moor, the deer tracks, the tree.'

'Tree?' said James, stumbling after her.

'There was a tree, a lone Scots pine. Callum and I used to walk to it. We'd sit and he'd read to me. Poems, passages from books he loved. We'd make love, too, under that tree. I have to find out if it's still there.'

He wished she hadn't told him that. He couldn't be told about other people's sex lives without imagining the act in progress. Now he was trotting just behind Bibi, in his mind a vision of her lying prone under a tree, enjoying a few moments of ecstasy, not as a young woman, but as she was now – seventy-two and, as far as he was concerned, past it. He shook his head, shoving the thought from his mind.

Bibi had stormed ahead. She jumped a small puddle. 'It was always muddy here.' Pointed at a large boulder. 'That's still there.' Breathless, heart pounding, she reached the end of the pathway and clambered over an ancient wooden gate. 'There's the tree. Look what the wind has done to it. It's leaning over. It was upright all those years ago. It was so much younger then, and so was I. So young, I knew nothing. Didn't know how to light a fire, couldn't cook, didn't know one end of a vacuum cleaner from the other. Happy days.'

She left the path and waded through the thick growth of heather to the tree. James followed, glancing at his watch. The grass on the small hill below the tree grew densely green and constantly shorn by wind and weather. Bibi sat, drew up her knees and hugged them. The smells – heather, peat – the late afternoon breeze on her face, the sounds of distant curlew and lapwing brought back a rush of memories.

'The cottage wasn't like that at all,' she told James. The most accurate description she could think of was hovel. 'It was damp and cold. A dump, in fact.'

Callum had heard about the cottage from a friend who

knew the daughter of the farmer, Angus Cluny, who owned it. He'd written to Angus, telling him he was a poet with a young bride and was looking for somewhere to live while he completed his new book. He said they were a quiet pair who only wanted a roof over their heads and promised they would keep the place clean and leave it as they found it. Cluny replied immediately, saying he had no prejudice against literary types, and that if it was quiet Callum needed, then Farley Cottage was ideal. The rent, cheap even back then, was an absurd two pounds a month. Callum answered by return, saying they'd take it, and enclosed a deposit.

They had first arrived at the cottage in late December; it had rained all day. Six o'clock in the evening they had stumbled out of the rambling, rattling country bus, and looked round. Callum had the landlord's instructions on how to reach the cottage in his pocket, but it was too dark to read them. He remembered it was up a small track opposite the bus stop. The ground was soaked, and they clambered through mud and puddles, carrying all they possessed in two battered cases. The small gate was stiff to open, and the key hard to turn in the lock. But at last they stepped inside and looked round.

She remembered how cold it had been. They had stood in the kitchen, unwilling to remove their coats, stamping their feet and blowing on their fingers.

'Our first home,' said Callum.

'It's wonderful,' she told him. Plainly, though, it wasn't. 'Well, we'll make it wonderful.'

They were in the kitchen, a dimly lit room with a stone-flag floor. There was a huge sink by the window, a single cupboard, a table with four chairs; beyond that was the bathroom, which was equally sparse. A door on the left led into the living room. Here were two overstuffed and somewhat hard armchairs set before a fireplace. Judging by the depth of the chill and the tang of damp, nothing had burned in that fireplace for a very long time.

Callum found some coal in the small outhouse and set about lighting a fire, while Bibi made up the bed. They owned a pair of sheets, along with a couple of blankets, six cups and saucers and plates, two spoons, two forks and a radio; enough, they both thought, to set up a reasonable home. 'What more could anyone need?' said Bibi.

'Nothing,' Callum assured her.

That night they dined on cheese. Drank whisky. They had no pots to cook anything in, and no kettle to boil water for a cup of tea. The next day they'd walked six miles to the village to buy the things they needed. That had included an extra two blankets, since the temperature had dropped below zero during the night, and though they'd huddled close and made sweaty love, they'd still woken in the morning shivering. There had been a coating of frost on the thin and fraying bed cover.

The following day, Bibi had sat at the kitchen table with her life savings, just over a hundred pounds in cash. She divided it into small piles that she put into envelopes, marked on the front with what the money was intended for – rent, electricity, food, coal. She reckoned they had enough to keep them for a year. 'If we're careful,' she said. 'We don't need much.'

He had agreed. What could they possibly need when they had each other?

They had settled down to a daily round of cold, damp, smoky fires, burnt food, arguments and tears interspersed with bouts of tenderness and passion. Callum had always been passionate.

On their second morning at the cottage they had walked to the roadside telephone box three miles away. How odd it had looked, defiantly red in a drab winter landscape. 'Vivid and lonely,' Callum said. Bibi had phoned home to let her family know she was all right. It was then that she had found out that her father had cut her from his will and had forbidden anyone to mention her name in his presence. 'He is furious,' her mother told her. 'You're lucky I answered the phone. Please don't call here again. I can't bear it when your father is in one of his rages.'

They had agreed that on Wednesdays, at two o'clock, Bibi's mother would call the phone box to keep in touch. Once a week Bibi had walked to that telephone and waited for her mother to call. It was there she learned of her father's illness and his death, and that he had been adamant she was not to attend the funeral. She always thought of it as the bad news phone box.

But on the day of that first call home, she had put down the receiver and emerged weeping. Callum held her as she sobbed; he'd opened his coat, invited her in beside him and wrapped it round her. As he held her, the country bus had rumbled slowly past. Bibi saw the passengers lean into the window, watching them. Tongues were wagging. After that, they were known locally as the weird couple who lived on Cluny's farm.

She marvelled at how deceptive memories could be. Ever since Callum's death, their time at the cottage had come back to her as filled with sweetness, love and kisses, long walks, meals eaten at odd hours as Bibi learned to cook and talk. They had spoken about everything; their days had been filled with the sound of each other's voices.

But they had also fought, and how. They had shouted and screamed at one another. Bibi had stormed out of the house at least once a week and stamped up the track to her tree, mumbling to herself about how vile Callum was. She had wept buckets under this tree.

What intrigued her was that even though she could now recall the arguments, and some of them had lasted for days – they could fight, go to bed, make love, and wake in the morning, still fighting – she couldn't think what on earth they had argued about.

There had, of course, been the money fights. But then, she thought, everybody argues about that. She had discovered one morning, when reviewing her envelope situation, that Callum had been dipping into several of them and removing pound notes – and now and then a five-pound note – and spending the cash at the pub in the village. He'd told her he was going to the library to catch up on his reading, and indeed, he brought books home, but he had spent most of his time drinking.

'How could you?' Bibi had said. 'You know we have a plan.'

'Oh, plans are boring. They stop you being spontaneous.'

'You have spontaneously drunk our money. My money, actually.'

'And what fun it was,' he said. 'Living isn't just getting by. It's meeting people and talking, hearing their stories. It's that moment of happiness when you take a drink of beer or whisky and let it slip back over your throat, and you look round to see if there's anybody about who might join you in a glass or two and a little bit of conversation. You know nothing, Bibi. Stop fretting about money. We'll get by. Something will come along.'

That was when the fight got serious. It had lasted a week. They had shouted and screamed, Bibi had flounced out of the cottage. Callum had gone to the library, waving a couple of notes in her face as he left. 'Don't wait up for me.'

She smiled at her memories. How foolish she'd been to believe a man like Callum would stick to her primitive financial arrangement. Of course he needed to drink, to sit at the bar in some old pub and chat. Chatting was what he loved to do. He needed to listen to opinions, the crazier the better, hear gossip, and he needed to expound about his own thoughts, dreams and beliefs. Now she thought that she should have just shrugged her shoulders, put on her coat and gone with him. It would have been fun.

She rummaged through her handbag to find a photo of Callum she kept there. She stared at it fondly. It was a picture of him standing beside the car, wearing his long black coat, his favourite red scarf wrapped round his neck. He had his hands shoved deep into his pockets and was staring quizzically at the camera, smiling, but only slightly. She stroked his face. 'That's you. Always a bit quizzical.'

She remembered how they'd walk that track, him in his pale twill trousers and tweed jacket, her in that navy dress, tight at the waist, he loved her to wear. She'd be bare-legged, old tennis shoes on her feet. They'd hold hands. He always, winter and summer, wore suede boots, elasticated at the ankles. He had learned how to re-sole them when holes appeared. 'Poverty,' he told her, 'teaches you a lot.' He could darn his socks, sew on buttons; he knew how to bake bread. 'Needs must,' he said.

When they had no money for food, he had caught trout in the stream that ran behind their cottage. And he had poached pheasant, using raisins soaked in whisky to lure them into the garden. He'd told her pheasants could not resist an alcoholic raisin or two. In the morning, they would find the birds slumped and drunk on the lawn. Callum would wring their necks, and hang them in the small shed where the gardening tools were kept, before plucking them and roasting them with apples he'd stolen from the local farmer's garden. He'd come home from his long walks, pockets stuffed with them.

Bibi could see him yet, coming up the garden towards her, eating a small and somewhat acid apple, swearing it was delicious. But they roasted well, she had to give him that.

Here under the tree – their tree, they called it – Callum would pull papers from his pocket, and read to her.

'A poem for you,' he once said.

'For me?'

'Just for you. This is it. *How do I love thee? Let me count the ways.*'

'That's lovely, it's wonderful,' she thrilled. 'And you wrote that? This morning?'

He had smiled. He certainly hadn't denied it. She had been so enraptured, she could hardly breathe. He continued.

'*I love thee to the depth and breadth and height/ My soul can reach, when feeling out of sight/ For the ends of Being and ideal Grace.*'

Sitting here now, Bibi could bring to mind every detail of his reciting that poem to her. He'd been sitting facing her, one leg extended in front of him, the other bent. He'd clutched his knee. He had gazed at her intently. It had been just after four in the afternoon, and hot. In the field beyond the moor, a skylark rose, singing. He'd moved closer to her.

'*I love thee to the level of everyday's/ Most quiet need, by sun and candlelight.*'

Tears had slipped down her cheeks. 'Beautiful,' she whispered. 'I never knew you could write something so beautiful. You are so clever.'

He reached over, held her face, and continued. '*I love thee freely, as men strive for Right; I love thee purely, as they turn from Praise.*'

This, she thought, was the most perfect moment in her life. It was exquisite.

'. . . *I love thee with the breath,/ Smiles, tears of all my life! – and, if God choose,/ I shall but love thee better after death.*'

'Callum,' she'd said. 'That is perfect.'

'And it's for you.'

'That is the most wonderful thing I've ever been given.' She had put her arms round him, and kissed him.

He'd slid his hands, such soft hands too, up past her knees, stroked her inner thighs. 'Let me count the ways,' he'd whispered.

Bibi grinned, remembering this. She rocked slightly, laughing.

She was aware of James coughing and pointing at his watch, but she ignored him. She didn't want him there. Some memories were too juicy to be interrupted – the things she and Callum had got up to here on this small hill, under this tree. 'I want it back,' she said.

She drifted back to her golden past – drunken pheasants on the frosty morning lawn; sneaking out to catch, by moonlight, forbidden fish from the landlord's river; the delight of taking bread, bulging in its tin, from the oven. They'd held their hands over it, to warm them. 'Oh,' she said. 'Wonderful times.'

She wanted to be alone. It was late, it was cold, but she didn't want to move. She hadn't forgotten much about her days in the cottage, but the scents and sounds of this place made everything she remembered more vivid. Little things came back: the way he'd lean over as he spoke to her; gaze ahead so she always thought he could see things she couldn't. Sometimes he'd lie with his head in her lap as they talked, comparing childhoods, exchanging opinions. She wanted to relish all this, and James being here spoiled it. So when he coughed and moved in front of her, trying to tell her how cold it was and how the light was fading, she pretended she couldn't see him. Couldn't he take the hint? Did he not realise this was a special place and she was reliving a very precious time? She stared ahead, smiling slightly, and slipped back forty years to when she was young and deeply in love.

It was a relief when she saw James starting back across the heather towards the road. Now she could get on with dreaming in peace. It was beautiful, and painful. There had been so many wonderful moments that she hadn't thought to relish as she lived through them. It was only in recollection that she realised how special they'd been. She knew that when she and Callum had lived at the cottage, they'd often been cold and sometimes hungry. She had on occasion come up here to this tree to get away from him, and cry. He never did understand the benefits of a good weep. He had, from time to time, mocked her inability to cook, and his superior knowledge on just about every subject they discussed made her feel stupid.

She had felt stupid when, years after he'd recited it to her, she had come across the poem in a book. It was such a famous verse, she was sure the whole world knew it, except her. What if she had mentioned it in company and claimed it to be Callum's? How awful, how embarrassing.

'You bastard,' she had said. 'You didn't write that at all. It was Elizabeth Barrett Browning. I let you have your way with me on account of that. I was entranced.'

She'd thrown the book at him. She hadn't meant to hit him, but she had, catching him on the left cheek, just below his eye. To her shame, it had bruised badly. Callum didn't mind, though; he said he was the only person in the world who could claim to have been mugged by Elizabeth Barrett Browning.

Two days after she had thrown the poetry book at him, in a rare moment when the children were out and they had the flat to themselves, he had found her in the living room. She was busy cleaning, had a bright yellow duster in her hand.

'Have you forgiven me for the poem?' he said.

'For wooing me with something written by Elizabeth Barrett Browning, claiming it to be your own?'

'I never said I'd written it,' he said.

'No, but you let me believe you had. It's still a lie.'

'You loved it.'

She said she had only loved it because she'd thought he had written it for her. 'Now I feel stupid. I must be the only person in the world who didn't know that poem. I left school at fifteen, there wasn't a lot of literature in my life.'

'But have you forgiven me?'

She looked away from him, refused to meet his gaze. 'No.'

He had taken her chin in his hand, turned her face to his. 'How do I love thee? Let me count the ways. There's missionary, then you on top.' He counted on his fingers. 'I like it when I take you from behind.'

'Callum,' she'd said, a little shocked. She glanced swiftly round the room, making sure there really were no children about. 'That's filthy. And anyway, that's only three.'

'My love,' he said. 'Wouldn't it be grand it we could do it where we stand? Four.'

'We are not doing anything where we stand. Some child could come home any minute and find us.'

He had laughed as she flounced out. She had gone into the kitchen and started to busily wash the dishes. As she furiously wiped, she became aware of him standing watching her, laughing. She turned on him, then started to laugh too.

'Callum,' she told the photograph she still held, 'I forgive you for the poem.'

Of course she forgave him. How could she not? He had recited to her a poem he'd learned by heart. He had probably even learned it for her. He had given her a beautiful moment. She had forgiven him so much; she named two of her children after the poet – Beth and Liz. And besides, when he had whispered Elizabeth Barrett Browning's words to her, he had meant them.

Stories of Mermaids and Mud Pies

Celia was watching a film when the phone rang. It was eight in the evening. Peter was out at a meeting of his golf club committee. Olivia was upstairs doing her homework. Celia had put her favourite film, Ingmar Bergman's *Fanny and Alexander*, on the DVD player. It was a story she loved to see unfold.

There was a party early on in the movie, a scene Celia thought exquisite. It was everything a party ought to be: laughter, dancing, elaborately dressed people celebrating life. She remembered with some distaste the parties Bibi and Callum had thrown. They had been nothing like the one in this film. The music at those parties had been jazz – Charlie Parker, Miles Davis – and people had shuffled about close to one another, rather than join hands and frolic from room to room, faces lit with joy. The food had been long French loaves with cheese, ham and a selection of salamis, nothing like the sumptuous feast on the screen. There had been drink, bottles of whisky, gin, vodka and wine laid out for guests to help themselves. But there ought to have been a huge crystal punch bowl, brimming with a fabulous concoction made from champagne, fruits and other things – Celia didn't know what, really.

At her parents' parties, Celia wore a blue silky dress and

bows in her hair. She always dressed up, though her mother told her it wasn't necessary.

'It's a party,' Bibi would tell her. 'We want people to relax and enjoy themselves.'

Celia never agreed with this. Parties were special, guests should put on their glad rags. The night should be aglow with light, razzle, glitz and utter opulence. Not that her parties were like that; they tended to be more like the ones Bibi and Callum had thrown. Still, she could dream.

She was irritated, then, when halfway through her favourite scene, the phone rang. It was James.

'Hello,' she said. 'How are you? How's Liz?'

'We are nowhere near Liz's yet,' said James. 'I don't really know where we are. Your mother wanted to see the cottage she lived in when she got married, so we took a detour.'

'That's nice,' said Celia. 'What's it like?'

'It's a cottage,' said James. 'Then she wanted to do the walk she and Callum used to take. We went up a track, across a moor to a tree, where she sat down. She stared ahead for a long time sort of smiling, a bit vacant, actually. I can't seem to get through to her.'

'Has she had a stroke?' said Celia.

'I don't know, do I?' said James.

'Well, is one side of her face numb, has she lost feeling in one arm, is one eye shut?'

'Not when I last saw her,' said James.

'When was that?'

'About half an hour ago. I couldn't get a signal on the phone. I had to come here.'

'Where's here?' said Celia. She could feel panic rising.

'Back at the cottage, about two miles from the moor and the tree.'

'You've left her alone?'

'I didn't know what else to do. I thought you might know. She just sat down under the tree and told me she and Callum used to come here to make love. Then she said, "I want it back," and drifted off into her own world.'

'Get back to her. Get her out of there. Smack her on the cheek if you have to,' said Celia.

'I'm not doing that.'

'It's eight o'clock at night. You have to find somewhere to stay. Oh, just get back to her, then find a bed and breakfast. And phone me back.'

She rang off. Stood, hands in pockets, staring ahead. She needed to talk to somebody, but who? Not Roddy, obviously. He didn't seem to care about anything these days. She dialled Beth's mobile. She could hear the clatter and hum of a restaurant in the background when Beth answered.

'Our mother is sitting under a tree on a moor somewhere in the middle of nowhere,' said Celia.

Beth said, 'So?'

'It's late. She probably hasn't eaten. I don't know where she's going to sleep tonight.'

Beth asked what she was expected to do about it.

'I don't know,' said Celia. 'I just needed to tell somebody.'

'Isn't James with her?'

'Yes. But he doesn't know what to do. She's just sitting

189

there, lost in some reverie. It's where she and Dad used to go to make love.'

'I think you've just told me more than I need to know,' said Beth.

'Well,' said Celia, 'they were young once. It's so annoying. I should have taken her myself. I shouldn't have left it to James. He knows nothing about human frailties. Why couldn't she just go and see Liz, then come home again? Why don't people do what they say they're going to do? Why don't they do what they're told? Why do they have minds of their own?'

'Celia,' said Beth, 'if you could sort that out, you'd be up for a Nobel prize.' She paused, then, 'Actually, I think that you have just told me more about yourself in a few questions than you'd ever want me to know.'

Celia said nothing. Could this be true? What did it mean? That she was bossy and intolerant?

'I'm on a date right now,' continued Beth. 'I'll speak to you tomorrow.' She switched off her phone and smiled at the man across the table. 'My mother's sitting below a tree somewhere in the Highlands. I think she's dreaming about her youth. It is, apparently, where she and my father used to make love.'

'Your mother sounds interesting,' said Bradley.

'I suppose she does. I don't really think of her as interesting; perhaps I've known her for too long – all my life. When I think of her, she comes to me struggling through our front door with bags of vegetables from her allotment. Potatoes, mostly. It was a big family, not much money. We ate a lot of potatoes.'

'You look well on it,' he said.

Beth smiled and said she hadn't at the time, she'd been a fat little thing.

He told her he had been too.

'I was spoiled rotten,' she said. 'My father called me his little dumpling. He used to take me on long walks and feed me chocolate.'

'Potatoes and chocolate could explain why you turned into a dumpling,' he said.

She nodded. 'He was a poet. He died when I was thirteen.'

She still missed him. He'd taken her along the Water of Leith and made up stories as they walked. He told her there were mermaids in the river who made birds out of mud, and when the sun came up all the birds flew away. He said bears lived on Arthur's Seat and they came out to play at night when the park was empty, and she had to leave a square of chocolate on a rock overlooking the pond for them to eat. They'd know she was their friend. At home he'd write the stories, and she'd draw pictures of bears, mermaids and birds flying into the morning. She still had the book they'd made together. When she'd cried at night, afraid of the dark, he'd sat by her bed holding her hand. She was safe, he'd told her. She'd always be safe; Black Eagle, her Indian chief, was looking after her. At night, he stood at the end of the bed watching over her as she slept. She believed it then. Sometimes, alone and sleepless in her flat, she wished she still believed it.

'Two years I've known you, you never told me any of this,' Bradley said.

'I know, but I don't talk about it.'

It pained her to talk about her father. He hadn't ignored his other children, but it was obvious Beth had been his favourite. He'd doted on her, and in the end this had embarrassed her. The grief she'd felt when he died had been unbearable. She had slipped into a silent world, stopped working at school and eventually lost her friends. She had failed to get the qualifications necessary to get into university, and had, until she met Bradley, held a series of dead-end jobs. About six months after the funeral, she'd been seized by rage. She was furious at her father for dying. How dare he? How could he do that to her?

'I wish it had been you that died and not him,' she'd said to Bibi.

Bibi had said, 'So do I.'

Beth felt her cheeks flush and hated herself for that.

'You were a kid,' said Bradley.

She said she knew that, but still thinking about saying that shamed her.

'Kids say things they don't really mean all the time; forget about it.'

'You would know,' she said.

He was divorced, had two sons who lived with their mother. When he and Joanne had separated, the flat above the garden flat the family lived in had become available. Bradley bought it. Now the boys spent as much time with him as they did with her. It was an arrangement that worked well. Joanne was still Bradley's business partner; they had daily discussions about work. He still did the garden, he mended fuses, unblocked her sink and had only a week ago helped her paint the kitchen. But there was no question of them getting back together. Their only problem was sex.

Both Joanne and Bradley had new relationships – Joanne with Steven, Bradley with Beth. Neither of them was willing to let their new lovers disrupt their comfortable situation. They did not want their sons coming across strangers in the bathroom or kitchen in the morning. Joanne always slept in Steven's bed, Bradley in Beth's. And there were to be no new babies. That would ruin everything.

For Beth, this was a problem. She was eight weeks pregnant, and had told nobody. At first, she'd thought she would get rid of it. But the more she thought about it, the more she wanted a child. She wasn't keen on having a baby – the mess, the sleepless nights, the nappies, the dribbling filled her with dread. A child, though, she thought, a child would be lovely. She wanted to talk to it, to tell it stories. She wanted to leave chocolate on the rock at Arthur's Seat for the bears and to watch mud piles to see if they turned into birds that flew away. She wanted to relive her happiest times. She was sure her father would approve.

After her teenage rage had quelled, she'd found a kind of calm. It started the day she was walking home from school and had seen her father across the street. She had rushed over and caught up with him. 'Dad,' she had shouted, running along the pavement. 'Dad. It's me.' The man had turned, looking baffled. It wasn't Callum, of course it wasn't Callum. Close up, Beth could see this man looked nothing like him and had apologised, flustered.

From then on, she had believed that Callum was out there in some silent, lonely place filled with light and air, watching her. This thought was unshakeable; she didn't really believe her father was dead. He was waiting to come back.

He would have hated that she became the lost and lonely soul who sat on the stairs at parties and spoke about death. He would have worried that she walked the same paths they had walked together, alone after school, looking for him. He would have cried to know that since he died of cancer, she was sure she would also die of cancer, and spent a long time in the shower checking her body for lumps. But he would love her to have a baby, he would love her to tell that child his stories. Beth believed this would make her happy again. Abortion was out of the question.

She didn't know how to broach the subject of her pregnancy to Bradley. It would, she was sure, be the end of the relationship. But right now, it was good to know he thought her mother was interesting and not, as she believed, a woman who had worked out her grief nurturing an allotment and who knew a hundred different ways to cook potatoes.

James jogged back up the track to Bibi. He cursed himself for leaving her alone. What if she had died sitting under that tree? How would he explain it to Celia? What would he do with the body? Cover it up with his sweatshirt, then run back and phone whoever it was you phoned when someone died under a tree in the middle of nowhere?

But Bibi was alive and well; she saw him coming towards her, running up the heathered path, face red and wrought with worry, and waved.

'Where the hell have you been?'

He told her about not getting a signal on his phone and running down to the road that passed the cottage. 'I was worried about you. You drifted off into some kind of dream. A coma, I thought. I phoned Celia. She thought you might have had a stroke.'

'I wish you hadn't done that. Celia will only fuss, and she'll phone other people to discuss my health. A stroke, indeed. I was basking in memories. I didn't want to be disturbed.'

James told her he'd been worried because it was getting dark and they didn't have anywhere to stay tonight.

'Of course we do,' said Bibi. 'I booked ahead.' She heaved herself to her feet and dusted down her trousers with her hand. 'We have rooms in the village.'

'You knew we were coming here? You said we were going to see your daughter.'

'And so we are. But I have stops to make along the way. Places I want to see again.' She sighed and looked around. 'This place is exactly as I remember it, hasn't changed at all. That's a comfort.' She started across the heather to the path that led back to where they'd left the car, James stumbling behind her.

'I'm old,' she said. 'I don't know how it happened, but it did. My life slipped by one day at a time and suddenly I was seventy-two. Seventy-two, I say to myself, that's really old. Only I don't feel old, not inside, anyway. Only my body lets me down. I get stiff, aches and pains here and there. I know I can no longer run for a bus. But really I just feel like me.'

She thought she had been living so long there was barely a sound, sight or smell that did not evoke a memory.

'These days I am living through are full of mourning and shadows and memories, and do you know?' She turned to James and smiled. 'I'm enjoying it enormously.'

Round and Round

Bibi's trip bothered Celia. 'I don't like her going away like that. She's getting on, and this trip is so disorganised. Look at what happened yesterday, she ended up sitting under a tree in the middle of nowhere,' she said to Peter.

'She was lost in memories,' he said. 'She was fine. She phoned you, didn't she?'

'Yes, at eleven o'clock at night, after they'd been to some pub and had fish and chips and a pint of beer. And I'd spent the whole evening worrying. I couldn't enjoy my film for worrying.'

'But she was fine. She went to see the cottage she had shared with Callum when they were first married. I think that's lovely. I wish we had spent our first married years tucked away in a cottage in the country. It would have been like a two-year honeymoon.'

'And that's another thing,' said Celia. 'She once told me that cottage had been cold and damp and they'd spent the whole time they lived there arguing. Now she's saying it's painted white and beautiful with polished floors and rugs and a garden full of flowers, just like she remembered it. It wasn't like that at all. She's going senile.'

'She has simply airbrushed her memories a little.

Painted them rosier than they actually were. What's wrong with that?'

Celia shrugged and said that nothing was wrong with that, and she supposed everybody did it at some time. 'But it's not good to lose your grip on reality.'

Peter said, 'Sometimes, Celia, it is wonderful to lose your grip on reality. You should keep that in mind.'

She said, 'What do you mean by that?'

'Your mother has allowed herself to paint a rosy picture of her past. What's wrong with that?'

She said she supposed nothing was wrong with that.

'Your problem is you keep hugging those memories of your mother and father arguing and how sometimes there wasn't a lot to eat. You know it wasn't like that all the time; you must have had some fun.'

She agreed with that.

'So be like Bibi, remember the good bits and gloss over the rest.'

She told him she'd find that hard to do. 'You don't know what it was like.'

He told her he had a pretty good idea, she'd talked about it often enough. 'But you hardly ever talk about Graham. That's odd. No, actually, it's more than odd. It's weird.'

'You know what happened,' said Celia. 'I've told you often enough. One day he was there, the next he wasn't. I remember us all sitting at the table; Bibi was serving supper, and I asked where he was. Bibi said he wouldn't be eating with us. Then he was still gone the next day and the next, and nobody would talk about it, though I asked and asked where he was. I walked all over town looking for him in the places where he used to hang out. Nobody had seen him. I phoned all his friends, they didn't know anything. Damn it, Peter, you know I hate talking about this.'

'It just strikes me as weird,' he said. 'Didn't Bibi or Callum say anything?'

'Eventually they said Graham had gone to America. After that I watched the post; I was even late for school for weeks waiting for the post to come. But he never got in touch, and after I kept on and on at Bibi about it, she said she didn't want to talk about Graham any more, and please not to mention him to her.'

'So you didn't,' said Peter.

'It was obviously upsetting her. So I didn't. Time passed. I grew up, I went to university. I met you. But I still think about him. God knows, I've done what I could to find him. I've looked up telephone directories for all the major cities. I even thought of hiring a private detective. But I didn't. Now I just google his name every week or so.'

'But nothing,' said Peter.

'Nothing,' she agreed. She picked up her car keys. 'I have to go. I'm late now.'

He told her he was sorry. 'But I still think it's weird.'

From down the hall, she shouted that she thought it was weird too. And that there was something her mother wasn't telling her. 'But God knows what it is.'

At lunchtime, when the surgery was empty, she phoned Roddy.

'Celia,' he said. 'I was just going out.'

'I just wanted to keep you abreast of our mother's journey. She went on a little detour to see the cottage she and Dad lived in when they were first married. She went into a daydream under a tree on a moor somewhere. Now she's saying the cottage was beautiful when we all know it was dank and miserable.'

'So?'

'I don't know. I worry about her.'

'She'll be fine,' he said. 'She's always fine.'

'Don't you ever feel angry? When you think back on our lives in that flat, when you think about her and Callum?'

'No. Should I?'

'Don't you think we were just there, the children? All of us simply the by-products of their great love affair? I mean, sometimes it was as if we didn't really matter and they fought and made up and fought again and made up again.'

'Christ, Celia, you're not actually saying you have some sort of complex because your mother and father loved each other. That's the nuttiest thing I've ever heard.'

'I don't know. Sometimes I feel that we didn't really matter to them. They were so caught up in their relationship.'

Roddy told her to grow up.

'Also,' said Celia. 'Who was that woman?'

'What woman?'

'The one,' Celia told him, 'who turned up. She was American, had long hair. I remember her sitting at the kitchen table, crying. I must have been about three or four.'

'That would have been Polly.'

'Who was she?'

'Somebody they met when they were in New York. She lived near them, I think. She was some kind of artist.'

'What was she doing in our flat?'

'Visiting, I suppose.'

'But she was sitting crying. Why would she do that?'

'She was upset about something. It was a long time ago, and we were kids.'

'Only,' said Celia, 'I remember I got up in the middle of the night. I'd had a bad dream and I went looking for Bibi. And she wasn't in bed with Callum, she came out of another room. I think it was the one that woman was sleeping in.'

'What are you saying here?'

'I don't know. I'm just telling you what I remember.'

'I think you are remembering wrong. She'd maybe been talking to the woman.'

'You don't think . . .?'

'Think what? That our mother was having a fling with a woman when our father was asleep in another room? No, Celia, I don't think that. And neither should you. Forget about it. It's past, history, over. Now I'm going to have my lunch, goodbye.' He put down the phone.

Celia sat holding the receiver, listening to the humming dialling tone. Well, that's me told, she thought.

She had recently spent some time considering her childhood. It struck her that she and her brothers and sisters had been ignored; they had brought themselves up. There had been no music lessons or dancing classes. Any sports they had taken up, they had pursued on their own. She had been in the school hockey team, but never once had either parent turned up to see her on the pitch. She thought about her daughter, Olivia, and how much time and effort she put into bringing her up – the music lessons, the homework she helped with, the long conversations about sex and drugs, books she encouraged Olivia to read, plays, ballets and films she took her to. I had none of that, she thought. Of course, they had all been encouraged to read, and there had always been music playing. But, really, there had been very little individual attention. She supposed that when a person had as many children as Bibi and Callum, it was hard to spend time with one of them without causing jealousies among the others. Except for Beth, of course. Beth had been given everything she wanted. But that, Celia thought, had been to ease the guilt and pain Bibi and Callum felt about losing Graham.

Mealtimes back then had been fraught with squabbles. Preparing food twice a day for a family of five children and two adults, seven people, was, Celia decided, not so much cooking as catering. Bibi hadn't ever eaten much, though. She would sit at the end of the table quietly drinking a mug of tea, watching the fray. Once, Celia and Liz had fought over a leftover roast potato. They had turned to Bibi to arbitrate on this vegetable issue. Celia thought it rightly hers, as she was older than Liz. Liz thought it ought to go to her; she'd been playing hockey and was hungrier. Bibi had sighed, risen from her chair. 'So arm-wrestle for it,' she'd said. 'It's only a potato, it's not the end of the world.'

Once, Celia had related this story to her daughter, who had listened with muted interest. All Olivia had said at the end of the tale was, 'So, who got the potato?'

'Liz,' Celia had told her.

Olivia said, 'Ah. So you still have potato issues with your mother.'

Celia had stared at her and said, 'That's not the point. I'm trying to show you how hard it was for me as a child.'

'Seems to me,' said Olivia, 'that if a small quibble over a potato is all you have to complain about, you must have had a happy childhood. My friend Chrissie is being bounced between her parents as they go through a nasty divorce. And Amelia's dad has just been made redundant when his firm went bust; now they're moving to a smaller house and her mum has taken a job at a supermarket to help pay the bills, plus her dad's been diagnosed with stomach cancer. They have something a lot bigger than a potato to worry about.'

Celia had said nothing, but had felt a little shamed and petty. Thinking about this now, she cheered herself up thinking how grounded and assured her daughter was. A result of excellent and sensitive parenting, she decided. Proof that all the individual attention and caring actually worked.

Roddy went to his usual lunchtime haunt, a small place that, as well as selling plates of soup and sandwiches, was also a bookshop and art gallery. He liked it here; the staff were friendly and the clientele more arty than the people who frequented the pubs that served business lunches. Also, the soup was good. Usually he ate with a book propped on the pepper grinder in front of him. He did this to indicate that he was alone, and happy to be so. And it helped to keep him from musing.

But today, his conversation with Celia had stuck in his head; he couldn't get rid of it. He slowly supped his bowl of spicy three-bean soup and pondered his life's decisions. He knew, of course, that he'd married Ruth not just because he loved her, but also because both their fathers had disapproved of the match. Callum, his father, had said he was a fool to get wed to such a neat and prissy woman. 'She'll make you miserable. A woman whose only aim in life is to have a perfect home in which she compiles lists of things to be done, lists of things to be bought, lists of where things are to be kept, lists of things she has served to dinner guests will only bring you heartache.'

Roddy had told him he was a fool not to recognise the worth of an organised soul mate.

Ruth's father had told her she was marrying into a family of disorganised, disreputable and scruffy hippies. So how could they resist getting hitched? Getting married against their parents' wishes was the only defiant thing either of them had ever done together.

'You married our mother against her father's wishes,' Roddy had said to Callum.

He hadn't disagreed.

'There you go,' said Roddy. 'Like father, like son. Round and round.'

Now he could see that there was a difference. His

mother and father had fought, argued and made up and laughed a lot. By the time Callum died, he and Bibi were companions. Roddy and Ruth never argued, so they never had the joy of making up, and they rarely laughed together. They ate at the same time every evening, went to bed at the same time, got up again at the same time. And they did it all quietly. They spoke in muted voices. They never, as Bibi and Callum often did, put on a record and said, 'Oh, remember when we bought this and we played it the night Jenny and Frank came over and we all got drunk. Oh, I love this track.' He thought that he and Ruth had let their lives slip away as they worked at being decent, ordinary people who got along with their neighbours. Now he thought that there was nothing wrong with disturbing the neighbours once in a while, say, every two or three months or so, by playing an old Jimi Hendrix track or something by The Pogues, or maybe even a bit of *Così fan tutte*, at full volume. They could do it to him, he wouldn't mind.

He had words he was fond of – twilight, whisper, hallelujah. Though he'd noticed that in the world in which he moved, none of them came up very often. No matter how hard he tried to twist conversations and emails so he could use one of them, he rarely succeeded. He couldn't really tell a client to come to his office at twilight to be told in a whisper that a loan application had been successful, and that the parting word might well be hallelujah. No, that wasn't any kind of commercial dialogue.

His favourite word, however, was yes. It was lovely, the

most beautiful word in the language. It could be whispered and it could be shouted from the rooftops. It was affirmative, optimistic and comforting. He'd once asked Ruth about her favourite word, and had been told it was *clean*. She loved the clear, crisp and precise sound of it, as well as getting comfort from cleanliness itself. She was a woman who was unhappy if the space she occupied wasn't pristine and organised.

She was close to their daughters, Helena and Florence, spoke to one or other of them every day on the phone. They visited her often; her home was a feminine place, and Roddy had often felt excluded from the female chat about female things.

Helena was married with a year-old son, Duncan. Roddy loved the boy, would take him on country walks whenever they visited. He would tell him the names of birds and flowers they came across. They chatted a lot; or, at least, Roddy chatted; Duncan listened. But it seemed to Roddy that the child listened in wonder.

'That boy's as bright as a button,' he'd told Ruth.

'Of course he is,' said Ruth. 'But why tell a baby the names of flowers?'

'He is full of wonder,' said Roddy. 'Every single thing is new to him. He sees things as they are.'

Helena, Duncan's mother, worked three days in an art gallery. She was assertive and fussy and demanding. Walls had to be pristine white, lighting just so. Roddy wondered if her colleagues feared her and artists kept out of her way. But he was wrong. The artists whose work she hung loved the respect and care she took over their paintings.

Florence lived with her partner in London – Camden. They had a large upper flat that was messy, cluttered with books and discarded clothing neither of them had the time or energy to put away properly. She worked in the City, but had recently discussed her new dream of giving up her professional life to become a plumber.

'Go for it,' Roddy said. 'Great money and you're doing something real, worthwhile. There must be a lot of women who'd prefer to have a female plumber. Someone they could really talk to about their plumbing problems.'

'Yes,' said Florence. 'That's what I've been thinking. Just get up in the morning, put on jeans and a T-shirt, look at my job sheet and off I go in my van. The problems I'd have to deal with would be practical, physical. Not the same as dealing with office rivalries and egos.'

'Exactly,' said Roddy. 'You could fit us up with a hot tub in the garden.'

Ruth had glared at them both. She didn't know how she would deal with telling her friends her daughter was a plumber.

Ruth suspected Roddy had affairs; he'd been unfaithful, she imagined, in thought, word and deed, probably with his younger colleagues. They were usually long-haired, leggy women who, in their free time, talked about their new cars and their holidays. She was wrong. Roddy had never had an affair. He had no interest in any of the ambitious young women who walked the corridor outside his office. He had not been untrue to her in word or deed, only in thought.

He dreamed of a soft, sensuous woman who'd say yes –

yes to everything. She had no name in his imaginings, and he could not really picture her face. He knew, however, that it was warm, full-lipped and gentle. Yes, she'd say when he suggested a film they could go to, a meal they might cook together, a CD they'd listen to, a walk they might take. Yes to evenings in bed together, yes to breakfast under the duvet, yes to an impromptu weekend away.

He knew what he wanted, and it wasn't anything a bright young thing could offer. He hungered for conversation, a humorous, sexually inviting woman with a throaty laugh who would hold his hand in the street and in bed and who would talk to him. And who would smile and say, 'Yes.'

The only thing that vaguely perturbed him about this was that the woman he dreamed about was rather like his mother. Not in looks, he told himself, but in nature. He wanted to have what Bibi and Callum had.

He finished his soup, and went to the small art gallery at the back of the coffee shop. A painting caught his eye. It was a snow scene, or an impression of a snow scene, a mass of white with small, mostly black figures moving through it. Here and there were splodges of blue and red. Trees were stark, leafless, pointing upwards. He sat on a bench nearby to stare at it. He sighed. 'God, I wish I could paint. God, I wish I was a genius of some sort. But I'm not. I am only me.'

A woman he hadn't noticed turned and said, 'I know. I'm the same. I'd love to be really good at something. Without all the pain and angst, of course.'

He smiled and apologised; he hadn't realised he was speaking his thoughts out loud.

'Oh, don't say you're sorry. I so agree with you. The only thing I can do really well is make gingerbread.'

'Is it soft and slightly sticky and a little bit chewy, with nuts and raisins?' asked Roddy.

She told him it was.

'Sounds lovely,' said Roddy. 'If you can make it without sweat, tears and frustration, maybe you've got the whole genius thing sussed.'

She told him she hadn't thought of that. Perhaps he was right.

They walked round the room, looking at the rest of the paintings, commenting on the ones they liked. But Roddy kept returning to the snow scene. He said he thought he might buy it.

'You should,' she said. 'It would cheer you up.'

'Do I look like I need cheering up?'

She said that in her experience, everyone needed cheering up. 'I know I do from time to time.'

He looked at his watch. In twenty minutes he had to be back at work. 'I don't suppose I could cheer you up by buying you a cup of coffee? And they do very good gingerbread, too.'

She smiled and said, 'Yes.'

'Do you know?' said Bibi. 'I think Callum loved me long before I started to love him.'

They were on the road again. Going, James realised, in

the wrong direction. 'This way,' Bibi had said, pointing to a road that was not the road that would take them to Gairloch, and Liz. He'd sighed, and had done as he was told.

'Yes,' continued Bibi. 'He was ready. He was older than me. I just got married, I didn't think about what it meant. I just thought it sounded grown-up to be somebody's wife.'

James changed gear, stared at the road ahead and didn't answer. They were travelling along the side of Loch Ness, wide, pewtery grey water ruffled by a small wind. He wondered if he would see the monster and kept shifting his gaze to watch the surface. At any moment a prehistoric head could rear up and look back at him.

'It's very deep,' said Bibi. 'There could easily be something huge and mysterious and ancient living in there.'

'You believe that?'

'I find more and more that I want to believe in anything that defies explanation. I like the mysterious. In fact, I hope the monster's in there and they never find it. It pleases me to think that it's lurking in the deep, knowing we're looking for it and keeping itself a secret.'

She told him to take the next left turn. The road got suddenly steep, single track as they moved up into the hills. James always marvelled that all this landscape was out here. He'd spent his life so far travelling the same city rat-run, to and from work and home again. It had all been buildings, and here it was trees bent by years of wind and weather, and mountains thick with heather and bracken. He asked where they were going.

'Back to where I spent the first part of my life. Home,' she said.

'Where you began,' said James.

'I began in that cottage,' said Bibi. 'I only really began after Callum found me. Before that I was lurking, keeping myself a secret.'

James wrestled with the steering wheel. The twists and turns in the road were hard to manoeuvre in an old car without power steering. 'Like the monster,' he said. 'Huge and mysterious.'

'I was never huge, never mysterious. I was young, ignorant and moon-faced. A face as blank as a bum. No expression, no life, no knowledge. Nothing.'

'Wonder what he saw in you,' said James.

'I may have had a face that lacked character. But I do believe – indeed, I was often told – that it had a certain beauty. I had cheekbones. I think Callum saw a chance to make his mark on somebody. He fancied himself as a mentor. My ignorance was astounding. Say what you like about young women these days, none of them are as blindingly ignorant as I was.'

Home

Once a week, Bibi trudged the three miles to the lonely telephone box to wait for her mother's call. There was never anybody in there; she thought she might be the only person who used it. There was comfort in hearing that familiar voice. Bibi hadn't realised until she left how much home and family had meant to her.

She had learned some simple home-making skills. The cottage looked less forbidding than it had when she and Callum first arrived. There were pictures on the walls, checked blankets draped over the chairs, an array of postcards from friends (all Callum's) and things of interest snipped from newspapers and magazines pinned up in the kitchen, and an assortment of found objects on the mantelpiece – a pretty pink stone, a ram's horn, a sprig of heather. It looked more homey.

But it wasn't really home to Bibi. Home was still that vast mansion, Knightly House, set in rolling grounds. What she missed was space. She couldn't get used to a living room so small, it only took a few steps to cross from the window to the fireplace. At Knightly, a person could stride about. There was air and light, even if it was often chilly. And there was always room to be alone. At the cottage she and Callum bumped into one another; they did small sideways dances to get out of each other's way. The only real space was the wide, wild and empty landscape beyond their front door.

There was also the problem of silence. Up till now, Bibi had rather relished it. Mostly because there wasn't a lot of it. There had always been people coming and going; the phone rang often, dogs barked, doors slammed. There had been voices.

At the cottage, all they heard was the sound of cattle nearby, a lowing that did not so much break the silence as amplify it. Inside, Callum worked. He set up a table in the corner of the living room, where the fire was. The only sound was his pen scrutting over paper. In time, when she had mastered a typewriter, Bibi would type up his poems, essays and journalistic pieces. But for now he put his words on paper with a fountain pen, a Parker so beloved he couldn't bear anyone else to touch it. As he worked, he wouldn't suffer any noise that disrupted his flow of thoughts, so the radio did not get switched on till he had finished for the day.

Bibi spent her time in the kitchen, reading cookbooks and novels she got from the library in the village. Once a week she walked there to shop and to select a fresh batch of reading material. She was working her way through Dickens and Agatha Christie, and had mastered sponge cake, fruit crumbles and stews. The days of burnt food were over.

Still, it was a joy to talk to someone she knew, rather than the local librarian or the woman in the post office or the man who owned the grocery store.

Once she had complained of feeling nauseous.

'You are taking precautions, aren't you?' said her mother.

'Of course I am,' said Bibi. 'I'm very careful. I wash all the vegetables, I make sure the milk doesn't go off. And when I'm walking to this phone box, I always face the oncoming traffic.'

There was a long silence. Then her mother said, 'We should have talked more when you were younger.'

'Perhaps,' agreed Bibi. 'But we are talking now.'

'I meant about sex. About contraception. That sort of precaution. Have you been to a doctor? Have you done anything about not getting pregnant?'

Bibi said she hadn't.

'Why not?'

'I didn't like to,' said Bibi. 'I was too embarrassed.'

'It's a doctor, for heaven's sake,' said her mother. 'He'll be used to talking to women about all sorts of things.'

'I have never spoken to *anybody* about that sort of thing,' Bibi told her.

It was true. Bibi hadn't had any real female friends when she lived at Knightly, and there certainly hadn't been any sex education at the village school she'd attended. Her brothers and sister had gone to boarding school, but by the time Bibi came along the family were already suffering financially. Her father had decided that he'd spent enough on educating his children, also, he didn't believe in educating girls. Besides, it would be a good idea to keep one at home to help with running the house and the estate. He had not mentioned any of this to Bibi.

She knew that babies came into the world, and that the pleasures she and Callum indulged in nightly were part of that process. But she did not know anything about preventing them. That was the stuff of whispers, giggles and nudges in the playground. Nobody had talked about it when she was around. She came from the big house; she wasn't invited to join in any of the naughty talk.

'But what about Callum?' said her mother. 'He certainly would know what to do.'

'He said it doesn't matter once you're married. That's the joy of it.'

Her mother said, 'Ah. I think you may be pregnant. You should talk to your husband and you should definitely see a doctor.'

Not long after that, they'd hung up. Bibi trudged back to the cottage where Callum was in the kitchen, making a pot of tea. He asked how her mother was doing, and what she'd said.

'She thinks I may be pregnant,' said Bibi.

He seemed delighted. 'Are you?'

'I don't know. I just feel sick a lot.'

'When did you last have a period?'

'None of your business.'

'I'm your husband. Of course it's my business.'

'I can't remember,' she said. 'Ages ago. I thought it was handy. I hate having periods. Also, I didn't have to buy sanitary towels in the chemist. I hate doing that. They stare at me. They think you and I are arty and weird.'

Callum had come to her, helped her remove her coat and led her to a chair. He'd made her tea, knelt by her as she sipped. 'A baby,' he said, stroking her stomach. 'It'll be a boy. But we'd better get you to a doctor.'

So began Bibi's monthly, then weekly trips to the doctor's surgery. She'd had to sit in the waiting room on antenatal clinic afternoons, in a row with a dozen or so other pregnant woman, all with their stockings rolled down and all clutching a small bottle containing their urine sample. She hated it even more than buying sanitary towels from the chemist's shop.

It was then that she became aware of what she called the secret world of women. She would look at women in the street or on the bus and think they knew all about being a woman, and she didn't. She felt clumsy and stupid. Trundling home on the bus, she looked round her. There were all sorts of women aboard, small, fat, tall, young, old, rich and poor. And they knew the secrets. They would have been passed on to them, mother to daughter, friend to friend, aunt to niece, grandmother to grandchild, but nobody had bothered to pass on anything to her.

These women would know how to peel a potato (though Bibi knew this now, she hadn't when she first got married, had stared at the lumpy, mud-caked things in puzzlement. It had taken her half an hour to peel four of them, and then she didn't know if that was too many or too few). These women would know about changing sheets, folding napkins, arranging flowers, cleaning burnt pots, sweeping floors, cooking pork chops, managing a budget, changing nappies, ironing, and that strange thing she read about in magazines – keeping your husband happy. Why the hell should I keep him happy? Bibi had thought. Why isn't there an article for him to read about keeping me happy?

She thought that all the women she saw, in fact all women everywhere, would know the things she didn't. They would do the things she and Callum did in bed, and they would all know how to have a baby. More importantly, they would know how *not* to have a baby. Except me, she decided.

Now she pointed to an impressive gateway, two pillars, both with a lion atop.

'This is it,' she said.

They turned down a long, tree-lined drive, James crouching over the wheel, looking round. In front of them was a huge house, three storeys high, with a sweeping curve of steps leading to a magnificent front door. And this was wide open. Everywhere James looked, he saw extravagance and wealth. 'You lived here?'

'It didn't look like this in my day,' Bibi told him. 'It was scruffier then. I preferred it.'

James said, 'Wow.'

'It's all so pretentious.'

They parked, got out of the car and looked round at the other cars parked here. BMWs, Jaguars and other expensive models. They made the Volvo look old and tired. Oh well, thought Bibi, I am old and tired, too.

'There's a croquet lawn and everything,' said James.

'Absurd,' said Bibi. 'I do believe they have even scientifically worked out the correct depth of gravel to give a satisfactory crunch underneath your feet.'

She stopped at the foot of the steps to look round. She had known the place would have changed, but at the same time had hoped it hadn't. As they'd crunched up the drive, she had almost expected to see the old tumbledown house with two black Labradors lying dozing on the steps. This new opulence unsettled her.

The house was painted pale honey, the colour of castles in fairy stories. The door was glossy black and at the top of the stairs leading to it were two stone lions, couchant. The lawns on either side of the driveway were clipped to such perfection it looked as if it had been done with nail scissors. Once that grass had been long, mowed only three or four times a year. At the far end had been a wood, mostly Scots pines. In spring it had been carpeted with bluebells. In early summer, giant rhododendrons, pushy incomers, Bibi thought them, bloomed. It was the home of rabbits, red squirrels, pine martens, crossbills, finches and goldcrests. Mornings, before the rest of the household was awake, Bibi had sat at her bedroom window and watched deer slip silently out of that wood to graze on the neglected lawn.

Now the wood was gone, the trees felled, their roots bulldozed out of the ground. It had been replaced by a terraced rose garden complete with fountains and sculptures of cherubs. This was not gardening, Bibi thought, it was vandalism.

They climbed the sweeping stairway and went inside. They wafted through scents of lilies and jasmine, felt their tired and scruffy shoes sink into thick, plush carpeting. Bibi looked down and said, 'For heaven's sake.'

'You left this for that little cottage?' said James.

'I keep telling you, it wasn't like this when I lived here.

There was no carpet, for a start. This was tiled and there was always a reassuring amount of mud underfoot. There were coats hanging up, walking sticks, a line of boots, and there was always a dog or two lying on the steps.'

It was dawning on James that they didn't fit in. This was not the sort of place where a person in baggy jeans and hooded top was welcome. Bibi didn't look too bad, though her linen slacks were wrinkled and sagged a little at the knees. She'd shoved up the sleeves of her pink sweater, which, he noticed, had a long thread hanging from the hem. Her glasses were perched on her head. The shoes definitely let her down – Puma trainers which still bore the stains from yesterday's tramp through the heather. There was, however, something about the way she stood looking round; her shock had disarmed her. She looked uncomfortable. A place like this demanded poise and confidence.

A man in a perfectly pressed suit and gleaming shoes approached; he smiled, wrung his hands and asked if they were members.

'Members?' said Bibi. 'I have never been a member of anything in my life.'

'I'm afraid, madam, this club is for members only.'

'Nobody had to be a member when I lived here. I was born here.' She pointed to the ceiling. 'Up there in the room above this. My birth was attended by two midwives from Inverness and a doctor. My father was getting drunk in the library at the time.'

The man continued to smile, but only because he didn't know what else to do with his face.

'He did the same when my brothers and sister were born. He always felt cast aside when my mother was producing another offspring.' She turned to James. 'Actually, he spent a lot of time getting drunk in the library even when nobody was being born. He drank a lot.'

The man's eyebrows shot up, but apart from that his smile remained fixed.

'Well, don't just stand there, fetch us some tea. We'll be through there, in what used to be the morning room.' She took James's arm and led him into a large room overlooking the croquet lawn. 'We'll sit by the window.'

They sat facing each other on matching pale green sofas. The man hurried away.

'What was this room like when you lived here?'

'It wasn't dark red with a white dado, that's for sure. It had, if I remember correctly, rather splendid William Morris wallpaper. How foolish to remove it. Hilary, our maid, used to light the fire every morning. We'd let it die later on, and she'd light one in the drawing room and the dining room, then a fire in every bedroom, poor soul. By the time I left, she was the only maid, and we only had a fire in the drawing room. But by then she was well past seventy and not really up to lugging buckets of coal up a couple of flights of stairs. What a ghastly life. I have often wished I'd apologised to her before she died.'

A woman in a neat black suit and crisp white shirt appeared.

'I know, members only. But this used to be my home. I wanted to see it again.'

The woman said she was Marcia Green, public relations

manager of the Knightly Country Club, and she'd love to hear more about the house.

Bibi said that she and her young companion needed a cup of tea. 'The Knightly Country Club,' she said. 'I am the last remaining Knightly. I don't recall being asked if you could use the family name.' She didn't know if she was the last remaining Knightly. She didn't know where any of her relatives were, or, indeed, if they were still alive. But she wanted to sound imperious.

'It was sold to our company as the Knightly Estate. Though it had been through two owners since the Knightlys lost it in the early sixties.'

Over tea, elegantly served with a plate of shortbread, Bibi recounted her family history. Marcia Green took notes. The house had been built in 1802 by Bibi's great-great-grandfather, who'd made a fortune dealing, rather dubiously, in cotton in Jamaica. She suspected slaves were involved. Her great-grandfather had added to the fortune by dabbling in tobacco and importing silk. He added the library and had built the shooting lodge.

'It's now rented out for guests who wish to self-cater,' said Marcia.

Bibi said, 'Hmph,' and continued. Her great-grandfather had also travelled across America in a covered wagon and had been involved in skirmishes with the Sioux. He had staked a claim in California and discovered gold.

'When he returned he was fabulously rich and lived a lavish life in London. And when he came up here, in August, to shoot, he brought many famous people with him. Dickens stayed here, Disraeli and the great Sarah Bernhardt. They played croquet on the lawn.'

Marcia said, 'Goodness, how exciting,' and scribbled enthusiastically.

'My grandfather carried on the tradition. He made pots of money selling whisky, single malt, of course, to gangsters in Chicago during the Prohibition era.' Bibi stopped and looked round. The room was spacious, had sofas placed here and there, each with a low table in front. 'This place is littered with sofas,' she said. 'The fireplace hasn't been replaced.'

Her father had sat in front of that fireplace in a battered leather chair reading *The Times* every morning. He drank coffee which was served in a silver pot with a long spout. He hated to be disturbed. There had been a leather Chesterfield here, by the window, and on the wall opposite there had been a huge dresser where the morning papers had been laid out.

'Do you know,' she said, 'Hilary used to iron the papers before my father read them. And his shoelaces, I remember that, beautifully ironed shoelaces.'

Marcia sat, pen poised, and looked at James.

He shrugged. 'She does that. She drifts off into her memories. She's old.'

Bibi heard that and vowed to have words with him as soon as they were back on the road.

Her father had a dog, Kipper, who followed him everywhere. The family knew when Humphrey was talking to the dog. The words were harsh. 'You bugger, you're a worthless lump of lard, a foul-breathed, tick-infested mutt.' But the voice was soft. Kipper would drink in the insults joyously, tail thwacking against the dresser. When the dog had died, her father had cried. Bibi had been surprised; she hadn't thought grown men did that. Her mother had told him to pull himself together.

Her mother had rarely come into this room. She would leave her car keys on the dresser when she came in from one of her committee meetings, then pick them up again on her way out to another meeting next day. She'd throw her coat on the sofa for Hilary to hang up, and got cross if it was left lying.

'Poor bloody Hilary,' said Bibi.

James and Marcia exchanged glances.

Bibi's memories of this house were of standing alone in rooms. Her mother had little time for her. 'Go play, Bibi. Find something to do.'

After her father had read his freshly ironed *Times*, he'd go to his study to phone his bookmaker. The gardener kept the grounds; Ian, the gamekeeper, looked after the grouse moor; Cook ruled the kitchen, and Hilary did everything else. 'Poor bloody soul,' Bibi said again. 'Whatever happened to them all?' she said.

'Who?' asked Marcia.

'All the staff we employed,' said Bibi. 'After my father died and the estate was sold, what happened to the people who worked here? They'd have been left without homes and probably hadn't the money to find somewhere else to live.' She turned to Marcia and James, who'd been watching her. 'We were awful. I used to suspect Callum was jealous of us, our big house, our money, or at least the

223

money he supposed we had. But he was right. People shouldn't be able to ruin other people's lives. I'm beginning to think we were utterly dreadful.'

She stood up. She shouldn't have come here. This was becoming painful. Sitting in this room, remembering how it had once been, had brought back something she'd forgotten about her childhood – loneliness.

She had tiptoed through life. She had spent a lot of time peeping through half-open doors, or crouched on the stairs watching Hilary bustle about, box of cleaning materials in hand, muttering to herself as she went. Bibi had hidden in the bushes, spying on the gardener. She barely remembered speaking to any of them. But then she barely remembered speaking to her parents. They hadn't communicated.

That was why I loved Callum; he taught me to talk. That night, when he'd taken her for a drink in the local hotel, they'd sat and spoken to one another for hours. They'd walked over the moor, talking. They'd lain in bed, talking. Mornings, they'd lingered in the kitchen, talking. 'We chatted for forty-odd years,' she said. 'That's what makes a love affair – sex and conversation.' She smiled. 'Time to go.'

In the car, James said that her parting had been a bit sudden. 'I think that woman wanted to hear more stories. I think she might have showed us round.'

'I'd had enough,' said Bibi. 'I didn't want to see any more. I'd rather keep it in my head the way it was.' She didn't want to look at the little room on the top floor that had once been hers. It would be painted and primped up.

All frills and fancy, she thought. It had been sparse when she'd occupied it. But she remembered the deer in the morning, and lying in bed hearing owls hoot and foxes bark, sounds of the night. 'Sometimes it's best not to go back.'

She opened a pack of mints, unwrapped one for James and one for herself. 'I used to hate my father for what he did. Cutting me out of his will, refusing to let anyone mention my name when he was about.'

'A bit nasty,' James agreed.

The road was steep, the view stunning. The gorse was starting to bloom. Bibi sighed. 'But now I think it's just what he did. When crises come at us, we often behave dreadfully. I did, I know. I did something really awful. What about you? Has life ever reared up and bitten you on the bum?'

James said it had. And thinking about himself standing yelling in Vicky's garden, he told Bibi he'd behaved badly.

Bibi unwrapped another mint. Popped it into her mouth and said she had an awful lot to be sorry about. 'If I apologised on the hour every hour for the rest of my life, it wouldn't be enough.'

James said she must have done something really terrible.

Bibi said she had. 'But I'm not telling you what it was.' She unwrapped another mint and gave it to him.

They reached the bottom of the hill and turned towards Inverness.

'Did Dickens really visit that house?' asked James.

Bibi said nothing.

'Did you meet him?' James went on.

'For goodness, sake, how old do you think I am? He died well over a century ago.'

'I didn't know. We didn't do Dickens at school. It was all Shakespeare, and then I wasn't paying attention.'

This was familiar. Hadn't she been ignorant about a famous poem by Elizabeth Barrett Browning? 'I think you must be dumber than me,' she said.

He sulked. They did not speak until they reached the outskirts of Inverness and Bibi told James to stop at a hotel. 'Time for lunch,' she said.

He didn't want anything to eat. He wasn't hungry. 'And I'm not dumb.' He slumped in his seat, shoulders hunched, looking out of the side window, away from her. He was filled with the silent implosive rage of the recently insulted.

'I'm buying,' she said. 'I don't expect you to pay for anything on this trip.'

He said he didn't care; he wasn't hungry, and repeated that he wasn't dumb.

Bibi said, 'So be it,' and went in without him.

Sitting at her table, eating grilled salmon, she watched him slumped in the car looking miserable. She summoned the waiter and told him to take some sandwiches and a glass of orange juice out to her driver. 'Can't have the staff go hungry.'

The waiter crossed the parking area outside carrying a tray of neatly cut sandwiches and a glass of juice. Bibi smiled as he indicated the old lady inside who had asked that her chauffeur be given a bite to eat, and James sulkily took what he was served. He was too hungry to refuse.

'Excellent,' she said as she got into the car later. 'Splendid meal. I hope you enjoyed your food too, young man. Let's get on down the road.'

They drove on in silence, then Bibi said, 'Anyway, Dickens never did stay at that house. I lied. I lied about everything. The covered wagons, fighting the Sioux, selling whisky to gangsters – all lies.'

'Was that the terrible thing you did?'

'Good heavens, no. That was just me amusing myself. The terrible thing I did was truly terrible. That was fun.'

James said it wasn't right to lie to people.

'I told that woman what she wanted to hear. It will make excellent reading on the website. And you enjoyed your shortbread, didn't you?'

A Professional Smiler

At work, Beth's title was Marketing Liaison Assistant, but mostly she answered the phone, placed adverts and, on occasion, manned the reception desk. When presentations were being made in the boardroom, she brought in the coffee and pastries.

Bradley, her lover, owned the company she worked for, something that set her apart from her colleagues. She no longer suffered snide remarks about what naughty things she might have had to do to get the job, but there were still awkward silences when she entered a room and interrupted people complaining about the hours they had to work or some extra duties they'd been asked to do. She was never included in any silliness, jokes or even office politics. Everyone worried that she might report back to Bradley.

Judith Whitley ran the Marketing department. She was eight years older than Beth, and tended to keep any juicy jobs to herself, Beth was the constant junior, and thought she was getting too old for that. She did, however, get to do all the evening entertaining of clients.

Judith had two children, and, Beth supposed, the accompanying guilt complex. She arrived in the office at eight in the morning and always left at five. Beth assumed that this was one of the trials of being a working mother. Judith needed to get home to her kids. Beth's job, then, required a lot of smiling. She was, she thought, a professional smiler.

Odd when she thought about it, because in private she rarely smiled. Her face fell into a natural glum expression. She insisted this was simply what her face did when she wasn't doing anything with it. In shops assistants often told her to cheer up, and workers on building sites would whistle and call, 'Smile, darlin', it may never happen.' She found this irritating, but struggled to flash whoever was commenting on her glumness a small upturn of her mouth.

Recently, she had found this harder and harder to do. When asked to smile, she was aware of twisting her face into a grimace. Of late, she had been crying a lot. The slightest thing could set her off – forgetting where she'd put her keys, dropping and breaking a cup. Last week, she'd been reduced to tears when traffic lights she'd been approaching turned from green to red before she could get through. She didn't know what was happening to her.

She was finding it hard to concentrate at work. Nights, she always woke at three or four in the morning, and never could get back to sleep. She'd make herself a cup of tea and watch television. She was hooked on old medical dramas; she had also become quite knowledgeable about Italian football, and felt very fond of the people who signed programmes for the deaf.

She followed her horoscope in a newspaper and found she was on the cusp of dramatic events which would change her life. She supposed being pregnant was dramatic, and would change her life, but this wasn't what she was looking for. She was hoping for something wonderful to happen in the next half-hour or so. Recently, Saturn had entered her sign for a six-week stay. She thought this to be a bad thing.

'Saturn has entered my sign for a six-week stay,' she said to Judith at work.

'Really?' Judith said. 'It has just left mine after a two-year stay.'

'What happened?' asked Beth.

'My dog was run over. My son was diagnosed as autistic. My husband told me he was having an affair, and my mother died.'

'Not good,' said Beth.

'A bit more than that,' said Judith. 'Tragic is how I'd put it.'

Beth said sorry. She hadn't known.

'No, you wouldn't,' said Judith. 'You never ask about my life. You seem only to be interested in yourself. You come in here every day looking glossy, and you spend your time smiling at everybody except me.'

Beth said she was sorry again. She knew they didn't speak much, 'But you rush off on the dot of five.'

'And why do you suppose that is?' said Judith. 'I have to pick up my son. My husband is no longer around to do it. And I used to have to get home to let my mother's carer away. She lived with us for the last few years, until she died.'

She didn't tell Beth she thought her work excellent. She suspected Beth was after her job, and with two children to care for, one at a special school, she couldn't afford to lose it. At monthly meetings she mentioned Beth quietly, damning her with faint praise. Judith was stressed. She took Temazepan, often swallowing more than was prescribed, and this made her woozy. Beth didn't speak to her, she thought, because Beth wanted her job; Beth slept with the boss and Beth's father had been a poet. She rather disliked Beth. It never crossed her mind that Beth didn't speak to her because she rarely spoke to Beth.

'You don't know what it's like out in the real world, do you?' she said now. 'You have no idea what some people go through.'

It hadn't been a good day for her. Her son had taken a serious tantrum when, distracted, thinking about a press feature she was trying to arrange, Judith had put the milk on his cornflakes before the sugar and had given him orange juice in the wrong glass. Calming him down, getting him ready for school had taken a while, making her late for work. She hated arriving when Beth was already at her desk, smiling and saying good morning.

'I suppose I don't,' said Beth.

At five, as ever, Judith left. Ten minutes after she'd gone, Beth switched off her computer, took her coat from the cupboard and walked out of the office.

The street was busy. Rush-hour traffic streamed past. The air smelled of ozone from the sea and of booze and food from the pubs and restaurants nearby. Tables cluttering the areas outside cafés and bistros were crowded with people who all seemed to be engrossed in interesting and lively conversations. She would not be involved in any such thing for some time because Bradley's ex-wife had gone on holiday for a month. Under the rules of their relationship, she was not to visit him, lest her presence upset the easy flow of his home life; he would come to her. But he wouldn't be doing that for the next four weeks; he'd be in charge of the children. This depressed her. Her conversation with Judith had depressed her. It would be the weekend soon, and she knew that if she did not phone round her few friends to see if anyone wanted to go out on Saturday night, she would, from Friday evening till Monday morning, talk to nobody. And this depressed her even more.

Her flat, a small warehouse conversion – one room, really; a kitchen and living room with a gallery bedroom reached by a spiral staircase – was five minutes' walk away. She walked slowly, wondering if there was anything on television tonight, and going through the contents of her fridge deciding what to eat. The more she thought about her evening ahead, the slower she walked. She stopped. She couldn't face going back to her flat. She'd busy herself, cook up some pasta and every few minutes gaze at the phone, willing it to ring. The silence made her miserable. She wanted to be somewhere comforting.

She turned, made her way to Leith Walk and took the bus uptown. She would go home, to her mother's flat. She would sleep in her old bedroom. It would be silent there, too. But it would be an easy, familiar silence. It would be bearable.

❊   ❊   ❊

James would always remember his first glimpse of Liz. She was standing at her front door when he and Bibi arrived. She was wearing jeans, a white T-shirt and black waistcoat, an outfit he rather liked. She was small and had long brown hair that she swept off her face, a kind of nervous reaction when she realised who was visiting. As he braked and switched off the ignition, he looked across at her. The expression on her face worried him. It was a mix of shock and disbelief. He wished he hadn't come here.

On the journey, Bibi had been nervous. She spoke too much.

'I'm not so sure about this now,' she had said. They had been on the long and beautiful road that led into Gairloch. The views were stunning, treetops and the sea beyond. 'Too late to turn back, I suppose. I wish I hadn't come,' she said.

James asked why. He was enjoying himself. He was driving along a strange and beautiful road, music was on the radio, he had his elbow propped on the open window. This was what he'd dreamed of doing.

'Liz won't want to see me. I haven't been up here for three years. I shouldn't just drop in on people, especially people I gave birth to. I should have let her know I was coming.'

James agreed with that, but didn't mention it. 'It'll be fine.'

'No, it won't be fine. Your children don't want you just

appearing at their front door. They like to know you are on your way so they can dust and polish and stock up their larders. They want to pretend their lives are wonderful and make sure there's nothing to criticise.'

James said nothing. He suspected that this might be true.

'Also, my children are all so much brighter than me. They know much more than I do. When I was young and my parents were alive, I thought they were more worldly-wise than me. Now I think my children are cleverer than me. Not fair. Why didn't I get a chance to be the wise and worldly one?'

James said he didn't know.

He saw Liz's expression change as Bibi climbed out of the car. She smiled and came to meet them, thumbs hooked over the belt of her jeans.

'What a surprise, I can't believe it. What brings you here?'

'Just wanted to see you,' Bibi said. 'A whim, really. It's been a while since I last came up this way.' She kissed Liz. 'You're looking well. A bit thin, though.'

Liz smiled.

'Where is everyone?' asked Bibi.

'The children are inside watching television. Drew's not here.'

Bibi said, 'Ah.' She turned and introduced James, and explained who he was. 'I twisted his arm to persuade him to bring me here. Celia was making a fuss about my driving.'

'Same old Celia,' said Liz. She kissed her mother's cheek. 'It's wonderful to see you.' Then she shook James's hand. Her nails, he noticed, were rimmed with mud. There was a tightness round her eyes that did not go away when she smiled.

'I noted the expression when you saw us arrive,' said Bibi.

'Surprise,' said Liz, 'and worry that I haven't enough to feed you.'

'We've brought goodies,' said Bibi. 'We shopped. Can't arrive out of the blue like this without bringing some food and wine.'

Liz said that wine sounded good. 'It's a treat these days.'

She went ahead of them into the kitchen, picking up toys, shoes and discarded coats and sweaters as she went.

Bibi said, 'What's the point? I've seen the mess.'

Liz smiled and said that she'd been meaning to clear up, but hadn't got round to it.

'Not for some time, judging by the state of things,' said Bibi. She looked out of the window. 'And the garden needs a bit of a cleanup, too.'

'I'll get round to it,' said Liz.

James looked out of the window. He saw a large plot, planted with rows of vegetables that seemed to be battling for space among nettles, thistles and other weeds he couldn't name. Hens moved about, pecking the ground, making soft clucking noises. Looking out towards the front, he noticed more weeds, and, across the narrow road, a strip of untamed ground in front of a line of trees. Two cows lifted their heads and stared vacantly back at him. My God, he thought. This really is the middle of nowhere. There was nothing but land and cows and sky.

'Is there a pub round here?' he said.

'There's an inn a few miles along the road,' said Liz. 'Not far really.'

'I don't want to go. I just wondered what people did round here.'

'They work. They watch television. They cook dinner. Same as everywhere,' said Liz.

James nodded.

'Just open the wine, James,' said Bibi.

He did as he was told, but could not help gazing round as he did so. He'd never seen anything like this before. The furniture was old; not desirably so, just old. The chairs round the table were painted an assortment of colours; the table was kept steady by books of varying thickness placed under the legs. The ceiling sagged badly enough for James to fear it might fall in at any time. He hauled the cork from the wine bottle, watching the plaster above him for signs of cracking and caving in.

The table was covered with a dark red oilcloth and was jam-stained and becrumbed. Once, Bibi's kitchen units had been similarly messy, but now they were pristine. He wiped them.

Liz was clearing the breakfast dishes as Bibi examined the wine glasses. When Liz's back was turned, adding the cereal bowls to the pile of unwashed crockery in the sink, Bibi took a tissue from her handbag and wiped them before pouring the wine.

There was one chair in the room. It was covered in a tartan rug. James thought it looked dubious; it wouldn't stand the strain of anyone sitting on it. Not that they could; it was heaped with coats, jackets, sweaters and school bags. It bothered him that the place was dusty, and it bothered him that this bothered him.

He hadn't always been fastidious. This had happened in the past six months. He'd get out of bed to put his shoes neatly side by side, if he'd been so careless as to get into bed without making sure they were in line first. He hated that in himself. He dusted his room regularly, opened the window to let in air, and vacuumed every Saturday morning.

Bibi would stand in the doorway, watching. 'Since you've got that thing out, you can do the rest of the flat while you're at it.'

Now she handed him a glass of wine. He stared into it, checking for dust and crumbs.

Bibi glared. 'It's fine.'

Sometimes he thought he was going mad. This obsession he had with neatness and cleanliness rather upset him. Still, he thought, if he was going off his head, he was doing it in the perfect company.

Two children, skinny, with freckle-scattered faces, appeared at the door and stared.

'Say hello to your grandma,' said Liz. 'And this is James.'

The children nodded at him.

'Am I not getting a kiss?' said Bibi.

The girl, Lara, ran into Bibi's outstretched arms. 'Oh, lovely,' said Bibi. 'Aren't you getting big?'

Louis refused. He wasn't into kissing.

'Excellent,' said Bibi. 'Keep to your principles. Though

you might change your stand on kissing in a few years' time.'

Louis shook his head and said he wouldn't.

'Well,' said Bibi, 'this is wonderful. Liz, isn't it time you started cooking?'

She cast a slow eye round the room, saw the mess, remembered the state of the garden and thought that she was witnessing despair, weariness and loneliness. She knew there was something her daughter wasn't telling her. This explained the look on Liz's face when she'd seen her arriving. She hadn't wanted her mother to see this mess. Well, Bibi thought, if I lived like this, I wouldn't want my mother to see it either.

They had a pleasant meal, chatting, reminiscing. Bibi made friends with her grandchildren and drank too much wine. 'I'm allowed. At my age, if my liver's damaged, I think, How much worse can it get?'

When Liz took Lara and Louis upstairs to bed, Bibi leaned over the table and hissed, 'There's something awfully wrong here.'

James said, 'Is there?' He thought Liz was untidy. She came from an untidy family; it was in her blood.

'There is a tension,' said Bibi. 'Liz keeps giving the children warning glances, telling them to keep their mouths shut. And she has never once mentioned Drew. Not once.'

'So,' said James. 'You said he was away at university. Maybe there isn't much to say about him.'

'Nonsense. A person always mentions the person they're married to. It comes up in conversation. It's natural. And look at the mess. I see problems here.'

James said, 'Do you?'

She leaned further towards him. 'You are blind. I'll tell you what I think. He's left her.'

'You think?'

'I think,' said Bibi. 'There is absolutely no sign of him in this house. Not a shoe, not a sweater, not a jacket hanging in the hall, not anything. That's what's happened, I'm positive.'

'But you can't be sure,' said James. He was leaning over, also whispering.

'I know the signs. Callum left me once.'

'I thought you left him, in New York.'

'Yes. Technically I did. But he didn't come after me, so in a way, he left me.'

James didn't quite get the logic of this. He frowned.

'Oh, for heaven's sake. He stayed behind. He spent over a year sleeping in friends' apartments, on their floors or sofas. He had an affair with Polly.'

'You never told me any of this,' said James. He had, over the miles they'd travelled, become caught up in the story of Bibi and Callum.

'That was coming later. Right now, I have to get to the bottom of this Drew business. And I have to sort things out.' She leaned back and refilled her glass.

'Isn't that interfering?' asked James.

'I'm her mother. Who is going to interfere if I don't? Anyway, it isn't interfering, it's caring.' She nodded at him, making sure he knew she was right, then swigged and leaned forward again. 'There are issues at stake here. This house, for example, is his. He bought it outright. What if he wants to move back in and throws her out? What if he sells it from under her? Where would she go? She has no money.'

She leaned back. Swigged a little more, and smiled. She had a mission. She relished the thought. She hadn't had a mission in years.

James, not wanting to get involved in family matters that had nothing to do with him, stood up and cleared the table. He said he'd wash up.

Liz returned to the table. 'I've put Lara in my bed, so you can sleep in her room. James will have to make do with the sofa.'

Bibi went to bed early; she said she'd had a bit of a day and needed to sleep. James and Liz took the wine through to her small living room to chat. It was more comfortable than the kitchen.

It was a small room, the ceiling low, beams exposed. The floor was polished pine and the sofa on which they both sat was old, rescued from the side of the road where a couple who owned a holiday cottage had placed it to be removed by the bin men. Liz had re-covered it in blue velvet and made red and green cushions to decorate it. Behind them the wall was shelved, each shelf filled with books, CDs and odd things she and Drew had found at church sales and boot sales – an old green decanter, an ancient typewriter, a little cup with a fat hen painted on the side. A wood-burning stove sent out a thick and soothing heat. That and the wine went to James's head. He fought the urge to sleep.

Liz asked what it was like to lodge with her mother.

'She's a bit bossy and critical, actually.'

'Yes,' said Liz, 'she's all that.'

'But the flat's lovely. I love it.'

'Oh yes,' said Liz. 'The flat's wonderful. It is filled with golden light, reminds me of Florence.'

James said he'd never been there.

'Oh, you have to go. It's beautiful.'

James said he would. He shifted in his seat; he had a suspicion Liz was going to cry. Oh please don't do that, he thought. He wouldn't know what to do.

But Liz slapped her knee and rose. 'Time for bed, I think. I have to get up to get the kids to school. And I've probably had way too much wine. I'm not used to it.'

She disappeared, then came back with blankets and bed linen. 'Make yourself comfortable,' she said. 'I hope you won't be too hot. We never let the stove go out, even in the summer. I think the place would get horribly damp if we did.'

They hovered close to one another for a moment, smiling. James had a strange impulse to kiss her. Nothing passionate, just a polite parting peck on the cheek. He resisted, but wondered what had got into him. He never did things like that.

Feeling Safe

'I'm married,' said Roddy.

Erica said she knew that.

'Is it that obvious?'

'Yes,' she said.

They were in the coffee shop, having lunch – soup of the day, spicy lentil. He told himself he hadn't come hoping to see her, though he'd enjoyed her company over coffee yesterday. They had exchanged names; she was Erica Baines. 'Roddy Saunders,' he told her, holding out his hand for her to shake. They hadn't exchanged telephone numbers.

No, it was the soup he was after. Still, he acknowledged an uninvited jolt in his stomach when he saw her coming in, but put it down to indigestion. Though he couldn't do anything to stop his face creasing into a smile when she crossed the room and asked if he minded her joining him.

Their conversation moved easily from agreeing about the deliciousness of the soup to a film about Picasso they'd both seen on television last night, and that led them to discuss more personal things. Like being married.

He told her he'd bought the painting of the snow scene he'd admired. He was going to hang it in his office. 'In the bank round the corner. I'm the manager.'

She said she hadn't ever met a bank manager who wore a pale linen suit and a pink shirt.

He shrugged. 'Sometimes I just can't face the grey pin-stripe.'

She nodded. She could understand that. He asked what she did.

'I'm a barmaid.'

'Really?' he said. 'You don't look like a barmaid.'

'You think I should wear a low-cut frilly blouse and a miniskirt? I should also have my eyes caked in blue shadow, presumably.'

'Sounds good to me,' he said.

She smiled, made a face and said she didn't think so. 'I'm assistant bar manager at The Hideaway, a job that suits my needs perfectly.'

'And what are your needs?' said Roddy.

'I have no need to be bar manager. I don't want the responsibility and I don't want to stay after closing time to do the tills. I like my life. I am free during the day to go to art galleries or the cinema, or just to stroll about. I have many friends – I need friends. I am a single mother, though my son is grown up and at university. Oxford. I need to see him every once in a while.'

'That's it?'

'Yes.'

'You don't need a husband, then? Since you haven't mentioned one.'

'No. I'm not married. Either because I don't want to be, or because nobody I wanted to say yes to asked me. I can't decide which.'

'And you like saying yes?'

'Oh yes. It's my favourite word. So, what's your story?'

He told her he had two daughters who were wonderful. And that his father, a poet, had freaked when he'd said he was going to study accountancy and take up banking. 'So that's what I did. I think it was about shocking him and a need for something secure. I have memories of living on potatoes and having the phone cut off. My parents lived messy lives. They fought and made up a lot. I wanted to get away from that. Now, I think they were right. They enjoyed themselves.'

She agreed that they probably did, and asked what his wife was like.

'Very organised, hates clutter. Still looks good. Actually, she was the sort of girlfriend you could take home to your mother.' Except for his mother; she disliked Ruth on first sight and had told him she'd make him miserable.

Was he miserable? He was a man of many hobbies. Over the years he'd taken up, and abandoned, guitar lessons, Italian classes, astronomy, golf, painting and tennis. Now it was photography, something he'd enjoyed for several years. His big passion had been for making furniture. He loved the smell and feel of wood. How its colour deepened as he applied oil and polish. His pieces – tables, chairs, dressers – had been built using methods taught to Roddy by a carpenter he'd worked for part-time when he was at college. Bibi and Callum had encouraged him in this, and had tried to persuade him to give up his accountancy course and pursue a career as a master joiner and cabinet-maker. He had refused, partly because it had annoyed his parents, and partly because Ruth had convinced him there was more security in life at a bank. Now, he hated his job. And he and Ruth had mastered the art of living together without having a conversation; indeed, without staying in the same room as one another for very long. So, yes, he was miserable.

'How lucky you are to have a poet for a father. Mine was a coalman,' said Erica.

He had an image of a little girl with long golden hair being hoisted into the arms of a tall, hearty, smiling man whose teeth gleamed against his blackened face

'Would you like to go out with me?' said Erica. 'We could have dinner.'

Roddy had heard about this, women asking men out. He had never thought it would happen to him. He said, 'Yes.'

'Excellent.' She wrote her address and phone number on a napkin. 'Sunday. You can pick me up around seven o'clock.'

James hated digging. He hated it when his face was close to the ground as he prised weeds from the overturned earth, and he hated shoving the spade into what looked to him like wind-shrivelled, merciless ground. He also hated standing alone in this godforsaken weed-raddled garden. He felt he was a solitary figure in a desolate landscape. Bibi had asked him to do this; he was beginning to hate her for that. Seagulls screamed, yakked and laughed overhead. He hated them, too.

Bibi brought him a mug of tea, looked with disappointment at how little he'd done and asked how he was getting on. He told her he was fed up, and that he had agreed to drive her, not to dig gardens. 'Look at this place, it's a dump.'

Bibi agreed, but wasn't going to admit it. She told him it had its charms. Looking round the garden, she saw that nature was claiming back the land that had been taken from it.

'I suppose you're going to tell me that house is charming too.' James pointed back at the building.

Bibi turned. She hadn't yet seen the back of Liz's home. It did look a little neglected from the front. This, though, was awful. It was tumbledown. Obviously Drew's enthusiasm for renewing the roof had waned halfway through the task. There were tiles missing; it sagged inwards in the middle. The paint on the doors and windows had peeled off. There was a crack in the wall at the far end reaching from the top window to the ground. 'Goodness,' she said. 'It is a bit run-down.'

James said it looked to him like the place was about to *fall* down. 'It isn't safe.'

As she considered the house, noticing the gap where the wall ended and the roof began, and how ill fitting the windows were, and how the crack, which was worryingly wide, seemed to go right down into the foundations, Bibi smiled. This was what that cottage she'd shared with Callum when they'd first married had looked like. It hadn't in any way resembled the house they'd seen with its gleaming white paint and roses growing round the door. It had been a dump, like this. It had also had that familiar greeny-black look – rising damp. She thought it absurd she should feel a rush of nostalgia for such a thing. But there it was.

She turned to explain to James about loving the most inappropriate of places because they had become home, and found him staring up at the gulls circling, skimming wildly overhead.

'I hate these birds. They look like they're speed-dating, whirling about.'

Bibi said she knew nothing about such matters, but that these birds knew things humans didn't. 'Weather,' she said. 'They're in a flap about some weather coming.'

By the time Liz returned from work, Bibi had made lunch: tuna sandwiches and tomato soup. Liz sat stiffly, shooting her mother the occasional resentful glance. 'I didn't ask you to clean up.'

'Well, I did. It gave me something to do,' said Bibi. 'I don't like just sitting.'

Yes you do, thought James. I've seen you just sitting often.

The room had been dusted, the tablecloth wiped, the sink units scrubbed, the floor vacuumed and the chair cleared of the pile of clothes and books. The place was verging on habitable.

'It's not right, coming into someone's home and cleaning it. It's like you are criticising me,' said Liz.

'I'm only trying to help,' Bibi said. 'There's such a thing as hygiene, you know.'

James thought, You should talk.

'While we're talking about this,' said Bibi, 'I paid your electricity bill, and your phone's reconnected.'

'You've been rummaging through my letters,' said Liz. 'Interfering.'

'Of course I am interfering. It's what I'm here for. If nobody interfered with you, you'd be sitting in the dark with no way of getting in touch with anybody.'

'I don't need a phone,' said Liz.

'Yes you do. What if something happened? You'd need to let people know. What if I died? How would you find out about it?'

'You could send me a letter,' said Liz.

Bibi glared at her. 'And how could I do that if I was dead?'

'How could you phone if you were dead?'

Bibi said, 'It's good to know you can just pick up a phone and keep in touch.'

Liz nodded. 'Still, you shouldn't look through my mail.'

'I'm very acquainted with final demands. I've had them often enough. Yours was in full view on the table. I didn't sneakily peek at anything else.'

James said, 'You two aren't going to argue, are you?'

Bibi and Liz both turned to him and said, 'Yes.'

'In which case, I'm off.' He took his sweatshirt and, pulling it over his head, left.

'That one knows nothing about being human,' said Bibi. 'I suspect he avidly avoids confrontation.'

She busily gathered the dishes on the table, took them to the sink and started to wash up. Her back to Liz, she said, 'Drew has left you, hasn't he?'

'Yes.'

'And you didn't tell anybody.' Bibi ran hot water into the sink and clattered the dishes into it.

'No,' said Liz. 'I thought he'd come back. Then when I realised he wasn't going to, time had passed and I didn't know what to say. I'd have told you in the end.'

Bibi said she knew that. 'Has he found someone else?'

'Yes,' said Liz. 'He doesn't come back often. It's awkward. It's a long journey and he has to stay the night. The children wonder why he sleeps on the sofa. He phones them. Though, obviously, not recently.'

Bibi, still washing the dishes, asked Liz if she'd thought what she was going to do.

'No,' said Liz. 'What is there to do? I don't have any money. I have a job, but that doesn't pay much.' She stared out of the window, watching James pick up weeds, shake loose earth from their roots and toss them into a green garden bag.

'So you're going to stay here,' said Bibi.

'You sound like you disapprove,' Liz said. 'You have no right. I've seen photographs of the cottage you lived in with Dad. It was worse than this. He told me there was a layer of frost on the bed in the morning, and you used to sleep wearing a big jumper and a woollen hat because it was so cold.'

Bibi smiled; she'd forgotten that. 'Yes, it was cold. We spent a lot of time in bed, but mostly because it was the warmest place to be. I wanted better for you.'

She hadn't wanted any of her children to know the depth of chill she and Callum had known when winter hit that cottage. There had been ice on the inside of the windows, waist-deep snow – sometimes they'd been cut off for weeks – frozen pipes and a chill that cut through to their bones. They had lain in bed arguing who would get up first to light the small paraffin heater in the kitchen. Neither had wanted to do it. Now and then they had stayed in bed all day because they'd run out of wood and coal for the fire. It was romantic only as a memory. Living through it had been hell.

She went back to washing the dishes. There wasn't going to be an argument after all. Pity, she thought, because Liz could do with one. It would get rid of her pent-up tensions, and all sorts of interesting information spilled out when people were angry.

Of course, Liz didn't really do anger like her other children did. When she was an infant, she'd been a contented little thing. She hadn't protested if her brothers and sisters had snatched one of her toys from her. If she was sitting in the middle of the floor, playing with her building bricks and blocking any indoor toing and froing, all anyone had to do was pick her up and put her down somewhere out of the way. She would accept that and carry on. She rarely cried, and never screamed. Not good, Bibi thought; a person has to scream from time to time.

Liz looked at her watch. In an hour she'd have to drive into Gairloch to pick up Louis and Lara from school. Once they'd been happy to let one of the other mothers bring them home; they'd even happily go to friends' houses to play. But since Drew had left, they'd insisted she pick them up.

Normally, this would be her time for lying on her bed, dreaming and worrying. She couldn't do that with her mother here, and she missed it. She had a lot to worry about. Last week she'd received a letter from Drew asking why the phone wasn't working, and telling her he needed to get in touch, he was filing for divorce. He had told her he would look for a job as soon as he passed his final exams and, obviously, he would send money to support his children. But, he'd said, in time she would have to find somewhere else to live. Once he'd graduated and found work, and he didn't know where that would be, he'd need the money from the sale of this house to put down a deposit for a new one.

Obviously, he'd written, *I will give you as much time as possible to find somewhere. And I will help towards a deposit on your rent. But I've spoken to my lawyer and I find that, as it is my house, bought outright before we married, and as you contributed no money towards the purchase, I can sell it whenever I want.*

Excellent idea to get all the bad news into one long letter, she had thought. She hoped it had taken him a long time to write, but knowing how he flew at life and was prone to bursts of enthusiasm, suspected it hadn't. Still, he had said sorry at the end, just before *Love, Drew*. An odd thing to write, since he plainly didn't.

For a few days she had tried to push this new problem aside. This was how she usually dealt with worrisome things – ignore them and they might go away. But eventually she asked Mr Talbot, the local lawyer. Fifty-six years old, he'd left the area only to get his degree; after that he'd returned and never left. He came by the shop where Liz worked every day to pick up his newspapers and to buy a packet of five cigars, his daily allowance. He asked Liz if she and Drew owned the house jointly. She told him no, it was Drew's. 'He bought it outright before we married.'

Mr Talbot said, 'Ah.' And had she contributed anything financially towards the maintenance or any extensions?

'No,' said Liz. 'My mother gave us some money when we told her we were coming to live here. We bought the wood-burning stove, a fridge and a cooker and some gardening stuff.'

Mr Talbot stroked his balding head and said, 'Ah,' again. 'The news is not good. He is entitled to sell the property as sole owner. However, he will have to provide for his children, and since they live with you, I think we could get some of the money from the sale there.'

'But he can sell?' said Liz.

'Yes,' said Mr Talbot. 'He most definitely can.'

Thinking about this now, Liz decided she needed to go upstairs to lie on her bed and indulge in a wave of worry. But she couldn't. She stared out of the window at James digging, tossing weeds into the large garden bag, stopping now and then to look up at the wheeling gulls, and thought he looked as miserable as she was.

Beth stayed the night in her mother's flat. There was comfort here. She'd gone straight to her old room at the end of the corridor. It was the smallest of the bedrooms, unchanged since she'd moved out eight years ago. On the wall was a framed photograph of Bibi as a child standing on a rough tangled lawn with a black Labrador, alongside several photos of herself with her father. On the shelves were a selection of her favourite childhood books – *Little Women*, *Danny the Champion of the World*, *The Wind in the Willows* and all of Callum's poetry. There was also her collection of soft toys and the cup she'd won for being on the winning team of an inter-school debate. On her bedside cabinet were several books about death, which she put in a drawer out of sight. She wondered what her state of mind had been when she was twenty, and worried it hadn't improved at all.

She made up the bed with the pink striped duvet cover that had been her favourite as a child, undressed and climbed in, and started to cry.

She woke at six in the morning, feeling better. The bout of weeping and her first full night's sleep in months had been good for her. She was hungry and went through to the kitchen to rake for food. There wasn't much in Bibi's fridge, but there was yogurt and fruit in James's. She took it, then made some toast and settled down at the table to eat. It was so comfortable here, she couldn't believe she'd been so foolish as to move out.

She scanned the bookshelves for something to read, came across Bibi's kitchen diaries and took them out. Bibi never would let anyone read them, 'You can have a good look when I'm dead,' she said. But since she wasn't here, she'd never know.

There were ten of them, covering the past fifteen years – she didn't make an entry every day. There were another fifteen in Bibi's bedroom. Nobody had read them, either. They were mostly a record of what the family had eaten and what work she had done in the allotment. But here and there were details of conversations with Callum and some of Bibi's private thoughts. They were written in a selection of hard-cover notebooks. Some entries were long and some only covered a few lines. A lot of it wasn't dated. The last one had been on the evening before she left.

Off tomorrow. Glad James is driving. Not having a licence bothers me. Didn't used to, but now I worry. I must be getting old. Got the car insured, too. So I am legal. There's a first time for everything. Actually, I only got the motor insurance because James once asked me about it. I lied and told him I was properly covered. Didn't want to get him into trouble, so I stumped up. Aren't credit cards wonderful?

Soon I'll see my Liz and Lara and Louis. Looking forward to it. Could do without seeing Drew, never liked him. He's cocky and bumptious, jumping from one big idea to the next. A man with too many master plans and no will to see them through.

I never was one for plans. It angered Callum. I always said you couldn't map out your future when you never knew what was going to happen. He said I was a fool. He said I had a mind like a ping-pong ball in space, bouncing about, never landing. I said that if you wanted to make God laugh, tell him your plans. Huge argument, made up in bed – Beth, nine months later. Maybe she can plan.

Intended to have salad for supper, couldn't be bothered. Had some cheese and wine, well, I'm going to die so why not.

Callum never did believe in God. I find it hard not to. My childhood was full of religion. I prayed every night. And prayed often during the day. I was a skinny, whispering child, filled with dread of all the things that might happen, and never actually did. Maybe my prayers were answered.

Callum hated religion. It was ugly and manipulative, he said. He didn't believe in God, or heaven or hell. You died and that was that. I was shocked when he told me he didn't think he had a soul. How could he say such a thing? We'd been married for a month, I think. I'd been making love to a man who seemed to me, at the time, heathen. We were in bed; I jumped out, didn't want to sleep beside someone with such diabolical opinions. He laughed, he always laughed at my religion, lifted the covers and told me to get back in. I wasn't wearing anything at the time, and it was cold in the room. 'Come here,' he said, 'let a sinner show you heaven.' I did. How could I resist? Getting sweaty together under the blankets with all that frost and chill outside, that was heaven. I miss him. I still pray, though he'd disapprove. I pray every day for Graham.

Beth thought, She's going to die? Then decided it was just Bibi making an excuse for eating unhealthily. Interesting about the result of the plan argument, though. She was shocked to find her mother wasn't qualified to drive, and had careened about town in that Volvo, after Callum died and wasn't around to stop her. 'She drove all over the place,' Beth said. 'She drove me to Yorkshire to see Roddy. She drove to London once. She could have been arrested.'

At nine she phoned her office to say she wasn't well. 'A virus,' she said. 'I felt it coming on yesterday. I think I'll need a few days.' Later she went to her flat, packed a bag and took a taxi back to Bibi's. She would stay here with her fictitious virus and her depression. It felt safe.

Jolted Memories

Celia had agreed to water the plants in Bibi's flat while she was away. When she'd been on the phone earlier in the day, Bibi had asked if the plants were happy. Celia had said that of course they were. 'Glossy-leaved and smiling,' she had said. This was a lie; tending the plants had slipped her mind.

She stopped by the flat on her way home, and stood for a moment, listening. She thought she heard someone moving about. A burglar, perhaps, though there was no sign of a break-in. 'Hello,' she called. No answer. She hesitated before shutting the door behind her. Perhaps she should phone Peter and ask him to come over and go through the rooms with her. She stood listening, holding her breath. Then shouted, 'Hello, hello,' again. Listened some more and decided she was being ridiculous. She was imagining things.

Still, she went through the flat, opening doors, sticking her head into every room, checking. She thought it odd that Beth's bed was made up. But that was Bibi. Celia thought her mother had never accepted her youngest child had left home, and kept her bed ready for her return.

Beth had been under the bed, eyes shut, trying not to breathe. She'd been in the living room, enjoying a dreadful afternoon movie about a woman suffering from amnesia, when she'd heard Celia coming up the stairs to the front door of the flat, rattling her keys.

She had jumped up, switched off the television, picked up her coffee cup and run down the corridor to her bedroom. She had heard Celia shout, 'Hello,' but hadn't answered. She didn't want to see anyone or to talk to anyone. If Celia found her here, she'd have to explain why she was skipping work. Indeed, she would have to tell Celia why she was here and not in her own flat. And that would mean admitting to wanting to cry all the time, feeling like she was in a tunnel staring out at the world, feeling hopeless, useless and heavy limbed. She wondered if Celia, always so bright and efficient, would understand. No, Beth decided, she didn't want to talk to anyone. She wanted to hide. So that was what she had done.

She stood in her room listening to Celia stride the flat, opening and shutting doors, shouting, hello, hello. When she'd heard her approaching her bedroom, she'd scrambled under the bed, still clutching her coffee cup. She lay pressed to the floor watching Celia's feet. It was dusty, Beth noted, and in the corner was the pink sock she remembered searching for many years ago when she was thirteen. There it is, she thought. I loved those pink socks.

It was a relief when Celia turned and left the room. Beth crawled out from her hiding place and brushed herself down. She heard Celia fill the watering can Bibi kept in the kitchen, and walk about tending the plants. She heard her return to the kitchen and put the can back under the sink. Beth sighed, relieved. Celia would leave now.

But no, she heard Celia coming back down the corridor and going into Graham's old room. She sat on the bed still holding her cup, wishing her sister would go away.

But Celia had no intention of leaving just yet. She was sitting in Graham's room, stunned to find it exactly as it had been when he'd lived here. Unlike the other unoccupied bedrooms, this one was dusted. It was exactly as she remembered it – the Jam, kung fu and motorbike posters were still on the wall, science fiction books and graphic novels on the shelves, a pile of heavy-metal tapes on the cabinet along with his tape deck – and she hadn't been in here since she married Peter sixteen years ago.

Bibi never would talk about Graham. She'd clam up, or she'd walk away saying, 'Don't ask me about him. I don't want to talk about it.'

Celia went back to the kitchen. It had broken her heart when Graham left, and she'd quizzed her parents endlessly about what had happened to him.

'Where is he? When's he coming back?'

'He's gone to America,' Callum had told her. 'Don't know when he's coming home. One day, soon.'

'Why doesn't he write or phone?' she'd asked.

Callum had said that when you went to America for the first time, there was too much to see, too much to do. 'You just don't think about writing a letter or making a call.'

In time Celia too had left home and had been caught up in her own life. But Graham's sudden disappearance still haunted her. He was her brother; there was only a year between them. How could she forget him?

Her childhood was here, in this flat. She could never

return without seeing things that jolted memories. The sofa where she and her brothers had fought about which television programme they'd watch. The area just outside her father's study door where they'd always tiptoe in case they disturbed him at work. The kitchen table, scene of many squabbles and family debates about music, books, films and, if she remembered correctly, the best way to fry an egg. What an odd thing to discuss, she thought. But it had been ongoing for several days.

Celia had said she liked them the way her mother did them. But Graham and her father preferred them over easy. 'Over easy, over easy,' Graham had chanted. Very American, she thought.

It was one of her earliest memories; she must have been five at the time. But, there it was in her head – all of them talking about fried eggs, and a tension in the air. Bibi had been sitting at one end of the table, her father at the other. She and Roddy had been sitting opposite each other, and Graham was at the end, beside her mother. It was before either Liz or Beth were born.

Celia pictured it. 'I liked the way Polly cooked eggs,' Graham had said. Her father had agreed, and Bibi had been angry at that. 'Oh you would,' she had said. 'Polly does everything better than me.'

Then Callum had said, 'Oh for heaven's sake, Bibi. We're only talking about eggs. You're not jealous, are you? Polly's gone home. Nothing happened. She fries a mean egg, give her that.' Then he'd looked at her, his head to one side. His expression, Celia recalled, had been slightly quizzical.

She vividly remembered the American woman who had come to stay. When she thought about it, it seemed odd. For a long time, before her father got ill, people were always coming to stay. Writers, painters, musicians and academics who were in town for the Festival, or lecturing or touring, or maybe just friends visiting. The house hummed with guests. But Polly had stuck in Celia's head.

Once, when she was in her early teens, she'd asked Bibi about Polly. 'Oh, goodness,' Bibi had said, 'fancy you remembering that. You must have been five at the time. Yes, Polly, we met her in New York, years and years ago. She came to see us; she stayed for two or three weeks.'

There was nothing in this flat that did not have a memory attached to it. She even remembered having to stand on tiptoe to reach the doorknobs. And there had been a time when her eyes were level with the top of the table.

She had been standing gripping the table, peering over at her mother and Polly as they talked. The atmosphere had been tense. Polly was crying; Bibi was leaning her elbow on the table, hand cupped in her chin.

She vaguely remembered Polly saying, 'I have a right.'

Celia wasn't one to pry, so it wasn't without guilt that she went into her mother's bedroom, opened the door of her bedside cabinet and took out the black lacquered box that contained her private papers. She found Bibi's will, her birth and marriage certificates, along with Callum's death certificate. There were Mother's Day and Valentine's cards that Celia and her brothers and sisters had made at school for Bibi. Locks of hair, carefully labelled and kept in small polythene bags. There were also some old black-and-white photographs Celia had never seen before. Bibi, Callum and another woman at Arthur's Seat, all smiling; Bibi and the same woman in this kitchen. There were the remnants of a meal on the table in front of them; Celia and Graham were there too.

Beneath the photographs was an airmail letter. Celia, knowing she shouldn't, opened it up and read. It was headed *Polly Woods, New York*.

My dear Bibi,

It is spring, my favorite time in New York. I am slowly getting my life together. But (and I know you won't want to hear this) I miss Callum, and I miss my Graham even more. Hardly an hour goes by that I don't think about him. I still cry nights.

I am on the roof of my building as I write. I have bought a cat to cheer me. I called her Bibi, after you. I am so grateful to you. What a heart you have!

This is for the best, I know it. But I am in awe of you. You took Callum back – I don't know if I could have found it in me to do such a thing after such a long separation. And you took Graham to bring up as your own. Such kindness, such forgiveness – good things will happen to you, I just know it.

I sold two pictures last week. Now I have enough to keep me till November, at least. Meantime I have made some resolutions. I will quit drinking. I will be kinder to people. I will try to be like you.

I cannot tell you how much I love you. I will pray for you. I hope some day we will meet.

All my love,
Polly

It had gone awfully quiet. Beth, sitting stiffly on her bed and desperate for a pee, wondered if Celia had left. She didn't want to stay hiding in this bedroom any longer than necessary. She slipped into the hall and tiptoed down the corridor, peeked into the living room. It was empty, as was the kitchen. Excellent, she thought, I'll catch the end of the truly terrible film.

She heard a sound in Bibi's bedroom, a rustle, a movement, a sigh, and went to investigate. Celia was sitting on the bed, rummaging through the black lacquer box where her mother kept all her secret treasures. She saw her sister take out a letter, open it and start to read.

Afraid of being discovered, Beth fled back to her bedroom.

Celia put the letter back into its envelope. Swiftly replaced everything as it had been in the cabinet, hoping it looked as if nothing had been disturbed. Then she went back to the kitchen, picked up her handbag and car keys, and left.

Beth returned to the living room. From behind the curtain she watched Celia get into her car and drive away. That's not right, she thought, reading Bibi's personal letters. That's prying. Of course, she had read Bibi's diary. But the diaries were on open display in the kitchen; anyone could pick them up and look at them. That was different.

The Rain Routine

Louis and Lara bothered Bibi. They didn't behave like the children they used to be. They were mini adults. They didn't bicker or barge about, they never raised their voices, and they tidied up their toys and books before going to bed. Bibi thought it wasn't natural. She remembered them as they had been when they'd visited her in Edinburgh eighteen months ago. They'd skateboarded down the corridor, fought over the television remote, burst into rooms breathless with excitement at some piece of trivia – there was a new flavour of ice cream in the shop, they'd seen a man with a dog that had only three legs, there was a huge spider in the bathroom. They'd been noisy, annoying at times, and fun. They were full of the stuff of childhood that Bibi loved. And she loved children.

She watched in unspoken surprise when Louis took three buckets from their place at the back door, carried them upstairs and placed them in a row, several feet apart on the landing. The weather the seagulls had been predicting had arrived. James had stood in the garden watching it rolling in – darkness, wind and a sudden merciless downpour. He fled indoors and told Bibi he'd never seen anything like it. 'There's nothing between you and the weather in a place like this.'

Bibi, observing the placing of the buckets, said he'd stood like a fool waiting to get drenched. 'We get proper, healthy wet rain here. It's good for you.'

James said he doubted that, and taking the towel that was hanging on the back of the kitchen door, started to dry his hair. He came and stood beside Bibi and saw the bucket ritual.

'What's this?'

'I should imagine,' said Bibi, 'that it rains indoors as well as out.'

James said that was just wonderful. As he spoke he heard the steady dripping of water into a plastic container. He could not hide his horror. 'This is terrible.'

Bibi confronted Liz, who was in the living room reading a magazine, two years out of date. 'Your son just put a couple of buckets on the landing.'

'It's what we have to do when it rains. He's used to it.'

'You can't live like this,' said Bibi. 'Get the roof fixed.'

Liz asked, 'What with? I haven't any money.'

'It's an insurance job,' said Bibi.

'It would be if we had any insurance. Drew bought the house outright. No mortgage, no demand to get buildings insurance.'

'Why didn't he fix it himself?'

Liz said he'd meant to but hadn't got round to it. 'He did the front bit, but lost interest. He moved on to alternative methods of central heating. He didn't get round to doing that either. He left us to go back to university.'

Bibi said that she hated Drew. 'I hate that he's abandoned you in this house. It leaks.'

Liz got up and headed for the kitchen. 'I know.' She turned to James. 'The buckets will need emptying soon. They fill up quickly when it rains like this.'

James said she should get bigger buckets. Liz told him that they'd be too heavy when full.

'You know all about it,' said Bibi. 'It's a rain routine. It's no way to live.'

'Like you didn't bring us all up in poverty? I remember you struggling up the stairs with bags of potatoes and making huge pots of soup with cheap vegetables. You sitting at the table with a cup of tea, not eating because there wasn't enough to go round.'

'I was frugal for a purpose, for Callum, so he could write. I was born to be frugal. It's an art. I was good at it. You are not. You are living in a leaky house with two depressed and insecure children. I hate seeing you this way.'

Liz said, 'Don't bring my children into this. They have nothing to do with you.'

Outside the wind rushed round the house, rain drummed on the windows, and the dripping became a steady run of water.

'Your children have everything to do with me. I'm their grandmother,' said Bibi. 'If it wasn't for me, they wouldn't be here.'

Liz told her she was interfering. Bibi said of course she was interfering. It was her job. 'You'll miss me when I'm gone and not doing it any more.'

Liz said she wouldn't.

Bibi told her that wasn't a very nice thing to say.

'I'd miss you but not the interfering,' said Liz. 'I'd better go and see my depressed and insecure kids. They'll have overheard you, and they get upset easily these days.'

James went upstairs to empty the buckets on the landing.

Alone in the kitchen, Bibi started to cook supper, rattling pots and furiously chopping vegetables, something she'd always done when she was fighting with Callum. It wasn't her house, and she didn't think she had any right to take over the preparation of meals. But kitchens were her natural domain, and she couldn't help herself.

Liz sat on the sofa, lifted Lara on to her knee and kissed her. 'How're you doing?'

Lara told her she didn't like it when people fought. Liz agreed; neither did she.

Lara asked, 'Where would we be? Grandma said if it wasn't for her we wouldn't be here. So where *would* we be?'

Florence, Liz thought. She explained that Bibi was her mother and had brought her into the world, and in turn she'd brought them into the world. 'So if my mother hadn't given birth to me, I wouldn't have been here to give birth to you. We wouldn't have existed.'

The concept of not existing was beyond Lara. She sucked her thumb, looking confused.

Louis said, 'So everything's Grandma's fault, then?'

Liz pondered this. Perhaps, if her mother hadn't painted such a romantic picture of her days in the cottage with Callum, she herself would have been more cynical about Drew's vision of living the good life, self-sufficient and not a wage slave. She knew this wasn't really true; she'd been swept along by Drew's dream, and had willingly left university to join him in pursuing it. But it was good to blame someone. So she said, 'Perhaps it is.'

'I think,' said Celia, 'Graham was the child Callum dreamed of. He was the wild one – moody, quick-tempered. He never worked at school, he was rude to his teachers. He got excluded regularly. He'd sit in his room playing his music, hardly talking to the rest of us. He was the stuff of adoration.'

Peter said that a good way to get adored by people was to ignore them.

Celia nodded and agreed. It was eight o'clock. They had finished their evening meal and had lingered at the table drinking coffee; neither of them could face clearing up.

'I think Callum understood Graham, he knew how to handle him. The rest of us just worked at school, came and went, had mates and lived our little lives. I'm sure we were a disappointment to him. We didn't rebel. Actually, Bibi and Callum were such a pair, I think we all grew up looking for a bit of peace and quiet. Except Graham.'

Her most vivid memory of her brother was of him leaning against the kitchen wall, thumbs hooked on the back pockets of his jeans, watching with scorn as Bibi and Callum bickered about the correct way to gut and cook a salmon they'd been given. 'Who cares?' he'd said. 'It's a dead fish, for God's sake.'

'He was good at being scornful. He had a fizz about him

– imploding energy. He always looked like he knew things you didn't, and he wasn't going to tell you what they were. And the girls that hung about him, you should have seen them, a new girlfriend every week. They used to come to the flat all the time, and when he wouldn't talk to them, which was often, they'd sit in the kitchen and talk to Bibi. Graham was the perfect teenager, a junior James Dean.'

Peter said, 'You miss him.'

'I think about him every day. Can't help it. When someone just disappears from your life, you are left wondering and waiting.'

Celia had thought Graham would come back. That he would reappear as abruptly as he'd left. So she had waited. On the first day of his disappearance, the family sat round the table as Bibi served supper, and Celia asked where her brother was. 'He's not coming home to eat,' Bibi told her. The next morning, when Graham still wasn't there, she had asked where he was. 'He didn't come home last night,' Bibi said. After days of quizzing, Callum finally admitted, 'He's gone to America.' Then to Bibi, 'Well, they have to know sometime.'

'When's he coming back?' Celia asked.

'We don't know,' said Callum.

'Why has he gone?' Celia wanted to know.

'He wanted to go,' said Bibi. 'He has always wanted to go to America.'

Every day she'd come home from school and ask if there had been a letter or a phone call from Graham, and she'd been told no. At last Bibi had said, 'Please don't ask about him any more. I can't bear it.'

Celia flooded her parents with questions. Where is he staying? Whereabouts in America? What will he do there? 'I mean, he doesn't even know anybody there.'

'He's Graham,' said Callum. 'He'll make friends. He'll meet people.'

At night, lying in her room, Celia had heard Bibi and Callum talking; low voices, murmurs drifted through to her. Once she'd heard Bibi say, 'I know it's all my fault. I know I should have done things differently. You don't need to keep pointing that out to me. I admit it, I'm to blame.' And she'd cried.

After a month with no word from his missing son, Callum had gone looking for him. He'd flown to New York. 'I'll cover my old stamping ground,' he'd said. 'Look up some friends. Somebody must know something.'

He'd returned after three weeks looking frail and tired. It was then that Celia realised her father was broken-hearted. 'Nothing,' he had told Bibi. 'Nothing. They left the city, went to Canada. I don't know where. There's no sign of them anywhere.'

'Them?' Celia had asked. 'Who is them?'

'He's with an old friend,' Bibi said. 'Someone we once knew.'

Celia said, 'At least he's with somebody. He's not alone, then.'

Callum had said, 'No, he's not alone.'

Now Celia said, 'Graham was the talented one. He did well in his art class, got great marks for his essays. It all seemed effortless for him. He never worked at it. Not like me, the family swot.'

Peter said that she'd done well. Her family, he knew for a fact, were proud of her.

'Yeah, but Graham was the one. He was the star.'

Peter took her hand, kissed it. 'Not to me he isn't.'

'I don't know where he is. I have almost forgotten what he looked like, and I doubt I would even recognise him. I could have passed him in the street without knowing it. It leaves a void, a hole in my life.'

'You've got issues about people leaving without telling you where they're going.'

Celia agreed with that. 'Thing is, the shame. I don't understand that. The grief, the guilt, the sense of loss, I get all that. But Bibi was full of shame, I remember that. What was that about?'

Peter said it might be that she hadn't told Graham he was adopted.

'Perhaps,' said Celia.

'Well,' said Peter, 'you'd better go back to the flat and have another rake about, see what you can find. Now that you've taken up snooping, you might as well keep on snooping.'

Being Naughty

It was pointless, Bibi thought. This ground was raddled with stones. It needed to be dug and sieved, dug some more, fertilised, raked and treated with kindness. She could tell that nothing much had grown here. It was clear to her that Drew and Liz had, in a lather of eagerness, planted as much as they could, then waited for a glorious crop to appear. 'All enthusiasm and no brains,' she said. 'All they provided was nibbles for the rabbits.'

She dug some more, shoved the spade into the earth, heaved up some soil and turned it over on to the ground. More stones. She sighed. Whenever she thought about Drew she had a vision of a man hurtling through life, arms spread and hollering. 'A fool,' she said. 'Like me.'

This morning, she'd been alone in the kitchen with Louis. He'd asked her if it was all her fault.

'Is what all my fault?' asked Bibi.

'All this.' He'd spread his arms to indicate not just the room they were in, but the house and the garden beyond.

'Why is it my fault?' said Bibi.

'Because you said if it wasn't for you we wouldn't be here.'

Bibi thought about this and told Louis he shouldn't listen to other people's conversations.

Louis pointed out that he hadn't been listening. He'd heard, he couldn't help hearing; Bibi had been shouting.

Bibi said, 'Ah.' She'd give him that. 'But none of this has anything to do with me.'

'So why did they come here?' asked Louis.

'They wanted to have a home, where they could have a good life. Somewhere that would be good for children. I gave them some money to help them along.'

'You helped,' said Louis. 'So it *is* your fault.'

Bibi said she didn't think so and had gone outside to consider this accusation. She liked the air here. It was soft, scented with sea and hills. She looked at the garden. James had dug half of it, complaining vigorously about how he hated it and how it was ruining his shoes. She thought she might finish the job; a bit of physical labour always clears the head, she thought. She plunged the spade into the ground, heard the rattle of stones and tutted. 'Rubbish soil.' She dug some more. 'My fault indeed. Anything goes wrong, blame your mother. That's what they're there for.' She yanked out some weeds. 'Everything's my fault. Teenage pregnancies, me, I did that. Binge drinking, I showed the world the way. Global warming, my fault. I left the lights on one night. Blame me for everything.'

She finished a row, started another. Sweating now. She thought about Liz. Always the quiet one, too uncomplaining, 'Should have taught her to scream and shout and stamp her foot.' She dug some more. 'She was too quiet. People always ignore the quiet ones. They slip through life unnoticed.'

She remembered Liz as a child – the one who always did as she was told. 'She avoided confrontations,' Bibi said, panting and digging. 'She hated arguments. But then, she would. She saw a lot of them.'

She stopped digging and stood, casting her mind back. Liz had been about eight when Graham left. 'Plenty of arguments at that time. Callum blamed me for the whole catastrophe. Liz would have heard all that. She sloped off to her room when we were fighting.' Then, Bibi remembered, during the next few years a gloom had fallen on the flat, and all conversations led back to Graham. 'Poor girl, growing up and us talking about her missing brother all the time. We let her go and didn't notice. She ran into the arms of the first person who paid attention to her.'

She started digging again. 'If I hadn't taken Graham on in the first place, none of this would have happened. If Callum and I hadn't gone to New York, he wouldn't have met Polly and Graham wouldn't even have been born. Then again, if I hadn't stamped out in a fury Callum wouldn't have been free to sleep with Polly. If I had noticed that blue and white striped shirt in the wardrobe, I wouldn't have stormed back to Edinburgh, leaving Callum alone . . .'

She left her spade in the ground as she waved her arms, going through all this. 'It's a domino effect: one thing goes wrong and a whole trail of disasters follow, and it all started with me being obsessed with a woman across the alley kissing a man I thought was my husband. So, all that's happened is definitely down to me. Ach. Damn and bugger, everything *is* my fault.'

Louis and Liz, at an upstairs window, observed Bibi standing alone in the vegetable patch, waving her arms and talking to herself.

'Do you think she's gone mad?' asked Louis.

'Sometimes,' said Liz. 'Mostly I think she spends a lot of time on her own; she talks to herself.'

James was washing the car, a chore he infinitely preferred to digging, when Bibi approached him.

'James, I need you to do me a favour. I want you to take Liz out for the evening. You could go to the inn along the road for a drink. I'll give you some money.'

'I agreed to drive you. There was nothing said about digging or taking people out.'

'I think Liz is in the doldrums. She's just sitting in this ramshackle house not making plans for her future. An evening out will help clear her head. She has important decisions about her future to make.'

James thought an evening out, a few hours in a place where he wasn't worried about the ceiling falling in on him, might be a good thing. He agreed.

Inside, Bibi met Liz coming down the stairs. 'I need you to do me a favour. I need you to ask James to take you out for the evening. It would do him good. He's spending too much time with an old lady.'

Liz said she didn't want to go out for the evening. 'I don't like leaving the children. Not since Drew left. They're still upset and confused.'

'I can look after them,' said Bibi. 'I know all about children. It would only be for a couple of hours. They'd hardly know you were gone. Please, I'd be very grateful.'

Liz had always found it hard to say no to her mother, so she said she would go out with James. 'But only for a little while.'

Bibi said, 'Wonderful. Go out and ask him. Do it now, before you change your mind.' This was splendid. Liz would invite James out, and he would agree to go. Bibi had made sure of that. She would have the children to herself for a while. She'd help them let off steam, tell them stories and send them to bed happy.

Roddy told Ruth he'd joined a photographic club, he'd be late. 'Don't wait up.'

Ruth said she wouldn't.

He picked up Erica and took her to a country hotel some miles out of town.

'Good choice,' said Erica. 'I don't think anybody you know will see us here.'

He smiled and said he hoped not. 'I don't want a huge row with my wife. I want us to part amicably.'

'Is that possible?' asked Erica.

Roddy thought it was. 'We hardly communicate any more. I think she'd be glad to be on her own again. She's got a lot of friends and she might not be too old to find somebody else.'

'How do you know she hasn't done that already?'

'Ruth? I don't think so, she's not the type. She's very straight. She likes an ordered life. An affair might be messy.'

'Do you still have sex?'

276

He shook his head. 'That's an awfully direct question for a first date.'

'I don't think so,' she said. 'I like to know these things. I mean, if you're not sleeping with your wife, you might be looking to sleep with me. And that's not on the cards. Not on the first date, anyway.'

'Well, best to get that out of the way. I wasn't planning to sleep with you, either.'

He ordered duck. She wanted fish.

'Red or white?' he said.

She told him she usually drank red wine. 'White doesn't agree with me.'

He told her she would have to drink most of the bottle, he was driving.

'Fine,' she said. 'Suits me.'

He told her he found her very matter-of-fact. Actually, she reminded him of his mother, but he didn't tell her that.

'I am matter-of-fact,' she said. 'I didn't used to be. But I started to find dealing with people who didn't say what they meant hard to do. It cuts through the layers of social nonsense if people are honest. I can't be doing with all the diplomacy and politeness and innuendo you get these days. Life's too short.'

Now, Roddy thought, she was sounding like his father.

He told her about himself. How he'd become a banker mainly, he thought, to annoy his father. And had married a polite, careful, strait-laced girl mainly to annoy his mother.

Erica asked what the wedding was like.

'Very odd, now I think about it. Two sets of people who didn't mingle. My family and her family. Her mother was all in pink, from large hat to shoes. My mother wore a long dress, cheesecloth I think, with a floppy straw hat and lots and lots of beads. My dad wore a claret-coloured velvet suit. I don't know where he got it, borrowed it I suppose. All the other men were in morning suits. At the reception my family and friends hogged the bar; Ruth's lot sat at little tables and chatted amongst themselves. Her family arranged it all. They'd hired a band that played dance music. Then my father phoned some people he knew and they turned up with their instruments and played Celtic folk rock with guitars, pipes, whistles and drums, and my lot danced and Ruth's lot looked on.'

Erica said she wished she'd been there. Roddy didn't have to ask which group she'd have joined.

'Then I worked in a bank up north and eventually ended up here. Two lovely daughters, one grandson I adore. That's me.'

'Did you take your kids camping in France or Italy?'

'Holidays in Cornwall,' he said.

'Have you had an affair, then? Since your marriage is so unsatisfactory.'

Roddy told her no.

She had dropped out of university – 'Something I regret' – to travel with her then boyfriend across India, then Australia. Back home, she'd worked in a club in Camden, then with a small theatre company, 'Running errands, helping with scenery, prompting, and playing insignificant walk-on parts.' After that she helped some friends set up an art gallery in the Lake District. 'A happy time,' she said. 'Then I got pregnant and decided to keep the baby. I have made occasional good decisions.' There had been a spell working in a tourist office and a short time in a radio station. 'I fetched up here because the man I was with bought a hotel. We were going to run it together. But he didn't like the life. He sold. We split. I took the job I'm in because the hours suited me. Here I am.'

'You've had an interesting life,' he said.

'Compared to yours I have. Roddy, you've shocked me with the way you've spent your days on this planet. I think you get nothing out of ten for being brave and nothing out of ten for doing what makes you happy. Nothing out of ten for life, really.'

He said he knew that. 'I've been thinking about it a lot. Time to change.'

When the time came, she insisted they split the bill. 'No protests, I asked you out. Really I should pick up the tab.'

This embarrassed him.

'Don't be silly,' she said. 'It's how things are done. You'd better start getting used to it, if you want to see me again.'

He told her he did.

He drove her home. They sat in the car chatting. He told her he didn't want coffee, he'd had enough already. Any more and he wouldn't sleep.

'And since there's to be no sex, hardly any point in you coming up to my flat,' she said.

'I wouldn't say that. I like to talk.'

'Still,' she said, 'I'm tired. It's time for bed.' Then she said, 'Would you like to go to the cinema on Wednesday? There's a film on I'd like to see.'

He said he would, very much. But sometime he'd like to ask her out.

'Fine. You ask me out after we've seen the film. We can have a Chinese afterwards.'

'We'll go for a Chinese meal and I'll ask you out, then,' he said.

She nodded; that would be excellent.

It was almost eleven when Roddy drew up at his front door. The house was in darkness; he thought Ruth would be in bed. She rarely stayed up after half past ten. He locked the car, and stood a moment looking at the stars. The air was soft; summer was on its way and he felt more than happy – joyous. The sweetness of it all, a new relationship, a new friend. He felt lost in laughter. He could sing out loud. He could dance. He hadn't felt like this since he was seventeen.

Inside, he walked through the living room to the kitchen to check the back door was locked. He noticed a bottle of whisky and two glasses on the table by the sofa and thought that odd. Ruth never drank whisky. She must have had a couple of friends round, he decided.

He climbed the stairs, taking off his jacket as he went. He usually came to bed after Ruth, and had got into the habit of leaving the landing light on, rather than switching on the light in the bedroom and risking waking her. He put his jacket on the chair by the door, then bent down to untie his laces. Face near the floor, he noticed a pair of hush puppies and Argyll socks that definitely weren't his. In a heap, near to them, were a pair of corduroy trousers and a checked shirt. 'Not mine,' he said.

He stood up. Looked at the bed. Ruth was in her usual place, on her side of the bed, sleeping deeply. Next to her was Jim Finney, the farmer. They were both naked. Jim was on his stomach, hairy back exposed, brutish balding head on the pillow. His mouth was open and he was snoring. As was Ruth. They were not entwined like lovers. They looked like a couple who'd been sleeping in the same bed together for a long, long time.

It wasn't really that his wife had been sleeping with another man that caused Roddy's rage, though that hurt. It was the sight of a man he loathed lying warm and content in his bed; indeed, on his side of the bed, looking relaxed as if he belonged there. Roddy felt betrayed, usurped. The red mist descended. He gripped the end of the bed – antique, cast-iron, bought when Ruth was in her phase of country cottage decor – and in a heart-pounding fury heaved from the floor, eyes bulging, shaking with effort. He held it for a few seconds and let it crash down again. The room buzzed, the floor shook, the clang resounded through the house.

Ruth sat up, clutching the duvet. Jim leapt to his feet, shouting, 'What the hell?' He was ready for a fight, and was not the sort to think that having no underpants on did anything to mar his dignity. Roddy stood trembling, his face contorted, but not, as Ruth thought, with hurt and fury. His pain was physical. Lifting an iron bedstead containing two people, one over seventeen stone, had been too much for him. He'd done something dreadful to his back, and was in agony.

He walked stiffly from the room, and only when he was out of Ruth and Jim's view did he bend double, clutch the small of his back and whimper. He staggered to the spare room, and eased himself on to the bed. The pain was excruciating. He lay in a cold sweat, mumbling curses and listening to the scramble of Jim shoving on his clothes, thundering down the stairs and out the door.

Ruth tiptoed down the corridor and stuck her head into the room. 'Roddy? Are you all right?'

'No, I'm not. Go away,' he said.

'I think we should talk.'

'I don't,' he said. 'Just go away. Go a-bloody-way.'

'I think you need to know he means nothing to me. It was just the attention. I felt wanted.'

Roddy reached for a pillow to support his aching back. Ruth moved in to help.

'Get away from me,' he said. 'Don't come near me. I told you to go away. Get out.'

She stood a moment, said, 'It's your fault as much as mine. You never so much as speak to me, far less touch me,' and left.

He lay in the dark, closed his eyes. The pain was awful, it hurt to move, it hurt to breathe. The shock, though, was slipping away. He shivered and slowly eased himself under the duvet. Bloody cow, he thought. Bitch. Effing woman. Who'd have thought it? Ruth having an affair. He was consumed with rage. And beneath that was a small bubble of relief. Now he would not have to tell her gently he wanted to leave her. He could just go. He was free.

It hadn't been Bibi's intention to break the sofa in her daughter's living room. She'd only wanted her grand-children to let off some steam and had instigated some boisterous games. As soon as Liz and James had left the house, she had turned to Louis and Lara, clapped her hands and said, 'Let's have some fun. Let's be naughty.'

At first, the children had been reluctant to do anything that was against the household rules. But there was something irresistible about charging from room to room, out the front door and round the house in a high-speed game of chase. Not that Bibi could run at all quickly. She was the greasy monster chasing the poor lost orphans she wanted to eat for her supper. She wielded a soup ladle as she cackled and lumbered after them. She hid behind doors and jumped out at them, sent them squealing, tumbling out into the garden. She came after them waving the ladle, shouting, 'Where are those children? They look very tasty to me.' More squeals.

That game over, Bibi studied her grandchildren and thought they looked wonderful. They were red of face, panting and smiling. That's how children ought to be, she thought. And wondered aloud what they should do next. 'I know. Let's jump on the sofa.'

Louis said they were definitely not allowed to do that.

'Who's to know?' asked Bibi. 'I won't tell. Will you?'

'No,' they said.

'Let's do it,' said Bibi. 'Let's be naughty.'

It proved to be a popular activity. Bibi didn't join in. She supervised, thinking sofa-jumping would do nothing for her knees. They bothered her.

At first it went well. Leaping and landing on a soft surface is always pleasing, especially for those who are under ten. It just got a bit out of hand. The children went too far, leapt too high, landed too roughly. The old piece of furniture creaked. Then, when Louis climbed on the arm and threw himself with abandon on to the cushions, it snapped.

'Oh dear,' said Bibi. 'I don't like the sound of that.'

Louis slid to the floor and stood beside her, looking dumbstruck. 'What are we going to do?'

'We are going to have some hot chocolate. After that, you and Lara are going to bed. And I will fix the sofa. Nobody will know. I don't tell tales.'

Half an hour later, Bibi surveyed the damage. It was worse than she'd thought. The sofa was, under its cushions and throws, wooden. Three of the base slats had snapped. 'Dear me,' she said. 'Tricky.'

Rummaging through the kitchen drawers, she found an old tube of Superglue and a ball of string. 'Excellent,' she said. 'Won't take me a minute.'

It took two hours. She was tired from being a monster and supervising the jumping, and needed to lie down. But she managed to glue the broken slats together, then wind a tight string binding round each of the breaks. She carefully put the sofa back together – slats, main base cushion, throws and scatter cushions. 'Nobody would guess,' she said. But she didn't test her handiwork by sitting down on it. She went to bed.

❀ ❀ ❀

It was after midnight when James and Liz got home. Mostly because they'd drunk too much, they stumbled and clattered into the house. Bibi heard them, and sighed. It was an old, old habit she'd thought she'd given up – this business of not sleeping properly till she knew everyone was home and safe.

The pair had gone to the pub and drunk beer. At first they'd talked about Bibi. She was the only thing they had in common. They agreed she was bossy and devious and energetic, and her age didn't come into it. That was how the woman was. It bonded them to admit that, despite all her faults, they both liked her. 'Don't really know why,' said James.

He told her about his life in Manchester and his affair with Vicky. 'Though it wasn't really an affair; we never did go to bed together.' It was like confessing to a stranger on a train. He didn't imagine he'd see her again after he and Bibi left.

'She was too young,' said Liz.

'*I* was too young. She was a lot older than me really. In the end I behaved like a prat. I was a fool. I stood in their garden yelling her name and the whole street was out looking at me. I don't think I was sane at the time.'

'I definitely wasn't sane when I said I'd marry Drew. I was dizzy with romance and dreams and Florence.'

'Actually, when I think about it,' said James, 'I don't think Bibi was in a balanced frame of mind when she and

Callum decided to marry. She was running away from her father.'

'Love,' said Liz. 'Who needs it?'

James said he didn't, that was for sure. He fetched them another two pints. By their third, they'd stopped talking and started chattering, leaning towards one another, agreeing on tastes in music, films they liked, and sharing embarrassing moments from their pasts.

Liz was heady; alcohol made her flirty. At eleven o'clock she suggested they go for a swim. 'It's warm enough.'

'No it isn't,' said James.

'Come on,' said Liz. 'Let's just walk on the beach. It's ages since I did that. Me and Drew used to do it all the time. We'd swim at night, naked. It's the loveliest thing in the world. My father wrote a poem about it.'

They drove a couple of miles along the coast, parked, and walked to the beach. Liz took off her shoes, curled her toes into the sand, then ran to the water's edge. She waved to James to join her, but he wouldn't. He was wearing his best designer trousers and didn't want to ruin them. She was cold on the way back to the car; her jeans were soaked from the knee down. He put his jacket on her shoulders, and kept his arm round her. 'Soon have you home.'

Then he asked about the poem. 'Was it any good?'

Liz shrugged. 'I think so. I don't read poetry that much. He wrote it after a stay in St Ives; dedicated it to all his children. Later, in a book of his collected poems he dedicated it to Graham – the lost child.'

James said that Bibi never spoke about Graham.

'He went away, just walked out, when I was about eight.

I don't remember much about him. He was tall, moody, had a lot of adoring girlfriends. He went to America. That's all I know. Except that Bibi and Callum fought about it for ages afterwards. I hate fighting.'

James said so did he.

'My mother and father loved a good fight. I think they got off on it. I'd hear them arguing about something, then Bibi would say, "OK, you win this one. Though it's my turn to win, you won last time." They just fought for fun. I hated it.'

James thought he would have too.

'And they had a running-away rota. When all of us kids were playing up, bickering about food, which was what we usually bickered about, Bibi would say, "It's my turn to run away." Callum would say, "OK. But I get to do it next." I sort of thought one of them would go missing when I was little. Of course, they never did.'

'But it worried you,' said James.

'Yeah,' said Liz. 'I can see now it was only a way of keeping sane. They had a lot of mouths to feed and very little money. I suppose it amused them.'

Back at the house, Liz went upstairs to take off her damp clothes and put on her dressing gown. James waited in the kitchen. Bibi heard Liz going into her room, then a few minutes later coming out again and tiptoeing softly back down the stairs. She didn't like the sound of that.

'You might have put the kettle on,' said Liz.

James told her he'd been drinking beer, and now he wanted more beer. Liz joined him. They opened the cans Bibi had bought for Drew, not knowing he wouldn't be there.

'Let's go to the living room. It's warmer.'

Bibi heard them move across the hall. She hoped, in vain, that they wouldn't sit on the sofa. She held her breath, waiting for the cries of horror when it broke beneath them. Nothing. She smiled. Congratulated herself on her handiwork. She was quite the expert with Superglue and string.

James and Liz sat side by side, and if they noticed the sofa was sagging towards the middle, pushing them closer than they intended, they were both too drunk to mention it.

'You going to stay here?' said James.

Liz said she didn't know. 'I've nowhere else to go. Unless I go back to my mother in Edinburgh. There's enough room, but if I did, I'd feel like I'd failed.'

'Failed at what?'

'At this life. Even though I'm beginning to think I don't really like it.'

'If you're going to fail at something, best to fail at something you want to do. If you fail at something you hate doing, it's like a double waste of time. Failure after years spent on a hated project.'

'Who told you that?' said Liz.

'My father,' said James. 'He also told me to look after my shoes.' He held his foot up and considered his trainers. 'He wouldn't approve of these. And all that digging hasn't done much for them.'

She put her hand on his knee and said, 'Sorry.'

He looked at her and smiled. So she kissed him. She didn't quite know what had got into her, except more alcohol than she was used to; this wasn't the sort of thing she did. Ever.

James was shocked. But only for seconds. Then he folded her into his arms and kissed her back. He loosened her robe, eased her down on to the sofa, and kissed her again.

This, Liz thought drunkenly, was thrilling. Making love while her mother slept in another room, something she hadn't done in years, not since she was a teenager, was exquisitely naughty.

It was a swift and energetic burst of passion. They were both spent and sweaty. James looked down at Liz, touched her cheek, thinking that now was the time to pay her a compliment. He was about to say she was beautiful, but at that moment the sofa snapped dramatically and collapsed. They crashed through the broken slats to the floor; cushions and ruined wooden frame caved in on top of them.

They scrambled from the debris, pulling on their clothes. Liz looked at the ruins of her sofa. 'Well, talk about the earth moving.'

James said they could have been injured.

'But we weren't,' said Liz. 'And we'd had our fun. So it's fine, isn't it?'

'Can we fix it?' said James.

'We can burn it,' said Liz, pointing at the sofa. 'I think it has finally died. A cremation is in order, and we'll get a few days' heat from that.'

James contemplated a night on the floor. He'd have liked an invitation to Liz's bed, but that had a child in it.

Liz thought about life with nowhere comfortable to sit, and heard the call of a flat in Edinburgh, filled with golden light, that had central heating, two sofas and several empty rooms. Increasingly, she was tempted to go there.

Beth moved in to her mother's flat. She had gone home, packed a suitcase and brought it back with her. She spent most of her time in bed. She lay watching the dust shifting in the shafts of sunlight streaming in through the window. Every now and then she'd get up and go to the kitchen to make tea. She'd bring it back to her bedroom to drink.

Mostly, though, she slept. She hadn't thought it possible to sleep so much. It was all she wanted to do. Even when she needed something to eat, she had to force herself to move.

She dipped, occasionally, into Bibi's diaries, opening one at random and reading. They told of planting and pruning and feeding plants, talks with her gardening cronies, things she'd seen – a fox, a goldfinch.

Tonight, Beth was discovering her mother's thoughts on her father's death.

It's been over a year now. I miss him, but I have almost stopped thinking he will come back. I hear a sound in the flat, and I don't think it's him moving about. Of course I talk to him. But I accept he won't answer. Friends say I was lucky to have known such a close marriage, but that I should get over it. I should expand my life – take classes in something, meet new people. I don't think so. I think now it is time to be lonely. I have to learn to live with it, I have to let loneliness in.

It was a new thought to Beth. She'd always sought company. Let loneliness in – she could do that, too.

That Went Well

Four o'clock in the morning, Celia sat at the computer in Peter's study, looking for Polly Woods on the internet. She liked the night and the silence, only the hum of the computer and the occasional car swishing past outside. The room beyond her desk lamp was dark. It added to her feeling of being a voyeur, spying on another's life. She enjoyed that.

The number of diverse people who shared a name always surprised her. There was an academic Polly Woods, a Polly Woods who was missing, and a Polly Woods who had died in 1834. None was the one she was searching for.

She found a magazine interview, written four years ago, with a Polly Woods who had owned a café in Toronto's harbour area. Flamboyant arts scene figure talks about New York's beat scene and her affair with minor Scottish poet.

Celia hoped Bibi never got to read that. He was never minor to her, she thought.

According to the article, Polly's collages, done during her stay in Greenwich Village when she'd been part of the famous beat scene, were now enjoying a resurgence of favour and were fetching reasonably high prices at auction.

'I used everything that was part of my life, part of me, to build a picture of what it was like to be fragile in a frightening, changing world. So there would be bottle tops, dead flowers, along with my toenail clippings and pubic hair. I was, I am, a deeply sexual being.'

'Oh yuck,' said Celia.

In the top left-hand corner was a photograph. Polly was wearing a green silk suit; her head was wrapped in a vivaciously coloured turban thing.

'I have known heartache,' Polly said. 'My best work came out of that.'

She had decided New York held too many painful memories for her, 'Every street in the area I was living in brought back moments that had been wonderful at the time, but became hard to revisit. I needed to get away.' At this point, according to the article, she had taken a long sip of her coffee and looked out of the window.

'All that happened at a time when I was reunited with my son, Graham, who'd been living with his father in Scotland. That was the best thing that ever happened to me.'

'No mention of Bibi,' Celia said. 'Now why does that not surprise me?'

'It was a traumatic time for Graham and me. He'd run away from his father. We knew he'd be looking for him. We went on the run, which is not as exciting as it sounds. We lived in Chicago for a while, moved to Seattle, before coming to Canada. It was the logical thing to do, since Graham was a British citizen and it would be easier for him to settle here. So we came to Toronto, and things took off for me. I started the coffee bar, and, well, here I am, part of a vibrant arts scene.'

Polly confessed to being an unfit mother. 'I drank,' she said. 'I had always felt insecure. Always lonely. Graham's father couldn't cope. I don't blame him, really. He took the boy back to Scotland and brought him up with his wife. I thought about the boy every single day. I knew if I didn't kick my habit I'd never see him again. So I did, though it wasn't easy.'

The interviewer said she had a voice like old velvet. A voice that suggested a life fully lived, a life of many sorrows.

'Too many cigarettes, probably,' said Celia.

'Then one day, when he was coming up for eighteen, I wrote to Graham. And he came to me. I do not think there are words to express the joy I felt. We had a lot of talking to do. He's my best friend now.'

Celia said, 'I think there has to be more to it all than that.' But it was early morning; birds were starting to sing, the flow of cars outside was getting heavier. Five o'clock. She could get a couple of hours' sleep if she was lucky. She had a busy day ahead.

Ruth had pretended to be asleep when, early in the morning, Roddy had shuffled into the bedroom to get clothes from his wardrobe. She had lain in bed listening as he showered, dressed and went downstairs to make coffee. Then she'd watched from behind the curtain as he crossed the drive to his car.

He was wearing jeans, a poloneck and his leather jacket. She wondered where he was going, dressed like that, and wondered too if he'd be coming back. After he'd gone, she went downstairs, made coffee and sat, worrying.

She ran through sets of scenarios. The worst one was getting thrown out of the house, getting cited for adultery in a messy divorce and ending up living alone in a tiny flat earning a meagre living stacking shelves in a supermarket. She had no qualifications.

She imagined that when her daughters found out what she'd done, they'd side with their father. And there was no point in looking to Jim Finney for help. He would not leave his wife. The farm was in her name.

She wondered if there was anything she could say to Roddy to induce him to stay with her. She rehearsed speeches. She could tell him she'd only slept with Jim once. It had been a silly mistake, an impulse. It meant nothing. At her age it was flattering that a man should find her attractive. 'It's you I love. It's always been you,' she might say.

She went upstairs, showered, dressed, then stripped the bed. She could wash away the night's doings. A bit of soap helped in all sorts of situations. After that, she went back to the kitchen to worry some more. She always did her worrying in the kitchen; the living room was too comfortable for such intricate thinking.

Guilt and fear made her leaden. For the first time in her life, she did not dust and vacuum or phone a friend for a chat. The thing that bothered her most, that chewed into her imaginings, was that everyone she knew would find out she'd been sleeping with a man who was generally considered to be boorish. Though he'd been considerate and kind to her; he'd brought her flowers and frilly underwear. Still, even if she did defend him, she knew she'd be a laughing stock. It was unbearable.

At four o'clock Roddy returned. He walked stiffly into the kitchen, sat down and winced. Ruth asked if he was all right.

He said he was fine, he'd pulled some muscles in his back. 'The doctor says if I take it easy it will heal in a couple of weeks.'

'What the hell were you doing for this to happen, Roddy?' Dr Rogers had asked.

'Moving a bed,' said Roddy.

'Why didn't you get Ruth to help you?'

Roddy had told him Ruth hadn't been available at the time.

Now Ruth sat at the table and asked if that was where Roddy had been, at the doctor's.

'There and other places. I quit my job.'

She stared at him, taking this in. 'Why?'

'I hate it and I'm not very good at it. I think they were happy to see the back of me. In fact, the word euphoric comes to mind. I suspect they were about to do something about me anyway.'

'What will happen?'

'I will get a pension. Reduced, of course, since I'm retiring early. My assistant will step in for the moment, though I think he'll get the job. He's very keen. And as I have several weeks' holiday due, I will not go back. Everyone's happy. Especially me.'

Ruth said, 'What are you going to do?'

'Think,' said Roddy. 'Spend some time wondering what the hell I've been doing with my life. I also saw the lawyer and filed for divorce.'

Ruth's insides turned over. 'Just like that. You saw the lawyer. You didn't talk to me.'

Roddy shook his head. 'Nothing to talk about. I saw you, Ruth. I came into the room and you were in bed with Jim Finney.'

'Don't you think we should have talked before you did this?'

'I caught you in bed with another man. I don't want a polite conversation.'

Ruth said, 'Couldn't we . . .'

Roddy said, 'No.'

'You don't know what I was going to say.'

'I do. Couldn't we try again? Couldn't we work it out? No.' He put his hand on his back, leaned into it, trying to ease the pain. He desperately wanted to lie down.

Ruth said, 'All the years we've been together and you won't give me a chance to explain.'

Roddy said, 'No.'

He told her he'd met someone, but nothing had happened. She had just reminded him of how a relationship was meant to be. 'We talk. She makes me smile. I'd just about forgotten about that. She gave me nothing out of ten for the life I've led. And she was right.'

'I think nothing out of ten is a bit cruel,' Ruth said.

'We've bought a house, nice furniture, a couple of cars. We have two beautiful daughters.'

'Our children I don't regret,' said Roddy. 'But Ruth, what were we thinking of? We got married and that was it. We settled down, we saved. We did nothing. We bought a house and sat in it. Ruth, we wasted our young lives playing at being old. The list of things I haven't done is endless. I'm ashamed of myself.'

'We were being sensible.'

'I don't want to be sensible any more. I want to waste my older life playing at being young.'

'You're going to go to rock concerts and backpack across the world?' she sneered.

'Backpack maybe. Rock concerts, I don't think so.' He got up. 'I'm going to lie down. My back's killing me.' He headed for the door. Ruth watched him go. She was in hell. Her stomach chuned.

She pleaded, 'Don't divorce me on the grounds of my adultery. I can't bear to think what people will say. They'll talk about me behind my back. There will be whispers and silences when I enter a room. When they find out I slept with Jim, they'll laugh at me.' She broke down, weeping.

'For God's sake, shouldn't you have thought about that before you did it? Before you took your knickers off. Really, couldn't you have done it with someone else? Why him?'

Ruth said, 'He made a pass. I was flattered.'

Roddy sighed. 'I find that I wish you'd been seeing someone I liked. God knows why. Perhaps I think it would hurt less.' He asked how long it had been going on.

'Two years. I'd leave the bedroom light on if you were out, so he'd know the coast was clear.'

'God,' said Roddy, 'we are pathetic. We can't even have a decent fight. You have a tepid affair with a man you clearly don't like. And I don't even feel like yelling and throwing things. Do you know what? I'm relieved. I have a good reason to divorce you. It's finally over.'

Head in hands, Ruth wept. 'I'm begging you, please, please don't do this. I'll lose my friends. I'll be utterly alone.'

'We'll separate,' said Roddy. 'I'll go. I have rented a flat. You can have most of the savings. I'll need something. You can have the house. I don't want it. Everything I hate is here. Now, please, I have to lie down.'

It wasn't a good Monday morning in Liz's house. The children were tired and irritable. They'd gone to bed late, and high on the sweets and hot chocolate Bibi had given them. Liz was hungover and embarrassed at her alcohol-fuelled passion of the night before. She avoided looking at James, who was also feeling sheepish. He thought his overenthusiastic performance had led to the broken sofa. He didn't know what to say to Liz. He would offer to buy a new one, but hadn't the money.

Bibi ached all over. 'Too much running around,' she said. 'My old body isn't used to it.'

Liz, on her second glass of orange juice, asked what she meant by running around. 'And when did they go to bed, by the way?'

'We played games,' said Bibi. 'Chasing and jumping. We were letting off steam. Can't remember when they finally went upstairs.'

Louis said it was half past ten.

'You know they go to bed at eight on a school night. And you got them high on sugar,' said Liz.

'And you were high on alcohol,' said Bibi. 'I heard you coming home.'

It was Lara who helped the argument along nicely when she came into the kitchen, pointed furiously at Bibi and said, 'You said you were going to fix the sofa.'

Bibi took a long drink of tea, contemplating her reply. 'I did fix it.'

Lara told her it was really, really broken now.

Liz said, 'What do you mean? You said you'd fix the sofa? Did you break it?'

'We were having a little jumping session on it. But it wasn't up to the strain. I did a job on it with Superglue and string.' She went through to the living room to see how her handiwork had held up. 'This sofa was never like this when I went to bed.'

She returned to the kitchen. 'I think someone else must have been jumping on it.'

She saw the abashed expression on both Liz and James's faces as they glanced at one another, then looked away. 'Oh, for heaven's sake, the two of you.'

Lara asked if they'd been jumping on the sofa too.

And Liz said it was time to go to school. 'No more silly questions.'

When they'd gone, Bibi turned to James and said, 'I

rather think we have outstayed our welcome. It's always lovely to see visitors arrive, and even lovelier to see them go away again. Still, I think it all went well.'

James said, 'You do?'

'Oh yes. My grandchildren will always remember me. But we should go tomorrow. We'll say our goodbyes with a splendid meal tonight, then go and see Roddy. I need to say goodbye to him.'

'Surely you'll say hello first,' said James. 'Visiting someone to say goodbye sounds like you're about to die.'

'Did I say goodbye? Sorry, hello, then goodbye, is what I meant.'

He said he was going outside to get some fresh air.

Bibi agreed he might need it and told him she was going into Gairloch to shop for tonight's meal. She took the car keys from the top of the fridge, where he'd left them last night. He watched in horror as she lurched along the road, crunching the gears. He was afraid she was buggering up the clutch.

'Graham Woods,' said Celia. She was in her surgery, changing the CD for a patient who'd told her he'd rather get a filling to Frank Sinatra than Mozart. It was one of those moments when her brain was on automatic. She wasn't using it for anything in particular, so it did a little musing on its own.

Her assistant and her patient looked at one another, puzzled.

'Of course, Graham Woods. He's taken his mother's name.'

She turned and apologised. 'Sorry, I was just thinking about something.' As Frank sang 'Fly Me to the Moon', she picked up the drill and said, 'Open wide.'

Found

Beth miscarried. It was early evening when she started bleeding. She was in the bath and saw the water turn pink. She climbed out, she sat on the bathroom floor, one of Bibi's old towels pressed between her legs, rocking back and forth. She wondered if she should call an ambulance. Perhaps she could bleed to death, she didn't know. Sweat beaded on her brow and upper lip, ran down her face. She stood up, thinking she should go lie in her bed, and blood gushed onto the towel. Tight pains ran across her stomach and lower back. She cried out, took some extra towels and crawled on all fours to her bedroom where she lay, face to the wall, rocking and weeping. She was a failure. Couldn't get along at work, didn't have many friends, couldn't keep a baby inside her. She felt hopeless, very afraid and sweated shame. No, she wouldn't call an ambulance. She didn't want to see anybody; she didn't want anybody to know.

At home, Celia looked up Graham Woods on the internet. She had often looked for Graham Saunders, and found nothing. But there, almost on the first click, was Graham Woods.

ISLA DEWAR

He owned a couple of restaurants in Toronto. He was a fashionable figure. He was married with a young child. He said in an interview he owed a lot to his mother, Polly. 'She's seen me through a lot of bad times.'

There were several restaurant reviews. One said: *The lamb was a joy, tender and pink inside. Served with his renowned dish, Bibi Potatoes, a combination of thinly sliced potatoes, onions, garlic and Gruyère cheese, it was rapturously delicious.*

'Bibi Potatoes,' said Celia. 'That's him. That's got to be him.'

She clicked on a newspaper interview with him in his home, and found a picture. Graham was sitting on a large cream sofa with his wife, Carol, and his son. He was tall, wearing a black shirt and jacket. His hair was cropped short. Celia touched his face on the screen. 'There you are.'

Then she went through to her own living room to tell Peter. 'I've found my brother.'

Bibi cooked what she called her last supper. 'We're off tomorrow. I don't expect you'll be seeing me for a while.'

Liz said, 'Perhaps we can come and visit you in the summer.'

'That would be wonderful,' said Bibi. 'But don't bother being polite. I know you'll be glad to see the back of me.' She was roasting lamb and making her famous potato creation with onions, garlic, cream and Gruyère cheese. 'Everyone loves my potatoes.'

They lingered at the table after the children had gone to

bed. There wasn't anywhere else to sit. At ten Bibi said she had to go upstairs. 'Got a long journey ahead. Don't you be late, James.'

Left alone, James looked awkwardly at Liz and said he was sorry.

'What for?'

'Last night. I got a bit carried away.'

'So did I,' said Liz. 'In fact, I think I started it. I enjoyed it, apart from the sofa collapsing, of course. We had fun. We're grown up. I think we can still be friends, can't we?'

James smiled and nodded.

Liz felt proud of herself. She'd always wanted to say something like that. It was almost as good as saying that golden light reminded her of being in Florence.

Roddy was sleeping when Celia phoned. 'I've found Graham. He's in Toronto.'

'Toronto?' said Roddy.

'He owns a couple of restaurants. I googled him. He has changed his name to Graham Woods. His mother's name.'

Roddy said, 'Ah, so that's why I couldn't track him down. How did you find out?'

'I figured it out. I found a letter to Bibi from his mother when I was watering her plants. Why were we not told?'

'I don't know,' said Roddy. 'Obviously I knew. I remember it all. Bibi and Callum were scared they'd lose Graham. I know they tried to treat him like they treated the rest of us. But he was precious; they thought Polly would come back and steal him away. They meant to tell you. But Liz got ill with meningitis, and they almost lost her. I think it scared them; they couldn't bear to think they might lose another. Then Beth came along, then Dad got ill. And before that he was often away. I think they just kept putting it off.'

'So how did Graham find out about Polly?'

'I have always thought she wrote to him and sent him a ticket to come and see her.'

Celia remembered. It had been when they were doing exams at school. Graham had been at home, studying. He'd have been alone in the house when the post arrived.

'And he went,' said Celia.

'He went and didn't come back. He phoned, but he was angry and he quarrelled with Bibi, then Callum. Apparently, Polly had come to Edinburgh years before to get him back. Bibi and she fought over him; our mother won. She had adopted him; Polly didn't have a leg to stand on. But Graham said he should have been asked, they should have given him the choice of who he wanted to be with.'

'How old would he have been. Four?'

'Yeah, about four.'

'He couldn't have made that sort of decision at that age,' said Celia.

'Actually, I think he could. I remember Polly coming over.'

'So do I,' said Celia. 'I remember her sitting at the table, crying.'

'Yeah,' said Roddy. 'I remember her with Graham. They adored one another. There was a bond. I saw it.'

Celia said she was thinking of going out to Toronto to see him.

'I think you should get in touch first,' said Roddy. 'Don't just turn up.'

'I would never just turn up. I'm not like our mother.'

'How is she, by the way?'

'Fine, I suppose. I haven't heard anything since she phoned to nag me about the plants. How are you?'

He told her he'd hurt his back but he was fine. Celia told him to take care, and she'd let him know what happened when she got in touch with Graham.

Roddy rang off. He went to his small study, switched on his computer, typed *Graham Woods*, and there was his brother, chef and restaurateur, wearing a chef's hat, expounding about the importance of using fresh local produce.

Well good for you, thought Roddy. You got away, you did what you wanted to do.

The moment Graham had come into his life was imprinted in Roddy's mind. A Friday, five o'clock, and Bibi had been at the sink, peeling potatoes. Wasn't she always? he thought. Poor woman must have peeled tens of thousands in her lifetime. No wonder she always ate pasta now. The radio had been on; Celia had been in her high chair, swinging her legs and fiddling with the house keys Bibi had given her to distract her till the food was ready. Roddy had been doing his homework, writing a composition – as they called an essay back then – 'A Day in the Life of a Dog'. He'd heard someone opening the front door. Bibi heard it too, and turned.

'Is that someone coming in?'

He had looked up. There in the doorway was his father in his long black coat; he was holding a baby.

Bibi dropped the potato peeler. 'You,' she said. 'What are you doing here?'

'I came home,' Callum said.

'What's that you've got?'

'What do you think?' said Callum. 'A baby.'

'Yours?'

'Mine. And Polly's. I've brought him to see you.'

Callum had seemed his usual nonchalant self. Bibi had been pale, shaking.

Roddy didn't know what happened next. He'd been sent from the room.

When he came back to eat his supper, Callum and Bibi were at the table. She was feeding the baby with a bottle, saying, 'This is a mess.'

'No it isn't,' Callum had said. 'It's life. It's what goes on.'

'You expect me to take in another woman's child?'

'My child,' said Callum. 'We could give him a good home.'

'You think you can just come back?' Bibi said.

'I think we can make a home. I think we can raise children. I think there's a lot of love here.'

Times had been hard, Roddy remembered that. Bibi had taken in students' theses to type. She'd sat at the kitchen table, working. She'd worn a coat and fingerless gloves to keep warm; she said they couldn't afford to keep the electric fire on.

At the supper table, Bibi had said, 'I don't want

someone else's child. Every time I look at him I'll think of you and her together.'

Callum said, 'You'll come to love him.'

There were nights and nights of voices. Talk, explanations, arguments. Roddy remembered lying in the dark listening to the murmurs drifting through the flat. He remembered feeling scared. Everything was about to change.

Then one day, a week later, Callum was out. Roddy was in the kitchen; the radio was on. It was always on. The baby had been crying and crying. Bibi had been ignoring him, trying to make a pot of soup. She'd given up, crossed the room to the crib – the one Roddy and Celia had both slept in – and stared down at the tiny red-faced infant, his fists clenched, beads of sweat on his brow.

'What are we going to do with you?' Bibi had said.

The child howled.

'Oh for goodness' sake, come on then.' She'd picked him up, crooned soft words, kissed the damp brow and, jiggling him to comfort him, heated a bottle.

That was it, Roddy thought. Graham was in. He stayed. Callum did too. He'd been away for almost eighteen months, but seemed to think he could return, and without much of an explanation, slip back into their lives. And, in a way, he was right. It was how he was – relaxed, confident. He'd slept on the sofa, at first, but in time he'd made his way back into Bibi's bed. She never could resist him, Roddy thought.

❊   ❊   ❊

The next morning at six o'clock, James packed the suitcases into the car while Bibi kissed Liz goodbye.

'Look after yourself. If you're short of money, get in touch. I don't like to think of you being without electricity. Say goodbye to the children. I've left them presents. Books and toys. No sweets, I know you disapprove.' She stood back, considering her daughter. 'It's been wonderful to see you. Remember me kindly.'

'It's been wonderful to see you too. I'll phone, I promise.'

Bibi said, 'Good,' and got into the car.

James lingered. He and Liz smiled at one another. James, suddenly shy, ran his fingers through his hair. Liz did the same.

Look at them, thought Bibi. Hovering round one another, making similar gestures. What's that about?

'Thanks for coming,' said Liz. And she kissed his cheek.

'Kissing,' said Bibi. 'I do not like the look of that.'

James got into the car. Reversed out, and, as they set off along the road, tooted.

'What were you doing kissing my daughter?' said Bibi.

'She kissed me,' said James.

'So I saw,' said Bibi. 'Well, we've got a long journey ahead. I think I'll tell you about Graham.'

Bibi's Letters

Next day, at lunchtime, Celia went back to Bibi's flat. She watered the plants, then went to the bedroom, looking for more information about Polly. She searched through the papers in the bedside cabinet, found nothing. She rummaged through drawers; still nothing. By now, she was obsessed by the woman from New York. She felt no guilt about prying.

She stood, looking round the room; she was sure there had to be something in here – a letter, more photographs, Graham's birth certificate.

Her eye wandered along the line of books on the shelf above the bed. Bibi, she recalled, had a habit of putting precious things in favourite books. Bibi's precious things were varied. They could be recipes, poems, train tickets to places she'd loved visiting, holiday photographs, flowers pressed between pages, letters. One by one she removed books, flicked through the pages, and put them back.

At last, in one of her father's books, she found a postcard and a letter. The first was from Callum to Bibi. It was in a volume that contained the famous 'Floating' poem. It was a silly seaside postcard; its message said, *Now I know what exquisite is*.

Celia put the postcard back into the book and thought

she was glad at least someone knew what exquisite was. She opened the letter.

Bibi,

    I am now back in New York.

    I will never forgive you. I am a mother, I have a right to my child. I know I agreed to your adoption of Graham; it seemed sensible and proper at the time that you become his legal guardian. I was delighted that my son would be with his natural father, and brought up in a loving household with brothers and sisters. But at the time I was not myself, I was an alcoholic. I admit it. I am still an alcoholic. I always will be.

    I gave up my son because I loved him.

    We all agreed – you, me and Callum – that should I ever feel capable of looking after Graham, you would let me have him. Then I turn up at your home, and you and he deny it. You refuse to let me take him back to the States with me. How could you? You said you had given him a stable home and that disrupting his life could upset him for ever. I don't think so. You have gone back on your word, and in time you will pay for that.

    I will have my Graham.

    Bringing in your lawyer to tell me I had no legal right to claim my own child was hideous of you.

    I know I behaved abominably. I got drunk, I threw things, I called you a thieving whore. I did some terrible things. But I was in hell.

    I think I will always hate you. And believe me, when he is old enough, I will find a way to tell Graham who his mother is, and that she has always loved him.

    Polly

PS I enclose some money to pay for your neighbours' windows. I apologise for breaking them. I never did have a very good aim, and besides, at the time of throwing the stones, I was not in any way sober. I am now.

Celia carefully folded the letter, put it into the book and replaced it on the shelf. She left the flat, then sat in her car staring out through the windscreen. Polly must have allowed Bibi to adopt Graham, then, after several years, changed her mind and come to claim him.

Now that she thought about it, Bibi and Callum had always treated Graham differently. Nothing over the top, but they'd been protective of him. He had not, for example, been allowed out on his own. If he'd wanted something from the shops, Celia or Roddy had been forced to go with him. Sometimes she would catch Bibi looking at Graham, and the expression on her mother's face had been one of worry and apprehension. For years, Celia realised, her parents must have thought Polly would come back to Edinburgh, snatch her son and take him out of the country.

Roddy will know what happened. Roddy must always have known; he was old enough to remember Graham coming into the house. She wondered why he had never mentioned this, and why her parents had never told them Graham was their stepbrother. I wouldn't have minded, she thought. Then she thought, Broken windows? What was that about?

She shook her head, started the car and drove off.

Beth, standing at the window, watched her go.

The bleeding had stopped. The baby was gone. A tiny, tiny thing, but perfect. It had slipped from her body onto her mother's green-and-white-striped towel. She had gazed at it, horrified and awash with guilt. 'Sorry, sorry,' she said to it. Then trembling she'd wrapped it in a fresh towel and put it with all the bloodied towels in a plastic bag, then dropped them into the rubbish bin at the back of the building. She lay on her bed for hours, numb with grief. She hated herself and hated her body. It was an awful, messy thing and it had given her the worst, bloodiest night of her life. In the morning, she phoned her office to say she was still ill and didn't know when she'd be back.

'You'll need a doctor's certificate,' said Judith.

'I had a miscarriage,' said Beth. 'My baby died.' She sobbed down the phone. 'I wanted that baby. I was going to tell him stories about mud pies that turned into birds and flew away.'

Judith told her to take as long as she needed. 'Just look after yourself.' The girl's demented, she thought.

Beth blew her nose on her sleeve, wiped her eyes and said she would look after herself. But looking after herself was the last thing on her mind.

'And that,' said Bibi, 'was how Graham came into my life.'

'Did Callum love Polly?'

'Yes, of course he did. I loved her too for a long time. I was obsessed by her. I could see into her flat from my back window. I spied on her.'

'Creepy,' said James.

'Yes, I think I agree,' Bibi told him. 'I was lonely, though. Strange thoughts drift in when you are lonely.'

James supposed that might be true.

'I have often been lonely,' said Bibi. 'Callum was away a lot. I lived my life through him. Every time something is remembered on television, I think of Callum. The miners' strike in the eighties. I saw him in the background on the news. He was with the pickets. We gave all the money we could afford to the miners. And all the clothes the children had grown out of and that we still had lying around. Graham's jackets. His trousers all had holes in the knees. Celia's dresses, Liz's little vests and such. Then there were all the protests about Vietnam.'

Bibi had been doing the ironing in front of the television when she'd seen Callum being yanked up from where he'd been sitting and thrown into a police van. 'He got fined, I remember. That was my savings for a holiday in Mull gone.

'I've been in the background all my life,' she said. 'Except for when Polly came back for Graham. I surprised myself then.'

Polly had written to ask if she could visit for a few days. *I'd love to see you both again, and, of course, I am just desperate to find out all about Graham*, she'd said. She arrived on a Wednesday morning in August, sweeping in, arms spread, shouting, 'Well hi, everybody. Isn't this just wonderful.' She was wearing tight jeans, a silk shirt that tied at her waist and very high heels. For the whole of her stay, everything about Polly – her clothes, her bright chatter, her tan – made Bibi feel dowdy.

'Still,' she told James, 'I was sure Callum and I were being very modern and liberal. We were open enough to let the son I'd adopted have a good relationship with his natural mother. I was pretty smug about it.'

Celia had just started school and only Graham was at home all day. At first, he had been wary of Polly. He'd never before met a woman who talked like this, looked like this, smelled so perfumed. But in time, he was smitten; he adored her, sat on her knee, put his chubby arms round her neck and kissed her. Polly had taken him for walks and to the zoo; she had bathed him, put him to bed, read him stories. She had picked him up and thrown him, squealing, into the air, caught him and kissed him. 'I was fine with it all. I was happy to see how well they got along. I just let them get on with it,' Bibi said.

Polly had started to make jokes about taking Graham home with her, bringing him up herself. 'I think I'll take you home in my suitcase, and in New York I'll have you all to myself. We'd have fun.'

Graham had been, in his four-year-old way, enthused. 'Yes, we'll go in an aeroplane.'

But as the jokes continued and seemed to be getting serious, Bibi had said, 'You're not having him. He's mine now. You gave him up. He belongs here.'

Polly had said, 'You can't deny me. I have a mother's right.'

'You gave that up,' said Bibi. 'You left him with us.'

Voices were raised.

'Of course, Celia saw none of this. She was at school by then. Roddy, too,' Bibi said to James now.

Polly's few days spread into weeks. She admitted she didn't want to go; she couldn't leave Graham, 'I just love him.'

One afternoon, when the boy was having a nap, Polly had found Bibi in the kitchen and told her she'd had her son put on her passport. 'I still have his birth certificate. You sent it to me when the adoption was completed. You said I might want to have it. You have a copy.'

'And why is Graham on your passport?' asked Bibi.

'I'm taking him back to New York with me. I'm his mother. I want him.'

Bibi told her she couldn't just whip the child away. 'You'd disrupt our home. It would upset Graham and everybody else.'

'He's mine,' Polly insisted. 'You agreed that if I got better I could have him back. Well, I'm better. I want him.'

'We agreed no such thing,' said Bibi. 'We said you were welcome to come and see him any time. That's all.'

'He wants to come. I have told him all about my life over there, and the school he will be going to and the friends he'll have. I've shown him photographs of my apartment with the room I have prepared for him.'

'How could you do that?' said Bibi. 'You think you can just snatch him away after we've done all the work. Who got up in the night to feed him? Who changed his nappies? Who bathed him and washed his clothes? Who nursed him through teething? Who was there for his first step and held him as he learned to walk? Who has bandaged his little cuts and grazes? Who taught him to speak? Who stayed up with him all through the night when he had chickenpox? NOT BLOODY YOU!'

This last howl from Bibi brought Callum, who had been writing an article about the beauty of football, from his desk. He found Bibi and Polly looking at one another, wild-eyed with rage. They were straining forward towards each other. The veins in Bibi's neck were bulging.

He was holding Graham. The child had been crying for some time, but neither Polly nor Bibi had heard him. His face was red, nose running, his jaw juddering as he gasped and howled. Both women reached out for him. But Callum handed him to Bibi.

He put his arm round Polly, and suggested they go out. 'To get some fresh air and let everyone calm down.'

He collected Polly's bag, already packed – she'd been planning to quickly take her son and go – and together they left the flat. Bibi sighed, kissed Graham and took him to the living room to distract him with his toys.

It was seven o'clock before Callum returned. Bibi was getting worried; she had started to imagine he'd left her and was headed for New York with Polly. If she can't have my son, she'll take my husband instead. But there he was, standing at the kitchen door, looking drained. 'She's gone,' he said. 'I took her to the station and put her on the London train. She flies back tomorrow.' Then he'd gone to his study and poured himself a whisky.

'He always did that when something bothered him. He slipped away to his study to brood.'

Polly, as soon as Callum had left the station platform, got off the train. She walked the length of Rose Street, visiting pubs, drinking vodka. Then she came back to the flat.

It was late; outside, drenched by street lights, Polly was standing bare breasted, shouting, 'Child stealers. Liars. Thieves. These people have ripped my child from my breast.'

Callum and Bibi were in the living room. They looked at one another in horror.

'She must have got off the train,' he said.

'She must have been drinking,' Bibi said. She'd pushed Callum towards the door. 'Go down and talk to her.'

Polly picked up stones from the kerb and threw them, screaming, at the window. But alcohol had rendered her aim useless. She broke panes in the flat below; smashing glass and shouts shattered the night air. Bibi and Callum's neighbours had phoned the police.

Bibi watched as Callum put his arms round Polly. 'This won't work. Look at the state of you. Nobody would let you have a child when you behave like this.'

And Polly had screamed, 'Bastard. You've stolen my child.'

Blue lights, and more noise. The police arrived. By now, most of the people who lived in the street were at their windows, watching. Some had come outside to get a better view.

Polly had shouted, asking them if they were enjoying the show and if they liked having child abductors as neighbours. Then, when a policeman approached, telling her to calm down, she had taken off her shoe and hit him with it. 'These people have my son. I want him. He's mine.'

Bibi watched as Polly was manhandled into the car and driven away. That was the last time she saw her.

Callum had gone to the police station with her.

'He came home at about four in the morning. Polly had been cautioned. They didn't press charges. Mostly because she was so hysterical, and I think they felt a little sorry for her. She was told to leave the country. She'd be met at London, taken to Heathrow and put on a plane.'

Now, James said, 'Goodness.'

'Bloody mess,' said Bibi. 'She sent all the children presents at Christmas. But Graham always got something special. He knew there was somebody called Polly in America who thought the world of him. But we never told him that she was his mother. We should have done that. I just put it to the back of my mind and hoped everything would sort itself out. A fool, me.'

Roddy apologised to Erica. He was sorry to drop in unexpectedly, but he had to talk to somebody. 'Most of my friends are her friends too. Ruth doesn't want anybody to know what happened.'

Erica said that was understandable. 'But they'll find out. Scandal always comes out.'

He liked it here. The room was large, painted pale grey, prints on the walls and a large cream-coloured sofa to sit on. He leaned back and winced.

'Your back?' asked Erica.

He nodded.

'Bloody stupid to lift a bed with two people in it.'

He said he knew that now. 'But the red mist came down. I was in a rage. Do you know what really pissed me off?'

'Other than seeing your wife in bed with another man?'

'It was the duvet cover,' said Roddy. 'That bloody pink duvet cover in that pink room and he looked like a prat lying there. Everything in the bedroom, the curtains, the walls, the sheets, is the colour of Elastoplast. I hate it. I thought, this is what I must look like in bed, head on a pink pillow, surrounded by things I hate. I have worked to pay for this. I realised that my journey through life hadn't been on a highway after all. It was a little B road with scummy cafés and no neon lights. I was furious.'

'With yourself?' asked Erica.

'Yes. It shames me to admit that when I examine it all. I don't really care that Ruth slept with another man. I'm enraged, though, that she was shagging *that* man. And that he was in my bed and that that bed was pink.'

Erica laughed. She put her hand to her mouth to try and hide her amusement. 'I'm sorry,' she said. 'I can't help it.' She asked what he was going to do now.

He said he was going to take time to think. 'Then a course, probably photography. I'll have the full mid-life crisis. I'll wear a leather jacket, drive my Harley Davidson. I might backpack. I might take up the cello. Get a few tattoos, get my ear pierced. There's a whole world to be explored. First, I'll let my family know. Ruth will talk to the girls. I'll tell my ma.'

'What will she say?' asked Erica.

'She will be delighted. She never liked Ruth.'

The Journey's the Thing

It took Bibi and James six hours to reach the outskirts of Edinburgh. James wanted to go to the flat – he fancied a night in his own bed. Two nights sleeping on the floor in front of Liz's wood-burning stove had been warm but uncomfortable. But Bibi said no, she thought they should keep going.

'I've got into the rhythm of being on the road. It suits me. I could go on travelling, spend the rest of my life in a car, seeing things, stopping in new places every night.'

She started humming 'Born to be Wild'. James asked her to please stop.

'Don't you like my singing?'

'No. It's distracting.' He was worried about the car. 'I think there might be something wrong with the clutch.'

'Nonsense,' said Bibi. 'They don't make cars like this any more. These old things can go on for ever.'

James said he didn't think so.

They took the bypass and headed towards the Borders, and at two o'clock they stopped to fill the car and eat at a small roadside café near the garage.

'I've never understood why a woman would take a man back after he's been unfaithful,' said James. 'Didn't it bother you that your husband slept with that other woman and had a baby?'

'Of course it bothered me. We did things in bed and I'd wonder if he'd done them with someone else. If Polly had taught him some tricks.'

James looked down at his sausages and sniffed. He hated it when Bibi talked about sex. Still, he would have liked to ask about the tricks; they might come in handy.

'But after New York he didn't have affairs very often. It was the flirting he enjoyed. It pleased him to think he was still attractive; he needed the boost,' Bibi continued.

They ate in silence for a while, then James asked if not letting Polly have Graham was the terrible thing she'd done.

'The terrible thing is I was happy about it. I was secretly filled with glee. I'd got Polly back for sleeping with my husband. I wanted revenge. She was so gorgeous and witty, with beautiful clothes; she made me feel a frump. She'd be laughing with Callum and the children. I'd be in the kitchen getting sweaty. I wanted to hurt her.'

James said bright and witty people could have that effect on you. 'But you should have told Graham you weren't his real mother.'

'You think I don't know that. Callum wanted to. I said wait till he was old enough to understand. Time passed. He was such a restless child, always on the move. There never seemed to be a moment. He'd come home from school, drop his books, change into his jeans and disappear till suppertime. Then it was out again. He never studied. Got dreadful reports from his teachers. He played heavy metal music and the Jam in his room. And I never seemed to be alone with him. There were always these girls hanging about him.'

James thought it would have been good to have a lot of girls hanging about. This had never happened to him. 'I hardly had any girlfriends when I was at school.'

Bibi told him he could make up for it now.

They lingered too long over lunch. James said they should take the motorway. But Bibi said they were just a whoosh, all traffic and no landscape. They'd take the B roads and they'd take their time. They headed for Carlisle.

Bibi said, 'He looked for Polly everywhere when she left.'

James said, 'Graham?'

'Yes. He couldn't believe she'd gone away without him. She'd told him she was taking him to New York. He looked under the bed, behind the wardrobe, everywhere. It was heartbreaking to watch. And he never forgot her. Every Christmas, he'd look at her parcel and be full of excitement because it was from Polly. You're right, I should have told him.'

It was after five when they rattled into Carlisle. James still wanted to get on to the motorway.

Bibi said, 'Nonsense. Travelling is all about the journey. We shall take a spin to Penrith, then Keswick and Windermere. On to Kendal, then to Ilkley. It will be a trip.'

'It will be dark,' said James.

'It will be twilight. The best time of day. We might see owls or deer, foxes, all sorts of things. This is what makes a journey memorable.'

'This is what uses up petrol, and I'm sure there's something wrong with the car.'

'I keep telling you, it's a Volvo. Nothing ever goes wrong with a Volvo. Now we need to stop for a cup of tea. And I need a pee.'

James said this all sounded like she was putting off getting to Roddy's house. He was right. Not that she didn't want to see her son; it was just that she didn't want to arrive uninvited at Ruth's front door. She knew she wouldn't be welcome.

Liz got home at lunchtime and looked through her mail – a couple of circulars offering her cheap car insurance, a catalogue for cashmere jerseys, and a letter from Drew, which she opened; the rest went into the bin.

Liz,

How are you? Hope the kids are well. I miss them.

Actually I'm writing to let you know that I have contacted an estate agent about the house. He will be calling round on Thursday to look it over and assess its value. He'll come at half past one so Lara and Louis won't be there to get upset about it, and he should be away in time to let you get to the school to collect them.

Hope this isn't too much bother. I'd also be grateful if, when potential buyers come to view the house, you would show them round.

Thanks.

Drew

Liz reread the letter several times, then said, 'I don't think so.' She didn't want to see an estate agent's face when he looked at the sagging ceiling and the huge crack on the outside wall. And there was rising damp and probably woodworm. Imagine, she thought, if someone came all the way from Glasgow or London to look at the house. They'd be dreaming of a holiday home by the sea, thinking about putting in a hot tub, planning barbecues on the patio. And they'd see this.

'Then there's the sofa. I can throw it out, but it won't be gone by Thursday.' She put on the kettle. 'Spacious country cottage,' she said, 'wood-burning stove, large garden well stocked with nettles. Kitchen ceiling an excellent conversation piece, intriguing air-conditioning through crack in wall. Roof well ventilated.'

She threw the letter down. Picked up the phone, dialled the number of the school and told the head teacher she was taking Lara and Louis out of their classes. She was moving to Edinburgh.

James had managed to travel for miles without changing gear. He'd swung round corners, shot through small villages, praying that there would be no policemen and no late-evening wanderers walking down the middle of the road. He'd been doing a steady forty miles an hour. The clutch had bust.

Beside him Bibi slept like a baby. She had drifted off outside Keswick, saying they were in for a treat scenery-wise.

He finally stopped at the side of the road and got out. He opened the bonnet and peered at the engine, thinking, Why am I doing this? I don't know how to fix it. He looked about him. The road was empty. He listened; he could not hear the sound of another car approaching. He would have to walk back to Keswick to get help.

James took the travelling rug Bibi kept on the back seat, and spread it over her. He tucked her in. He left a note telling her the clutch was buggered and he'd gone to get help. He closed the car door carefully and stood breathing in the smell of evening. Then set off.

Bibi woke. It was dark. She was cold and she was alone. She had no idea where she was. Somewhere a rabbit, ensnared or caught in a fox's jaws, shrieked. It was this that set her mood – fear.

Where was James? She clutched her travelling blanket and let her mind fill with possibilities, all of them dire. He had been abducted or murdered, she thought. She'd read about such things. People pretending to be stranded in remote places stopped the car, then assaulted the driver, stealing his cash and either killing him or taking him away to kill him later and dispose of the body. Then again, he might have been taken ill, called an ambulance and been whisked off to hospital. Or maybe he'd just abandoned her. She threw off the blanket and got out of the car. She stood looking up and down the road.

Her heart beat faster. She had no idea where she might be. The last thing she remembered was being on the A66. She thought it wrong of James to leave her here; whatever had happened, he should have woken her. She decided to drive away. But peering into the car, she saw the keys were not in the ignition, and after rummaging through the glove box, she found that her mobile phone was also gone. That would be it: someone had stopped the car, accosted James and stolen the phone.

She got back into the car, wrapped the blanket round herself and said, 'Well, Callum. What do you think of this? A fine mess.' It was then she saw the note. He's broken my car, she thought.

She sat sucking mints and talking to herself for two hours. She remembered the day she'd run away. She had waited at Perth for Callum's train to arrive. She'd had hours to wait, but hadn't left the station in case she missed it. She might wander too far and not be able to get back in time, so she had waited. She'd been aware that the guards had been looking at her. 'You needing help, love?' one had asked.

'Just waiting for the Glasgow train.'

'That's three hours, darling. You should take a stroll round town.'

She'd shaken her head. 'I'll wait here.' So she'd waited, and indulged in dread imaginings. Her father had found out and had Callum arrested. What for, she couldn't exactly say. But her father was a powerful man locally. Or, then again, Callum had changed his mind. He wasn't coming. He'd gone off the whole idea of marrying her.

Then, when the train came in, there had been Callum, knocking on the window, signalling her to join him. She'd cried.

'What's wrong?' he said.

'I thought you'd changed your mind. I thought you weren't coming.'

'No,' he said. 'Running away to get married to the laird's daughter. I wouldn't miss that. Best time of my life so far.'

She smiled. Saw in the distance whirling lights shimmering in the dark. 'The cavalry is coming, Callum,' she said.

The tow truck stopped in front of the Volvo. James jumped out and came to see her. 'You all right?'

'I'm fine. You've broken my car.'

'I told you the clutch was buggered miles back.'

'It's a Volvo,' said Bibi. 'Volvos don't break down. They go on for ever.'

It didn't happen often, but right now she felt frail, old and vulnerable. 'I thought you'd abandoned me.'

'Nah,' said James. 'Had to walk a bit, then I got to a garage. I took your mobile in case I needed it. We have to get in the truck,' he said. 'He'll take us to Roddy's house.'

James helped her from the car, led her to the tow truck and put his hand on her arm as she climbed in. Then he spread the blanket over her.

The driver asked if his grandma was all right.

James said she wasn't his grandma. 'She's my friend.'

Ruth was standing at her living-room window when she saw the truck arrive. Its lights, flashing orange, filled up the night outside, reflected round the room. It was one o'clock in the morning, and she was still waiting for Roddy to come home.

Who the hell is that? she thought.

She saw Bibi get out, and stand a moment rubbing her knees.

Oh my God, thought Ruth. It's *her*. What's she doing here? She pressed her palms together. 'Please God, do not let her stay long. Thank you.' Started for the door, stopped, resumed praying. 'Sorry, God. Amen.'

As she bustled to the front door, Ruth thought, Pork chops. I could grill them with mustard and Gruyère on top, and some potatoes with sea salt and rosemary. No, she won't want anything like that at this time of night. Sandwiches. I'll have to make up the bed in Florence's room. Bloody woman, I hope this is a flying visit. Can't stand her.

She flung open the front door and cried, 'Bibi! This is a wonderful surprise. How are you?'

Bibi also flung open her arms. 'Ruth. You are looking well.'

They embraced.

'This is a dramatic arrival. What happened?'

'The car broke down. We got towed. It's all very exciting.'

'And who is this?' said Ruth, pointing at James.

'This is my chauffeur, James. He's actually my lodger. I twisted his arm so he would drive me here.'

Ruth told them to come inside, she'd put the kettle on.

Bibi thought she'd rather have a drink, but said, 'A cup of tea would be lovely.'

They sat exchanging living-room chat, a little too loudly, James thought. It occurred to him that women were not very good at disliking one another. They tried too hard to hide it. Men would just ignore each other, or speak as little as possible. Men were better at not getting along with someone; they weren't bothered if it showed. Women, though, were better at getting on together; they chatted, giggled, and shared things like lipstick, gossip and sympathy. He was proud of this observation, and decided to share it with Bibi once they hit the road again.

'And where is Roddy?' said Bibi.

'Away on business,' said Ruth. 'He should be back tomorrow.' She slapped her knees and stood up. 'This is terrible of me. You must be starving. I'll make you sandwiches.' She made for the door, turned and said, 'Is there any reason why you're here? Or is this just a surprise visit?'

'A surprise visit,' said Bibi. She smiled and said, 'Don't worry, we won't stay long.'

Ruth, on her way to the kitchen, and out of Bibi's hearing, said, 'Good.'

I'll Tell You Mine,
If You Tell Me Yours

In Bibi's flat, Celia was watering the plants. She did the geraniums and herbs in the kitchen and walked out into the hall on her way to the huge plant in James's room. It was lunchtime; her mind was full of thoughts of Graham and whether she should get in touch with him, and if she did what should she say? She looked up, saw Beth standing, silent, pale, still, wearing a white nightdress, in front of her, and dropped the watering can. 'Oh my God.'

Beth didn't move.

'Beth, what are you doing here? You gave me the fright of my life.'

Beth looked at the pool of water on the floor and said, 'So I see.'

Celia asked again what Beth was doing here.

Beth said, 'I've been living here.' Her legs were feeling unreliable. They didn't feel like they were going to hold her up any more. They were shaking. She went into the living room and sat down on the sofa.

Celia followed. 'Are you all right?'

'I had a miscarriage.' She leaned forward on her seat,

elbows on her knees. She didn't look at Celia. 'I lost my baby.'

Celia sat down beside her, put her arm round her, stroked her arm. 'I didn't know you were pregnant.'

'I didn't tell anybody. It would have become obvious soon enough.'

'You're shivering,' said Celia. 'You should be in bed.'

Beth nodded.

Celia led her back to bed. She filled a hot-water bottle and slipped it under the duvet at her sister's feet. 'Perhaps you should come home with me. You'll have company.'

Beth said she didn't want company. She wanted to be here. 'I like it here.'

'You should see a doctor,' said Celia.

'Don't want to see a doctor. Don't want to see anybody. Don't want to talk to anybody.'

Celia asked if it had been Bradley's baby. And did he know?

'Of course it was Bradley's. And no, he doesn't know. He doesn't want any more babies.'

Celia said that Beth must tell him and asked if Beth was eating.

'Not hungry,' said Beth.

'You have to eat,' Celia told her. She went to the kitchen, looked in both the fridges and in the cupboards. 'Nothing,' she said. Then went back to Beth. 'I'll have to go out and buy some food.' She paused at the door. 'How long have you been here?'

'Since Bibi left. I saw you look through her secret things.'

Celia said, 'Ah.'

'Don't worry about it,' said Beth. 'I've been reading her diaries.'

Celia asked what they said.

'They're just about things she planted, things she cooked, and being lonely. I like them.'

'I'll go and buy something for you to eat,' said Celia. 'Then I have to get back to work. I can't cancel my appointments this late in the day. I'll come back this evening.'

Beth said she didn't have to. 'I like being alone. I don't want to talk. I can't think of any words I want to say.'

Celia told her to keep warm. She left the flat, then sat on the stairs, got out her phone and dialled Bibi's mobile.

Roddy turned up at ten in the morning. Bibi and Ruth were having a late breakfast; James was in the shower. Roddy was wearing jeans and a leather jacket, he hadn't shaved, and he didn't look to Bibi as if he'd been on a business trip.

Still, he was delighted to see her. 'Saw the car, knew you were here.' He leaned down and kissed her, then poured a cup of coffee and sat opposite her.

He and Ruth exchanged a curt nod. She didn't ask if he'd had a good trip. Bibi knew there was something they were not telling her. 'My car is broken,' she said. 'So if you want to get rid of me, you'd better help me find someone who'll fix it.'

Roddy promised to get in touch with a garage. Ruth stood up, sniffed, and said she'd better shop if Bibi was going to stay. 'Supplies are low.'

When she'd gone, Roddy reached over and took Bibi's hand. 'I'll tell you mine if you tell me yours.'

'I don't know what you mean,' she said.

'I mean you know something's going on and are dying to find out what. And I know there's some reason for this trip to see Liz, then me. So I'll give you my truth if you give me yours.'

'Why should there be a reason? I just wanted to see you.'

'Ma, I know you. I'm the one who knows you best. I saw you sitting in the cold, wearing that big coat, typing theses for money. I was there when Celia was born. I saw Dad come home, carrying Graham. I saw you pick Graham up and fall in love with him. I saw Polly outside our flat, throwing stones at the window, screaming. I saw it all. I know you, and there is a reason for this trip.'

'You saw Polly that night?'

'She was half naked. You bet I watched.'

'You never mentioned it.'

'I didn't know what to say. I was a kid. I'm mentioning it now.'

Bibi told him to go first. 'Where were you last night?'

He told her about Erica. 'Just a friend, at the moment. But I am hoping for more.' He said that he was divorcing Ruth, and he'd quit his job.

'Well, good for you,' said Bibi.

He told her everything.

'You found her in bed with another man? Ruth? I don't believe you.'

'It's true. I promised not to tell anyone. I've told Erica, now you. I'm not doing very well.'

'It'll come out,' said Bibi. 'These things always do. Make sure you're out of the way when it happens.'

'Now you,' he said. 'Why the big trip?'

'I am going to die.'

'Rubbish.'

'I am. The doctor left me alone in his consulting room and I peeked at my notes. I haven't got long. I wanted to see you to say goodbye.'

He held both her hands in his, leaned back and studied her. Over the years, he'd known quite a few people who were terminally ill; none of them had looked as healthy as Bibi. They'd had dreadful coughs, a grey pallor; they wheezed, they'd lost weight, some could hardly walk. Right now, Bibi glowed. She'd had a good night's sleep, a hot bath, washed her hair, and moisturised then made up her face. He'd never seen anyone look less like they were on the brink of death. 'Are you sure?'

'Oh, yes,' said Bibi. 'Right now, some terrible clot may be coursing through my veins on its way to my heart. Then, *bam*, I'm gone.'

He put her hand to his lips. 'I don't want this to happen.'

'I'm ready,' said Bibi. 'It was a terrible blow at first. But I'm old. I thought about it deeply. I don't quite believe in these things, but I'm hoping Callum is somewhere waiting for me. My affairs are in order. I'm ready.'

Roddy said he really didn't want to hear this.

'You are the executor of my will. I don't know who'll want my furniture. But it used to belong to my mother. I'd like some pieces to stay in the family. The money for the flat is divided equally. But give James my car, he'd like that.'

Roddy nodded. He still didn't believe her.

'I may have to leave you all with some debts. I've run up quite an amount on my credit cards on this trip – petrol, meals, stuff for Liz and her kids.'

Roddy believed that.

'You must promise not to tell,' said Bibi.

He promised. But thinking about his promise to Ruth, Bibi wondered if he could be trusted.

He got up, walked round the table, kissed the top of her head. 'I'll phone my garage, see if they can do something about your car.'

At the door, he turned. Bibi was helping herself to a third slice of toast. She spread it thickly, took a bite, then, sensing he was watching her, turned to meet his gaze. 'Really,' she said, cheeks bulging, 'I'm dying. I saw it in black and white.'

Roddy said, 'Right.' He still didn't think it was true.

Bibi sat for a moment contemplating her death. She hoped it would be quick, painless, and that she'd be in her bed at home when it came for her.

Her phone rang. It was lying on the table where she'd put it this morning after James had given it back to her. It was Celia. 'It's Beth.'

Sublimely Happy, Ha, Ha, Ha

'Soup,' said Beth. 'Is that all you can think of? Soup doesn't cure everything.'

'It cures a lot,' Bibi told her. 'It's nutritious and easily digested. Eat.'

She had arrived an hour ago and found Beth in bed, facing the wall. Not really knowing what to do, she had done what she did best – bustle and boss. 'You're not going to lie there feeling sorry for yourself. You'll have a bath. You're looking a bit grubby to me.'

Beth had obeyed. Bibi put fresh sheets on the bed, and from the supplies Celia had brought in made a pot of carrot soup.

Beth, back in bed and feeling better, lay listening to the sounds from the kitchen. The radio was on; there was the clatter of cutlery and pots. She could hear Bibi talking to herself. It was a comfort. So lovely to lie doing nothing, to be looked after; she wondered why anyone grew up and left home.

But not prepared to admit any of this, she had grumbled when Bibi brought her a bowl of soup, bread and grapes and cheese on a tray. Then stayed by her bed to supervise the eating of her meal.

Grudgingly Beth had taken a few mouthfuls. 'It's quite good.'

'Of course,' said Bibi. 'I made it.'

Beth said, 'I really wanted that baby.'

Bibi reached over and touched her hand. 'You would. It's a heartache to lose it. Nature can be cruel.'

'I don't know what got into me,' said Beth. 'I never wanted a baby before. One day I saw a woman carrying a little boy along the street. He was so beautiful. She was chatting to him, and he was laughing and cuddling her. I thought, I want one of those.'

Bibi said she knew the feeling.

'After that, there were babies everywhere. I hadn't noticed them before. In fact, I hadn't really liked them. They were messy and noisy. If someone with a couple of kids came into a restaurant where I was eating, I'd get really annoyed. Then I wanted one, a little baby of my own.'

Bibi said she knew. 'I'm old and I still get those feelings. I remember how it was to have a baby, to hold them and smell them. The smell of a baby is magical. I remember how I'd smile when they yawned or sneezed, and how I'd watch mine sleep, little fists clenched on the pillow. Then I remember the truth. Not just that I'm way past having a baby, but how awful it can be.'

Beth looked at her.

'The mess, the noise, the tantrums, the worry. The fuss you have to go through just to get out the door, putting on coats and shoes and gathering the stuff you need to take with you. Running around bent double trying to catch them before they do some damage to themselves or some-one's property. Then there's parents' day at school, I hated that. Then they start asking for things you've never heard of, making you feel really old. Oh, it all just goes on and on and on.'

'You haven't put me off,' said Beth. 'I want to take my child for walks along the river and look for mud pies that change into birds and fly away.'

For a moment Bibi looked bewildered, then, 'You want to pass on the stories your father told you.'

Beth said, 'Yes.'

'An excellent reason to bring someone into the world,' said Bibi. 'Now get some sleep, we've got a busy day tomorrow. First we'll go and say hello to Callum, tell him all that's been happening. Then we must have a look at the allotment. I want to see how my sweet peas and broad beans are coming along. Now, I have some phone calls to make. I must ring Celia to tell her how you're doing, and Roddy to find out how my poor old car is getting along.'

She phoned Roddy first and was told the car was in a garage and that one of the mechanics had found a replacement clutch on the internet. 'It'll be fixed in a few days. We'll look after James.'

'You'll have to pay for the car for the moment,' said Bibi. 'I'll give you the money back.'

Roddy asked what would be the point of that, since she'd probably use one of her new credit cards, and he'd have to pay that bill when she died. 'I'll pay for the car.'

'You won't have any money when I die,' said Bibi. 'Not now you've left your job.'

Roddy told her he'd probably take on some accountancy work to pay his way through an adult education course. 'Photography, probably. Then furniture restoration. I'll be a student for the rest of my life.'

Bibi said she thought that an excellent plan, and rang off. After that she phoned Celia to tell her Beth was on the mend, and to give her news of Liz and Roddy. 'And,' she would say, 'there's a wet stain on the floor in the hall. Did you spill water and not wipe it up? And who has been reading my diaries? They're in the wrong order on my shelf. And someone has been rummaging through my private things. That's such an adolescent thing to do, Celia.'

In the morning, Liz locked her door and walked to the car. 'That's it. It's over.'

She had packed the boot with as much as she could take on a single journey. The hens had been given to a neighbour, and she'd said goodbye to the few friends she'd made. She got into the car, pulled the seat belt round her and started the engine.

'It's going to be a long journey,' she told Lara and Louis. 'So don't start asking are we there yet for at least two hours.'

She was filled with relief. Now she would not have to see the house she'd been living in for years through the horrified eyes of strangers. It was her happiest moment in ages. She reversed out of the drive and drove off. She didn't look back. She didn't want to see her home as it was now. She wanted to remember it as it had been when she and Drew had worked on it together, when it had been part of a dream. She didn't intend to ever come back.

Bibi and Beth took Callum a large bunch of daisies.

'He always liked them. He said they were the simplest of flowers, unpretentious. He thought my delphiniums were a bit above themselves. He liked poppies, too. He loved them because they grew everywhere. Just planted themselves down wherever they fancied, and grew.'

Beth said that was true.

Bibi said, 'Well, Callum, I've got such a lot to tell you. I don't know where to start. I saw Roddy, and Liz. He's going to be fine. I'm a bit worried about her, though.'

Beth left her to it. She'd chat to him later. She wandered off, looking at gravestones. She sat on a bench and watched Bibi animatedly telling Callum her news. Her mother's voice drifted across to her. 'The car broke down in the middle of nowhere. Your car, you'd have been cross about that . . .'

Beth smiled. A small wind shifted through the trees behind her; she looked up and realised how long it had been since she noticed the little things that went on around her. She'd been coming and going to and from a job she hated. She'd been seeing a man she adored, but only on his terms. It was time to change.

It took Bibi a good fifteen minutes to tell Callum of her adventures. She came and sat beside Beth. 'We'll get going to the allotment now. We can have a picnic. You can help with the weeding. There's nothing like some fresh air and a spot of gardening to clean out your mind. You smell the ground, hear birds, see some weeds needing to be yanked out. And that's all you think about. Sometimes you can even fool yourself that you are sublimely happy. Ha, ha, ha.'

It was late afternoon when Liz parked outside her mother's flat. 'Here at last,' she said. They all stumbled out on to the pavement and looked up at the window.

'What if she's not in?' said Lara.

'I don't think she will be,' Liz told her. 'I've got a key. Your grandma insisted everyone in the family had a key. She used to say that the flat would always be home.'

The only stop she'd made on her journey was at a supermarket, where she'd bought the children sandwiches and orange juice. She'd phoned Drew from there too. She knew he wouldn't be in and left a message: 'If you want to sell the cottage, you sell it. You show people round. I'm not doing it. If you want to contact me, I'll be at my mother's.'

They climbed the stairs and unlocked the door. 'Isn't it lovely here?' she said.

'Bathed in golden light,' said Louis. He sounded a little bit sour.

'Yes,' said Liz, not noticing. 'This is where we're going to stay till we find a place of our own.' She sighed. 'I love it here.'

❊   ❊   ❊

Roddy phoned Graham at his restaurant in Toronto. It was three in the afternoon; he reckoned it would be ten o'clock in the morning over there. He wasn't sure what he would say, but he thought it had to be done.

One of the waiters answered and Roddy asked to speak to Graham Woods.

'Who's calling?'

'His brother, Roddy.'

He was asked to hold on. It seemed like an age before Graham came to the phone.

'Hello.' An odd accent, a little bit Scottish but mostly Canadian.

'Hey, Graham. It's Roddy, remember me?'

'Of course I remember you. How are you?'

'Well. You?'

'I'm fine.'

'Long time no speak,' said Roddy.

Graham agreed.

'We found you on the internet. I've been wondering about you for a long time.'

'Me too,' said Graham.

'Thing is,' said Roddy, 'it's Bibi. She is going to die.' He thought about this. It was too dramatic. 'Well,' he went on, 'she says she's going to die. I'm not sure I believe her, but she's convinced, and I think she'd like to see you before she goes. She'd like to know that you've forgiven her.'

'Have I?' said Graham.

'Of course you have. She only wanted the best for you. She thinks about you every day.'

'Does she? I thought you might all have forgotten about me.'

Roddy said, 'No.'

He heard pages turning. 'I'm looking through my diary,' said Graham. 'I can't get away for a couple of weeks. Do you think Bibi can hang on that long?'

'To be honest,' said Roddy, 'I think she'll hang on for another twenty years. But she's got this into her head. Frankly, she's looking very well. I just think it's time you got together again. Spoke to one another. Made up. Face it – she's over seventy. She is going to die someday.'

Graham said he knew. He'd been thinking about that. 'How is she? How are you all? What have you been doing?'

They spoke for an hour. Then Graham said he had to go. 'It's nearly lunchtime. Busy for me.'

Roddy said he was sorry to have kept him so long.

'No,' said Graham. 'It's great to hear from you. I think about you all a lot. I've told my wife about you. She'll come over with me.' He said he'd phone to give Roddy his flight details. 'Meet me at the airport,' he said. 'I don't want to face Bibi without some support.'

When Roddy hung up, Ruth asked who he'd been speaking to for such a long time.

'My brother in Canada,' he told her.

'I didn't even know you had a brother in Canada.'

'Yeah, well I have.'

She said that was a long time to spend on a long-distance call. Roddy told her she wasn't paying for it.

'I just wanted to phone the girls. I have to let them know what's happening. Unless you want to do it.'

He shook his head. 'You do it. You're a lot better at lying than me.'

He found James sitting in the living room reading a newspaper, keeping out of the way. 'I'm off to the cinema and a Chinese with a friend. Want to come?'

James said, 'Please.' He didn't fancy an evening alone with Ruth.

It'll Be a While Then

Bibi stood at her front door, listening. 'Did we leave the television on?'

Beth said she didn't think so.

'Only it's booming,' said Bibi. She went to investigate and found Lara and Louis, side by side on the sofa, watching an afternoon movie.

'Well, surprise,' said Bibi, voice light, trilling above her bewilderment. 'What are you two doing here?'

'We've come to stay,' said Louis.

'That's wonderful,' Bibi told them. 'Is it a school holiday?'

The two children both shook their heads.

'Where's your mum?'

'Putting her car in your garage. She doesn't want to pay for parking.'

'Good thinking,' said Bibi. 'Well, better put the supper on, I expect you're all hungry.'

Cooking was what she did when she was upset, angry, confused or bewildered. She shrugged at Beth. 'You'd better go and say hello to your niece and nephew. I didn't know they were coming. But I can figure out why they're here.'

'They wanted to see you again,' said Beth.

'I don't think I'm the attraction,' Bibi said. 'I think the main attractions are comfortable seats, plenty of hot water and central heating.'

Liz arrived, breathless. She'd been running, worried about leaving her children alone in a strange flat. 'I thought you'd still be at Roddy's,' she said. 'I put my car in your garage. I thought it would be empty. In fact, I didn't think you'd be here.'

Bibi said, 'Well, I am. I live here. What brings you here?'

'Drew put the house on the market. I didn't want to be there when viewers saw it.'

Bibi nodded. 'So how long will you be staying?'

'Till I get enough money to find a place of my own.'

'How long will that be?' asked Bibi.

'After Drew sells the house.'

Bibi said, 'It'll be a while, then.'

James picked up the Volvo. He said goodbye to Roddy, who'd driven him to the garage, thanked him for his hospitality, told him to give his love to Erica, who he'd liked a lot, then headed for Manchester. He wanted to see his old haunts again.

The estate where he'd grown up was the same – old grass, grey rather than green, graffiti, a shop with boarded windows. He hadn't really noticed how rundown and sad it looked. He thought he couldn't live here now. He'd seen too much to settle in a place like this. Once, it had been home.

He drove past the garage where he'd sold cars. Shiny rows of motors on the forecourt, and inside, through the huge glass windows, he could see young men in suits moving about. That used to be me, he thought. He didn't go in; he wasn't the same James. He knew he had nothing to say to anybody in there. He smiled. He'd had some good times, when he thought about it.

Finally he drove to the street where Vicky lived. He parked. Wondered if he should go up to her front door and ask to see her. Perhaps not. He'd been a fool the last time he called. He wouldn't be welcome. He sat a while, remembering how he'd stood on that front lawn shouting her name. It still embarrassed him. He hadn't known he could be so passionate, so angry.

He was just about to drive away when he saw her. She was walking down the pavement on the other side of the road. She was wearing shorts and platform boots and a tiny sleeveless red top. Between the shorts and the top was a slice of tanned bare midriff. She had shiny rings in her navel. Her hair was long, past her shoulders, and as she walked she swept it from her face. She was with two similarly dressed friends. They were giggling. He heard her say, 'I was like, sooo not going to go out with him . . .' And the other girls laughed.

She looked across at him. He slid down in his seat, holding his breath, praying she hadn't seen him. 'Cool car,' she said. Then they all went inside.

He could hardly believe how young she looked. Why hadn't he noticed? he wondered. If he saw her in a bar for the first time now, he wouldn't dream of approaching her.

Her face, though beautiful, had that young look, as if it was waiting for life to happen to it. She looked street-smart, and slightly silly. Back then, he thought, his own face had looked open and without depth. It had needed a few more expressions.

It occurred to him that he'd never love anyone like he'd loved Vicky, and felt a twinge of sadness about that. But at the same time, he was awfully glad about that.

He started the engine, turned the car and headed for the motorway. He'd drive all the way to Edinburgh; he'd drive all night. Windows rolled down, cans of Coke to drink and the radio tuned to a rock station. He'd enjoy the ride.

Not a Woman on the Verge
of Kicking the Bucket

'Of course my blood pressure's up,' said Bibi. 'My flat is full of people. It's stressful.'

'It isn't up much,' said Dr Burns. 'You need to relax and cut down on the alcohol.'

'There's Beth, Liz, her two, and James. The television is on all day. They are always phoning people and making cups of coffee. I like my peace. I need a bit alcohol in the midst of all this. I don't even get to sit and do my crossword in the morning.'

'But the hospital was pleased with you after your last checkup.'

'Liars,' said Bibi. 'You can't fool me. I know what's happening. I think it appalling you don't tell people the truth. We need to know if we're going to die. We have to say goodbye to our families and friends, sort out our wills, make peace with ourselves.'

The doctor agreed. 'But you're not going to die.'

'I am. You don't need to try to fool me.'

He looked at her file. 'Your blood pressure was fine at the hospital. Your cholesterol was fine; liver's fine; you're not diabetic, not overweight. My God, Bibi, you'll outlive us all.

I'd say you've got at least another twenty good years in you.'

Bibi said, 'Rubbish. I saw my file. The consultant was called away and I sneaked a peek at it. It said no medical intervention was advised.'

Dr Burns said, 'I think you must have looked at the wrong file. Probably the person coming in after you.'

Bibi said, 'Nonsense.'

'If the doctor had finished with you, he might have taken your file with him as he went out. He'd hand it to the clerical staff to be put away till your next visit.'

She went back in her head to her hospital checkup. Certainly there had been an old woman in a wheelchair in the waiting area when she left. But she'd been too devastated to pay much attention. She tried to relive the moment when the consultant had been called away. Had he been carrying a file? She scowled, willing herself back to that consulting room all those weeks ago. Now she pictured it in her mind, in the vision that came to her, he definitely had a file in his hand.

'Oh my goodness,' she said. 'I think you may be right.'

'I think you shouldn't go jumping to conclusions. You didn't tell anybody you were about to pop off, did you?'

'Only Roddy. And he didn't believe me. But it has cost me dearly. The petrol for my trip, the things I bought, meals, presents; I even had the car insured. I thought my family would pick up the bill once I was dead. I thought, why shouldn't they? They'd get a bit for the flat and the garage. I thought they'd be able to afford it.'

The doctor told her not to get overly upset sorting it all out. 'Your blood pressure.'

Bibi left and walked slowly towards home. She stopped at the internet café, bought a cappuccino and paid for some computer time so she could email Roddy.

Hello Roddy,

Not going to die after all. Sorry about that. The doctor says I'm fine. I looked at the wrong file. All I can think of is that poor soul whose medical records I read. She was in a bit of a state.

Hope you're well.

Love,

Bibi

She logged off, finished her coffee and headed back to her flat.

Roddy didn't get the email. He'd moved into his flat and his computer was still in its box. He'd put up the snow scene picture he'd bought and was spending his time watching DVDs and listening to music. He thought he was born to be idle. Tomorrow he was driving to Edinburgh to pick up Graham, his wife and Polly at the airport. He hadn't told Bibi anything about it, and was worried about this.

He'd spoken to Celia at length, though. She thought everyone should come to her house.

'I can prepare some food, we can make it a party. I can't do a sit-down meal, I don't have enough chairs.'

Roddy said that sounded fine to him.

'I think Graham and his wife should stay at Beth's flat.

It will give them freedom to come and go as they like. Bibi's flat is too full. There are queues for the bathroom. And I think Polly should stay with me. I don't want her and Bibi under the same roof for days on end. They'd probably fight. And maybe Bibi's not up to the strain of it all. She might really be going to die.' Then she said, 'No, she's not.'

Roddy said, 'That sounds great. I think Bibi's fine, too. I don't see how anybody can eat as much as she does, and do the things she does – all that gardening and walking to her allotment – and be on the verge of kicking the bucket.'

Celia said she'd thought that too. 'I wish you hadn't told me, though. I worry all the time now.'

Roddy said so did he. 'But listen, when she was staying with us, and you phoned to tell her about Beth, she ran up the stairs to pack. She ran, Celia. Two steps at a time and she wasn't out of breath. Is that someone who is at death's door?'

Celia said it wasn't. 'And she's cooking for everyone. And bossing. And playing with Lara and Louis and still walking to her allotment every day. I don't see any sign of her flagging.'

Roddy said he'd see her tomorrow. 'Are you coming to the airport?'

She told him she was. 'Peter's going to bring Liz, the kids, and Bibi to my house. We told her we're having a family party to celebrate her return from her trip. James is bringing Beth.'

Roddy said, 'Excellent. Six o'clock arrival. See you then.'

Things Bibi Was Good At

They stood, Celia and Roddy, watching the passengers from the London flight swarm in. Moving through the throng, three exquisite, perfectly dressed people wafted towards them.

'That's them,' said Celia. 'My God, look at them. His jacket must have cost more than my car.'

'Pretty cheap, then,' said Roddy.

She told him to piss off. 'Look at them.'

They were tanned, gym-toned, expensive people. Graham and Carol looked to be in Armani; Polly wore a silk suit and a soft-brimmed hat. It was evening, in Scotland, and her eyes were hidden behind sun-glasses.

'I've got three lasagnes crisping brownly in the oven. They won't eat food like that,' said Celia.

'They will tonight,' said Roddy.

The nearer Graham, his wife and Polly got, the more heated and desperate the whispers between Celia and Roddy became.

'The last time I saw Graham he was wearing a sleeveless denim jacket with Black Sabbath printed on the back. He had spots.'

'He's grown up,' said Roddy. 'You don't have spots any more either.'

'We should have hired a caterer,' said Celia. 'We should have booked a room at the Prestonfield House hotel. Something posh.'

'And who is going to pay for that?' said Roddy.

'I don't care. I'd mortgage my house not to have them see my lasagne.'

And then they were all together. Mixing, mingling, exchanging air kisses and saying how wonderful this was.

Graham introduced his wife. 'Carol, this is Roddy, my big brother, and Celia, my sister.'

Polly stood back, observing all this.

Celia thought, That's her. That's the woman I saw crying in the kitchen years ago.

Celia and Graham greeted one another warily, both staring at each other's faces, noting how much they'd aged.

They drove to Celia's house, where Bibi and the rest of the family had gathered. She was exasperated. 'Where are Celia and Roddy? Our first family get-together in years and they're not here.'

Then they had walked slowly into the room – Graham, Polly and Carol behind them.

It had been a moment Celia and Roddy had been dreading – Bibi meeting Graham and Polly. They'd imagined an emotional greeting. Outbursts of weeping.

But Bibi stood still, staring at him. In all her years of wondering where he was, he'd stayed as he was the last time she saw him. A boy approaching eighteen, in a denim jacket, sleeves ripped off, heavy metal badges badly sewn on, and a scornful look on his face. She'd forgotten he might have grown up.

'Graham,' she said. 'At last. There you are.' She'd put her hand to her lips, and looked away. Tears in her eyes. 'Callum should be here.'

Graham went to her, pulled her to him. 'You're just the same.'

Bibi said, 'I don't think so. I've got old.'

'You're not old. You'll never be old,' he said.

'Oh, I am,' said Bibi. 'I'm old, and I've missed you.'

Polly had been watching this, and stepped forward. 'Hello, Bibi.'

Bibi turned and saw her, drank her in. It was the same woman who had fascinated her more than forty years ago. The woman she'd spied on from her flat in Greenwich Village. She was older, but still beautiful. She'd lost her look of bewilderment and insecurity. Her face had firmed; she looked wise, humorous, witty even.

'Well, Polly,' said Bibi. 'You look wonderful. Look at you and look at me. You win.'

Polly said, 'I don't think so. You've aged well.'

Bibi said she was pleased to know she was good at something, even if it was only ageing. There was an odd silence. They stood looking at one another, a roomful of people suddenly thrown together with whole life stories to exchange, and nobody knew where to start.

Then Bibi took Graham's hand. 'Look at you. You're a man. And so handsome. You look like Callum.' She took him to the table to heap a plate with lasagne he didn't want for him. 'You have to tell me everything. Every minute of everything that's happened to you since you left.'

Graham said he would. 'Tell me about Callum first.'

'We missed you,' said Bibi. She thought she'd leave it till later before she told him how much he'd cried, and how they'd fought. 'He looked for you everywhere. Sometimes, I think he walked the length of New York.'

'He went to New York?' said Graham.

'Oh, yes,' Bibi told him. 'Looked up everyone he knew. Searched in all of Polly's old haunts. Couldn't find you.' She knew she would never tell Graham how paled and wretched Callum had been when he returned to Edinburgh. It had been then, Bibi thought, that he'd started dying. It had taken ten years, but yes, she knew it had begun when Graham went away. No, she definitely could not tell him that. Too much guilt to lay on him. I'll take all the blame, she thought. I'll take all the guilt. I'm old, and guilt? I'm used to that.

But after that, the evening was a swirl of laughter, wine, slightly burnt lasagne, mango sorbet and memories.

Celia came face to face with Polly. She stared at her. 'I remember you,' she said.

'You were sitting in my childhood kitchen crying your eyes out,' she didn't say.

Polly said, 'You must have been five years old last time I saw you. Look at you now. And a dentist. You must make a pile of money.'

Celia smiled and said, 'Not where I come from.' She noticed that the only people eating her food were her family, and James.

Graham had brought photographs – his restaurants, his children, his home.

'He's got a pool,' said Olivia. 'Cool. Why can't we have a pool?'

Peter said because they hadn't room. And also they couldn't afford one.

James didn't say much. He felt out of place, lost in this gathering.

Liz worried they'd all be up late. Lara and Louis had started a new school. She didn't want them to be tired in the morning.

Olivia was hoping to be invited to Toronto. She wanted to swim in the pool.

Polly proposed a toast. 'To reunions,' she said. 'And to Bibi. She is something. I never met anybody like Bibi.' Then she said, 'You have a dish named after you. Did you know that? Bibi Potatoes.'

And the swirl went on.

'Bibi Potatoes,' Bibi said to Roddy. 'It's not very Nellie Melba, is it? I'd rather have a pudding named after me.'

Roddy, who'd drunk too much wine, said, 'It could have been worse. It could have been turnips or sprouts. Don't complain.'

'Potatoes,' Bibi said to Graham. 'Is that the dish with Gruyère cheese, onions and cream?'

'And garlic,' said Graham.

'And nutmeg,' said Bibi. 'And a little tarragon, when it was available.'

'Tarragon,' said Graham. 'That's the flavour. I never could get it exactly the way you made it.'

Bibi smiled. 'I used dill sometimes, too.'

Graham nodded. 'I knew there was something else.'

At ten, Liz left. She had to take the children home to bed. 'They're tired,' she said. James drove her.

Polly stood beside Bibi. 'He looks a little like Graham,' she said.

Bibi said she knew. 'That's why I rented him the rooms. He's nothing like Graham, though. He's quiet. He wants to be a mechanic. He's starting a course in the autumn. Celia helped him with that.'

Polly said, 'She's lovely, your Celia.' Then she linked arms. 'Let's find somewhere to talk.'

Bibi said the kitchen was quiet at the moment.

Bibi sipped her wine. Polly drank Diet Coke, 'I'm still a recovering alcoholic. Always will be. But I enjoy a cigarette in the evening. You've got to have a vice, I think.'

'Oh yes,' Bibi agreed. 'Tell me about Graham. Did you get along as soon as you got together?'

'Yes,' said Polly. 'We did. But I had no idea what to do with somebody his age. He had no interest in anything other than music and beer and girls. He was wild. I was forever getting up in the night to go fetch him from parties and clubs and gigs. He'd be drunk and cursing. I suppose I understood; I'd spent a long time being drunk and cursing.'

'I remember,' said Bibi.

'I kind of embarrassed you there,' said Polly. 'Sorry about that.'

'I'm sorry too,' said Bibi. 'Callum and I argued about that till the day he died. He thought we should have brought Graham out to visit you. You'd have visited us. We'd have phoned and written. We'd have been a big extended family.'

'He was always a dreamer,' said Polly. 'He couldn't see that a wife and a husband's lover or ex-lover might not exactly get along.'

'No,' said Bibi. 'He never did understand that.'

'I adored him,' said Polly.

'So did I,' said Bibi. 'I think Callum always had a place in his heart for you. You were more exotic than me.'

Polly said it was all a sham. 'A show I put on. I'm still the same unsure person inside. Look at the trappings I need.'

Bibi considered the silk suit, the designer shoes. 'I can't afford such things.'

'You don't need them,' said Polly. 'You never did.' She asked what had happened after she went back to New York.

'We fought, Callum and I, about you. About Graham. We always fought. But this was worse. He felt bad. I just felt that I had won. I wanted to hurt you. I thought you were so much more interesting and beautiful than me.'

'No,' said Polly. 'I was never that.'

'We brought Graham up. But he was the difficult one. Callum loved him for that. He always liked a rebel.'

'I got the worst of him. I didn't know what to do with him. I actually wanted to send him back.'

Graham had been difficult. Polly hadn't really known what it would be like to have a teenager around. She had sent Graham a ticket to New York, a letter telling him she was his real mother, and photographs of him with her during her stay in Edinburgh, along with a couple of pictures of him with Callum in her tiny flat in New York. 'I wanted him to come to me. Mostly, I wanted to hurt you. You'd got Callum. We moved around, Graham and me. I thought you'd be looking for us.'

'We were,' said Bibi. 'Callum went to New York. He looked for you. I think he also got caught up with old friends.'

'In time we moved to Toronto,' said Polly. 'I set up a coffee bar. Graham drifted from job to job. He had too many girlfriends, he hung out with a crowd that I, to my utter surprise, disapproved of. I never thought I'd disapprove of anybody.'

'Children do that to you,' said Bibi. 'They change your point of view.'

Finally, in order to keep an eye on him, Polly had brought him to work in her coffee bar. She hadn't wanted to. She feared he'd be rude to the customers. In fact, he never was. The people that hung about there reminded him of the people who hung about his old home in Scotland. He had, however, been rude to the women who cooked the food Polly served. He claimed he could do better.

Polly, used to his absurd boasting, had said, 'OK, go ahead, do better.' And he had. He had a feeling for food. Oh, he made mistakes, he had his disasters. But Polly had seen something in him and packed him off to catering college. 'If you're gonna do it, do it properly.'

When he finished college, she had set him up in his own

restaurant, a small place at the harbour. For two years it had looked like she was going to lose her money. But slowly word had spread, the place became fashionable, and so did Graham. He'd come out of his kitchen and chat to his customers; he made them laugh, sometimes he'd sing to them. A night at Graham's was a night to remember.

He had married Suzie. For a year or so they were happy, but she didn't like the hours he kept. She spent every night alone. Graham would come in at two or three in the morning. She would leave at half past eight to go to work as a biologist. They hardly saw each other. She left him for her boss.

Graham had taken it badly. He worked. He had tantrums in his kitchen, shouting at staff, swearing, but his food was still wonderful. He survived. He wrote a cookery column for a newspaper; he appeared on television. He opened another restaurant. He spent time with Polly, who always told him he should find himself another wife.

Three years ago he met Carol. She had come to interview him for a magazine, and hadn't, at first, liked him very much. 'Arrogant arse,' she said.

Graham had told her his father was a poet. 'You're kidding,' she said. 'I don't believe you.'

'No, really, Callum Saunders. Look him up. I took my mother's name when I came over here.'

He thought this must have done the trick, because she started going out with him, and two years ago married him. When she was four months pregnant, she had ordered a book of Callum's poems from a bookshop. It was out of print, and it had taken the owner some time to track down a copy.

Carol had given the book to Graham. She'd said, 'There's a lovely poem in it. It's about floating! It's dedicated to you, I think. The lost child.'

'When you're floating, float,' said Graham. 'I remember that. But I never read the poem. I hate poetry.'

'You must have heard him say it,' said Carol.

'Probably,' said Graham. He read the poem. It triggered memories of his old life. The times in that flat, Callum writing in his study, Bibi working at the sink. 'Potatoes,' he said. 'She filled us up on potatoes – mashed, roast with rosemary from the allotment, dauphinoise, duchesse. I'd forgotten that. We all hung about the kitchen, arguing.'

'Well, there you go. A happy childhood and you turned into a delinquent, according to Polly. Shame on you.'

'And that was us,' said Polly now. 'Working through tantrums. Growing up, just like everyone else.'

Bibi said, 'He's so grown up. It took me aback. I was half expecting a boy in a denim jacket with his upper lip turned up at me. And there he is, a man, a respected chef who named a dish of potatoes after me.'

'It's what he remembered,' said Polly. 'It's famous. Many people think it was the making of him.'

Bibi said no. 'It had nothing to do with a dish. You were the making of him.'

Didn't We Have Fun?

Years ago, Bibi and Callum had gone to Toronto. Callum had been invited to a poetry festival. They had walked along Bloor Street, Younge Street and Yorkville Avenue. They'd strolled by the lake. They'd eaten in restaurants and explored the harbour area. And all that time, Graham and Polly had been living there.

We might have met, Bibi thought. If we'd walked down the right street at the right time we could have run into one another. This reunion, this getting back together, could have started then.

It would take a lot more than an evening. It would take a year, maybe two or three. Graham and Polly and Carol would stay for a few days. They'd have meals together, they'd exchange memories, they'd talk. So much time to make up.

One day in the not-too-distant future, she would go out to visit him. She'd stay at his house, meet his son, and walk through the streets he'd walked in the years she was looking for him. We have to take it a step at a time, she thought.

'Let's go back to the party,' she said to Polly.

In the living room, Graham was drinking wine and talking about the poetry book Carol had bought him. 'It's got a lovely poem in it.'

366

' "Floating",' said Bibi. 'He wrote that after he'd been to St Ives. He had such trouble with it. Stamping about, shouting at everybody to be quiet. He'd spoken about it too much, spoiled it, really. Like opening the oven when the bread is still cooking. That's how he described it.'

Graham stared at her. 'Yes, I remember that. He was in a state, and you got pissed off. You were in the kitchen. Roddy was at the table. I was under it.'

'You spent a lot of time under that table,' said Bibi. 'I think you felt safe there.'

'Anyway,' said Graham, 'Callum came storming through; you were in the kitchen at the sink and you got pissed off.' He paused because all this had happened a long time ago, and the picture in his mind was from the point of view of a child under a table – legs, voices. ' "For God's sake," you said, "why can't you just float? When you're floating, float." '

'That's right,' said Bibi. 'And he went off and wrote his poem.'

'But you said it,' said Graham. 'He got the credit. People quoted it. He had to read it out everywhere he went. And you said it.'

'But I didn't write the poem. I only said that line.'

'Still, you said it.'

'You are the only person that remembers that,' said Bibi.

Graham nodded. 'I remember.'

The next night, Graham, Carol and Polly had dinner with Bibi. She made them her potato dish and roasted a couple of chickens. Graham thought her cooking better than his. 'It's the dill. I should have remembered.'

Afterwards, while everyone else sat at the table, Bibi and Polly took their coffee to the living room. 'It's comfier here.'

Bibi opened the windows. The night was balmy. They remembered Callum.

'He loved you too,' said Bibi.

'I know,' said Polly. 'But you won.' A velvet voice, filled with admiration and regret.

'Maybe. It was lovely, but sometimes there was no money and too many mouths to feed and the electricity had been cut off, and, really, that wasn't a load of laughs. You had a career, lovers, I should imagine. What if I'd gone away, and you'd stayed with all the children? You wouldn't have thought that was winning.'

Polly said, 'When you put it like that, perhaps I wouldn't. Still, he stayed with you, and I loved him. I had the odd lover, but I only really wanted him.'

Bibi said, 'I think he'd have been happy if he could have had us both. But we wouldn't have stood for that.'

'No,' said Polly. Then, 'Can I ask you something? Something personal? What was he like at the end?'

'Ill,' said Bibi. 'Very ill. Weak and a bit repentant. He had cancer of the liver, but when you're old it doesn't have the same effect as when you're young. He took a long time to die. It was then we became real friends.'

'But right at the end,' said Polly. 'Were you with him then?'

'Yes,' said Bibi.

'What were his last words? If you don't mind telling me. I'd like to know.'

Callum had taken her hand. 'It was all dreams and anger, wasn't it?'

'No. We had some lovely times.'

'I think I wasn't very good. I never wrote what I wanted to write. What seemed wonderful in my head came out all wrong on paper.'

She told him not to be silly.

'No, I'm not being silly. I was never as good as the others – the people I met and mixed with. There were always those who were better than me.'

'No,' said Bibi. 'They weren't. Nobody was as good as you. And you were always wonderful when the lights were off.'

'Yes,' Callum had said. 'Wasn't it wonderful, all of it? Didn't we have fun?'

Bibi turned to Polly. 'Those were his last words. "Didn't we have fun?"'

Polly said, 'Oh, I like that. And didn't we? You spying on me – oh, I knew about that, I played up to you. Then you running away and me having an affair, and a baby, then giving him to you and then wanting him back and us fighting, then me screaming outside your flat. Didn't we have fun?'

Bibi said, 'Yes, we did, didn't we?'

'You miss him,' said Polly.

'I do. But he isn't gone. Not completely. I keep him here inside. I don't have to remember to think about him. I think about him all the time.'

That was one of the consequences of marriage. She'd always known that the day would come when one of them would go and the other would be left behind. She'd thought that for the first time when she'd been on the platform at Perth station. The train had pulled in, Callum had leaned out of the open carriage door, waving, calling her name. For a second, just before she'd started to run towards him, she'd thought, one way or another, one day you'll leave me, and I'll spend the rest of my life being lonely.

I Forgot to Float

After a week, the three went back to Canada. Bibi would go out to spend Christmas with them. Meantime, she would email every few days and tell Graham about her allotment and nag him to take Omega-3 tablets, and sometimes she'd send him a recipe. He always thanked her.

Roddy started a photography course, and saw Erica several times a week. James took a work experience job at a garage, something to do till his course started in the autumn. Liz looked for work. Sometimes, in the depth of the night, Bibi heard her slipping down the hall to James's room. Bibi would shake her head. She supposed they were young, and that was what young people did. 'Sex,' she said. 'It's the ruination of us all.'

Beth said she'd go back to her job soon. 'I have to get my head together first,' she said. She still saw Bradley. She still wanted a baby. But she stayed with Bibi. 'I like it here.'

The flat was full of voices. Bibi heard them. The chatter of children, James making breakfast in the morning, Liz nagging Louis and Lara to hurry up, it was time for school. The radio played, but it wasn't on the station Bibi liked to listen to. The phone rang, but it was rarely for her. There were more dishes to wash, and someone always got to the newspaper before she did.

She'd lie in bed, listening. 'Voices,' she said to Callum, 'I missed the voices. I wanted them back. Only now they're here, I sometimes wish they'd go away again. This isn't what I planned. But then what is? How you must be laughing at me. I was floating, and I forgot to float.'

ISLA DEWAR

Secrets of a
Family Album

Obsessively neat Lily, a writer who writes about writers, is asked to interview the enigmatic journalist and photographer Rita Boothe. Leafing through a book of Rita's from the early seventies, Lily notices a picture of an incandescently sexy young woman sitting in a limousine swigging Jack Daniels. It's her mother, Mattie.

Lily isn't shocked. She's jealous. She wants to be like that, beautiful, abandoned. But Mattie is no longer meltingly gorgeous. In their neglected house, she and her husband scrape by and bicker. Upstairs, Grandpa flirts on the Internet. Marie, Lily's sister, is facing a custody suit and her brother Rory avoids coming home.

Lily is usually the one to sort the family out, but she's tired of being boring and dependable. She wants to let go, be a woman of wicked mystery and intrigue. Like the one in the photograph.

Praise for Isla Dewar's novels:

'Observant and needle-sharp – very funny' *The Times*

'Both wise and funny' Shena Mackay

'Breathless . . . appealingly spirited . . . sparkiness, freshness and verve' *Mail on Sunday*

'Genuinely moving and evocative' *Scotland on Sunday*

0 7553 0082 3

R

headline
review

ISLA DEWAR

Getting Out of the House

Nora was devastated when her mother, Maisie, told her she preferred her older daughter, Cathryn. Heartbroken, but not altogether surprised. After all, Cathryn was clever, good looking, just about perfect, really. Nora was awkward, and prone to daydreaming and telling fibs. Who wouldn't prefer Cathryn, Nora thought?

But now, living in Edinburgh, removed from her child-hood home and her volatile mother, Nora is happy. She has a lover she adores, a close circle of friends with whom she can banter and joke, and a job that befits a dreamer and fibber. Life is beautiful. But when Maisie's world unexpectedly falls apart, she and Cathryn think it obvious Nora be the one to pick up the pieces. Nora doesn't think it obvious at all.

Escaping her family was Nora's first step to self-fulfilment. But when she has to deal with betrayal and the surprising consequences of a love affair, she finds, at last, a way to forgive and even learn to love the people she left behind.

Praise for Isla Dewar's novels:

'Isla Dewar's novels occupy a unique and instantly recog-nisable world . . . She is a fine observer of the nuances of family life . . . evokes atmosphere and place powerfully' *Scotland on Sunday*

'Observant and needle-sharp – very funny' *The Times*

'Strong characters, sharp dialogue and a haunting sense of place' *Eve* magazine

0 7553 2590 7

headline
review

Now you can buy any of these other bestselling
books by **Isla Dewar** from your bookshop
or *direct from her publisher*.

FREE P&P AND UK DELIVERY
(Overseas and Ireland £3.50 per book)

Keeping Up With Magda	£7.99
Women Talking Dirty	£7.99
It Could Happen To You	£7.99
Giving Up On Ordinary	£7.99
The Woman Who Painted Her Dreams	£7.99
Dancing in a Distant Place	£7.99
Secrets of a Family Album	£6.99
Getting Out Of The House	£7.99

TO ORDER SIMPLY CALL THIS NUMBER

01235 400 414

or visit our website: www.madaboutbooks.com

Prices and availability subject to change without notice.